CW00858678

ADVANCE PRAISE FOR **RECKONER**

Reckoner *is a deftly crafted coming-of-age story by novelist Douglas Rappaport that is about grief, forgiveness, and human connection. A truly compelling read from cover to cover, Reckoner lingers in the mind of the reader long after the book itself has been finished and set back upon the shelf. While very highly recommended, especially for community library Contemporary General Fiction collections, it should be noted for personal reading lists that Reckoner is also available in a digital book format.* —Midwest Book Review

Other than getting some sense of a detox center from TV or movies, or possibly from what acquaintances with first-hand experience may have described to them, most readers will be unfamiliar with such a setting and the people there—staff as well as those being treated. And with an epidemic these days of widespread addiction to a range of illegal and prescription drugs, many readers will be curious about such places and find more to connect with in a fictional account such as this one, that virtually puts them there, than in what most journalism offers, as factual news reportage. So, like Ken Kesey's novel One Flew Over the Cuckoo's Nest, *its story having taken place in a mental institution,* Reckoner *provides an interior view of an otherwise unfamiliar place.... It's a novel very relative to our times, not only for younger readers approximately the same age, and of a similar mindset to Miles', for instance, but for any contemporary readers aware of the serious situations so many people are dealing with today.* —John Pahl, Fiction Editor for Dunes Review

Douglas Rappaport has done an amazing job of combining a very touching story filled with lonely characters all in search of the same two things: love of self and love of others, with an approach that is so introspective it could lose readers if not properly handled. But Rappaport handles it beautifully. Kudos to Douglas Rappaport for pulling off this most ambitious and engaging project. —Viga Boland, Readers Favorite

If you decide to read Reckoner...*and you should...prepare yourself for a very different journey into literary fiction. Rappaport's approach might initially confuse you: it will take a while to figure out just what he is doing. Once you have figured it out... or think you have... you'll find yourself wondering how much of what you are reading is actually taking place in the real world and how much is occurring in the narrator's mind. And therein lies the challenge to the reader to keep on reading. If you do, you will be rewarded by a most touching story that somehow takes you where other writers rarely go: inside your own mind.... Time and again, as they read Reckoner, readers will recognize themselves tuning out what is going on in their immediate vicinity while their minds meander into other times, places and spaces... and the trip is fascinating!"* —Vianvi.com

Rappaport crafts a tapestry of voices in this often moving YA/New Adult novel about a protagonist struggling to find wholeness. The voices of the various narrators--many of whom are in recovery or battling addiction—are solidly rendered and distinct. Small details and pivotal moments alike serve to create a slice-of-life story that also deals with fundamental issues of identity and redemption. Rappaport's mosaic approach is unique, while the novel also offers an unusual blending of psychological rumination and plot-driven circumstances. Miles Rockefeller is a sympathetic, troubled character who evolves from challenged and splintered, to broken, to hopeful. —Booklife Prize 2020

RECKONER

A NOVEL

DOUGLAS RAPPAPORT

MISSION POINT PRESS

Readers are encouraged to go to www.MissionPointPress.com to contact the author or to find information on how to buy this book in bulk at a discounted rate.

MISSION POINT PRESS

Published by Mission Point Press
2554 Chandler Rd.
Traverse City, MI 49696
(231) 421-9513
www.MissionPointPress.com

Cover art and design by Mark Pate

ISBN: 978-1-950659-87-6
Library of Congress Control Number: 2020923518

Printed in the United States of America

Dedicated to all you human beings, especially those in recovery from drug and alcohol addiction.

ALSO BY DOUGLAS RAPPAPORT

One Day the Weatherman (a novel)
Victim of Circumstance (non-fiction)
The Great Deceiver (a stageplay)

CONTENTS

PART ONE
CROW CATCHES A CATERPILLAR

9

12:12

People ruin everything....

This was what Miles Rockefeller was thinking when the two young women invaded his sanctuary, promptly setting up their sunbathing towels in the virgin grass just as he was finally feeling some peace from watching a wedge of geese ascend over the water. The girls were talking about drugs, which seemed to be everyone's favorite topic of conversation at the rehab facility—at the same time exchanging their growing list of withdrawal side effects in an effort to name something the other person hadn't experienced yet. Or, better still hadn't heard of before, or even thought possible.

"It's 12:12," one of them said to the other. "Make a wish."

"What?"

"12:12," she repeated, glancing at her wristwatch again as if she suddenly didn't believe it, which reminded Miles that no one had their cellphones anymore.

"I thought that was only at 11:11?"

The other one scoffed, followed by a, "Whatever."

Just then, as if saving him from the girls' ridiculous banter, Miles heard over the loudspeakers: "Miles R., please come to the nurse's station. Miles R., to the nurse's station."

Heading back toward the main building, Miles felt irritation that they paged him so often; worse, they had to repeat his name in such quick succession that it was humanly impossible to respond to the first announcement before the second one seized the air. He also found it peculiar—although he understood the whole anonymity thing, attributed to everyone's so-called "disease"—that only a first initial was used for last names when addressed by the staff or printed on the

ID badges. First names were apparently okay, but no last names—although, in the cafeteria the day before, while Miles told a story to his table-mates, he accidentally blurted out his last name, causing him a mini-stroke upon the realization that this circle of addicts could now Google him once they returned to the real world of cellphones and social media. The punchline, however, was that his captive audience didn't even notice his gaffe.

He realized early on at the rehab center that the other addicts were all narcissists, only interested in their own backstories. Everyone else's seemed to bore them. Once in a while, if they somehow caught something during someone else's backstory—good listening skills weren't an attribute of most addicts—they would buzz in and say, "I didn't know you were in for opiates?" ("In" being code for "addicted.") This, in turn, would greatly upset the storyteller, who would then bark back like a rabid dog: "I told you twenty times I'm in here for benzos and opiates! Why do you think they have me on subs!" This, in most cases, would get a response something along the lines of: "You're on subs?" Which, of course, would only infuriate the storyteller even more. And if your backstory involved something non-drug related, such as an operation you had undergone, forget about it. Only a drug addict could be disappointed if you told them your injury was chronic, rather than from some grisly accident— although it wasn't a good idea to use the word "chronic" in a non-drug related story. Your thesaurus skills needed to be top notch.

Miles was always amused by the back and forth of con- stant confusion that permeated most of the conversations he overheard around the campus, so long as they didn't involve him. The more drug classifications people were in for, the prouder they seemed to be. If you were in just for alcohol, that didn't seem to impress anyone, even if you supposedly beat down three cases of beer or four pints of vodka a day.

But if you were in for heroin, for example—which was never a solo item—people knew immediately that you were probably addicted to everything else as well, and were therefore more interesting to talk to.

Entering the main building, Miles held the door open for three guys who were headed outside, two of whom were staff. They were known on campus as a "PSA," although none of the addicts could agree on what the acronym stood for. That was the other thing—you could stand there all day and hold the door open for people, and hardly anyone would ever say "thank you" unless they worked there; even the latter wasn't absolute. It was as if they didn't even notice you holding the door open for them, and just figured it had magically opened on its own—or worse, that they were *entitled* to have the door opened for them.

As the thankless three passed him, Miles realized the entourage was on a one-way trek toward the parking lot. It was an official escort out of Shangri-La, and he knew the guy being taken away. It was Devin L.

"Devin!" Miles called out to him. "What's going on?"

Devin turned his head to the side, his lips twisting in a Joker's smile. This wasn't a good sign, despite the fact that he usually looked like that. It was something else that didn't seem right.

"I pissed hot," he said proudly, without a hint of guilt.

When escorting someone off the premises due to a violation, the staff members always seemed to walk faster than normal, like they were trying to get a ticking bomb off campus without it prematurely exploding. Miles had heard Devin clearly and knew the ramifications of what he had said, but couldn't come up with a quick enough response before he and his entourage vanished into the ether.

"Hey Miles," a voice suddenly said from behind him. It was one of the girls from Miles' group counseling. She was twenty, but looked fourteen and had a knack for saying crazy things out of nowhere. It was as if the drugs she had abused were still in her system—heroin, molly, alcohol, benzos and opiates, if he remembered correctly—filling every pore, unable to escape. She was also famous for adding "spoiler alert" in the middle of her backstory whenever she told it, as if the listener hadn't yet realized—or more likely, forgotten—that she was an addict.

"Hey Sasha," Miles said, realizing that people usually looked like their names. Sasha looked like a Sasha, mostly because of how she wore her hair. Devin looked like a Devin—although he looked so high at the moment that he could have answered to any number of trust fund names.

Sasha gestured toward Devin, disappearing back into the real world: a dream which still took place with or without the addicts. Time was wickedly cruel, especially for those inside this bubble where the gears of the universal clock had some-how stopped moving forward.

"Looks like Devin's escaping Alcatraz," Sasha said matter-of-factly, as if they were actually on that concrete island in the middle of San Francisco Bay.

The loudspeaker came on again, still beckoning Miles to the nurse's station, just in case he had forgotten.

Miles started. He had completely forgotten where he was headed because he'd been so completely mesmerized by the site of Devin walking off the grounds. "I gotta go," Miles said, turning toward the door, which he still held open for no one in particular.

"Did you do the homework yet?" Sasha called after Miles, already several paces away. The worried-sounding tone in her voice made the question seem like it held life-or-death con-sequences. Miles hadn't yet done the current assignment for the group counseling sessions he and Sasha attended, but he didn't really care enough about it to engage in a conversation with her, especially since he was late for his medication.

One of the nurses was about to call for him again when

Miles entered through the half-open accordion doors. They never seemed to open the doors completely, as if they didn't want anyone to know they were actually there, behind the wizard's curtain, doling out the magic pills everyone so needed, especially the ones in detox whose bodies were endlessly betraying them.

The heavy-set male nurse—who usually worked the graveyard shift and played cool Pandora songs super loud on his iPad—eyed Miles' name badge, even though he knew Miles. The medical staff followed a strict policy, posted on the main door: NO BADGE. NO MEDICATION. NO EXCEPTIONS.

"You're due for your pheno," the male nurse said, monotone, like it was something he was tired of repeating. As Miles sat down, he handed him a tiny paper cup with the phenobarbital in it and a slightly larger one containing water. The pill itself was almost as big as the cup that held it, but this didn't matter to Miles, who had recently become an expert at swallowing a handful of various-sized pills at the same time—something he had never thought possible, given he'd previously had trouble swallowing just one, even something as small as an aspirin.

"I'm only getting pheno now?" Miles asked, sounding like the paranoid drug addict that he didn't want to sound like. "I thought I was due for the anti-anxiety stuff."

The nurse turned back to his computer. "Not 'til 2:30."

"Oh," was all Miles could say. Arguing with the nurses about anything was a colossal waste of time.

The nurse half-smiled. "So, you looking forward to the Labor Day barbecue?"

Miles stared back, unimpressed.

The nurse's smile crept up like moss. "A little break in your diet, at least...."

"No, I won't be here for that, as lovely as it sounds. I'm actually leaving this afternoon."

The nurse glanced at a calendar hidden behind the computer, as if he wasn't sure what to trust—the month of September or Miles. He picked up a clipboard next to the phone. "I don't have you on the list for today," he said. "What day are—" He interrupted himself. "No, wait, you're still in detox. You can't be leaving today."

"I don't know. I'm not keeping count," Miles lied, since he knew exactly how long he had been a "patient" there. The addicts, if not referred to by just their first name and last initial, were designated as being "in recovery" and never anything else, medical or otherwise. Like labeling was a crime the rehab center refused to commit, so the word "patient" was never used—the irony of which was also never mentioned.

Miles wasn't much of a numbers person, but he knew, almost to the minute, when he would officially get his walking papers. If he were to tell the truth, he had just passed the halfway mark—two weeks—even though it felt more like two years, especially since he was still being detoxed, as the nurse had just pointed out. Miles had been detoxed at a prior facility, but that detox had gone too rapidly, or so he was told—particularly for someone coming off benzos. And so, he had to endure a second round. But the worst news, which Miles learned from the present medical staff, was that his body could still be withdrawing for up to a year, and that it would most likely be similar to a roller coaster—with the ups and downs, curves and thrusts utterly at random.

Miles didn't want to make eye contact with the nurse, who now glanced at the video monitor above the computer, as he knew what the nurse was about to say.

"I've got a line," the nurse pleaded impatiently, proving Miles' assumption correct.

Miles also looked up at the monitor. It was amazing, he thought, how one minute there would be no one getting their meds, and a second later a whole line of people suddenly appeared, like vampires materializing from thin air.

"See you back here at 2:30, then 5:30 for your dinner meds," the nurse said.

"I won't be here then," Miles countered, still not in complete control of the words coming out of his mouth. It was a bad day for his detox. He wasn't currently having hallucinations—at least not the visual kind—although he had recently started experiencing auditory ones, which in some ways were even scarier, as they teetered closer to believability and often had him answering someone who wasn't really there.

"Well, if you go to dinner early, as long as you're here by 6:00 that should be fine."

"Like I said, I won't be here then…I mean, I'm not going to dinner at all. I'm leaving this place just as soon as I can get a ride…but I'll obviously need my cellphone back first, so I can arrange it and stuff."

The nurse glanced at the video monitor again. "I have other people to get to," he said, his tone not as impatient as the words he chose. His manner of calmness every time Miles saw him was actually fairly impressive; perhaps it was a result of listening to music so profoundly, especially considering the stress of having a healthy dose of addicts nipping at him around the clock. (The ones who didn't nip only refrained from doing so because they were in half-comas already and couldn't nip anything even if they wanted to: for them, simply walking was the first, and sometimes only, hurdle.)

Miles scoffed. He didn't like it when the nurses ignored him. In some ways, it was the worst side-effect of them all. He glanced at the growing line on the video monitor, too, noticing his roommate standing at the front with that look of fear he always wore, subliminally screaming that there was no possible way he could deal with the day ahead, much less the next few minutes. He had droopy eyelids that almost covered his eyeballs, as if his eyelids alone were responding to his hopeless life and were just about ready to give up. The very sight of him irritated Miles to no end, mostly due to his jealousy of those who had no trouble sleeping—a minority population for sure. Miles hadn't slept in three nights. His roommate, Kirk, slept like a baby, even on his first night—a rare occurrence in a rehab center, unless you came in day one fucked up on downers. It was either one way or the other: lots of sleep or no sleep at all. Extremes in just about everything were the norm there. And what irritated Miles about Kirk even more was the fact that the guy would just get in bed at night and immediately go to sleep without moving at all; he would simply drift off in whatever position he landed on the mattress in. No getting comfortable, no finding the perfect angle for his body to lie, no fidgeting whatsoever. Just bam. Gone.

Rufus Wainwright's cover of "Hallelujah" started to play on the nurse's iPad. Both Miles and the nurse paused, realizing the very sound of their voices was a violent disturbance to that sacrosanct song. Even the other nurse a few feet away, who had been busy taking someone's blood pressure, seemed to freeze in the moment.

Miles wasn't one for "moments" anymore, even though this was a favorite song of his, which he immediately reminded the nurses of (as if it were a quiz show and he had just buzzed in). Then he blurted: "I *am* leaving today, for real." He realized just then, however, how silly this empty threat sounded. Empty threats were popular songs performed by the addicts, and it was a never-ending concert. Plus, even if it were true, the nurse probably didn't give a shit either way. Miles was merely a receptacle of medicine to them—as long as he didn't have a seizure or die during the transaction. Seizures seemed to be a common worry there, especially with the patients in detox where anything was possible.

"Be that as it may," the nurse responded, "as long as you're in my computer here, you still exist in my world, despite your own claims to the contrary."

Now the nurse sounded like an existentialist Santa

Claus—the latter due to the hearty laugh that followed—although Miles had no idea what an existentialist was, if anyone happened to quiz him on that.

The nurse checked his computer again; doing this seemed to be the one non-musical thing that brought him any type of peace or comfort in the miasma of rehab. "You're a minor, too, Miles, so I don't think you're going anywhere just yet." He laughed again. How annoying, Miles thought, since it now seemed a bit condescending, too. That was another thing about the nurses there: one minute they were your "BFF," and the next your worst, most immovable enemy.

"I'm not gonna be a minor for much longer."

"Then let me be the first to wish you a happy birthday in advance," the nurse said, smiling crookedly.

"This isn't a prison," Miles shot back, still on autopilot. "I can leave whenever I want...and I don't have any parents either, so no one can stop me." Miles said this in such a way that it sounded like fact, even though it was the furthest thing from the truth—and he knew it.

Miles gestured at the computer. "It does say that in there, right? That I don't have any parents?" Without waiting for an answer, Miles continued, "I mean, you probably know when my next shit's gonna be...in that fancy computer of yours." Miles glanced at the nurse's name tag. He had never noticed before that the nurses wore them, too. *Cody*, it read. The name tag didn't show a last name, or even just a last initial like the addicts had on theirs. He was simply "Cody."

Cody stared at Miles; this wasn't anything new or revelatory. The nurses were trained to wait it out until the addicts wound down their assorted tirades. Stopping them midstream served no purpose unless it involved other people, or, of course, violence. And Cody had a special button on his phone just for that. It made him feel like the President of the United States, or so he had joked to Miles on more than one occasion, as if he had forgotten the other times.

The addicts were always telling their sob backstories to Cody, or any nurse that would listen—Miles had witnessed as much, and naturally shared his own—so they had probably heard everything there was to hear. Whether an addict found out that they were adopted (the story Miles told), or that their partner had cheated on them (a story Miles overheard once), causing them to use drugs and alcohol to numb the confusion of it; or, worse, had been involved in a car accident while they were under the influence—maybe with the latter as a trigger, or something along those lines—and injured or killed someone innocent, more than likely someone the addict knew or even cared about. Almost everyone there had an irreconcilable past that they had to deal with, including most of the staff; and now, the current addicts—the ones whose bodies were betraying them due to withdrawal and, most likely, sleep deprivation—were without an artificial substance to help them through it (other than cigarettes, of course, as addiction seemed to be a lot worse than cancer—at least while in rehab). Most of the nurses felt for the addicts, especially Cody—himself a former addict—but they could never play favorites. All the kids had to be treated equally, or at least subject to a pretense of equal treatment.

In this circumstance, however, Cody played along. He stared, and kept staring, at the computer screen, which was like the Ark of the Covenant at the end of *Raiders of the Lost Ark*. If Miles or Cody looked at it directly for too long, their faces would melt off as surely as the ill-fated Nazis.

"It says here your next shit is going to be in forty-five minutes," Cody said flatly. Then he turned back to Miles and flashed that wicked smile of his. "So, now you know."

"Ha ha," Miles said, defeated, as he stood up finally from the chair that barely fit his ass. Not that Miles was necessarily a big person—he was just under 5'9" and 160 pounds—but the chair seemed too small for anyone above the age of nine. Every chair in the nurses' station, save for the ones the two nurses sat on, were too small for almost all the rehabbers, even the teenagers like Miles—despite his baby face, which made him look young enough to possibly fit. It was a sore point for Miles, since throughout Junior High and High School, "Baby Face" had been his nickname. His face was unconvincing in its plea that it would ever grow a beard; as a consequence, Miles didn't have to shave very often. To counter it, he grew his hair long, which was not appreciated by his most recent foster parents, the Kellys. Though he hadn't been born yet when the movie version of *Interview with the Vampire* came out, Miles was trying to emulate Brad Pitt's tortured eternal soul, Louis—minus the colored contacts, but with the attempted sideburns. Just as Miles was finally leaving the nurse's station, Cody said, "You know, if you tell someone to go to hell correctly, they will have no choice but to go."

Miles stopped. Cody flashed him a much friendlier smile—an unmistakable invite to Armageddon. Then, because it seemed like the only response, especially in light of the grin, he said evenly: "Go to hell."

Cody laughed despite it being the obvious punchline he had more than set up. Then he boomed to the waiting line outside: "Next!"

DRIVERLESS

"I can't stop the bad thoughts."

This was what escaped Kirk's mouth as Miles tried to sneak past him in the meds line without engaging in conversation, but after accidentally making eye contact, it was too late to prevent it. At first Miles wanted to keep walking, but then something stopped him—maybe the fact that he wasn't expecting Kirk to say something so raw, almost a plea. Of course, Kirk always seemed to be a moment away from some type of catastrophe. Although this was also true—to some extent at least, of all the addicts there—disaster, for Kirk, seemed to be constantly within arm's reach.

The girl sitting next to Kirk, whose name Miles couldn't remember—and he didn't want to stare at her badge to find out, lest she think he was staring at her tits—alternated between picking her scalp and pulling at her eyebrows. Her fingernails, reduced to nubs from biting and caked in various layers of nail polish, conveyed her life story like the rings of a tree depicted its age. Watching her hands tremble made Miles even more tense; when other people were anxious around him it added to his own baseline, which was already calibrated as nervous.

The guy sitting on the other side of the twitching girl—someone else whose name Miles couldn't remember, he forgot people's names almost the minute they introduced them-selves—was bitching to no one in particular about having to wait so long for meds. And he always seemed to be in line for meds, no matter what time it happened to be. If you didn't know where he was at any given minute of the day or night, the line at the main nurse's station was the first place to look.

"It's like they live in another time zone or something," he said, mostly to himself, even though everyone in line could clearly hear him.

Miles glanced at the name badge the guy had tied to one of his jutting biceps, rather than hung from around his neck like everyone else. His name was Sawyer—Sawyer R.—and his picture looked like it had been taken just a moment ago. His perfectly manicured, thin "Lincoln" beard—a feat in itself, as the rehab facility took all shaving items when a new patient checked in—along with his arctic blue eyes caused the girls to swoon over him, not to mention more than a few guys who secretly envied his brooding masculinity. With his equally short crew-cut, Sawyer was the furthest thing from Miles' doppelgänger imaginable. Possibly the most intriguing aspect of Sawyer's appearance, though, was a fairly big tattoo of Pee-Wee Herman on his right forearm, replete with Pee-Wee's signature gray glen plaid suit and red bow tie, which Sawyer flat-out refused to explain, no matter how many people asked him about it.

With the swagger of an older brother, Sawyer had introduced himself to Miles in the cafeteria not long after Miles arrived at the rehab facility. Whenever there was fresh blood, and after everyone had plundered the very popular "name-that-addict's-choice-of-poison-just-by-looking-at-them" game, friendly introductions were eventually carried out—and sooner than later if it proved difficult to get a consensus regarding the "name-their-chosen-poison" game. If the latter was the case, instead of the first question being the standard: "Hi, I'm so-and-so, what's your name?", it would inevitably be: "What are you in for?", as if the new person had committed a crime and had just arrived in prison rather than rehab (although some *had* committed crimes, and rehab *did* sometimes feel like prison).

"You look like someone I should know," Sawyer had said to him upon their first meeting, just north of the stale bagels.

"Really? Why's that?" Miles had asked back, which almost threw Sawyer off for some reason.

"Uh…thought you might be a fellow supporter of benzos," he'd said, half-grinning, apparently proud of his own addiction.

"Benzos?"

Miles looked around to see if anyone was watching them. If they didn't arrive on day one with an existing bout of paranoia, which was highly unlikely, the addicts quickly absorbed it into their bloodstream.

"Yeah," Sawyer said, not backing down from trying to figure out the addictions plaguing Miles. "I'm thinking benzos and opiates…." He studied Miles' face. "Maybe heroin?"

Miles felt unsure of what to say. It wasn't any of Sawyer's business, or anyone else there for that matter, what he had checked in for. He quickly realized, however, that they would just keep asking him until he confessed, so there was no point in challenging the inevitable. "Not a bad guess," Miles finally replied. "Although no heroin, sadly."

Sawyer seemed almost disappointed that Miles wasn't addicted to heroin. Addicts weren't necessarily rooting for the recovery of other addicts; the more drugs you were dependent on, the more satisfied they seemed to be. Unless, of course, they were in an AA or NA meeting. Only in those sacred spaces did the addicts cheer for one another to reclaim their lives. Addicts were walking contradictions, not to mention pathological liars, although they would never admit to either. Even if they bragged about taking fifty milligrams of Klonopin in one day without dying, their truth was a moving target as long as the listener believed their ever-changing backstories. And if enough people believed it, the addict would believe their own fiction.

"You deaf?" the twitchy girl said to Kirk. "The nurse just called for the next person."

Kirk, caught off-guard, didn't respond at first, which only increased Twitchy's impatience. Little did she know that Kirk was always caught off-guard by anything that happened to him.

Another addict appeared out of nowhere and sat down next to Sawyer, just as Kirk finally understood the situation and stood up to get his meds. This was standard operating procedure for the meds line: just as one person would get up, another one would join the back of the line, thereby keeping the number of people waiting the same. The newest member of the line was Peter K., who always had a smile plastered on his face, regardless of anything that might be happening around him, good or bad. Along with Sasha and three others, Peter was in the same group counseling as Miles, which was the only reason Miles knew his name. Peter's constant smile was usually disconcerting, because even when he relayed something horrific, like talking about how his step-father had fondled him as a child, that smile was always there. And if that wasn't enough, Peter's tenor, nasal voice and continuous sniffling—the latter a side effect from heroin detox—made it seem like he was allergic to life itself (though still happy about it for some reason).

"Hey, Peter," Miles said without thinking, for the last thing he wanted at the moment was to get into an uncomfortable conversation with him. Then again, almost every conversation with the addicts there was, in some way, uncomfortable.

"You coming or going?" he said.

"Uh…going I guess," Miles replied.

"Next!" came the sudden voice of the female nurse. This caused Twitchy to stand up as if she had just been electrocuted. Then she practically dove into the nurse's station, afraid that someone might steal her pole position if she didn't move fast enough.

"I guess I'm next," Sawyer said to no one in particular.

Miles couldn't help but notice the huge cross that hung from Peter K.'s neck. He had seen it before, but he'd never had the urge to say anything about it. "That's a big cross, man," Miles said. "Makes you seem like a missionary from Africa or something."

Sawyer, who was probably only joining the conversation out of boredom, turned to Peter as well. "You're super religious, huh?"

"Captain Obvious strikes again," Miles said.

Ignoring the comment, Sawyer continued, "So, if you're so religious, how did you end up in here? I don't know many other addicts that are as outwardly religious as you...at least not at first. You know, before they're born again or whatever."

"The Lord has always been by my side. And now, in here, even more so. His guidance and love will give me the strength to make it to the other side."

"The other side of what?" Sawyer asked.

"This disease...I mean, you know this is a disease, right? It's no different than cancer."

Sawyer scoffed. "Dude, this is not the same as cancer. People die from cancer. My mother died from cancer, so I know."

"People die from addiction as well," Peter said without losing stride.

"Well, yeah, overdoses and shit. But, I mean, cancer kills a lot more people. Like, if you have cancer, you're probably gonna die. Whereas with this, unless you OD or something like I said, it's not necessarily gonna kill you."

"That's not true, man," Miles piped in, despite not wanting to be part of this conversation anymore. "Drinking fucks up your liver. Haven't you heard of cirrhosis?"

"What are you, a fuckin' doctor?" Sawyer said.

Miles laughed. "You don't need to be a doctor to know that. It's common knowledge."

"Yeah, I was being sarcastic. I know you're not a doctor."

Sawyer was always having to tell people that what he had just said was sarcastic, as he hardly ever used the right tone to make his statements ironic-sounding.

At an off-campus NA meeting a few days before, someone had asked Miles what he at first thought was a rhetorical question. He'd been standing near the donuts and coffee, thinking this would be the first and last meeting he would ever go to, now that he had met the rehab's requirement, when a guy in a Yankees cap and a hole in his sweater asked him: "What do you think is the saddest thing in the world?"

"Excuse me?" Miles had said, looking around to see if perhaps this guy were talking to someone else.

"What do you think is the saddest thing in the world?" the Yankees fan repeated.

Miles wanted to answer, "Probably you, talking to me," but instead said, "I have no idea." He was still unsure why this guy was addressing him in the first place. Even though everyone there seemed friendly, addicts would usually say their name first when they approached someone new. It was that familiar catch-phrase: "Hi, I'm so-and-so and I'm an alcoholic/drug addict." But this guy, evidently, didn't want to bother with that step.

"The saddest thing in the world," the Yankees fan said, "is that you can't go back."

Miles could only stare at this man in the baseball cap. Beneath the brim, he had deep, dark bags under blood-shot eyes—a definite candidate for sadness, not to mention insomnia. And even though Miles was considerably younger than this alleged Yankees fan, he knew enough already from life to know that his casual-seeming statement was probably true.

"No," Miles finally said. "I guess you can't."

Even so, standing by the meds line, in only his second conversation with Sawyer, Miles had no idea yet just how true that sorrowful, heavy-eyed man's declaration would become.

He would never be able to go back.

Miles was in the cafeteria, standing by the cold beverage machine, busy drying his right hand and part of his arm. He had poured water over both when he forgot to put his empty cup under the dispenser before pressing the button (yet another side effect from his never-ending insomnia). He wondered, embarrassingly, whether anyone had noticed this unintentional comic routine, but then reminded himself that drug addicts weren't overly concerned with the rest of the world as a general rule. Someone nearby was even ironically blasting Frank Sinatra's "My Way" and, for some reason, no one was asking them to turn it down or use headphones. The addicts weren't allowed to use any type of entertainment device while in rehab—"Nothing that would distract them from their recovery"—so Miles was confused at first, but then realized the Frank Sinatra fan was a member of the janitorial staff, apparently on a break. Still, though, it was so loud! Couldn't anyone else hear it?

Also nearby, a young girl with a tattoo of a bleeding eagle on her left thigh sat reading a tattered paperback copy of *Even Cowgirls Get the Blues*. The addicts weren't allowed to read personal books either—unless, of course, it was "The Big Book" or something pre-approved by their counselor, the latter of which was near-impossible. The one exception on the approved reading list were any books by or about the reverend who had founded the rehab center, and whose name and legacy enshrined the facility.

"She's hot, huh?" someone suddenly said in Miles' blind spot, causing him to almost jump. "Shit, you're jacked," the voice continued. "Too much caffeine? What the fuck?"

Miles turned to see Sawyer standing there, also eyeing the

tattooed reader. "How the hell did she get approval to read that? Is Tom Robbins now required reading here?"

Miles glanced back at the girl. The paperback was in such ill repair that the author's name was almost completely torn off, as if someone had intentionally ripped it. Miles, not much of a reader himself, was surprised that Sawyer knew the writer of the book—if that was indeed who he was referring to. He didn't come across as someone who even knew what a book was, much less as someone who'd read one.

"You've read Tim Robbins?" Miles asked, unable to conceal the bewilderment in his voice.

"It's *Tom* Robbins…and what? You think I'm stupid or something?"

"No, I was just—"

Sawyer laughed. "I'm fucking with you." He looked over at the girl again, still immersed in her book. "My little sister read that, I think."

"Oh," Miles said. "I didn't know you had a sister."

Sawyer lost his grin. "Hey man, don't get any ideas. I'll fuckin' torch you if you say something about my sister."

"I wasn't—"

Sawyer laughed again. "I'm just being sarcastic."

"That's not sarcasm," Miles said; then decided to let it rest, not in the mood to teach Sawyer about the subtleties of ironic rhetoric. He filled his water glass, this time remembering to put the cup there first. But he couldn't stop his hand from shaking.

"You sleep last night?" Sawyer asked, repeating the most common question probably overheard at breakfast—but only so the person asking, under the pretense of appearing thoughtful, could talk about their own fight with the long hours of the night.

"Nope. Going on four nights now. I think I'm starting to hallucinate." Miles glanced at the janitor, who was still enjoying his cranked Sinatra regardless of whether anyone else was. "That's so fuckin' loud! Can none of the PSAs hear it?"

"What?" Sawyer said. "Man, I had the most fucked-up dream last night."

"Must be nice, dreaming...actually sleeping."

"Yeah, you look tired. Your eyes...ya know, you sorta look Asian. Is that from insomnia, or are you actually part Asian or something?" Sawyer grinned. "Seriously."

Miles laughed. "I'm a little bit of everything, I guess."

"A mutt," Sawyer said. "Nice...." He cleared his throat. "So, anyway, I was like twelve and in my old bedroom in the house where I grew up," Sawyer continued, like he'd never left off, cutting the air with his hand as if to erase the nuisance that was Miles' insomnia. "And I guess I must've been looking out my bedroom window or something because, all of a sudden, I saw a car crash into the house."

"Oh?" Miles said, popping his head up like a whack-a-mole.

"The weird thing, though, was that there was no driver in the car."

"What do you mean, no driver?"

"There was no one in the car. Like, it was driving itself."

"What the fuck does that mean?" Miles said. "I'm not down on dream symbolism, especially a driverless car. Unless it was chasing you or something. Chasing means something, I think."

"I don't think it was chasing me. It *was* me." Sawyer paused for dramatic effect.

"You're tripping, man," Miles said. "That makes no sense. What do you mean it was you? I thought you were looking out your bedroom window?" Miles rubbed his eyes with the palms of his hands. "I'm not following. Too early for me. No coffee yet." Miles started to walk toward his assigned table;

RECKONER

no doubt his table-mates were wondering where he was, especially since everyone needed to be accounted for.

"I *was* looking out my bedroom window," Sawyer said, trying to regain his one-man audience. "But I was also driving the car." This time he didn't hold for the punchline. "I couldn't see myself driving the car because I was coming from the future…. It was future me. I couldn't see future me because, in time travel, you can't exist in two different timelines at the same time. That's why I couldn't see myself."

Miles bit. "But why were you coming from the future? I don't get it."

"I think I was coming from the future to warn myself. Like—"

"Warn yourself about what?"

"That's the part I don't know yet. What the warning was. Because I woke up too quickly. I woke up before the invisible driver could tell me."

In his peripheral vision, Miles could see his table captain pointing him out to a questioning PSA who was evidently looking for him, making sure he had woken up for breakfast—not realizing, Miles thought, that you have to actually sleep in order to wake up.

Miles gave what remained of his attention span back to Sawyer. "So, you can hear future you, but you can't see him? That makes no—"

"I know it makes no sense. That's why it's a dream. I just know it was a warning of some kind, whether future me spoke or not. Like the crash itself was the warning…. I don't know."

"Maybe it's your future sponsor driving the car, and he's warning you not to relapse."

"Relapse?" Sawyer laughed. "This isn't my first time at the rodeo, my friend. If you factor in my age, I have almost no

31

chance of *not* relapsing. The cards are stacked against me… just like they are for you."

"What? The cards are stacked against me?" Miles didn't wait for an answer. "I haven't relapsed before. This is my first time in rehab."

"Well, trust me," Sawyer said. "The odds are still against you. You're destined for mission failure." He smiled askew, revealing a fair amount of his pearly whites. "Who knows," he added, not even trying to conceal his grin, "maybe it was you driving the car?"

PAINTED

"I just need a damn maze and a piece of cheese," Lilly said, adjusting herself on the couch's cushion for what seemed like the hundredth time. Her increasing anxiety, which seemed to prevent her from ever being "comfortable enough," as she sometimes described it to the shrink, was becoming so intolerable that she wondered why she even bothered with the meds anymore. "They're like sugar pills or something," she lamented, answering her tumbling thoughts out loud, this assertion having nothing to do with her previous cryptic comment. "What do you call it?"

"What's that?" Dr. Stevens said, as if she had woken him up from a sound sleep.

"You know, the fake pills, the ones that aren't supposed to do anything."

"Oh, you mean placebos?"

"Yes!" she said, a little too enthusiastically, her Tourette's-like outburst yet another side-effect of her anxiety. "My Ativans are like placebos. They don't do anything at all, as you can plainly see." She laughed at herself, thinking that she acted more like a Batman villain than a regular person most of the time. But how was a regular person supposed to act, she wondered? *Is there such a thing as a "regular person?"*

Now it was Dr. Stevens' turn to laugh. "I can assure you that the Ativan is working. If you weren't taking it, trust me, you'd be a lot worse. Sometimes the benefit of a medication can be felt more when it's absent than when you're actually taking it. But of course, that's just my personal observation. If you're concerned about the effectiveness of any of the medications you're taking, you should talk to Dr. Berg. He's the expert."

Lilly adjusted herself on the cushion again, thinking how ridiculous it was to lay on a couch in therapy. *Is it mandatory to lay on a couch in a psychologist's office?*, she wanted to ask someone who wasn't a psychologist. Why couldn't you just sit in a normal chair? Was it supposed to make you more comfortable physically while you became more *un*comfortable mentally?

"Let's get back to the maze," Dr. Stevens said.

"Maze? What maze?" She was agitated, and she didn't know why.

"Yes. A moment ago, you said something about needing a maze or a piece of cheese."

She mulled it over briefly. "Oh," she said, as if she had just solved a difficult math equation. "It was a maze *and* a piece of cheese, not *or*. You can't have a piece of cheese without a maze." She realized that she wasn't making a nickel of sense. "I mean, sure, you can have a piece of cheese without a maze, but you can't have a maze without a piece of cheese." She knew before Dr. Stevens replied that what she'd said probably didn't make any sense the other way around either.

"You can't?" Dr. Stevens asked. "So, at the end of *The Shining*, was Jack Nicholson's character looking for a piece of cheese in that hedge maze?" Dr. Stevens always made movie references during their sessions, which wasn't a great strategy with Lilly, since she didn't see a lot of movies.

"Jack Nicholson? What maze?"

Dr. Stevens laughed. "It doesn't matter. What I would really like to know is, who are you setting the trap for?"

Lilly just stared at him.

He tried again. "Who are you trying to lure to the piece of cheese?"

Still nothing, as if someone else had said the metaphor a minute ago and was no longer present in the office.

"Who do you think?" Lilly said after a long moment, not able to hide her anger or frustration. "My ex-husband."

Dr. Stevens moved forward in his chair. "Okay, good. So, Barry, then. You want to set a trap for Barry. What about the piece of cheese? What does the cheese symbolize?"

Lilly could only stare at him again, her face twisting as if she had just bit into a lemon. "I'm paying *you*. You're the doctor. Didn't you go to school for this?"

Dr. Stevens chuckled. "I'm just curious who or what you think the piece of cheese symbolizes. Of course, I have my own ideas. I just—"

Lilly looked at him as if she had just suffered a silent stroke and, therefore, couldn't comprehend anything he was saying.

"The student he met at Starbucks…the one he cheated with?" Dr. Stevens said. "I'm sorry, I don't recall her name."

Lilly noticed some water stains on the ceiling. Had they been there before?

Dr. Stevens studied her for a long moment. She hated it when he did that. *Just talk!* she wanted to scream at him. *What are you looking at?*

"Who cares what her name is?" Lilly said aloud. "And besides, I don't think she's the only one. I think he's cheated on me with other women, not just her." She scoffed. "If you can even call her a woman, that is. She's a girl."

"Why do you say that? About the possibility of other women," Dr. Stevens replied, then cleared his throat as if he wanted to activate the reset button.

"What about your son?" he said, as if it were the next logical question—a box that needed to be checked off.

"My son?" she echoed, without hiding her frustration.

Dr. Stevens waited. Lilly relaxed a little.

"Owen's an angel. He's an old soul, as they say." She laughed and wiped her nose. She wasn't sure whether she was having allergies or crying, so the laugh that escaped her surprised them both. "He's seventeen, but acts like he's *my* parent. He makes sure I'm up in the morning, have my coffee, get to the store on time—the store doesn't run itself, obviously. He takes care of me, and he doesn't judge or take sides." She laughed again. "Even after what his father did, he seems so understanding of both of us, including the divorce. I think most kids his age would be wrecked by their parents splitting up, especially an only child, but he seems so resilient."

Dr. Stevens scanned his bookcase, like he was searching for a certain title, before returning his attention to Lilly. "Theodore Roosevelt lost his wife and his mother on the same day," he said, without ceremony.

Lilly stared at Dr. Stevens. Was he saying that Owen could be president someday? Comparing her son to Theodore Roosevelt?

"He didn't allow the sadness of life to break him." A smile faded in from the corners of his lips. "Hope comes from the strangest places."

Before she could speak—accept the award that he was bestowing on her son—Dr. Stevens continued: "Owen might be playing this strategically. Maybe he hopes that you and Barry will get back together if he acts strong, doesn't take sides."

"Are you—"

Dr. Stevens revealed another smile. "As the inimitable Forrest Gump said, 'Sometimes there's just not enough rocks.'"

The interview question was: "Would you rather dance in the rain, ride on a train, or never have any pain?"

Owen sat in the cold, mold-smelling back office of the bookstore, glancing between the bowling-pin-shaped assistant manager and the shelves of discarded books that were, seemingly, not acceptable to sell in the store itself. Either that, or the employees were too lazy to restock or move them to a more sensible holding area. The occasional employee who entered the break room while Owen was in his interview seemed not to notice him at all, or anything else for that matter, other than the vending machine and the large clock on the wall. Some of them read books on their break: Tolkien and general science fiction seemed to be favorites.

"Mr. Owen?" the assistant manager said, unsure as to whether or not he had heard the question. "Rain, train, pain…. Which one?"

Both were aware that the question sounded like Dr. Seuss, which almost made Owen laugh out loud. Without thinking, Owen replied, "Well, dancing in the rain is off the table, since I'm not much of a dancer. Not a big fan of rain either, if I'm being honest. As for having pain, do you mean emotional or physical?" He was in some emotional pain just from the interview itself, compounded by the manager calling him "Mr. Owen," which was one of his pet peeves. Owen was his first name, not his last, and he felt being referred to in this way was just plain laziness—despite it being the "Southern" way.

The assistant manager seemed unprepared for this challenge. No one had ever asked for clarification on that part of the question, and even though Owen's response seemed to be perfectly reasonable, it still appeared to irritate the assistant manager—although he was the type of guy who seemed like he got irritated by most things.

"I can't say," the assistant manager said at last.

"Okay," Owen continued, figuring that the assistant manager wasn't going to clarify anything. "Then I guess I would rather ride on a train."

The assistant manager smiled, revealing a chipped tooth.

"Why would you rather ride on a train than never have any pain?" He glanced down at the question written in his pocket-size notebook. "Or dance in the rain?"

Owen unintentionally laughed out loud—the Seussian aspect was too much to bear. As if he were having a conversation with the fabled doctor of silly, instead of interviewing for a part-time bookseller position…by far the strangest interview he had ever experienced.

"Well," Owen began, "if you're on a train, then you're going somewhere and open to new things. I can't accept the pain answer, even hypothetically, because it might mean that you don't work as hard as you can, like you don't dig in and get your hands dirty, like you're afraid of being defeated by an obstacle of some kind, afraid to try something that might be too risky."

The assistant manager stared at Owen. It was apparent that "Chippy" had incorporated this question into his interviews just to fuck with people—same as his next question: "So who do you think would win in a fight, Spider-Man or Batman?"

Owen laughed again, although he was starting to wonder if the assistant manager threw these absurd questions at white people as well. "I'd have to say Batman," he said. "I'd pick Batman mostly because he's a lot older than Spider-Man and therefore more wise and mature, ya know? So, he would fight in a more intellectual way, which I think would ultimately win the day. Spider-Man can only shoot webs and swing around, so I don't think he'd have the physical edge either— not in the long run, at least."

Now it seemed as if the assistant manager wanted to punch Owen in the face. Owen, too, was starting to get irritated, even though he hid it well. He was only interviewing for a retail position, not the CIA—although he had to admit the last few questions were somewhat entertaining. He had never been asked such strange things before. If he was ever a

manager of something someday and was interviewing someone, maybe he would ask similar thoughtful questions, just
to see what kind of answers he would get. But not to fuck
with the person like Chippy seemed to be doing. Owen was
simply curious how another person might answer them,
especially since he knew that the assistant manager probably
wasn't going to tell him the correct responses—if there *were*
correct responses, which he somehow doubted.

After leaving the bookstore, Owen decided to walk around
downtown Raleigh, maybe get a latte at the nearby coffee
shop. He wasn't really sure how the interview had gone. The
only thing the assistant manager had said at the end was,
"Good convo." Regarding whether he got the job or not, or
how long it would take to find out, Owen had forgotten to
ask. Besides which, Owen didn't have any bookstore experience. He had applied because it was part time and not far
from where he lived with his mother. Although, to be fair,
she had told him that he didn't need a job, especially since he
was so busy with school. She wanted him to spend his free
time with her, doing "mother-son" stuff. And if he insisted
on working, why not just work for her at her boutique store?
But he needed to get away from her a little, get whatever
space he could. It was bad enough that she wouldn't let him
live in a dorm; ever since his father had moved out, she'd
become unbearably dependent on him (though Owen was
afraid of telling her so and hurting her feelings).

As he waited for his latte, Owen watched an older man,
maybe around his father's age, read aloud to his young son
from a children's picture book, using different voices for all
the characters. He was quite good at it, actually, and didn't
seem to care how loud his performance was, right there in
the middle of the coffee shop. From what Owen could tell,
though, no one else seemed to care. Owen wasn't sure what
was more impressive: the father's bravura, uninhibited performance, or the fact that no one seemed to notice it whatsoever.

He was so captivated by this not-so-private performance that he didn't even hear the barista calling his name from a foot away. But someone tapped his shoulder, and Owen picked up his drink.

As he left the coffee shop, Owen passed a cute girl that he thought, at first, was staring at him, but then he noticed she was sitting next to a guy, probably her boyfriend. He glanced at her and she smiled at him, but he was too nervous to smile back. Why was she smiling at him if she had a boyfriend? he wondered. With his peripheral vision, he looked behind him to see if, perhaps, she was smiling at someone else standing nearby, but all he saw was the counter with the sugar and creamer for the customers, and he doubted she would be smiling at an inanimate object. He wished he were the type of guy that could just go up to a girl and converse with her—but he would always talk himself out of it. Anyways, the likely possibility that she was sitting next to her boyfriend provided ample reason for him to keep on walking.

The loose fall air greeted him like a friend he wished he had. He stopped to breathe it in, but then, becoming self-conscious, quickly crossed the street. He walked toward two homeless men who were having a conversation and wondered what they might be talking about. He had once seen two very small children talking to each other in a playground, and had wondered the same thing. Each child seemed to be seriously engaged in what the other was saying despite it only adding up to gibberish, just like the homeless men in their own inebriated way.

"There's so many coincidences all the time that they call it serendipity," Owen heard one of the homeless men say to the other as he passed by them.

"Ser-en-dip-i-ty," the other one repeated, a syllable at a time, as if he simply liked the sound of the word.

Owen thought about serendipity. He knew it existed, because many of the other kids at school seemed to get everything they wanted, whether they deserved it or not. Owen, meanwhile, generally experienced whatever was the opposite of serendipity. It almost felt like he was cursed.

As a child, he had told his mother that he was more afraid of success than failure, to which his mother had replied, "You should be so lucky."

But his mother didn't get it. He wasn't talking about luck. Whatever had compelled him to say such a thing, especially at such a young age, had nothing to do with randomness. It had to do with the existence he was living with her, and that he knew would continue to no end.

After passing the two homeless men on the sidewalk, Owen was reminded of a Civil War documentary he had recently watched. Although he had been taken by some of the genius generals whose strategizing defied the odds, the curiosity that stayed with him concerned what happened to all the dead bodies on the battlefield. *Who picked up all those human remains?* he had wondered. *Or were they just buried where they fell?* The idea of collecting all those fallen soldiers strewn across the fields was incomprehensible to Owen.

Equally fascinating to him, if not more so, was another documentary he had come across recently about the life of Leonardo da Vinci. The man's God-like ideas and work weren't what captivated Owen, but rather the two years of his life when he was completely unaccounted for. Disappearing was something Owen often wondered about. He had heard of people just dropping off the map, but instead of being impressed by the lack of breadcrumbs in their wake, the question he could never shake off was whether or not they had told anyone—specifically their loved ones—what they planned to do before doing it.

MOTHER

Driving relaxed Lilly, and the longer the trip the better. But only if she was alone. Maybe this was because she didn't feel guilty when she drove by herself. With her favorite music gushing from the stereo—lately she couldn't stop listening to the bluesy voices of Sam Smith and Edwin McCain—she would devour every moment of her "me" time. Driving along the wooded North Carolina roads, she would often stare vacantly at the abandoned sheds and farms she passed, wondering what their stories were. *Who had lived there, and why didn't they live there anymore? Why was no one else claiming it? Didn't anybody care about the decrepit buildings, left to wither away without the slightest concern?* Once she had even seen a lone ice cream truck tucked away on some vacant property, with bushes growing out of it—the really old-fashioned kind of truck, not the white pedophile vans from the '70s and '80s—and actually started to become angry that whoever lived there had let it decay, denying present-day children their summer treat.

Occasionally, she thought about pulling over and looking at these haunted plots of land more closely, but then she would talk herself out of it, since she couldn't identify a good enough reason to do so. Then again, she couldn't really identify a good enough reason to do anything when she actually thought about it. What was the purpose? The other night she skipped brushing her teeth before going to bed, then felt guilty about it later. But it wasn't like anything bad was going to happen to her teeth, or, for that matter, herself, if she missed brushing them one time. Was someone, or something, going to appear out of nowhere and punish her?

Her parents were both deceased, but that didn't prevent them from visiting Lilly whenever they wanted. She didn't believe in ghosts and knew the random apparitions weren't real, but that didn't stop the ridiculous incidents from happening. She mostly saw her mother nowadays, since her father had been long gone and probably wasn't still hanging around purgatory—she didn't believe in heaven or hell, but she believed in purgatory—not to mention that she couldn't remember what he looked like anymore. She had started to forget what her mother looked like, too, but that was a stage of grieving she wasn't willing to accept yet, now or ever. Her mother had been her closest friend, and would have been a solid shoulder to cry on during this Barry ordeal. Then again, if she truly thought about it, was she remembering a type of mother that her own mother had never been? *The kind of mother you see on TV? The kind of mother who nails every Hallmark moment on the nose?* She knew people often remembered their loved ones as perfect angels, which no human could have realistically been when they were alive, but that didn't stop Lilly from casting her mother as a Mrs. Brady or a Mrs. Cleaver, who could solve any problem within a half-hour.

She hadn't really gone into much detail about her parents with Dr. Stevens yet; she'd been too consumed with what was going on with Barry to delve into her early life, especially since she had only seen Dr. Stevens a handful of times so far. Her long-time neighbor, Loretta, who couldn't stay out of anyone's business (especially Lilly's, for some reason), had recommended him, and despite the fact that he didn't take any insurance, she still made an appointment to see him. And without knowing why, she hadn't paused in the least about returning, even though his non-stop movie references were starting to set her aflame. Recently, he had quoted from that *Dumb and Dumber* movie—"We've got no food, we got no jobs...our pets' HEADS ARE FALLIN' OFF!"—and she had just stared at him, not knowing, once again, what the hell he was talking about. But yet she still kept coming back, as if there was a part of her that *did* get him, and his movie references, completely. Dr. Stevens, however, wasn't convinced of this, at least regarding *Dumb and Dumber*, and had followed that particular quote with: "Lilly, you can't control the uncontrollable. If your pet's head is going to fall off, then it's going to fall off. Complaining is just a fool's way of seeking peace."

"Heads don't just fall off," she had retorted, as if personally affronted.

Dr. Stevens laughed. "That's exactly what I'm saying." He paused, as if trying to come up with a different strategy. "But let's say your head could just fall off. Do you think you could stop it from happening?"

Lilly scoffed. "So now I'm the dog?"

"The what?"

"The dog, the pet."

He laughed again. "It was actually a bird, but that's not the point." Dr. Stevens seemed to know that he was now losing the battle over this particular analogy. "Worrying about something you can't control is just meditating on shit."

Lilly had stirred. She wasn't expecting him to curse; she always felt taken aback when someone of authority said a bad word. This had started when, as a child, she first heard her mother say "fuck," followed by her defining the word in ways Lilly never expected a parent to do.

"Well," Lilly said, not trying to be funny, "I think if there's a possibility that your head could just fall off, that would be a good enough reason to worry about it."

Dr. Stevens smiled, now seemingly out of frustration. He was probably wondering if she gave him a hard time on purpose, thus giving up any further attempt to explain accidental-bird-decapitation-as-metaphor.

Snapping back to the present, Lilly decided to pull over at

a lake park she was currently passing, a park that she drove by often but had never stopped at before. She turned off the car, got out and walked over to a bench that looked out over the water. The bench was empty, but a young mother played nearby with an infant; she didn't notice them until she sat down. She smiled at the mother, and then at the baby, but realized that the baby probably couldn't see her due to his newsboy hat, which was pulled down so far it covered most of his eyes. It reminded her of the old comic strip character, *Andy Capp*, who also preferred to wear his hat that way, although the baby obviously didn't have much choice in the matter.

She remembered when she first got pregnant with Owen. It was a surprise for everyone, especially the obstetrician, who, because of Lilly's t-shaped uterus, had told her and Barry that carrying a baby to term would be highly improbable. She'd gone through two miscarriages already, had just about given up hope of successfully getting pregnant when the miracle of Owen happened.

Before she had gotten pregnant the first time, when they were just beginning to try, Barry came home from work one day and made an announcement that Lilly would never forget, nor forgive him for, even though he would never know the profundity of his statement. He had said matter-of-factly, as if remarking on the weather: "I can't decide whether I want a kid or a dog." At first, she wasn't sure what he had said exactly, perhaps because her brain couldn't process his equating of a baby and a dog, as if either could be casually obtained—or disposed of. Although she had never been pregnant before, she was fairly certain having a baby was completely different than getting a dog. Accordingly, she had replied with as much sarcasm as she could muster: "Well, you let me know when you decide."

Lilly had no idea at the time this was the beginning of the end, the start of the downward slope on which their marriage would soon slide. She was simply overcome by his naked apathy. Back then, however, almost everything Barry did irritated her to an incomprehensible degree. Like how he would tell a long story—usually a boring one with no point—and then say near the end, "To make a long story short." She would then tell him that he couldn't say, "To make a long story short" after already telling the long story, but he didn't seem to get it. Their friends, when they were on the receiving end of his tales, would always laugh at this, as if Barry did it on purpose for comic effect, but she knew better, and would eventually just keep silent in front of company (other than letting out the occasional scoff under her breath when she couldn't help it).

Barry had lost his hair early, and although she didn't mind his baldness—she'd always had a bit of a crush on Andre Agassi and Vin Diesel—it infuriated her what he did in public whenever he saw another bald man. He would nod at them, and often they would nod back, as if they shared some kind of secret understanding. If he was near enough to another bald man, they would each seemingly stare at the other one's smooth head, like dogs sniffing each other's assholes.

As she sat staring blankly out at the lake, remembering Barry's antics, a grunt escaped from deep inside her belly, which made her face immediately flush with embarrassment. "Sorry," she said to the young mother, whose attention was on her *Andy Capp* baby. "I guess I was daydreaming."

The young mother looked up in a way that instantly told Lilly her apology wasn't necessary. "Excuse me?" she said.

Lilly stood up so quickly that she wasn't yet in control of herself, as if someone else had prescribed her movements without telling her. "I'm sorry for bothering you."

The young mother smiled, revealing perfectly white teeth. "You're not bothering us in the least," she said. "It's actually nice to see other human beings at the park once in a while.

Sometimes it seems like everyone else has died from some catastrophic event, and me and Eddie are the only survivors."

Lilly nodded at the baby. "His name is Eddie?"

"Yes," the young mother said. "I named him after his grandfather." She smiled again. "I love your hair, by the way. It's very Jennifer Aniston."

Lilly laughed. "Oh, right, the 'Rachel' look. I completely forgot about that." Lilly's face blushed again, this time in anticipation of what she was about to say. "People actually tell me that I look like her from time to time, but I don't think so." Lilly shook her head, as if she needed to clear something up to prevent further embarrassment. "The black version, that is."

"I was pretty young when that ran," the mother said, seemingly ignoring the last comment about Lilly's skin color—herself an African-American. "But I watch *Friends* re-runs when they're on. Same with *Seinfeld*."

Lilly tried to smile, but now she felt old. She had only turned forty a few months before—without ceremony, of course—but talking to this mother, who was just a toddler in the '90s, made Lilly feel like a grandmother, or whatever a grandmother might feel like since she didn't really know—at least not yet. The idea of Owen marrying someone and having kids—the thought of it made her feel giddy and spooked her at the same time.

As Lilly drove home from the lake, a home she now worried she would somehow lose in the divorce, her mind whirled with images from the past, most of which were unwelcome. What alarmed her the most, though, was the fact that these images once represented a happy time in her life—but now, thinking back on many of them, the memories flipped from virgin petals to the bitter thorns below. She remembered traveling by train as a student through various countries in Europe, on one particular winter stretch from Vienna to Neuschwanstein watching a young girl in the frigid corridors playing violin to no one in particular. Lilly had felt bad for this teenage performer, especially when the train conductor eventually appeared and asked her to stop playing. But during the few minutes of the lonesome musician's loose interpretation of one of the Kreutzer études, which Lilly secretly observed from her dark compartment, it felt as if they were the only two people in the world who, in some unnamable capacity, could still save humanity.

But whatever intrinsic hope Lilly had achieved as a naïve music student, some twenty-odd years before, had long since departed and was unlikely to return, due mostly to the frightening images she couldn't stop conjuring, a relentless nightmare that soaked her bedsheets and left her, more often than not, waiting terrified for the dawn.

HANGMAN

It was the radiator in his room, which sounded like a British car horn, that woke Miles from a profound sleep. He had finally beaten his insomnia—despite Kirk's best efforts to keep him from doing so—and was dreaming about a white dog when the radiator cap decided it couldn't take it anymore. This didn't wake Kirk, however, who, as usual, was busy wheezing his life away. In addition to snoring, Kirk had sleep apnea and refused to wear anything at night to dampen his affliction. So, every time Kirk blasted off his mattress in the middle of the night, gasping for air, it scared the living shit out of Miles, even if he happened to be awake at the time, which was usually the case. And if that wasn't enough, one of the graveyard-shift nurses would wake them both up every morning at 6:15 for breakfast, usually knocking so hard on the door that Miles thought they might unintentionally break it down.

Even though the radiator had pulled Miles out from a quasi-nightmare—in the dream, he hadn't yet determined whether the white dog was a threat to him or not—he was still irritated that he'd been woken up before the nurse's call-to-arms, especially since he had finally found a good night's sleep.

Of course, the graveyard-shift nurse didn't disappoint, hammering on their door only a few moments later. It was this deafening blow that finally brought Kirk back from whatever alternate reality he was actually the hero of. He sat up a little and rubbed his eyes, then looked over at Miles.

"Why do they always have to knock so loud?" he said, as if Miles somehow knew the answer.

Miles bounced up from his bed, for he knew that if he waited at all, getting up would be almost impossible to achieve. Then he shot a death glance at Kirk, which he didn't bother to hide in his voice. "Because that's what it takes to get you out of your morphine-induced coma."

"I'm not on morphine," Kirk replied dryly, not getting the sarcasm in Miles' voice.

Ignoring him, Miles went over to the thermostat—KILL ME was scrawled above it in messy handwriting, apparently a message from one of the previous "tenants"—and switched the heat to off. At his next group counseling session, when Miles casually mentioned the KILL ME message he had found scribbled above his thermostat, his counselor reacted poorly, to say the least, and insisted on knowing what room Miles was in so this message could be purged before someone reading it, such as Miles, took it as gospel. It seemed ridiculous to Miles to assume that, just because a former tenant of his room had left a particular message, Miles (or anyone else for that matter) would read it and then, because it was etched into the wall, actually kill themselves—as if the thought had never occurred to them until they read the words.

After turning the thermostat off, Miles went over to the solitary window and opened the blinds, all part of his morning ritual. If Miles didn't do it their room would stay dark all day long, since Kirk was too lazy to do anything, much less something so easy to achieve.

"It's too bright," Kirk whined, right on schedule.

"Then don't look at the window."

Miles made a break for the bathroom—being the first person to get there in the morning was a prize worth fighting for. "The sun's not even fully out yet," Miles added as he started to close the bathroom door. "Don't be such a pussy."

Twenty minutes later, Miles was sitting across from Sawyer in the cafeteria, only half-listening to his story of a block party he had attended shortly before going into rehab (the first time, as his current stint was his second).

"You couldn't tell the difference between a straight guy and a gay guy," Sawyer was saying, "because everyone had on sneakers."

Miles was staring at a nearby coffee dispenser, debating about getting a third cup, since they would stop serving regular coffee by the time he got out of morning prayer and meditation. He thought it asinine that they only served decaf after 9:30 in the morning. They were apparently afraid to keep serving "leaded" during the day when so many of the addicts had insomnia and were being given medication to help them sleep, but their idea of how long caffeine stayed in everyone's system was a bit cushioned, to say the least. Even Miles knew that eight hours was more realistic, which meant they could probably safely delay the decaf until 2:00 in the afternoon.

"…that's why sometimes I can see why it would be beneficial to believe in God," Sawyer was saying when Miles returned his attention to the conversation, which was more aptly a monologue with no audience in sight.

"What the hell are you talking about?" Miles asked. "I thought you hated organized religion."

"I do," he said. "Are you even listening? I'm talking about Old Chapel Hill Cemetery. I can't believe that people are just lying there. It's so weird."

Miles scoffed. "Yeah, that's pretty much how cemeteries work. Have you not seen one before? You know, it's where society puts the dead bodies…."

"Ha ha. I mean, it just sorta hit me after that party, when I was puking there."

"You puked in the cemetery? Like on a grave or something? What the fuck?"

"I don't know for sure. It was a while ago, and it was dark. I only know I puked because I saw some of it on my sweatshirt the next morning. Plus, my girlfriend told me how drunk I was the night before."

"Does this story have a point?" Miles said, still seriously considering another dose of caffeine, which he thought could possibly inject some purpose to the festivities. Even though he had finally slept the night before, he felt even more tired now than he did following the nights when he didn't sleep at all. This seeming phenomenon was something he didn't understand, and that he never got a good explanation for when he asked various doctors about it. He didn't really understand doctors, although recently he had discovered a secret word that opened all sorts of doors with the medical staff, as opposed to most other side effects, and that was "hallucination." He referred to it as the "H word" with the other addicts he had met.

The "H word" was also something Miles had more experience with than he would have liked, mainly due to sleep deprivation. As recently as the previous day, hallucinations had plagued him during a morning lecture in the chapel. Just as the speaker echoed one of the mantras of AA: "I'm sick and tired of being sick and tired"—a verse stolen from the '60s civil rights movement—Miles had stood up, thrown the hood of his sweat jacket over his head as if about to rob a convenience store, and somehow made his way to a nearby pillar where he proceeded to balance himself to keep from passing out. But it wasn't fainting that scared him most at the time; it was the dark shadows dancing on the back wall that he couldn't seem to escape or unsee.

"...yeah, it really baked my nerves," Sawyer was saying. He was telling yet another story about a different UNC party, where he apparently met Kate Upton—some supermodel that Miles had never heard of—but some other guy at the party had "cock-blocked" him, and his conversation with her (probably one-sided anyway, if it happened at all) was cut short. Sawyer was jabbering to such a degree it seemed he might run out of breath and would have to stop talking—but then, somehow, he kept going.

"You're like the fuckin' Energizer Bunny," Miles said, trying to get a word in edgewise, possibly two. "Wait a second. I thought you had a girlfriend?"

Sawyer paused for a few seconds, as if Miles' interruption were in a different language and he had to translate it before responding. "You mean that pink bunny with the drum?"

Miles laughed without meaning to. He had forgotten about the pink bunny's implied musical talent, proudly displayed by fervently pounding a bass drum that hung from its neck. If he had a bass drum around his neck, Miles thought, he would probably smash it all the time, too. He felt completely like the pink bunny, he realized, because he couldn't turn himself off either. His mind seemed to race twenty-four hours a day; no matter what he did he couldn't stop it, regardless of the different (non-addictive) tranquilizers the doctors at the rehab center prescribed him. He had told more than one doctor that he needed something more along the lines of a horse tranquilizer to take him down, as he felt he could pretty much beat anything else. Finally, at an appointment the day before, the head psychiatrist had smiled widely and shaken her head when Miles pleaded that no drugs worked on him, and that if he didn't sleep soon he'd go completely crazy. "Don't worry," she had said. "This will make you sleep. Trust me."

At the time Miles wanted to beat this new prescription, even at the cost of yet another sleepless night, just to show her that he knew himself better than she ever could, regardless of all her training. Even though, deep down, he knew she was only trying to help him, he was still irritated by the smug smile accompanying her overflowing confidence in her new magic potion.

But maybe he'd been provoked by the head psychiatrist, because he subsequently felt an added pressure to sleep, as if his insomnia somehow affected more than him. And one thing he knew for certain was that he couldn't take any more pressure. His insomnia was already self-defeating; he didn't need other people to assist in that endeavor. As it turned out, though, the self-righteous doctor *had* been right, for he finally did sleep the night before, despite every effort his brain had made to defeat her proclamation. He almost wanted to lie to her at his next appointment, tell her that her two PhDs were meaningless to him. "Go ahead," he wanted to dare her. "Keep trying to beat me. Because no matter what you do, you never will. I'm a lost cause."

Sawyer was still asking him about the pink bunny's alleged music talents when Miles finally got the strength to overcome his laziness and get another cup of coffee. When Miles returned to the table a minute later, half-expecting to find Sawyer upset about leaving him hanging, he asked Miles, instead, to get him another cup of coffee as well. "Being you're still up," he added.

"Does it look like I'm still up?" Miles asked sardonically, comfortably seated again across from Sawyer.

"Come on," Sawyer whined like a teenage girl, but even more annoyingly.

Miles could only stare back at Sawyer. He was too tired to argue. Besides, considering the time it would probably take to make him shut the fuck up about the coffee, he knew he should just get back up and fetch it for the lazy bastard.

"Fine," Miles grunted, popping back up and feeling more exasperated than humanly possible. "But you owe me—"

"I don't owe you shit," Sawyer said, without a hint of sarcasm. "I don't take orders. I only give them."

Outside in the morning sunshine following breakfast,

Miles leaned against a birch tree and watched the mutating clouds seemingly speed away from one another, as if sharing the sky weren't even a possibility. The sky, especially when it was clear, sometimes reminded him of the sea, which, for some reason, always made him feel lonely. He knew most people somehow felt better when they were near the ocean (or so he believed from movies and TV), but, for him, seeing the boundless waves and stirring whitecaps made him feel like an isolated island yet to be discovered. And Onslow Bay, the rehab center's handsome neighbor, wasn't much comfort either—other than the birds, which Miles had recently started to watch.

In addition to the geese, Miles loved to watch eagles float effortlessly above the bay. Some would even fly in small circles occasionally, or at least it appeared that way, as if just enjoying the simple act of flying and nothing more. Spotting the occasional bald eagle never ceased to thrill Miles either, especially since he had always thought the emblematic bird already extinct. For no particular reason outside of laziness, Miles had put the bald eagle in the same column as a dinosaur—an apparition as unlikely to see in real life as the T-Rex. But then a member of the staff had noticed him birdwatching one day and pointed out a couple of bald eagles scavenging nearby. Although Miles had now seen too many bald eagles to count (regardless of the fact that he might have been seeing the same ones over and over), every time he spotted that small white helmet on an eagles' head he felt he was seeing something that should have already been snuffed out by the phenomenon of evolution (or human interference, whichever came first).

Shortly after arriving in rehab, during the roughest part of his detoxing when most people prayed for death, Miles remembered something one of the PSAs said to him that he was sure he would never forget for as long as he lived. The profundity of this statement was made even more unique based on the fact that almost everything the PSAs usually said irritated him to no end. These self-help observations were especially annoying because they were almost always accompanied by a shit-eating grin, as if they knew all the secrets of the universe and were only too willing to share them. The staff seemed to start this uninvited verbal assault on day one, when they didn't know any of the addicts that well yet. Some of the ditties in regular rotation were: "Insomnia never killed anyone," and that other high-and-mighty mantra, no matter how dire the situation: "You'll be okay." He didn't need anyone to tell him that everything would be okay. What the hell did they know? They couldn't guarantee something like that, especially since it was highly probable that things would *not* be okay; based on percentages most of the addicts there were not going to get a happy ending, sadly including even the more optimistic cases. This wasn't a Hollywood movie, after all.

Miles had been feeling more than suicidal that day, both physically and emotionally (he was only on his third day of detox), when Cash, a bearded, heavily tattooed PSA with a lisp, somehow materialized from thin air itself. Like most PSAs, Cash had a talent for seemingly being everywhere and nowhere at the same time; he smiled, noticing Miles staring blankly out at the bay. (*Cash*...most of the staff members, with the exception of the medical doctors, were former addicts themselves, and many had names that seemed more like nicknames from their using days that they hadn't quite divorced from yet.)

"You alright?" Cash asked, sitting down next to Miles and eyeing his name badge. When Miles didn't answer straightaway, he repeated the question, this time addressing Miles by name as if he were a longtime friend.

"Huh?" Miles finally answered, confirming Cash's probable suspicion that Miles was unglued, or close to it.

"Whadya looking at?" Cash said, revealing that shit-eating

grin Miles would become all too familiar with in the coming weeks, not just from Cash but from almost every staff member, save the medical staff—at least in theory.

Cash followed Miles' deserted gaze across the undisturbed water. "See any bald eagles today?"

This was the first time anyone had mentioned bald eagles to Miles as something in the real world, and not just on money. "Bald eagles?" Miles echoed.

"Yeah," Cash said, pointing to an eagle that was presently searching for breakfast. "See that one there?"

Miles looked, but didn't say anything.

"That's not a bald eagle," Cash continued. "It's just a regular eagle. The bald eagle has like a white hat on."

"A white hat?" Miles said after a moment, as if unable to say anything other than repeating what he had just heard.

Cash laughed. "Well, it looks like a hat. The tops of their heads are white."

Miles continued to stare, this non-response the only one he could sustain; his brain was a labyrinth of torn silk.

"See that one there? That guy's a young bald eagle. You can tell even though he doesn't have a fully white head and tail yet. I think he's close, though."

"Close to what?" Miles said after a beat, as if everything that came out of Cash's mouth required a detailed explanation.

"Close to being an adult. His head is already starting to turn white, and his white blotches are becoming more solid."

They were both silent now, as if any sound other than the intimate ambiance around them would be profane. In the distance a guy played guitar, but since he was so far away Miles had to imagine the music he was carefully strumming. The only other noise that seemed to cut through intermittently came from the make-shift Wiffle ball field, where Miles could occasionally hear the sound of the bat making a connection and, shortly thereafter, someone yelling, "Safe!"

After eavesdropping on a few of these moments, Miles

said something that surprised even him, for he didn't realize he actually felt this way until it leaked out of him like pus from a puncture. "I don't want to live anymore," he said flatly, letting the weight of the words do what was necessary.

For some reason, though, as shocking as Miles felt his statement was, Cash didn't seem the least bit taken aback, like he was used to being the recipient of such confessions. But even so, Cash didn't respond immediately, as though he took the comment very seriously and wanted to give his reply as much consideration as possible. Because this was evident, Miles knew he was going to get an authentic answer and not a canned retort.

"See that?" Cash said finally, pointing upwards at a cluster of unimpeachable clouds. "That's why you can't kill yourself."

"Sorry?" Miles said just above a whisper, unsure of what else he could possibly say.

"Don't apologize," Cash said quickly, as if, once again, he already knew the script. "Don't ever apologize for how you feel, no matter how weak you think you might sound. Because if that's how you truly feel, then you're anything but weak."

"I just worry that I'll never be happy...no matter what."

"Eh," Cash said, once again without missing a breath. "Happiness is overrated."

Miles accidentally smiled, for he didn't really feel like smiling—at least not this much in advance.

"Pain is inevitable," Cash added. "Suffering is optional."

This time Miles didn't smile.

Cash laughed. "Sorry for all the platitudes."

"Platitudes? What's a plat—"

Cash laughed again. Then he patted Miles on the shoulder. "You'll be okay," he said.

Miles flinched from the comment, then flinched again a moment later when Cash's walkie-talkie went off—the volume set so loud that Miles wondered whether people in the next state could hear it. Cash pressed a button on the walkie-talkie to silence it and stood up to leave, no doubt answering the general page that had just blasted through the small black speaker. Before walking away, though, he read Miles' face and said, with yet another shit-eating grin: "Seriously, everything will be alright."

Then, just as he had arrived, Cash disappeared like a ghost, leaving a bitter acidic taste that Miles was already becoming too familiar with. *Fuck everyone*, Miles remembered thinking that day just after Cash left—although, if he were being honest, he'd felt that way just about every day since then, if not before. And now, walking past the bench where he and Cash had sat that day, which seemed like so long ago but really wasn't, he heard a loud buzzing coming from nearby. When he turned to find the source of this noise, Miles noticed a bee searching furiously for nectar among the bushes that lined the wooden fence—a fence that many of the addicts, including Miles, included in strategic daydreams about bounding across and landing in the bay below, sinking to oblivion where rescue was not an option. The punchline to this plan, however, was that the water below was shallow enough to walk through, barely making it to even a short person's waist. So, despite the fall possibly hurting a little, the water was nowhere deep enough to swallow up anyone's seemingly never-ending pain or catastrophic failures.

Miles didn't know whether it was the chemistry of the toxins vacating his body or a lack of sleep, or possibly both, but whenever he closed his eyes, regardless of how much light was or wasn't penetrating his vision, a film on an endless loop would play, with the back of his eyelids as the movie screen. He would always see the same images over and over again—the only variable being the order: a pair of female eyes with long lashes, opening and closing, sometimes winking at him; a close-up of a mouth with sharp teeth, sometimes smiling, sometimes not; a boy standing in the middle of a field, some-times with grand landscapes, sometimes without a boy; a bird flying in a clear blue sky, sometimes alone, sometimes in a flock; and, last but not least, a deformed hand. Miles didn't know what any of it meant; nor, disconcertingly, did any of his doctors. He thought it might be a side-effect from the detox, but none of his doctors would sign their name to that. He wondered, at times, whether he forced these extraor-dinary visions, but he knew innately that he did not; rather, they were somehow messages from his subconscious trying to tell him something—or perhaps trying to warn him?

The other addicts whom Miles explained these fantastical visions to—his cafeteria table-mates for the most part—thought they were cool, and if they were indeed a side-effect from something, to make goddamn sure that whatever he was doing to cause them wouldn't stop. Some of his fellow addicts even admitted to being jealous of these short films that played perpetually in the movie theater of Miles' mind, perhaps because it reminded them of drug-induced dreams they had once had (and were being presently trained to never have again).

Ironically, as much as Miles feared turning the lights off at night and going to battle with his chronic insomnia—a terror that chased him from the moment he relented to end the day—he began to actually look forward to the lights dim-ming in the coliseum behind his eyes so that this cinematic presentation could begin. And although the doctors didn't know what caused this strange spectacle, Miles began to psy-choanalyze the images on his own, innately knowing there had to be some type of meaning behind them all, some answer to the question they were trying to bring to the surface.

Looking back on it later, in real life outside of rehab, Miles would miss his old View-Master that he was never able to fully control—those past psychedelic images frustratingly irretrievable and likely extinguished. Ultimately, he would wonder whether that beautiful yet grotesque slideshow symbolized the ending of his childhood and the beginning of his penitence.

BITCH

Owen was halfway through a blueberry muffin when he realized it wasn't a blueberry muffin. He was at the downtown coffee shop close to the bookstore; even though it was only his second full week as a bookseller he was already tired of it, not to mention bored. Unlike the other employees at the store, he hated to take his breaks in the break room. To him, that wasn't really a break—he had to physically leave the store to feel like he was truly getting a reprieve.

Especially annoying to Owen was the fact that none of the breaks he got were very long at all. Even the "lunch" break, considerably longer than the break you got if you worked at least four hours in a row, seemed like an injustice. By the time he left the store, it was almost time to return. And he didn't think taking lunch in the actual break room would make much of a difference time-wise—not to mention the level of aggravation he would have to endure with the other employees who had the nerve to take a break when Owen did (despite the fact that none of the regular employees—i.e., non-managers—had the luxury of taking a break whenever they desired; it was always up to the manager-on-duty to decide who went on break and when).

He was staring at this so-called blueberry muffin—in point of fact, a banana nut muffin—trying to remember what kind he had actually ordered, when he suddenly heard someone talking to him (and a female voice at that), although she had to repeat herself before Owen finally looked up.

"What?" Owen said, even though he had clearly heard her the first time.

"Did anyone ever tell you that you look like Cam?"

"Who?"

"Cam. Cam Newton."

"Newton?" Owen echoed, like a crotchety old man with bad hearing. He made it so difficult for the girl to converse with him that he later wondered how she had mustered so much patience. He wouldn't even bother to talk to himself, much less believe a stranger would have the will to do so. If this was what it meant to work for a living, he didn't want to become an adult. It put him in a constant bad mood.

"The Panthers QB," the girl tried again, sounding somewhat dumbfounded, as if everyone should know who Cam Newton was, especially in North Carolina. "He's really hot," she added, in case he was in the minority.

Owen could only stare. She had long blonde hair that was partially braided at the top. She reminded him of a blonde Princess Leia, but with longer hair. After another moment, as if slowly waking from a deep sleep, Owen finally understood what she was saying, or at least caught the gist of it. "Oh," he said. "I don't really watch football."

This, too, embarrassed Owen. He felt it wasn't very manly to not know football, especially if a female knew more about it than he did. Despite trying to stay interested in a game on several occasions—especially on Thanksgiving, when there was nothing else to do—he just couldn't get into it. Like almost everything else in his life, it bored him.

"You look exactly like him," she said, apparently still trying to start some type of conversation. "And you have the same ears, too."

Despite her best efforts, Owen was still clueless that she was flirting with him, and he had no idea what she was talking about regarding his ears. Weren't his ears pretty normal? he wondered. Maybe they were somewhat small proportionally, but no one had ever said anything to him about his ears before.

"Ah, yes," he said, sounding like an old professor who had just gathered the academic information he was seeking; or, more characteristically, the long-awaited lab test results. "Do you like blueberry muffins?" he asked without thinking, then felt embarrassed yet again, worried that he now sounded like an idiot-savant or something.

She laughed and covered her mouth with her hand. She was seemingly self-conscious of either her mouth or her laugh, or possibly both, and now, with the unequivocal lab test results in, Owen felt like he was in love.

"I do like blueberry muffins," she said, then eyed the half-eaten muffin in front of Owen. "That doesn't look like a blueberry muffin, though."

Now it was Owen's turn to impress, or at least try to. "Would you like a blueberry muffin?" he asked evenly, or as evenly as he could, trying desperately to not sound nervous.

She laughed again, and again covered her mouth. After a few seconds of sheer terror Owen realized that her laugh just then was a good thing, or at least he prayed as much. He just didn't want to blow it, especially in a situation that didn't happen to him very often—if at all.

"Uh, sure," she said, "but I'm just gonna grab a coffee first. And I can get the muffin. No worries...but I appreciate the offer."

He was thinking that he had failed by asking her such a stupid question, but then she surprised him by setting her purse down on the table and adding: "Is it okay if I sit with you?"

His mouth tried to say "sure" or "yeah" but what eventually came out was "shyeah," the shy compromise. She laughed again—*boy, what a laugher,* he thought—and then said boldly, à la Arnold Schwarzenegger but cuter: "I'll be back."

Two minutes and seventeen seconds later she reappeared and sat down at his table just as she had promised—minus the muffin.

A golf ball landed at Lilly's feet as she was checking the mail at the end of her driveway. When she and Barry had bought the house just before Owen was born, the realtor had told them—in answer to Barry's question about the driving range, which skirted the periphery of the backyard—that only a very good golfer could hit the ball well enough to make it to their property. Be that as it may, there seemed to be an abundance of good golfers in the area, since they found themselves dodging balls quite often. One year, two days before Christmas, a stray ball actually hit Owen in the ankle and they had to take him to the emergency room when it swelled up afterwards. Why they had never complained or moved, though, Lilly couldn't answer. Barry had joked with friends over the years that it was sort of like they were living on top of an old Indian burial ground, like the family from *Poltergeist* who, defying logic of any kind, refused to move away until most of the damage had already been done.

Looking back, Lilly wasn't sure what she found more grating: the random attack of stray golf balls or Barry's stale jokes that only he found funny. He reminded her of those comedians that laughed at their own jokes, like Bob Saget, for instance—and she hated Bob Saget. She even referred to Barry as Bob Saget when she was really steamed, and right to his inflated, disproportionate face, but he never seemed to get the dig, which only magnified her irritation to a more oppressive level.

She lost her grip on all the shopping catalogs and miscellaneous bills that she had just pulled from the mailbox due to her raging effort to kick the golf ball back at the evildoers—a futile attempt to begin with, even sans the fact that her foot completely missed the target. Worse yet, her flat shoe went flying out from under her during this failed Rockette-like kick, causing her to lose her balance and plummet into the graveled driveway. Now wearing only one shoe, she wailed like the Wicked Witch of the West during her death-throes. Amplifying her heinous mood to an even higher degree, Lilly noticed her neighbor curiously observing from across the street, so she shot up, collected the scattered mail from the driveway and limped to the front door, cursing under her breath at each painful step of her unadorned foot.

Shortly after her evening bath—one of the few things that calmed Lilly down, especially in combination with the extended-release Xanax that helped her sleep—as she was strewn across the floral couch reading Richard Dawkins and sipping from a chardonnay (also a wonderful combination with the Xanax), she saw something white flash in her peripheral vision. Thinking she had just moved her head too fast, she continued to read about militant atheism and wondered whether or not she would be considered militant. She didn't think she was belligerent toward religion, at least not in general, but all those Bible-thumpers littering the south who often quoted scripture in an attempt to recruit the non-religious made her feel more than a little hostile. Lilly was a lifelong believer in "to each their own," but when people started to prey on other people's anxieties about death, offering them what they felt was a justifiable explanation to all life's mysteries but with no factual basis whatsoever, she wanted to stab them in the eyeball. *Jesus*, Lilly thought, *maybe I am militant? Why would I ever stab someone? And in the eyeball, no less?* It reminded her of a short story she wrote as a child called "Murder in the Face," which absolutely horrified her mother, who couldn't seem to make it past the title to the beginning of the narrative (not such a loss anyway, since the prose didn't come close to matching the *je ne sais quoi* of the title).

She was about to get herself another glass of wine when she saw the white flash again, and this time not just in her peripheral vision. Her heart leaped inside her throat, but instead of fear spreading throughout her body, it was unmitigated resentment that she succumbed to from being alone in the house—no Barry of course, but *where the hell was Owen? Was he working late at the bookstore? Were bookstores even open this late?*

She glanced at her naked wrist, expecting to see a watch there, but she had taken it off before getting into the bath. Now she was even irritated at the book she was reading, since it wasn't electronic; if it had been on her Kindle instead, then maybe she could see the time. Then again, she realized, it was so frustrating trying to figure out what time it was on the Kindle, as you had to press some button to get there. *Why wasn't anything easy?* she wanted to scream at anyone who would listen.

She was pushing herself off the couch—surely, she wasn't getting fat, was she?—when Lilly saw the white flash a third time. But now it wasn't just a flash. She could clearly see what the whiteness was, and it wasn't a car's headlights (as she had subconsciously written it off). Nor was it an early snowstorm—the other possibility. It was a white dog with red-hued eyes like a wolf, and it was standing on the lawn just staring at her.

Now her animosity toward Barry returned. She had begged Barry for a dog—preferably a female one, as dog penises bothered her, especially the "lipstick" aspect—starting back when Owen had entered the ninth grade. Knowing that her only child would be going away to college in four years (but, of course, not knowing that she would be divorced by then as well), she'd come up with the dog idea—although, at the time, more for company than security. But Barry had told her he was against getting a dog, mostly because he was a heartless son-of-a-bitch who had a dislike for all animals, which somehow included man's best friend. She remembered watching TV with Barry once; when a commercial came on that showed abused dogs Lilly had looked away, unable to bear such an appalling sight, but Barry stayed glued as if he were watching a Bruce Willis action movie (the first *Diehard* was his favorite movie—and she hated herself for knowing that).

Barry had been Lilly's high school sweetheart, so she had never intimately known another man, but when he wouldn't look away from that commercial about abused animals, as she did, she began wondering whether all men were just as insensitive to such things. If she were going to stab anyone in the eye, she realized, momentarily forgetting about the white dog that was still outside the window staring at her, it should be Barry. The religious extremists, or whatever category they fell under, were no match to her now-ex-husband. If the world had more "Barrys" in it than anything else, the whole of mankind was indeed in trouble.

She shouted, "Shoo!" through the window at the white dog, as if it could hear her through the thick panes. Not surprisingly, since it obviously couldn't, it stayed rigidly where it was, like some kind of sentinel protecting her—and not, as she first suspected, there to get her. But why did she need protection? *And from whom?*

She laughed out loud. Was she really asking herself existential questions because a stray dog was standing outside her house? She rose up from the couch—a harder task than she anticipated due to the Xanax and wine, not to mention the hot bath—and went to the front door. Why the dog was such an annoyance to her, she couldn't say; she just knew she wanted it to leave and stare at someone else. But why was it staring at her, anyhow? As if it were judging her, and for something she didn't mean to do....

Yet when Lilly flung the front door open to scream at the dog, it was already gone. She looked down the street in both directions, but the dog was nowhere in sight. Had she only imagined it? She was fairly stacked with Xanax and wine, but that shouldn't make her hallucinate...should it?

She yelled for the dog as if she wanted it to come back, as if it were her own dog—a stark contradiction to her original intent—but only because Lilly needed the animal to acknowledge her now; she needed it as evidence that she was still alive and could affect the world, even if just with her voice.

But the dog didn't return that night, or the next night, or the night after that. It wouldn't return until almost a year later, standing in the exact same spot it had stood on that first night—staring at her, either on guard or waiting to kill, beckoning her to do something she wasn't quite ready to do.

Owen had completely lost track of the time, and at the cost of his job; there was no "three-strike rule" at the bookstore, or even a two-strike one. But, then again, starting from back at his initial interview, he had a nagging feeling that the assistant manager had it in for him. Owen wasn't normally a paranoid person, but it seemed like the assistant manager wasn't his biggest fan and, as a consequence, was just waiting for him to slip up. But why had he even hired him, then? Were there no other good candidates? Or possibly no other candidates at all? That couldn't be; there were always people looking for jobs. Sure, he had taken too long of a lunch break when he first met Elodie—the football-watching blonde with the bad memory and the name that seemed misspelled—but it was so worth it. Surely, he couldn't have left her mid-flirt to return to a job he hated anyway. Plus, he didn't want to fuck it up like he knew he would if given the chance—Elodie, that is—and he certainly didn't want to mess with the all-important flow.

It wasn't until almost an hour had gone by that Elodie asked him what time it was; she didn't wear a watch because she already had a cellphone that told the time, so why did she need a watch?, she had asked when Owen glanced at her bare wrist, as if he didn't believe her. In actuality, though, he was looking at the tattoo near her wrist. It was a sideways number eight, which he found out later was the symbol for infinity. *But why did she have an infinity tattoo?*, Owen would subsequently wonder that day, after he had Googled the symbol. With no job now, he had all the time in the world to Google to his heart's desire.

Even after Owen looked at his watch to tell her the time, it still didn't occur to him that he was already very late in returning from his lunch break. Later, after he was fired, he would justify his empty-headedness (to himself, at least) due to being completely smitten by Elodie, which, coupled with the fact that he didn't like the job anyway, was just fine with him. However, it wasn't until he overheard someone at the next table say something about needing to stop at the bookstore after they finished their coffee that Owen realized he was fucked.

"I'm fucked," he had said, which for some reason resulted in Elodie laughing. After she covered her mouth again, which only made Owen forget *why* he was fucked, he impulsively asked her why she covered her mouth every time she smiled or laughed.

"That's a bold question," she said after a bit, possibly due to not expecting it, let alone having a good answer ready just yet.

"Sorry," Owen said, mad at himself for crossing the line. He wasn't a line crosser normally, which only frustrated him more, hoping it wasn't a fatal mistake. "I meant it in a good way."

Elodie smiled, which instantly let him off the hook. And this time she didn't cover her mouth, possibly due to the smile coming on so quickly. "I don't know," she said, deciding to come up with an answer after all. "I guess I'm a little embarrassed by my mouth."

"Why? What's wrong with your mouth?" he said sincerely.

Elodie smiled again, this time remembering to cover it, but then instantly dropped her hand from her mouth since the jig was now up. To Owen it seemed as if she were shedding her clothes, exposing her naked body to him for the first time.

"You have nothing to hide," he said. "You have a great mouth."

Owen couldn't believe he was being so assertive with her. Normally, when he was around someone of the opposite sex he didn't have the nerve to even say hello to them, much less look in their direction for too long for fear of being caught. Caught doing what exactly, he didn't know. But for some reason, with Elodie, even though he had only just met her, he felt freer to be himself—whatever "himself" actually meant.

"Thank you," she said, still smiling and still not covering her mouth. "You're sweet."

Owen smiled back without thinking about it first. He didn't seem to be in control of any of his responses to her, verbal or otherwise. Hopefully, he thought, he had a good mouth, too, but he really didn't know for sure. No one had ever told him—other than his mom, of course. She complimented him so much on just about everything that it made him uncomfortable; the frequency, alone, of her unabashed sentiments were enough not to be believed. Had his mother not been so emotionally bankrupt and repetitive, he just might have taken her adulation as truth—or at least some of it. And now he had to believe Elodie.

After Owen and Elodie finally walked out of the coffee shop, now more than a block away, Elodie remembered that she had left her cellphone on the table. Owen had gallantly offered to walk her to her car, hoping that with another few minutes to gain more confidence he could ask her out on a real date, like dinner or something. The only problem with this plan, however, was that Owen didn't have any money, especially now that he had lost his job on top of everything— an irony he didn't see presently, nor the bigger irony that was just a few seconds, and feet, away from him.

He was walking back to the coffee shop by himself after telling Elodie that he would go fetch it—hurriedly walking, that is, for he didn't want someone to steal Elodie's cell— when, out of the corner of his eye, he saw something green on the ground. Owen wasn't a person who usually found things, not to mention valuable things, or even the type of person someone would call "occasionally lucky;" but, on this particular afternoon, he would squash all of that. For when he stopped and looked down, more due to instinct than any-thing else, he realized the small green object next to his right foot wasn't a leprechaun, but rather the end of a leprechaun's rainbow: a hundred-dollar bill.

Owen couldn't believe his luck—nor again, see the irony—that he now had the money to take Elodie out. Of course, he still had to ask her, which he would do once he hopefully found her cellphone and returned it to her. But now that he had found the money, he was feeling much more confident. It wasn't the money itself, though, that had boosted his courage. It was the simple fact that, finally, things were starting to go his way.

TRUANCY

He awoke to the sound of seagulls, or possibly a woman getting fucked, but then he remembered that he was still in rehab and no one here was getting fucked—at least not in any enjoyable way. Before jumping out of bed, beating the 6:15 wake-up call, Miles thought about the first (and only) time he ever had sex. He'd run away from his foster home, his fourth one in as many years, and found himself at some type of pop-up carnival in a parking lot next to the mall. He had met this girl—Rhoda? Rhonda?—who may or may not have been working at the carnival. He was never sure, as he quickly found out the truth wasn't something she was entirely familiar with. What she was familiar with, however, was having sex. She couldn't have been more than a few years older than Miles, but she definitely knew what she was doing. Miles even asked her how many men she had been with; she had said (lied) that Miles was only her second.

To be fair, Miles hadn't been totally honest himself that night. He had lied to her as well, saying he *wasn't* a virgin, which she could quickly tell was complete bullshit, even saying so right to his face. Miles was even more humiliated when his massive erection suddenly went down and withered back into itself, like a turtle retracting its head (which, like the reptile, was more because he was scared as opposed to not turned on). Later, Miles would argue with himself whether or not he had truly lost his virginity that night, because he had never come (at least not inside her). He hadn't come until a few hours later when he found himself back at his foster house, masturbating to an old *Playboy* magazine he had

73

stolen from one of his foster brothers, who hid them in a tackle box under his bed.

Looking back on it, Miles wondered whether he couldn't run away from his foster home that night because of his unquenchable need to shoot his load, since he wasn't able to finish with Rhoda/Rhonda behind one of the porta potties next to the main carnival tent. Even if she hadn't called him out on his virginity, the smell of the porta potties was enough to kill his mood, regardless of the fact that it was his "first time."

"What the fuck?" Kirk suddenly exclaimed from under his sheets.

"Jesus, you scared the shit outta me," Miles said as he made his way toward the bathroom. "I didn't know you were up."

"Well I am now."

At breakfast a half-hour later, as Miles was on his second cup of coffee and trying to make his way through carton-based scrambled eggs, Sawyer told Miles that he was planning on leaving rehab in the afternoon, probably after lunch. "It would be best to get one last meal in," he said, "even though it will likely be shit. Who knows when I'll eat real food again…if you can call this real food."

"What do you mean you're leaving?" Miles returned quickly, somewhat impressed with himself for actually paying attention to what Sawyer was saying this time, especially on only a few hours of "true sleep," which, as far as Miles was concerned, was straight sleep without waking up at all during the night—something he was hardly ever able to achieve, even outside of rehab.

"Are you not listening to the words coming out of my mouth?" Sawyer said, enunciating each word in exaggerated fashion like Chris Tucker in *Rush Hour*, a movie Miles had never watched from start to finish but had seen enough scenes from to know that Sawyer was mimicking it.

"Yes, I am listening, as a matter of fact," Miles said, a little irritated that even when he was actually paying attention—for once—he wasn't getting any credit for it. "But I still don't understand. What do you mean you're leaving? Like, today? I thought you weren't out until next Thursday."

"I'm not," Sawyer replied, "but there's this guy that's coming around that doesn't come by very often…or never, actually."

"What the fuck are you talking about? Am I understanding this right? You're gonna leave rehab like a week before you actually get out?"

Sawyer nodded his head a little bit, enough to equal an acknowledgment.

"Why the fuck would you do that?" Miles asked. "What do you mean there's a guy coming around? What guy?"

Sawyer scanned the cafeteria with paranoid glances. "Shut the fuck up. Not so loud. Fuck!"

Miles lowered his voice a little. "Well, I don't get what the fuck you're talking about. You're talking crazy."

"What's the big deal if I leave a few days early?" Sawyer said, sounding like a normal, non-paranoid person again—at least for several seconds in a row.

"But why would you do that? Don't you have to finish because of a court order?"

"A court order?"

"Yeah, for that shoplifting you said you got arrested for. And the cops who arrested you said you were high as a kite, and then the judge forced you to go into rehab as part of your sentence?"

Sawyer was silent for a moment, as if remembering a fond memory and not the actual memory of getting arrested outside a Durham convenience store. "Well, fuck that shit. I don't need no judge telling me what I have to do. I do what *I* want to do."

Now it was Miles' turn to be reflective—but about what,

he wasn't sure. His mind had gone to sleep suddenly, which was not unusual for him, especially since his body was still detoxing itself.

"You sound like you're on Jerry Springer or something," Miles finally said. Though he had only seen the Jerry Springer show twice in his life, and only for a few minutes each time, he knew the reputation the show had, like most people did.

Sawyer laughed, which Miles wasn't expecting. In the short time Miles had known Sawyer, he rarely cracked up. "This has nothing to do with whether I got some dumb bitch pregnant."

Miles took a bite from the burnt white toast on his plate, then a sip of his coffee, which had gone cold. "Who's this guy you're talking about?"

"What guy?" Sawyer said, eyeing Miles' coffee. "Can I have some of that?"

"Fuck you. Get your own coffee."

"I don't feel like getting up."

"Well, I'm not your fuckin' slave. I'm not getting you coffee again. I've done it so many times, it's your turn now."

Sawyer snickered wheezingly, like air deflating from a tire. "Dude, it's never my turn."

Miles debated whether or not he wanted to get up to get another coffee for himself. "So you said there's this guy that comes around, or something?"

Sawyer thought about it for a moment. "Oh yeah...so I've never met this dude or anything, but he apparently has the best crack in the Triangle."

"Crack? Are you serious? Or are you talking about his ass crack, homo?"

Sawyer turned white and his pupils seemed to dilate. "Don't call me a homo, you fuck. I'll take you down right here."

Miles laughed. He'd never seen Sawyer this upset before,

so he thought at first that he was just joking around. "You'll take me down? Okay, Pee-Wee, whatever you say."

Sawyer seemed to be turning into *The Incredible Hulk* before Miles' eyes, which completely jarred him. For the first time in his life, Miles was actually scared of another person's possible violence toward him, despite the fact that they were in rehab presently and the chance of a full-fledged fight breaking out, and not getting stopped just as quickly, was slim to none.

"Don't call me Pee-Wee," Sawyer said, visibly holding his temper back.

"Chill out, man. I'm talking about your tattoo."

"Oh," Sawyer said, reaching over to grab Miles' coffee and taking a sip before Miles could stop him. "Shit, this is ice cold!"

"Hey man, get your own coffee!" Miles grabbed his coffee back and gazed into it as if looking for possible contamination due to Sawyer drinking from it. "That's what you get for not getting your own cup. Sorry it's not up to your satisfaction." The sarcasm not lost on Sawyer, for once.

"So, let me get this straight," Miles went on. "You're gonna leave rehab like a week before completing your sentence in order to buy crack from some dude? Do you hear how crazy that sounds? It almost sounds like the punchline to some stupid joke. I mean, are you hearing the words I'm saying? Single-digit days remaining in rehab…buying crack…hello?"

"It's *the words coming out of my mouth*, not the words I'm saying," Sawyer said.

Miles could think of nothing to say in response due to the cloud of confusion encircling him, which was also apparent to Sawyer—finally.

"You're jacking up the line from *Rush Hour*," Sawyer said calmly, as if the sudden rage he'd almost had a moment ago had been completely imagined by Miles.

Likewise, it took Miles another moment to get his sea legs back. "I'm not quoting some stupid movie," he said.

Sawyer smiled, the smile of someone completely confident with what he was about to say, like there was no denying the truth of it in any way whatsoever. "The punchline is that you're coming with me."

And it did turn out to be the punchline.

"Hey man, you can jack up your own life," Miles said to Sawyer a short time later, borrowing the word "jack" from Sawyer's somewhat limited lexicon, "but I only have two weeks left here myself. So why would I leave now when I'm so close to finishing, just to go with you down to North Carolina to buy crack? I think you're cracked in the head if you think I'm going with you. I don't even buy that you're gonna go, being you have a court order and all. You're not that stupid."

"You don't have a court order, too?" Sawyer asked, but then answering his own question said, "Oh, that's right. You don't. You're here because your foster parents made you come."

"My foster parents didn't make me do shit. I just needed to get away from them."

"Oh, I see. So, this is your idea of a vacation that you willingly went on?"

"Hey man, this place isn't so bad. I mean, have you not seen the bay out there? It's pretty awesome."

"Oh, that's right. You're a birdwatcher. I forgot."

"Don't knock it 'til you try it," Miles rebuked, not without some scorn. "It's totally amazing, just watching them soar and shit."

Sawyer stood up abruptly from the faux-leather chair.

They were sitting in the makeshift library—there weren't any actual books there, since the addicts would probably steal them out of boredom—adjacent to the cafeteria, although breakfast had ended some time ago. It was almost lunchtime now. "Well, while you're nerding out about birds flying over the water, I'll be getting fucked up down south, where apparently the real men are."

Miles laughed. "Sure, man, knock yourself out smoking crack. You'll end up back here in no time…or worse, in jail…or dead. You're a junkie, man. I mean, isn't this like your fifth time in rehab?"

Sawyer turned toward the French doors that led to the cafeteria, a good thing for Miles because it prevented him from seeing the rage percolating on Sawyer's face, like a tea kettle about to whistle. "It's my third time, asshole. But that doesn't mean shit. Trust me. If you ever go back to rehab, which you definitely will, you'll see that it doesn't mean shit. They throw some baby aspirin and *The Big Book* at you and expect you to proclaim Jesus as your savior or some shit. I say fuck Jesus and the donkey he rode in on." As he was heading through the doorway, he added: "Fuck this place…and fuck you."

Alone for a few seconds before people started filing into the cafeteria for lunch—the center seemed to revolve around meals—Miles repeated "donkey" a few times. "What an idiot," Miles said to himself under his breath as the incoming crowd made their way toward the waiting Sloppy Joes. *If Jesus actually existed and rode on anything*, Miles thought, *it would've most likely been a camel, not a fuckin' donkey.*

Walking against the traffic, Miles made his way outside toward his favorite spot to watch the birds. He didn't get too far, though, before one of the PSAs ordered him to turn around and go back to the cafeteria for lunch. Fortunately, it was Cash, and when Miles told him that he would be back in a minute, Cash let him go. Miles had no intention of returning anytime soon, which Cash probably knew, and made sure to conceal himself behind the birch tree in such a way that any PSAs or other staff members who happened to walk by wouldn't see him—unless, of course, they were specifically looking for him. Almost everyone there, staff and addicts alike, knew where to probably find Miles if he went missing (and Miles went missing a lot).

As he waited for some birds to show up—they seemed to be out to lunch as well—Miles scanned the rehab center's property, once again finding himself impressed at the level of care that seemed to go into everything there, from the smallest bed of flowers to the manicured lawns and impeccable foliage. Even the shrubbery on the south part of the suicide fence was spectacular; although, as Miles now knew, the only thing an addict could gain by leaping over this hedge was sheer embarrassment, death and/or freedom being entirely unobtainable here.

Finally, a couple of eagles entered the mid-day sky. Miles watched them for a while, completely lost in their effortless soaring—so lost, in fact, that he also completely lost track of the time, though he didn't have a watch on to know for certain. He often wondered why people still wore watches, since most people owned cellphones (when they weren't in rehab). So why on earth would anyone need additional reminding? Was it that hard to keep track of the time? For Miles, at present, the answer was an ironic and definite yes. Not only had he bypassed the lunch hour, but he was about to miss the afternoon lecture and meditation as well; granted, it was highly probable a PSA would soon find him and send him over to it, especially once he turned up on the missing list after not responding to his name during roll call. It was a funny thing, the roll call at rehab, as once your name got no immediate response some other addict, as sure as hell, even if they didn't know you at all, would pipe up with a possible explanation as to your current whereabouts. This, in turn, would be instantly confirmed by the majority, despite the fact this same majority probably had no real idea where the missing person was presently located. Miles found the whole thing ridiculous, and would often joke to himself that it was a good thing they weren't a jury in a murder trial or something, as they apparently could be swayed by the wind alone.

It was Cash who eventually showed up at the birch tree, of course just in time for Miles to make it to the lecture and meditation without missing a beat—not that any of the lecture would likely be something new that Miles hadn't heard before. No matter who the "guest" speaker turned out to be, the dribble they usually tried to impart on the addicts—though some lecturers were better at it than others—was recycled bullshit that all had the same message, and that was: "Don't fuck up again. Because if you fuck up again, you'll likely lose everything this time...if you haven't lost it all already."

This was fine with Miles. He had no concept of losing everything, as everything was something he'd never had to begin with. Maybe it was this very fact that made him agree to leave rehab with Sawyer—because, for Miles, at least as far as he knew, there was nothing at all to lose anymore.

DOMINION

Sawyer's father was former military—from which branch, Miles didn't remember, and he wasn't about to ask Lieutenant Colonel Ramirez to repeat it. Miles couldn't even remember which war Sawyer's father had said he fought in; Miles was horrible with US history, or any history for that matter, and his lack of basic retention skills didn't help. When Miles first noticed that he couldn't remember anything anyone ever said to him, he blamed it on the tranquilizers that he used to take, and then held the detoxing from these same drugs responsible, in addition to the fact he had left rehab before his body was probably ready. But as it turned out, that was only part of the explanation. He was just a bad listener, period. Miles didn't even know that Sawyer was Latino; whether or not Sawyer had ever mentioned that back in rehab, Miles had no idea. But that was inconsequential now. At the beginning of any relationship, if you missed the finer details the first few times around, it would eventually become too late to ask—and sooner rather than later. Miles couldn't even remember if Lt. Col. Ramirez had said anything when his son suddenly appeared at his front door—a son who was supposed to still be in rehab; a son who currently had a warrant out for his arrest; a son who only had to wait a few more days, but didn't.

Lt. Col. Ramirez had a very animated way of talking, and was clearly used to hypnotizing audiences with his war stories. As he spoke he acted everything out with only his upper body, as he needed an ornate wooden walking stick to help balance his weak legs—a straightforward cane was unacceptable to him—and since he had been on the front lines, which was where most of his stories took place, his graphic descriptions demanded theatrical gesturing.

Miles and Sawyer had only been out of rehab for a few days—"out" a loose term, of course—and the friendship they had started there continued to grow in the real world, which for people who had met in such an environment was not out of the ordinary. There is a certain type of intimacy that addicts share with one another—an understanding that, in a lot of ways, more than rivals their relationships with their sexual partners. In this way rehab relationships are more on par with the bond between soldiers who have experienced a wealth of devastation and death that a civilian could never understand, even with the glossy aid of Hollywood's best efforts. This members-only club of kindred souls, however, was foreign to Miles, who couldn't make any such connection while Lt. Col. Ramirez regaled his other listeners with tales of his fallen brothers.

On their second day there Lt. Col. Ramirez ended one of his stories with an unforgettable decree—one which was able to rouse Miles from his stupor and, for that matter, any living, breathing human being in near proximity. "That shit will pucker your ass," he had stated, the exclamation to that particular war story. He shot a look at Sawyer, who flinched in such a way that Miles wondered if the retired Lieutenant Colonel had ever physically abused his only son. Sawyer being his only son was a sore point, to say the least, for the former military man, who had been cursed with three daughters before God finally granted him a male offspring (three daughters who had cursed him back by wanting nothing to do with him now that they were adults).

"What's with your dad?" Miles had asked Sawyer that afternoon as they were leaving his house, walking toward his father's tan-colored diesel-guzzling Mercedes—an audacious contradiction, since the retired Lieutenant Colonel's every other sentence seemingly started or ended with "fuckin'

Germans" this or "fuckin' Krauts" that (though he hadn't fought in WWII). Then again, he was, if anything, consistent in his fanatical patriotism, since he tried very hard to make sure his hatred for the Japanese, Vietnamese, Koreans, and occasionally even the Russians (despite the fact that the Cold War had been long over) were equally dispersed.

"What do you mean?" Sawyer replied as they got into his father's diesel Mercedes. But before Miles could say anything, Sawyer continued, "Yeah, I know. He's a bit rough around the edges, but he's always been that way."

"Oh, because he was in the military?"

"Yeah, sure, but he hardened up even more when my mom left."

"Left?" Miles echoed, starting to feel a little lightheaded, again. Or had he been feeling this way for a long time, he wondered, and only now just noticed? He wanted to share this curiosity with Sawyer, but he knew Sawyer wouldn't listen. Detox complaints were not allowed.

Sawyer started the car, apparently not noticing his gaffe.

"I thought your mother died of cancer," Miles said, flatly.

"Oh…right. Well, she did, sort of."

"Sort of? You don't *sort of* die from cancer."

"Yeah, true."

"Your father was pretty old when he had you, huh?" Miles asked, although he said it more like a statement.

Sawyer nodded, then turned out of the driveway and gunned it down the street—no doubt to aggravate his father, who couldn't gun his own car anymore. If his dad hadn't been watching them through the living room's bay window, frowning, there was no doubt he'd have heard it regardless.

"My mom left when I was a kid," Sawyer said. "I was super little, so I barely remember her."

"That's pretty different than dying of cancer, just so you know."

"Yeah, well, I never saw her again, so it's basically the same thing."

Miles was silent for a moment, now riding a fresh wave of nausea. "I guess I could say the same thing," he eventually said, regaining himself, however briefly. "And about *both* my parents. But I didn't get the chance to even see them for a little bit, like you did with your mother."

It now seemed like a competition to see whose backstory was sadder, although there would never be a clear victor in this case; with addicts, nothing was more tragic than their own history, regardless of anyone else's.

"You okay?" Sawyer asked. But Miles couldn't answer straightaway, lest he throw up in the car right then and there.

"Oh," Sawyer suddenly announced, as if he had just figured out a difficult math problem. "You're still detoxing. That's rough, man."

Miles could only stare back at him. Then, finally, he said, "Yeah, because of you...because you made me leave rehab too early. And I was almost done!"

Sawyer laughed, but it wasn't the type of laugh that another person might like to hear—after telling a joke, for instance. "I didn't make you do anything," he said. "You're your own man. I can't make you do something you don't want to do."

"Oh, so—"

"Hey, you never know," Sawyer interrupted, abruptly changing the subject back and making the air even more awkward between them. "You might have been too young to remember...before they gave you away, or whatever."

"Who?" Miles said, sounding more confused than he wanted to let on.

"Your parents."

Miles regretted that he had shared some of this personal info back at Sawyer's house, and now even more details that he would have preferred to keep for himself—but, as usual, the words came out before he was able to stop them. Soon after the retired Lieutenant Colonel's colorful comment about ass-puckering, Miles was quizzed by Sawyer's father about his own background. If Sawyer had been reticent to talk about the true architects of his past when he and Miles were back in rehab, Miles had no such luck now. He was unable to hold back the truth—or rather, a version of events that Miles held as his truth—later attributing this unintentional disclosure to clandestine skills the retired military man presumably developed from interrogating prisoners (as opposed to any sudden weakness on Miles' part).

"I don't know who my real parents are," Miles had nakedly admitted to Sawyer's dad. "I've been in and out of foster homes most of my life, and the only thing I know is that my mother gave me up when I was a baby because she was dying of cancer or something." Ironically, Miles didn't realize he had just made up the same lie that Sawyer had previously used on him.

Ignoring the surprised look on Sawyer's face, probably due to this unexpected leakage of personal information (and perhaps recognizing the same lie), Miles went on: "I don't know who my real father is." And just to make sure there were no follow-up questions, Miles added: "That's all I know."

Unfortunately for Miles, however, there *was* a follow-up question, but it came from Sawyer, rather than Sawyer's father: "How many foster homes have you been in?"

Miles paused, as if contemplating the answer, although in truth he was ashamed to admit the number. "I don't know," he replied at last, gaining back the cloak he normally used with snoopy strangers.

In his father's Mercedes shortly thereafter, Sawyer asked, "So why have you been in so many foster homes?" But before Miles could answer, or come up with another lie, Sawyer said, "Oh, I know. Never mind."

"What?" Miles said, not a little bit curtly, now curious as to what Sawyer thought was the reason.

The car stereo blasted Joel Osteen's voice, though neither Sawyer nor Miles knew who that was; they just knew it was annoying, and loudly annoying at that. Sawyer quickly reached over and turned the radio down. "Where do you think we met, dumbass?" Sawyer said, replacing Joel Osteen's voice but retaining the high level of irritation that hung in the air.

It took a second too long for Miles to compute.

"You're a drug addict," Sawyer stated matter-of-factly.

"That's not why," Miles said a little too defensively, as he was unprepared to come up with any other explanation, even a weak one.

Sawyer punched some buttons on his phone until the Twenty One Pilots' anthem "Heavydirtysoul" countered back from the stereo.

"Really?" Miles asked, confusing them both as to whether he referred to Sawyer's deadpan verdict of Miles' life or the compelling musical cry to save his soul, which he innately knew indicated his soul and not Sawyer's: quite heavy, but not dirty just yet.

It was ironically near the end of "Semi-Automatic" when Miles found the Walther P99 in the glove compartment; Lt. Col. Ramirez apparently preferred that his handguns be German, too.

"What the fuck?" Miles blurted.

Sawyer glanced over and grinned. "Oh, that's called a gun. People use them to kill other people."

Miles picked it up and held it out. "Is it loaded?"

The Mercedes swerved as Sawyer reached over to grab the gun, but missed. "Shit, man, don't wave that around!"

Without a second's pause, Miles threw the gun back into the glove compartment as if it had suddenly bit him. "Oh my God, it *is* loaded?"

The car swerved again. "Fuck, don't just throw that! It could go off!"

"Then why do you keep a loaded gun in the glove compartment of your fuckin' car?"

"It's not my car!"

Miles tried to catch his breath. As if it were reading the moment and not just on shuffle, "Guns for Hands" started to pound out of the Harmon Kardon stereo.

"Have you ever used that?" Miles asked, not having any idea of the ways in which his new friend *had* used it.

"Of course not," Sawyer lied. "I'm not a fuckin' criminal."

Miles reached over and turned the stereo down. "Yet you had a court order to go to rehab—" Miles interrupted himself. "And then left early!"

Sawyer smiled again. "I don't know that I'd use the word *left*. I mean, we had to sneak out in the middle of the night—"

"Yeah, because of you. I wasn't serving out a sentence. I could've left whenever I wanted, and that's what I did."

"Well, I don't think your step-parents would be thrilled to know that you did that."

"They're my *foster* parents, not step," Miles corrected Sawyer. "And I don't give a fuck what they think. They could probably care less what happens to me."

"Then why don't you call them right now and tell them that you're out? See what they say?" Sawyer's Joker-like grin was now beginning to irritate Miles.

"Sure, and I'll tell them how I just found a loaded weapon in your car, too."

"Well, it would serve no purpose if it was *un*loaded, would it? Besides, my father has a permit to carry that." Sawyer turned the car into a gas station. "He has permits for all his guns."

"*All* his guns? Fuck, man, how many does he have?"

Sawyer stopped the car and turned off the ignition. "As many as it takes."

"Takes to do what?"

This time Miles didn't need to see Sawyer's face to know that he was grinning again—probably pleased with himself for being so witty.

"Wait here," Sawyer ordered as he stepped out of the car, like Miles was a dog. Then he said, "You want anything?"

"Nah," Miles said. "I don't have any cash."

"No worries. I got you. What do you want?"

Miles still couldn't think straight after having a loaded gun in his hand only a few moments before. "I don't know… whatever you're getting."

Sawyer slammed the car door and went inside the food mart, returning almost as quickly as he had left. He threw a bunch of candy bars and cokes into Miles' lap, then screeched the Mercedes back out onto the road before Miles could say anything.

"I got a couple beers, too," Sawyer said, pulling them out of his jacket like a magician pulling a rabbit out of a hat. "Here." He threw one of them to Miles as he accelerated down the street.

"Damn, man, you got a lot of shit—wait, I thought you were getting gas?"

Sawyer glanced at the almost-empty gas gauge. "Nah, we're good."

"How much do I owe you for this?" Miles asked.

The grin again. "I told you I got you," Sawyer said.

It had been Sawyer's idea to rob the convenience mart in Wake Forest, though Miles had no clue his friend had already robbed one convenience store that day, all while Miles waited innocently in the car. Miles also didn't know at the time that Sawyer was no virgin to armed robbery, which constituted the main difference between the two crimes that day: the first had been shoplifting. This time it was the real thing, with a gun ("Just to scare the cashier with," or so Sawyer told Miles).

"I won't use it unless I have to," Sawyer said in the car, prior to going inside.

"Unless you have to?" Miles repeated, aware that his heart was beating out of his chest.

Sawyer had told Miles that the court-ordered rehab he was doing when they met was for a DUI, but in reality it had been for *several* DUIs, as well as carrying a concealed weapon without a permit. Fortunately for Sawyer, he had only been caught with the concealed weapon once; had he been caught again, he would have been charged with a felony. Even luckier for Sawyer, he had gotten away with robbing a convenience store near NC State a few months before going back into rehab, and with a gun to boot, just like this time—though his friend who had done the robbery with him near NC State hadn't been so lucky. He got caught later, but wouldn't tap out on his friend, and was currently serving time in Boone.

As Miles sat listening to this NC State story in the car, all-the-while watching Sawyer handle the gun like a pro, like a killer he had seen only in the movies, Miles thought about the very real possibility that, if he did this with him and they were caught together, he wouldn't hesitate in the least to turn on Sawyer if that meant saving himself. *Fuck*, Miles thought, *I haven't even known the guy for a month!* Any sensible person would turn on someone like Sawyer, especially if they had to in order to save themselves. This other guy was an idiot, Miles decided. And Sawyer probably wouldn't hesitate to turn on him if the opposite circumstance came up, even if they had known each other for years rather than weeks.

Why this was Miles didn't know, but for years afterwards he would often dream about Sawyer's Pee-Wee Herman tattoo. Frequently during these nighttime visions, Miles would displace the tattoo in his mind, imagining it on other people and not Sawyer, like he was looking for Sawyer but couldn't find him, these decoys that shared his tattoo intentionally throwing him off the scent. It was like a movie he had seen once on TV late at night with one of the guys that previously played James Bond; they did a similar thing at the end in order to cause chaos and confusion—quite successfully, too, if Miles remembered correctly.

"You ready?" Sawyer said, crimping the semi-automatic at the same time.

"Ready for what?" Miles said, sounding like a little boy who is afraid a monster is either hiding in his closet or under the bed.

Sawyer laughed. "Don't be such a pussy." Then he softened a bit. "Nothing bad is going to happen, trust me." Now he sounded like a mother was maybe supposed to sound when she quelled the fears of a young son refusing to go to bed due to fanciful fears.

Suddenly, something Miles couldn't describe came over him. It seemed as if all the fear he had ever felt somehow drained away; not even the darkness, nor anyone or anything using it as a cloak, could ever harm him again.

In one dream years later, as Miles followed Sawyer inside the store (the wrong crime for Miles to be dreaming about), while staring at the gun in Sawyer's hand he noticed the Pee-Wee Herman tattoo missing from his friend's arm. This scared Miles more than the crime they were about to commit, for without the tattoo, something was missing that seemed integral to their mission. It wasn't long, however, before Miles found the tattoo again, just as they reached the cream-colored counter the cashier stood behind. But this didn't relieve Miles the way he thought it would, for now the tattoo was permanently etched on his own arm—and for all the world to see.

UNDERTOW

"…and that's why he doesn't buy green bananas anymore."

Owen smiled at Elodie, proud of himself for remembering the story correctly and not fucking it up, like he usually did when relating things like that.

"I don't get it," Elodie said.

Owen's smile faded as quickly as it had appeared. And he wasn't sure how to explain it any better. This was the way his mother had told him the story, and he had gotten it. Why wasn't Elodie getting it?

"Well, you know what green bananas symbolize, right?" Owen tried again, glancing around the coffee shop as though looking for someone else who had maybe accidentally overheard him and *did* get what he had said.

"But I don't understand why your mom said that to your grandfather. Does she like green bananas or something?" Elodie said, not without authenticity.

"No," Owen said. "My grandfather said that to my mom when she asked him about his mortality. You know, being he's in his nineties and all."

"Oh!" Elodie exclaimed as if she finally got it, even though it was obvious she didn't.

"Isn't that awesome?" Owen said, hoping she still might get it somehow. "Sums up mortality pretty well, huh? It's that tenuous. But at least my grandpa knows that—" He corrected himself. "*Knew* that. Although I heard later that he stole the line from a movie he had seen at the senior center. Forget what it was called. Of course, he's dead now, so he was right not to buy the green bananas after all." Owen smiled, once again happy that he was nailing this story; it was a story he had never told before, and a good one at that, even if it came from a movie. Maybe if he kept telling her great stories like this, she would relent and go on a date with him. Maybe she had been lying when she said she had a boyfriend. He was apparently gone anyway, like in rehab or something. And besides, Owen wasn't addicted to anything like her boyfriend apparently was, probably a plus. She had even told him she dated black guys, which was pretty cool since he had never dated a white girl—especially a pretty one like her.

Interrupting his train of thought, she suddenly asked him if he had any tats.

"Who?" he said too quickly, once again sounding like a senile old man with hearing issues. He wasn't trying to be funny, which was maybe why it was.

She laughed, probably not having any idea that he was beginning to fall in love with her—if only for the way she laughed. "You don't have any tattoos?" she asked, but not really in the form of a question; more like a statement.

"Oh," he said. "No, I don't...not yet, at least." He smiled, hoping it reminded her of Cam's smile—whoever the hell that was, since she had mentioned him, and his smile, more than once.

She smiled, too, which just about killed him. He had a furious hard-on—a throbbing erection that made his whole body quiver.

"If aliens do visit us someday and subsequently destroy us, I can't say I would blame them," Lilly said. "In fact, I might go one step further and say we probably deserve it."

Dr. Stevens leaned in closer, as if whatever she said next

might be a secret only shareable in a reverent whisper. "And why's that?" Dr. Stevens coaxed her.

Now it was Lilly's turn to shift positions, trying to make herself more comfortable on the couch in what seemed a never-ending battle.

"Are you uncomfortable, Lilly?" Dr. Stevens asked.

"What?" she said automatically.

He gestured at a velvet-upholstered chair directly across from him—a chair that, Lilly was embarrassed to admit, she hadn't really noticed before. How this was possible, and after all these visits, she couldn't fathom. Maybe he had only recently moved this chair into his office, she thought, as in today right before her appointment? But why would he do that? Just to mess with her sanity?

"Would you rather sit in the chair?" he tried.

"Oh, I didn't know I was allowed to sit there."

"Allowed?" he said curiously.

"I mean…I thought I had to lay on the couch. You know, because—"

He laughed, which caught her off-guard. Was he laughing at her? Because if so—

"You can sit wherever you want." He smiled. "There's no rule about where a patient has to sit." He scratched his temple above his right ear. "I guess the movies have done a disservice to therapy, the way they make it seem as if the patient always has to lie on a couch and talk about their mother." He paused again, thoughtful. "Many therapists I know don't even have a couch in their office, if that makes you feel any better."

"Feel any better?"

The smile faded from his face, but not in a disapproving way. He shifted in his seat again. "So why do you think mankind deserves to be annihilated by aliens?"

"Annihilated?" she echoed. It seemed as if she could only repeat anything he said. She couldn't concentrate, or even remember what she had been talking about when the whole furniture thing threw her off. Had she been talking about aliens? Why on Earth—or rather, off of it—

"You said that we probably deserved to be destroyed by aliens someday," he said, interrupting her thoughts, which were going around in circles anyway. "If they should ever visit us, I think you said?"

She stared at his face, hoping he would just keep asking her questions until something resonated and made sense of whatever the hell was going on; but that wasn't going to happen, and she knew it. She had to explain the alien comment, which she now remembered, although she had no idea why she had said it in the first place. "I don't know," she began. "I guess I'm getting pessimistic in my old age." She laughed, surprising them both. Had she just made a joke? *It probably wasn't a good joke*, she thought, but at least she was trying, right? Was Barry really making her this tongue-tied in her brain? *Fuck Barry and the whores he's probably still fucking*, she almost said out loud (*had* she said it out loud?).

"You look angry all of a sudden," Dr. Stevens remarked, throwing Lilly off again. Was he purely reading this from her face? Maybe he was a good shrink, after all?

She laughed again. "Maybe I just want aliens to exterminate Barry," she said, feeling a little alive, like she was temporarily in control of things—or at least the things that came out of her mouth, which was a start.

"Maybe so," he said, smiling at her. "Maybe so."

He had inherited a love for trash from his father. This unrepentant fact made Owen wonder whether other people suffered from this strange ailment as well—if it could be called an ailment. Was it really weird that he liked to throw things away? Or that he tore up all his trash a dozen times or so, as if the trash receptacle would only accept it if it were ripped up a certain number of times, or in small enough pieces? As a little boy, he had watched his father throw away trash in a similar fashion. But it wasn't like he was trying to copy his father. He simply enjoyed throwing things away. And like he told his mother—to a degree she could understand—it was better than being a hoarder. In fact, he was the opposite of a hoarder (whatever that was called).

Owen only thought of this because he had walked past a garbage bin on his way back to the coffee shop, bound to retrieve a hair clip Elodie had left behind. But the hair clip wasn't on the table they had just vacated, like she'd said it was; nor was it on the floor near the table, if she had instead dropped it, or if someone had accidentally knocked it off. It wasn't in lost and found either—and if a hair clip was what he thought it was, he doubted someone would steal it.

"Where are you going?" he asked Elodie once he got back to her car, exasperated, seemingly catching her just before she drove off. "I was getting your hair clip?" he said, posing it as a question, now confused about whether she had even asked him to go back to get it, or whether he had just gone without thinking: chivalry on auto-pilot.

She had started the engine and was turning up the music on the stereo. *Was she about to leave? And without me? Jesus*, he wanted to say out loud. He was doing her a favor, once again, by going back to the coffee shop to retrieve whatever she'd forgotten this time. She was always forgetting something, although it never seemed to be the same thing twice. Owen thought about everything he owned, realizing it would be difficult for him to forget a different thing each time, for he didn't own nearly as many things as she seemingly did. But he would never tell her that. He would just keep returning to retrieve whatever she had presently forgotten. As long as the possibility of being with her existed—not just sexually, but as a couple—he would continue to rescue whatever she needed him to rescue.

"I have to go pick up my boyfriend," she said. "His car broke down."

"Okay," Owen said, standing dejectedly on the sidewalk like a puppy whose owner just told it they couldn't play anymore—but would maybe play more later, time permitting.

"I'll call you," she said, accelerating out of the parking space.

"But you don't have my number!" Owen shouted as Elodie drove away, not realizing until a few seconds too late that this was the case. Regaining himself, at least temporarily, Owen walked the mile and a quarter back to his house, completely forgetting he had ridden his bicycle to the coffee shop and that it was still locked up outside of it.

Nearing home, Owen felt a sharp hollowness in his stomach. Elodie had driven away without his number; the only consolation was that he would likely run into her at the coffee shop again. As long as he kept running into her there, it didn't even matter if cellphones had ever been invented. Besides, it was probably a good thing they couldn't communicate by cell at this early stage in their relationship. Be it via text or a voice call, Owen knew he would most likely screw up if given the opportunity. He had done it in the past: accidentally hitting send on an incomplete text, or saying something stupid without thinking first.

Remarkably, however, Owen wasn't the least bit curious as to why he kept encountering Elodie at the coffee shop when she didn't even work there, or anywhere nearby for that matter. It was almost as if she were as fundamental to the coffee shop as coffee was, and, without her, it couldn't operate. Likewise, Owen was just as fundamental to the bookstore—had he still worked there. His mother was clueless to the fact that he wasn't employed there anymore. He went to the coffee shop instead of going to work, just to get out of the house and away from her ruthless neediness, and of course to keep up the lie. He would bring a book with him to pass the hours—anything by Stephen King—but had been fortunate enough the last few times to run into Elodie instead, who, for all Owen knew, was also using the coffee shop to camouflage herself. It might have been the only thing they had in common.

ABSTRACT

He had been dreaming about a painting, but not about *seeing* a painting, like one observed in a museum. In the dream, he *was* the painting, an intrinsic element of it, coalesced from composite colors. He was an abstract, a still-life, a landscape, an animal, a Christ-figure, a child. He was everything that matter contained; yet, when he woke, Miles wasn't quite sure if he contained anything at all.

But whatever uncertainties Miles had about his chemical make-up in relation to the fundamental elements of the universe, Sawyer would give no quarter. Aside from frequent trips to the bathroom to dry-heave because he was more nauseous than not, and the feeling that he was either too cold or too hot, his body consistently convulsing as if tiny tremors from a long-ago earthquake were still active, it became even more difficult for Miles to navigate the ridged terrains that were and weren't Sawyer. As Miles battled with what should have been the end days of his detoxing, those old, familiar poisons continued to flow through his body, unimpeded. And as each day outside of rehab added up, the more strength was gained by this sickly venom until, finally, the war was lost.

For the first time in his life, Miles had not only held a gun in his hand but had directed it toward another living person—this the unlucky cashier whose untimely shift coincided with a visit from him and Sawyer. But Miles had only agreed to hold the gun if it wasn't loaded, which Sawyer promised him was the case, but back in the car, when they had safely returned with the contents of the cash register in hand, Sawyer started laughing so violently that Miles knew he had been lied to.

To be certain of this, however, since Miles didn't know how to check, he aimed the gun at Sawyer's face, which quickly turned a sickly, pale yellow.

"Whoa!" Sawyer said, reaching out to tilt the gun in another direction, away from himself. "What the fuck are you doing? Are you fuckin' crazy?"

Miles put the gun down, careful to point it away from himself as well. "You've lied to me twice about that being loaded!" He shook his head. "I can't believe this."

Sawyer grinned, and if this wasn't a shit-eating grin, Miles didn't know what was. "I haven't left your sight," Sawyer said, even-toned, or as even-toned as he could get after all the coke he had done just before getting into the car.

"So?"

"Well, did you see me unload the ammo? After you complained the first time about it being loaded?"

"I was sleeping," Miles started. "So, anything's possible."

Miles thought about what Sawyer had just said, but the fact that he had been so incredibly stupid, not to mention naïve, was too much for Miles to accept about himself. He knew he had made mistakes over the years—plenty of them—and he knew he wasn't the smartest guy around; but this…this even he couldn't believe. And the fact that the gun was loaded—twice!—wasn't even the worst of it. He had just committed armed robbery! He had held up a convenience store for what? $200 and some change? Was that worth anyone's life? And if they were caught, which certainly wasn't out of the question, *he* had been the one holding the gun, not Sawyer. Sawyer, who had intentionally manipulated the situation so that Miles was the one holding the gun. *But wasn't all manipulation intentional?* Miles thought. This was no accidental design by Sawyer. Sawyer knew all along what he was doing, and Miles had fallen for it. And now Miles was a criminal just like Sawyer probably was (as he had probably lied about that, too).

Sawyer had been studying Miles while he was seemingly lost in thought. He turned the wheel and the car cut right. "Oh, lighten up," Sawyer said. "Everything's fine. No one got hurt, and now we have some spending money."

"Spending money?" Miles echoed. "Seriously?"

Sawyer contemplated this for a second. "Sure, we didn't make that much bank, but wasn't it worth it just for the thrill of the hunt?" Sawyer grinned again, even more shit-eating than before. "Just admit it. Admit that you got a woody from this, which is no small feat by the way, being you're wasted right now."

"Are you serious? You think I got off on this? *Any* of this?" Miles tried to collect himself. "This isn't whack-a-doodle," he continued, not sure of where he was going with anything coming out of his mouth. "This isn't a fuckin' joke. People's lives are at stake!"

Sawyer was already laughing and Miles hadn't noticed when it started, which was even more annoying. "Whack-a-doodle!" he tried to repeat between sobs of laughter. "Whack-a—"

"Shut the fuck up!" Miles shouted, hoping his voice would penetrate the noise that was Sawyer.

Sawyer was still in hysterics. "Whack-a-doodle!" He caught himself for a second. "Don't you mean whack-a-mole?" He went back into a frenzy. "Whack-a-*doodle!* How do you whack a *doodle?*"

Miles started to get out of the car, even though it was nowhere near stopped at the moment. Sawyer stopped laughing, abruptly. "Hey. Hey! What are you doing? Stay in the fuckin' car! Where do you think you're going?"

Miles sat back in the passenger seat, caged for now, and suddenly at a loss for why he was doing or saying anything at all. Was he saying something?

Sawyer's voice startled him, as Miles had completely forgotten he wasn't presently alone. "You do realize that you're still holding the gun, don't you?" he said, sounding like he was holding back a fresh bout of laughter. And if Sawyer started to laugh again, things were going to get bad—and fast, as Miles was silently filling up with rage. But first: nausea.

"Pull over!" Miles suddenly said, trying to open the passenger door again, and again without any concern that the car might not be stopped.

Sawyer quickly pulled the Mercedes off to the side of the road, auspiciously avoiding an accident with the car in the next lane, since he hadn't bothered to look first. But whether or not Sawyer knew that his friend was about to toss his load wasn't obvious; he was probably more concerned that Miles forgot to put the gun down when he started vomiting.

Miles was still feeling a little queasy when the evening news came on a few hours later, he and Sawyer watching it from a hotel room that was too nice for them (as Miles had told Sawyer when they checked in, though Sawyer wouldn't entertain saving any of the money they had stolen).

"It's house money," he had said, which the front desk clerk had overheard but probably didn't understand.

Several hours later, after piling up a huge room service tab that went beyond their illegal earnings, they still hadn't left the hotel. "We're famous," Sawyer announced proudly at the end of the news story regarding their robbery, which they had apparently gotten away with—at least for now. He turned to Miles, who was staring toward the bathroom as if trying to decide whether or not to expend the energy to get off the bed and walk all the way over to the toilet to throw up again—or, as he seemed more experienced at lately, dry heaving.

"You do realize," Sawyer went on, "that you're not puking because of the detox. You might feel fucked up and all from the withdrawal, but this other stuff is something else. What, I don't know. I'm not a fuckin' doctor. Maybe you're just stressed out."

"Stressed out?" Miles repeated as sarcastically as he could, given his present physical condition. "You think? I mean, we only just committed armed robbery, so why would *I* be stressed? I pull a gun on people every day. Didn't you know that?"

"Yeah, yeah," Sawyer said, as if a slight acknowledgment were enough to diffuse the situation.

Miles grabbed at his forehead, which was pounding so hard that he was certain his thumping pulse could be seen by others—or, at least, Sawyer, since they weren't currently around any other people. It felt like a sinus-pressure and stress headache rolled into one, then times a thousand. Miles was never good with numbers; he just knew that this was the worst headache he'd ever had, and with no close second.

The TV was blasting a commercial with a bunch of dogs driving a car. Miles could tell that the commercial was probably funny, if he happened to be in a different mood (which, of course, he wasn't); plus, it was so loud that he couldn't think straight. It was hard to concentrate on anything when your ears were practically bleeding.

Now the dogs were barking at a passing mail truck, which almost made Miles laugh out loud—bad mood or not. He didn't know what the commercial was for; nor did he really care. If only as a quick diversion, it was worth mentally stepping out of the conversation he was having with Sawyer, however briefly. Part of him—he almost laughed out loud again just from having this thought—wanted to pick up the gun, which still lay by the sink where he had rinsed the vomit off of it earlier, aim it at Sawyer's face, and then pull the trigger—perhaps even multiple times. And he would want Sawyer to see him aiming the gun at his face before pulling the trigger, pausing just long enough to see the awareness of impending death cross over him, mixed with the realization of who was responsible for it; pausing just long enough to see the defeat manifest in his eyes; pausing just long enough to see someone finally one-upping him—someone that, for whatever reason, had finally turned the so-called tables of control.

Coming out of the haze of this daydream, but without turning toward him, Miles said, "Why was I the one holding the gun, anyway? It's your gun, or your dad's or whoever, so how did I get stuck with being the armed one?" He looked over at Sawyer and held his gaze for a moment while he studied his face, although he wasn't sure why. Maybe he was curious whether Sawyer had a "tell"—a subtle physical twitch other people could use to get leverage on him. But if Sawyer did have a tell, which was doubtful, it wasn't something Miles was going to find out by simply staring at him.

Miles glanced at his hands, and then his fingers, as if searching for the culprit—a jagged nail. "But I guess that's how you wanted it," Miles went on, returning his attention to Sawyer's face, which, with a skillful rebound, displayed his signature smile.

"We're not gonna get caught," Sawyer said, as if it couldn't be challenged; as if he believed it to be true, and therefore everyone else had to believe it as well, whether they wanted to or not. Sawyer had a way, Miles was now realizing, of making anything he said sound true, regardless of how far it happened to fall from the bullseye. With Sawyer, there wasn't even a target to aim at; he just had to show people the arrow he was about to nock. And that was enough.

It was an overcast day with rumbles of thunder in the distance when Miles saw Owen for the first time from the diner's storefront window, though he didn't know his name yet, nor did he think he would ever need to learn it. He happened to be watching him walk down the street next to a blonde girl when, in a strange coincidence—Miles would later wonder whether all coincidences were strange—Sawyer said something off the cuff about them, which meant that they were both observing the same pedestrians.

"Look at that shit," Sawyer stated unabashedly. "A fuckin' interracial couple. That shit ain't right."

Not believing the words that had just come out of Sawyer's mouth, Miles said, "You can't be serious?"

"What do you mean?" Sawyer shot back defensively.

"You sound like a racist, and an uneducated one at that."

"Oh, so now you're correcting my English?"

"Fuck your English," Miles said. "Being a racist pretty much trumps that. Not to mention, I don't think most racists speak properly anyway, so I wouldn't worry about that part." Miles turned his attention back to the "interracial couple," who seemed to be perfectly content with one another. "This is 2017," he went on. "Not 1817."

"Hey man, I'm not a racist. I just don't think they should date outside their race."

"*They?*" Miles repeated. "Really?"

Sawyer just stared back. Miles turned to eye the subject of their conversation anew, but they had already passed out of view. "Why do you sound so pissed off?" Miles asked. "It's none of your business when it comes down to it. Leave them be. Other people can do whatever they want. You're not judge and jury."

This last part brought out Sawyer's shit-eating grin. "That's where you're wrong. I *am* judge and jury," he said, without the least bit of sarcasm or irony.

The waitress appeared from out of nowhere. "Do you guys need anything else?" she asked, writing on her notepad and then ripping the top page off, which she then placed on the table in front of them. "No rush on that. You can pay upfront." And then she was gone, not even bothering to wait in case they wanted to order something else.

"She's hot, huh?" Sawyer said.

Miles glanced over his shoulder, trying to see where the waitress had gone. Then he turned back to Sawyer. "I didn't really get a good look, to be honest," he said. "She seemed cute, though."

"No, not the waitress, shit-for-brains." Sawyer gestured outside. "The blonde."

"Oh," Miles said, glancing back out the window as if the couple would still be in view, even though he knew they were long gone by now. "I didn't get a good look at her either."

Sawyer's grin returned, uninvited by Miles. "Are you gay or something?"

"No, I'm not gay," Miles responded more defensively than he meant to sound, enunciating each word as if he were practicing a stage-acting exercise. "And you seem to have a strange fascination with strangers."

"With strangers?" Sawyer echoed uncharacteristically, sounding more like Miles.

"Yeah…" Miles started. "That blonde we just saw walking down the street."

The next moment was one that Miles would never forget for as long as he lived. It was what followed out of Sawyer's mouth—once again, without the slightest bit of falsity. "What would it take for you to kill someone?"

At first Miles didn't believe what he'd just heard, chalking it up to the white noise in the diner. But Sawyer was eagerly awaiting a response of some kind, so Miles, to buy himself more time at the very least, simply said, "What?"

"Do you think you could ever kill someone?" Sawyer asked again, this time enunciating the words so clearly that it was impossible for Miles to think he'd misheard even one syllable.

"Why would I..." Miles began, then bolted up from the table. "You're fuckin' insane."

Sawyer watched his lunch partner walk toward the door, an expression of satisfaction on his face, as if what was happening—Miles abruptly exiting the diner—was all according to script.

"Come on," Sawyer called out after him. "We're family now."

Miles stopped as if he were an AI-controlled character inside a video game, and someone else was governing his next step. Without turning around, Miles said, "You're not my family."

"I'm all you've got left!" Sawyer shouted.

But Miles was already out the door.

CONCESSION

When Owen awoke on Tuesday morning, despite a lack
of sleep due to spending the night with Elodie—which he
wasn't going to complain about in the least—he had a fleeting thought that someday, somehow, he might become something great, like even become president. He wasn't the type of
person who would normally have a thought such as that, but
after losing his virginity to Elodie (though there was a strong
chance this was only due to her getting way too drunk during
Monday Night Football), he felt like there wasn't anything he
couldn't achieve if he put his mind to it. Maybe he was just in
an optimistic mood due to finally having sex, and with a hot
girl to boot, but he didn't care. Regardless of what might be
behind it, he felt a euphoria that he didn't know was possible,
and now that he recognized it, he never wanted to let go of
the feeling. Even if life eventually threw him some curveballs,
which he imagined it would, he was going to power over anything that came his way because he was now indestructible,
like a steel fence nothing could ever penetrate. Even the fact
that Elodie was gone by the time he woke up was fine with
him. He didn't question it (other than the fact he was in *her*
apartment). If she had to be somewhere early—although she
had never told him that she had any type of job to get to—
that was okay. He had to look for work anyway himself, so an
early start wasn't the worst idea in the world. Plus, he would
probably see her later in the day at the coffee shop anyway,
after checking in with his mother (who thought he had slept
over at a friend's house).

He decided that he would just walk around and look for

work, maybe see if there were any HELP WANTED signs anywhere. He wasn't going to use the internet this time. He had found out about the bookstore job from Craigslist, but maybe he could find a better job this time by using a different strategy. It didn't help, though, that his mother kept calling him. She tried him three times in a row when he was inside a music store inquiring about their sign outside, but the truth was that he would have probably ignored her calls anyway. It was so annoying how she would call so many times in a row, as if after the first few times he would be adequately worn down and have no choice but to answer. She did this because it worked the first few times she tried it, but only because he thought there was an emergency or something since she seemed to be trying so hard to reach him. When he discovered that was her ploy, however, he didn't fall for it anymore, although he occasionally got nervous that one of these times it might actually be an emergency and he would miss it. But it was the classic case of "The Boy Who Cried Wolf," so it served her right if something important did eventually happen. She should learn how to call people once, and if they didn't answer, then so be it. *Leave a fuckin' message like a normal person!* he wanted to scream at her.

It turned out that the music store had already hired someone, and apparently a while back, but had forgotten to take down the sign in their window. "Sorry," the pierced, tattooed, skinny guy behind the counter said.

"No worries," Owen replied, and then exited the store faster than he thought he would, as if a girl had just rejected him, rather than the innocuous situation that had actually transpired. If that weren't enough, he also felt weird whenever he said "no worries" to someone, or when other people said it to him. He was hardly ever sincerely worried about something when someone told him not to be; likewise, he didn't think other people were that worried either when he said it to them. *What a stupid expression*, he thought soon after leaving the music store. He wished he hadn't said that just then, and he also wished that someone would tell him not to worry when he actually *was* worried about something, which was unfortunately more often than he would have preferred. If only people could get the timing right for this apparent command, maybe it would help him to not be so worried so much—but he doubted it. They were only words, and words weren't powerful enough to change a real-world situation…were they?

Because Owen tried to convince himself that he felt this way about words, he worried that he might never say "I love you" to anyone. He hadn't even said these three words to his mother, who, herself, didn't seem to have the ability to *not* say them to him. Whenever she told him this, which was, at the very least, once daily when he went to bed at night—was there a chance that he might not wake up the next day or something, and that was why she never missed this regular opportunity to tell him?—he couldn't even muster the energy to say just two words back, such as, "You, too." He would often guiltily beat himself up over this, because even if he couldn't say these three seemingly magical words to anyone, much less his own mother, was it that hard to say two words back that were just two syllables total?

Just before Owen met Elodie at the coffee shop later that day, he mused over the possibility that he might tell Elodie, a person whom he had only recently met, that he loved her, and not his own mother who he had obviously known his whole life (and who, unbeknownst to him, had struggled mightily, both physically and emotionally, to bring him into this world). He had actually almost told Elodie that he loved her the night before, just after they had intercourse, but the words wouldn't come out audibly for some reason when he mouthed them to her (besides the fact that she wasn't even in the bed next to him at the time). She was in the bathroom peeing, and had even advertised that she was going to pee because of something about getting a urinary tract infection. *Did she have an STD?* he wondered anxiously when she went to pee (again) at the coffee shop just after "running into him" the next day. She sure seemed to urinate a lot. Could he, too, be infected after only having sex once? he worried as he waited for her to come out of the ladies' room.

When she got back to the table a few minutes later, he only managed to mumble, "You okay?" before returning his gaze to the menu he was pretending to read.

She slung her gigantic purse over the back of the seat and sat down before answering, which only made him more tense. *Why was she stalling?* But then she smiled and said, "Of course, silly. I was just going to the bathroom. Why would something be wrong?" She reached over and patted his arm, which gave him a quick erection. "And don't you know that menu by now?"

"I don't know," he said, somehow answering both questions at the same time, the irony occurring to him that he was just able to say three words rather easily, but not the words he had thought he would say the night before to Elodie, or to his mother every single day of his life so far. He was beyond irritated with himself on both accounts, but then remembered that, also as of last night, he was no longer a virgin.

He looked around and wondered if anyone at the coffee shop could tell that he was no longer a virgin, that he'd had sex with the girl sitting at the table across from him. He was not only a man, he proudly decided, but a "manly" man— the type of man that had sex with women and then had coffee with them the next day. As a result of such a conquest, the rampant insecurities that had plagued him just minutes before vanished in such a way as to seem like they never existed to begin with, like a crazy myth that only crazy people believed in, not dissimilar to ghosts or extraterrestrials.

"I love you," he suddenly said, not realizing at first that he had said it out loud. But then, abashedly aware of what had just come out of his mouth, he wanted to take the words back, still inaudible to her, as if he had merely coughed or sneezed. This scheme, however, was stomped on by what came out of Owen's mouth next, the two words that normally followed such a bodily function: "Excuse me."

Elodie laughed and covered her mouth with her hand, which was not the reaction he was hoping for; the "hand" thing was too innocently cute for him to comprehend at the moment. He wanted to cover his own mouth with his hand to hide any of the words that had just come out of it—but it was already too late.

"Why are you excusing yourself?" she asked, the smile on her face only getting wider. "I think it's adorable what you just said."

Adorable, he thought. *What's so* adorable *about telling someone you love them, and for the very first time no less?* He didn't want to be adorable; he wanted to *be* adored. *There's a difference*, he wanted to tell her, and have her understand him, consequently correcting herself to admit she loved him, too. But she was never going to tell him that…at least, not to his face.

The phone call didn't go anywhere near as planned. It had taken Miles almost as much time to get his confidence up to place the call as the call itself lasted once he dialed the number. His foster parents, the Kellys, who were of Irish descent but definitely not drinkers, weren't bad people. They had good intentions, especially considering they adopted a child who had already been in four unsuccessful foster homes. They had even known about the drug and alcohol problems that had plagued Miles since he was ten years old, his propensity for violence—he had gotten into several dust-ups at school where the other boys didn't fare so well—but they were a God-fearing couple who felt that love and, of course, Jesus himself (if you asked him politely enough) could cure anything. And because of their keen ability to forgive under any circumstance, no matter what a person did, everything under the sun was somehow pardonable. But to be able to forgive someone for anything they did—this seemed unfathomable, even to someone like Miles, who was constantly praying for the kindness of strangers, even though he didn't really believe in God—nor luck for that matter. This was maybe the reason why rehab wasn't a successful arena for him, as he needed to believe in a higher power, starting with himself, and that was the one thing he definitely didn't believe in. As for luck, Miles saw that as a folktale, a children's story.

The act of forgiveness was something that Miles certainly respected, and often admired, but despite the Kellys' best efforts, he couldn't be tamed. Not by them; not by anyone. As a result, Miles made every effort *not* to think about them, or any of his other failed foster homes for that matter, since he hated the fact that he had failed all of them in some way. Even this—not ever thinking about them, after they had done so much for him—was unforgivable in his eyes.

So, when what was to be his final phone call to the Kellys crashed and burned like a plane with no engines, Miles wondered why he hadn't ejected himself when he first noticed that the plane was going down. This was a common occurrence for Miles—that of the pilot going down with the plane without ejecting, since he was either not observant enough of the failing gauges in front of him, or just didn't have the wherewithal to ever think about saving himself in time.

"So?" Sawyer asked, having just finished pissing on the side of the road and now back in the car, raring to go.

"Can't you ever do anything like anyone else?" Miles said, putting his cellphone back in his pocket, ignoring the fact that it was too big to fit properly. "You could've pulled over at a gas station or something."

"Don't you worry your pretty little head about where I choose to piss."

"What?"

"Just tell me how it went down. Did you call your parents?"

"They're not my parents."

"Sorry," Sawyer said quickly, although he didn't sound sorry at all. "Your step-parents or whatnot?"

"*Whatnot?* What the fuck—"

Sawyer pulled the Mercedes back onto the road. "Never mind. I've lost interest now." And the sad thing was that Sawyer *had* lost interest; he wasn't just saying that. If he had to wait at all for information, especially if the information wasn't entirely related to him, it was going to skid downhill, and fast.

They drove for a while in silence, with the radio unusually unattended. As they neared downtown, Miles felt a strange sense of foreboding, or perhaps just extreme paranoia from the drugs he had recently taken, that something inescapable was about to happen, even considering the ample warning time allotted to them. And with regard to the story that would play out in their heads for the rest of their lives—both completely fictionalized, and for different reasons—Miles and Sawyer, and the public for that matter, would never arrive at a consensus, thus creating (consciously or not) various timelines of untruths.

But the part of the story no one could argue with, and the most tragic, was what the victim had to say about the whole thing—which was absolutely nothing. For Owen was in a coma from getting shot just above his left ear and through his lateral sinus. In other words, whether it was Miles or Sawyer who had pulled the trigger, or someone else not yet known, the shooter had almost missed...

almost.

JUST

The phone rang in a way that Lilly had never heard before, and, she hoped, in a way she would never hear again. She was of the minority that still had a home phone, but the way the promotions with the cable company had been when she signed up, she had felt forced to get it. She didn't know if this was a good thing or bad thing, as the home phone reminded her of growing up, long before cellphones were around. And maybe this was also why she couldn't *not* have a home phone, as if it meant saying goodbye to her childhood and accepting the fact that she was an adult—a fact that, especially in light of what had just happened, wasn't something she was anywhere near accepting.

Lilly answered the phone just before Detective Garcia hung up, which was obvious from the delay before the detective said anything. Either that or the detective didn't know what to say, which was highly unlikely given her occupation.

"Hello?" Lilly said, almost sure this was a wrong number call, since no one usually called it on purpose except for telemarketers. Besides, she wasn't normally home during the day but had felt too sick to open the store that morning, which also wasn't typical of her. She hadn't slept much the night before, nor the last few nights in a row, and the exhaustion was starting to add up. Her recent bout of insomnia was also unexpected, given that she took prescription meds to help her sleep—what she took could likely take out a 300-pound man, much less a woman nowhere near half that size. But the last few nights something troubled her, something she couldn't quite identify—a surefire omen that something bad was only inches away from her, maybe even under her bed, waiting for just the right moment to strike and inject its deadly venom, ensuring the slow death she knew she deserved.

When the person on the other end of the line didn't say anything at first, and no pre-recorded telemarketing message started to play either, Lilly became filled with even more dread that something was wrong. Positive news usually came out in the open; bad news chose its reveal like a seasoned character actor, willing to hide in silence for just the right moment.

"Hello?" Lilly said again, not sure why she hadn't hung up yet—an option she later regretted not acting upon, because had she hung up before hearing the news, there was the possibility that it wouldn't be true, or have the ability to become true at a later time. At least this was her logic.

"Is this Mrs. King?" came the voice at the other end of the line.

"*Miss* King," Lilly corrected, now sure the world had ended and that she had something to do with it. The fact she wasn't legally divorced yet and still technically a "Mrs." was lost on her.

"And you're Owen King's mother?" the voice asked. Even though it was obvious that the caller already knew the answer to this question, they went through the formality anyway.

"Yes?"

"There's been a shooting. Your son sustained a gunshot wound—"

"What?"

"—to the head."

Silence. Then: "Is...dead?"

Another pause. Lilly shuddered.

"No, ma'am, he's not dead, but he's in critical condition."

"Oh my...God," Lilly said, finally able to say three words in a row. "Oh my God!"

The tan-looking man had been on the same page for far too long, and was probably fast asleep. When someone read a book *that* slowly, which Lilly always seemed to notice, they were most likely asleep and no longer following the narrative of the story they were previously immersed in—or at least pretending to be immersed in. But when you were asleep, you weren't pretending anymore. And now, like the tan man in the emergency waiting room, Owen was among those who weren't pretending anymore.

The cruelest thing, however, was the fact that the tan man in the waiting room would eventually wake up, and probably sooner rather than later considering the continuous chaos swirling around him. For Owen, though, whether or not he would ever wake up again was a question no one seemed able to answer, or maybe willing to answer. He certainly looked like he was going to wake up, Lilly thought, now in the room with her son, staring at his mummifying eyelids that tried so frantically to constrain his bolting pupils underneath.

Lilly was wondering what he was dreaming about when one of the nurses came into the room to check on him. *Was he dreaming?* she wanted to ask the nurse, unaware that she had just spoken this thought out loud.

"Most likely," the nurse replied, "but we obviously don't know for certain."

"What?" Lilly said, not having any idea at first what the nurse was talking about, then wondering what other thoughts she hadn't contained inside of her. *Am I even able to have private thoughts anymore?* she almost said out loud, again. *Or is that part of my brain now dead? Dead like Owen's seems to be?*

Why won't he wake up?

Where was he?

Was he even here anymore?

The nurse smiled at her, which made Lilly want to scream.

Why was the nurse smiling? Was she happy about this for some reason? She had no right to smile. She didn't even have any right to be in the same room with her and Owen!

"He's probably dreaming," the nurse tried again.

"Dreaming about what? What could he possibly be dreaming about?" Lilly cried out, knowing how ridiculous the question sounded but not caring even a little bit.

The nurse smiled again. "Well," she started, "of course we can't know what he's dreaming about, but we can pray that it's all good things."

The nurse was almost safely out the door when Lilly said, "Does he even know I'm here?"

"He's here, Mrs. King. He's here."

Alone now in the room, or, rather, alone with Owen, Lilly spoke to him as if he could hear her but chose not to respond—an irony, she knew, given this was how he usually acted when she spoke to him of late. But that was okay. Everything was okay. He didn't need to respond. She knew Owen could hear her loud and clear, although she was doing neither with her voice at the moment.

Later that afternoon, when Barry finally arrived at the hospital—*where the hell had he been?* she wondered, wanting to literally kill him—she told her future ex-husband that their son had twitched earlier in response to her, a sure sign that Owen could hear her and would return to this world soon. Barry seemed at a loss to understand what Lilly meant by "this world": was their son in another world presently? One in which he could go back and forth as he pleased?

"Since when are you so foo-foo?" Barry asked, visually pleased with himself for using the word "foo-foo."

"Foo-foo?" Lilly repeated. "Really, Barry?"

Barry could only stare back, apparently too afraid to reply.

"I'm not being foo-foo. Even the doctors have said that he can hear us—"

"Please," Barry interrupted, "they don't know. How could they? For certain, I mean?" Barry looked away, seemingly tearful—both of them allowing the silence of the room (other than the beeping machines) to wash over them.

Lilly realized that, for once at least, Barry was right. The doctors couldn't know for sure that Owen was in a place where he could hear them. *Was it because*, she wondered, glancing at the machines that kept her son alive, *when a family member spoke to their loved one in a coma, the patient's vital signs spiked or something?* Because, if this were true, she hadn't seen, nor heard, any spiking whatsoever when she told Owen how much she loved him. So, there was no way the doctors could know something like that. With powers such as these, they would also know exactly what people were dreaming *about*, and no one could know something like that.

A moment later, Barry said he was going to raid the nearby vending machines because he was starving. But Lilly didn't care that Barry was hungry. He had no right to eat anything now, or to be hungry at all for that matter. His son was lying only inches away, alone and dying. Yes, Owen was alone, Lilly decided, despite the fact that both of his parents were in his hospital room at that moment, and despite the fact that his mother was currently holding his limp hand—the same hand that had an IV in it. She had worried at first that by holding his hand—the one with the IV in it—she might accidentally dislodge it, and, by doing so, might hurt him; or worse, might disconnect him from necessary fluids he needed to stay alive, thus killing her own son.

In the stillness of the stale, disinfectant-smelling room, Lilly watched Owen breathe—in and out, in and then out—sounding more like Darth Vader than a normal person, and wondered how much, if any, of her son's breathing was his own work. Or whether these machines—these loud machines—were doing everything. *What else could these machines do?* she wanted to ask someone. Anyone. *Could they cook for her? Could they clean for her? Could they pick up the dry cleaning? Could they keep Barry from ever returning to this room with his Snickers bar? Could they make all of this go away, like one too-long late-night sugar-induced nightmare that could be solved simply by waking up?*

Lilly stared at the door, once again hoping that Barry might somehow get lost and not ever find his way back to the room. *Did Barry comprehend, to any degree, the magnitude of what had happened to their son?* she wondered. *Did he fucking realize that their son had been shot in the fucking head and would likely die—or, at the very least, probably be paralyzed and/or retarded for the rest of his life?* Either way, Owen would lose. Either way, they would lose. *Maybe Owen would be better off dead, rather than living out the rest of his life with some type of severe brain damage?* Or were they—her and Barry—better off if Owen died? It was a terrible thought, and she hated herself for even thinking it, but it was true, wasn't it? Wouldn't *everyone* be better off? She knew Owen wouldn't want to keep on living if it meant living in such a way—or, rather, dying in such a way. *For was it even living at that point? Or was it merely a type of prolonged death?*

"Did you want a Snickers or something?" Barry's voice came through the door before he actually did, returning to the room like someone's cellphone angrily ringing in an otherwise hushed movie theater. "I forgot to ask."

"You forgot a lot more than that," she almost said, but then stopped herself, for the last thing she needed was to get into it with Barry right now. She didn't have the energy to fight with him anymore—or, really, the energy to do anything anymore. She even doubted that she had the energy to get up off the chair she was currently caved into; or, if she somehow did get to her jelly-like feet again, the energy to make it across the stained, sterile floor and out the tombstone-heavy door—only to slingshot herself like a rubber-band back into that vast, yellow chair next to Owen's bed, and not ever returning to that "thing called life," as the purple Prince had once claimed.

She tried to ignore the Snickers comment, and worse, the way Barry was eating it and waving the already half-consumed bar in the air like a trophy, but she couldn't. "How can you eat now?" she said bitterly, as if she had just tasted something sour and, like a kid, couldn't hide her reaction to it.

"What?" Barry replied, still waving his Snickers in the air, and with a mouthful of chocolate that made anything he tried to say tacky-sounding, as if his lips were loosely connected to each other by an invisible string.

"Really, Barry? Really?" This was all Lilly could say at the moment, having now forgotten most of the words in the English language other than her future ex-husband's name and the word "really."

"What do you want from me, Lilly?" Barry was able to say, still with a mouthful of chocolate keeping him a few syllables away from full pronunciation.

"Just finish your fucking Snickers," she said, suddenly able to extend her vocabulary. "Jesus."

From a silent cue, Lilly and Barry both looked over at Owen, like they had forgotten someone else was in the room and their son had actually said something (which, of course, he hadn't). Then, as if his blemished boy had directed him to do so, Barry threw the rest of his Snickers into a nearby trash bin—though unintentionally with too much zeal, causing the candy bar to land with an agitated thud, corrupting the empty quiet.

"Sorry," Barry said.

"Sorry," Lilly repeated to Owen on Barry's behalf, as though the sound may have disturbed the peace of his slumber—a direct contradiction to what she actually wanted most in the world at that moment, which was for her son to come back to life.

"What's going on with that other boy?" Barry asked Lilly, giving the impression that they were already mid-conversation on some new topic. Lilly frowned; she had no idea what he was talking about.

"What other boy?" she said, feeling a little calmer now, as if the chance of Owen getting better had just been crystallized by something happening behind the curtain of their present reality, a successful magic trick that she didn't want to know the secret to—as long as the reveal was what she wanted it to be.

"The killer...the one who shot my son."

"*Your* son?" Lilly said, wanting to point out *her* son to him, as if Barry needed to be reminded of his role in this unfolding drama, a role that she would have preferred be played by someone else—someone who actually knew their lines and had the ability to sell an audience their veracity.

"I don't know," she replied. "Why does that matter right now?"

"Why does that matter?" he repeated, suddenly agitated. "Are you serious?" Then, not waiting for an answer, "He killed our son!"

"Oh, now it's *our* son?" She glanced at Owen, thinking again that maybe their shouting would wake him up. "And he's not dead!"

"What are you fucking talking about, Lilly? Did you get a brain tumor in the last five minutes?"

"A what? A brain tumor?" Lilly looked down at her hands. In the last five minutes, if anything, her hands now looked older; there were wrinkles where she hadn't noticed them before. She almost wished she did have a brain tumor, or something just as lethal, but quicker-acting, something that would drop her dead to the floor right then and there—more than dead, actually, if that were at all possible.

Barry softened. "I just want justice, that's all."

"Justice?" she echoed, like it was a foreign word she had

never heard before and didn't know the meaning of. She glanced at their son, subconsciously trying to respond to Barry just by looking at Owen, as if that alone were more than sufficient as a response.

Several moments passed, Darth Vader breathing so loudly in her ears that she thought she might go crazy; as if the rasping sound of Owen breathing in and out were the only sound left in the world—and it was deafening.

Barry was the first to break, but only as much as he would allow, especially in front of Lilly. Regaining himself enough to speak, he said, "I mean, I know it won't change anything... justice...whether he ever wakes up or not." He looked over at his son, who seemed to be fighting for every breath, and started to break again. "Maybe he's better off if he doesn't wake up?"

She was about to launch into him again, raging over his insensitivity for saying something like that about their son, as if he sincerely wished that Owen would pass on from this world. But she didn't question him, knowing deep down that he might be right, at least in regard to justice. Whether Owen survived this or not, justice didn't care. A dozen death penalties, a dozen life sentences—it didn't matter. Justice had no conscience, nor despair.

PART TWO
THRESHER

125

MITOSIS

He didn't realize there was a problem until he found blood on the pages of the book he was reading. At first Miles didn't know where the blood was coming from, but then he noticed something red in his peripheral vision—a rapidly growing red—and realized he had ripped a good-sized chunk of skin off the tip of his left thumb.

"Hey!" Miles hollered, hoping one of the guards would hear him this time. "I'm bleeding!" But by the time he got to the last syllable of "bleeding," he knew that his call to the one guard he could see from his cell, or even anyone within hearing distance, wouldn't be answered. He could bleed to death and it didn't matter to anyone. Not that he thought he was bleeding to death at the moment, but he knew that if he were, he would probably be ignored just the same. He was lucky enough to be able to read a book in his cell, and when he had visited the prison library a few days before and found a worn paperback tome by none other than Stephen King—a time-travel book about a guy trying to keep the Kennedy assassination from happening—Miles knew enough not to complain, at least not too much. Although he had never been in jail before, he figured he was doubly lucky for finding this type of book in the prison library, as opposed to a non-fiction book about something boring; or worse, a copy of the Bible, which seemed to be quite popular with many of the other inmates. That and books about the law—the law of getting the fuck out.

The other inmates, for whatever reason, had found God behind these concrete walls, or at the very least were searching for him, if only so they could pray to someone or something about getting out. Nothing made a godless man more religious than sheer desperation. And desperation was something Miles was definitely becoming more acquainted with since arriving there.

Even though he knew it would probably be fruitless, Miles shouted again for a guard.

"Shut the fuck up, you fuckin' pussy!" another inmate yelled back.

Despite his present circumstances, this almost made Miles laugh. Although he had only been in prison for roughly two weeks, it didn't seem like any of the inmates could put two words together without an expletive as one of them. Miles was consistently amazed at just how many versions of "fuck" they could fit into one sentence. Then again, if he were in here for much longer, he knew "fuck" would probably be every other word out of his mouth, too. Like God, "fuck" was apparently another deity worth praying to.

Without thinking, Miles put his cut finger in his mouth, and despite the metallic reminder of his blood sucked on it like a child instinctively sucking his thumb. Glancing at the Stephen King book in his lap (which, ironically, now had blood on some of its pages), he wished that time machines actually did exist—although where he would go with one, he had no idea. Would he go backward or forward? Neither direction screamed out to him as a better possibility. He guessed it was just the idea that he could go anywhere he wanted, actually being able to control the direction of his life in some way. If this concept of control was why a lot of the inmates prayed to God, then maybe it was about time Miles found religion. He had nothing else to lose, he figured.

The biggest thing weighing on Miles' mind, however, wasn't even his present circumstances. It was that he wasn't sure if Sawyer had been arrested, or even where Sawyer was. They had both been getting high at Bennett Place—this was the last thing Miles remembered—although he had no idea what had happened after that. This thing he was charged with—shooting someone—he had no memory of. He didn't even know who this guy was that he had apparently shot, other than that it was a black kid around his age, and that the guy might die from the gunshot wound.

What if the guy died? Miles worried, now thinking about this possibility. Would he be charged with murder? He didn't remember shooting anyone, and he figured he would remember something like that. In fact, he had no memory of ever shooting a gun, period, like at some stacked beer cans or something out in the middle of the desert—the kind of scene he only saw in the movies or on TV. Sure, he remembered holding the gun for a minute in Sawyer's car, but that was it…wasn't it? Or had they been fucking around with the gun at Bennett Place, too, pretending they were back in the Civil War?

Where is that motherfucker?

"Hey!" Miles screamed again, hoping a guard would hear him this time, or, more accurately, respond to him, as he was fairly certain that they could hear him. Everyone within one mile probably could. He was yelling loud enough that *someone* had to hear him—which, of course, also included the other prisoners.

"Shut the fuck up, Nancy Boy!" another convict immediately shouted back, enunciating each syllable in such a slow, rhythmic way that it sounded as if they were rapping the beginning of a song, rather than responding to him (Miles wished it was the former).

What the fuck was a "Nancy Boy" anyway?, Miles wondered. The other convicts definitely had their own lingo, but he was still learning it. Trying to translate some of the phrases they used was a good distraction, too: it kept Miles from thinking about where he was, why he was there, and, most importantly, at least for the moment, where the fuck Sawyer was.

He stopped screaming for a guard and decided to lay back down on the cot that was too small for someone even half his size—yet another challenge he realized on day one at the jail, and it wasn't entirely to his sleeping comfort. Until he made a friend that was bigger than him—preferably much bigger—he would be picked on by a whole lot of convicts.

The toilet situation was something that also caused Miles a fair amount of distress. To begin with, it didn't seem like they cleaned the bathroom area that much, if at all. Was cleaning it his responsibility? he wondered. Or rather, his and his cellmate's responsibility? It wasn't like he saw any form of housekeeping ever walking by, as if he were in a motel that offered maid service, some short Latino woman pushing a cart of wrapped toilet paper rolls and other supplies hollering, "Housekeeping!" before letting herself into his cell to clean it. And his cellmate clearly wasn't the type of guy who would get on his hands and knees to clean the toilet. Miles was lucky enough, he knew, that his cellmate wasn't raping him every night after lights out. His cellmate, whose name he didn't know (and Miles wasn't about to make introductions), kept to himself most of the time. Miles wasn't even sure if his cellmate had uttered a single word, like to another convict in the cafeteria or something. On some days, Miles wondered if his cellmate *could* say anything, as though he might be a mute. Either way, Miles came to realize, it was probably smart of his cellmate to keep his mouth shut.

Taking a shit in front of his cellmate, or anyone else who happened to walk by, wasn't something Miles felt comfortable with on any level. Of course, he knew most people wouldn't be comfortable with something like that, though his cellmate didn't seem to have any issues with it at all. He would just plop down and let it rip, not even caring if there was piss on the seat before he sat down (which there most likely was). Miles wondered if all the convicts were like him on day one, just in regard to taking a shit in front of other people; but whether they were or not didn't really matter, for when Miles had to go (and he tried so hard not to), there weren't any other options. Worst of all, whether it was Miles going or his cellmate, and at any time of day, diarrhea wasn't an anomaly. Outside of the anxiety from being incarcerated, this was probably also due to the slop served in the cafeteria as a substitute for real food. It was almost as if the prison *wanted* the inmates to have diarrhea—and all the time, not just some of the time.

Lying on his cot that seemed to be made of medium-sized marbles, and which felt as if they were dispersed in such a way that no muscle in your back was safe, Miles stared at the stained ceiling and thought about the Sistine Chapel, which one of his foster parents had told him about on an overcast school-day afternoon when Miles was home sick. From just the description of it, this tourist attraction sounded incredible, like something every person should have on their "bucket list," and which Miles now thought he would probably never see in his lifetime. Even if he somehow got out of jail, he couldn't imagine ever going to Europe.

Miles occasionally overheard other convicts talking about how many days they had been behind bars so far, or how many days they had left behind bars. Either way, it reminded Miles of rehab: the "prisoners" there also spoke of numbered days, and once the addicts were sober outside of rehab, the numbered days would start over, most likely running until the day they died (if they stayed vigilant).

But Miles had "broken out" of rehab early, and not long before his sentence was complete. Why had he been so stupid?, he wanted to scream, hoping that someone, even another convict, could give him a reasonable answer. And where was Sawyer at this moment? Who would break him out now from a place he actually needed breaking out from?

He wished he had never met Sawyer, for Miles felt that, some-how, the Pee-Wee Herman-tattooed ass-fuck was responsible for all of this—and that someday, he was going to pay.

He still couldn't believe he had gotten away with it. Of course, he hadn't been the one who actually pulled the trig-ger—although, truth be told, he couldn't remember for cer-tain. And the guy Sawyer had just slept with had no idea what kind of person had picked him up and then fucked him, and without so much as ten words in a row. They had only met the night before at a gay bar downtown, and the dominant/submissive dynamic was never in question, despite the fact that both were alpha males.

That morning, after Sawyer kicked this toy out of his bed, and then his apartment—they were all toys to Sawyer when it came down to it—he stayed in bed and stared at his ceiling, which, for some reason, made him realize that his rent had been due a few days before; worse yet, there wasn't much of a possibility that it would be paid anytime soon. *Oh well*, he thought, *fuck it. Fuck the landlord. Fuck everyone.* Maybe he would just go on a fucking rampage and leave all the wreck-age behind. That was how he felt, anyway.

The night previous, just before he went downtown to pick up a toy for the evening, a trending story on the internet seized his full attention. News stories on the internet, trend-ing or not, rarely interested Sawyer at all. But this one was about someone he had lost track of for a few days—and this news story proved his friend hadn't actually been taken away by "men in black" who believed they were both aliens (though, naturally, Sawyer had evaded capture). The truth was that Miles had been arrested by regular men—Raleigh

Police?—who believed he had attempted to murder a black teenager in cold blood.

Sawyer was finally back from whatever enchanted place the drugs had taken him, though, admittedly, he was still a little bit hazy, at least as far as his short-term memory was concerned. But he was always a little bit hazy anyway in his regular state (whatever that was). And his short-term memory had never been that good. Occasionally, and he had no idea why, a random synapse would fire off in his brain that would cause him to remember some image or sound bite or brief event that had happened when he was only single-dig-its-old—and yet, on the flip side, he couldn't even remember what he'd had for lunch that day. Was this how everyone functioned, Sawyer wondered, or was it just him and his drug-decayed mind playing masturbatory tricks?

The one thing Sawyer ever felt he was good at—other than taking an array of drugs and consuming large amounts of alcohol—was getting people, and really most people, to do whatever he wanted. And now he wasn't sure whether or not he had just achieved the near impossible, which was getting someone to do something as huge as killing someone else—someone else who was a complete stranger to them.

Still lying in bed but no longer staring at the ceiling, Sawyer wondered whether this was what Charles Manson was like. Was *he* like Charles Manson? He couldn't be; Manson was certifiably crazy. *But maybe I'm crazy, too?* Sawyer thought. Was that possible? Some considered Manson a genius—a sick genius, of course, but still a genius, especially when it came to manipulating other people. And Sawyer had that same talent. But did that mean he would be put away, too, like Manson, and be rejected at every parole hearing for the rest of his life?

No, he couldn't go back to jail—of this much, Sawyer was certain. The fact that he had already been imprisoned before was a secret he had kept from everyone, including his father. He was only a minor when he was arrested, but he'd had fake identification that somehow the police fell for (he didn't have time to remove the fake ID from his wallet), and they never even asked him about contacting his father, which was truly a godsend. So, Sawyer had never told anyone about his incarceration, just like the other big secret he kept from everyone—a secret that he was probably going to take to his grave, even though he wanted so badly to be out in the open about it. Living with this secret—a secret that he was ashamed of just the same because he knew no other response to it—was a way of life he couldn't keep his distance from, no matter how hard he tried. He also knew, of course, that the Bible didn't approve of this secret, just as his father wouldn't approve if he ever learned of it—and his father wasn't necessarily such a religious guy. He knew he would most likely go to Hell for it, regardless of whether or not he actually believed in Hell. There was no other possible outcome. In the endgame, Sawyer's lack of belief in a higher power wouldn't matter one way or the other; he knew he was going somewhere for this role he had no choice but to play—a destination that he would deserve no matter what he told himself at night in order to fall asleep. And it was nighttime—always nighttime—that was ripe for belief in things one couldn't see with the human eye; the dark kept most things hidden, especially the things it needed to keep hidden.

The night before, Sawyer had been mean to the guy he picked up at The Lamplight. He was always mean to them; he would never see them again anyway, since a long-term relationship was out of the question—or even a short-term one for that matter. Anything past a night was one night too many. He didn't need that kind of attachment, or drama, to play out in his life. *Bing bang boom: see you later, motherfucker.*

The funny thing—if it could be called funny—was that in "real life" (as opposed to cruising a gay bar like The Lamplight, where one could never hide), other people would often think that Sawyer was British, even though he had no accent to speak of. In such situations, when he knew someone was implicitly talking about him, he would overhear this type of exchange from nearby:

"Is he gay?"

"No, I think he's just British."

And Sawyer wished that he *was* British, or anything other than himself. He wished for this simple truth every day of his life, from the moment his eyes opened in the morning to the moment he finally fell asleep at night. And when he dreamed, he would dream of becoming the kind of boy who everyone liked, the kind of boy who never did anything wrong...

the kind of boy who, more often than not, would be mistaken for an angel.

CUTICLE

As a younger man, Barry often found himself falling in love with waitresses. He wasn't sure why exactly, although when he was considerably older and looked back on it— looking back on things was unabashedly a favorite pastime of his—he realized that it may have been because they responded to his needs, more or less, especially the ones who worked at the same bar he did and seemed to be in awe of the bartenders there—or so he had liked to think, since he had been one of them. Maybe he *was* a chauvinist, or had been as a bartender, he wondered now, just as Lilly had liked to point out to him back then, and still did twenty-odd years later. Lilly, ironically, had been one of the agog waitresses at the bar, which he liked to point out to *her*. Not that he identified as a chauvinist per se, at least consciously; maybe the loss of his mother at a young age had something to do with it, but he wasn't about to go to a head-shrink like Lilly had and listen to that Freud bullshit. Parents died, and that was just a fact of life; it was the order of things. Why someone needed to go to a shrink to figure that out, Barry had no idea.

"Get over it!" he wanted to scream at his wife, who was now threatening to become his ex-wife—and all because he had fucked someone else once. *Once.* But she wouldn't listen. Ever since her father died, things had just gotten worse between them. Her father had been a cheat as well, though the fact that she grouped her father with him was more than a little absurd. Cheating once wasn't a crime; cheating once was an accident, a slip-up. He certainly wasn't a serial cheater like her father apparently had been, though she accused him of it just the same, and without any real evidence whatsoever. What a joke the whole thing was, he wanted to tell her, but knew that wouldn't help his cause.

Lilly had changed over the years, and this even she admitted. She claimed she was much more secure now—secure enough to be alone the rest of her life if she had to be. But she had always been secure with herself. This hadn't changed. What had changed was that she had become much more of a—he hated to say it, but it was true: a bitch. Plain and simple. Especially after she started seeing a shrink and he boiled this paranoia inside her. But Barry was willing to stick it out with the marriage as long as she stopped seeing this whackjob doctor, as that would likely return her to her old self. Actually, he wasn't even a real doctor, Barry remembered, as he couldn't prescribe drugs to her. Lilly had to see someone else for that. Come to think of it, the drugs she was on were also probably turning her into a bitch. They were "bitch" pills, and if she stopped taking them, and stopped seeing a shrink, she would most likely return to her old self, and then they could move forward again like a normal married couple. This much he had to said to her, and more than once, but she had replied that there was no such thing as "normal," which he didn't understand at all. Sometimes, especially lately, he had no idea what the fuck she was talking about. *Probably more brainwashing from that fucking head-shrink of hers*, he had decided.

After Owen was shot, and by a white boy no less, he'd gotten a call from Lilly at the ER, where she was "fit to be tied" as they say. She was so unhinged, in fact, that he had no idea what had happened at first. During their brief phone call she was so hysterical it was almost like she was speaking another language which he couldn't quite understand, no matter how hard he tried to get her to slow down. All he'd been able to make out for certain was that some white boy, around the same age as Owen, had shot him point-blank on the sidewalk. From the sound of it, it was a miracle that he was even still alive.

The police had thought the shooting might be gang-related at first, but after he and Lilly told them that Owen wasn't part of any gang the police relented, as if they'd only made it up just to get a reaction from them, especially considering the white boy wasn't part of any gang either (that they knew of so far) and had no prior record. This latter part about the white boy not having a previous record made the shooting that much more confusing, as it seemed to be without motive, which, according to the police, made these types of cases much harder to solve.

That first day, Owen was in surgery for most of it, and although Barry would never admit this to another living person, one of his first thoughts had been that this tragedy, regardless of whether his son survived it or not, could possibly mend his marriage. He felt a little horrible for thinking this, but he also knew that it might be true. Their marriage was quite possibly the one thing they still had some control over—although this might have been debatable, too. Everything that day seemed to be debatable, not the least of which was what the doctors had told them in the waiting room.

"He could wake up tomorrow, he could wake up in a week, or he could wake up not ever," Dr. Popovich had said—for some reason more directed to Lilly than to him, even though he was standing right next to her. He was always standing right next to her. And Barry didn't know what was more irritating: the fact that Dr. Popovich had seemingly ignored his presence as "the father," or the fact that the foreign-sounding doctor had seemingly used incorrect English—though Barry wasn't a hundred percent certain about the latter. He wasn't an English teacher after all, and he didn't think he had to be. He didn't think he had to be anything other than "the father"—whether the doctors recognized him in this role or not. But he would make sure that they recognized him. Barry swore to himself this much. Otherwise, someone was going to get hurt—and not just the kid who had shot his son.

Barry had been biting his nails for at least an hour, if not more, and she couldn't take his nervousness any longer. It was only making her more anxious, and that was something she definitely didn't need right now, especially since she forgot to bring any Ativan with her to the hospital. How could she have remembered? It was enough to remember how to even drive a car, like she had somehow done to get to the hospital, much less remember any of her meds. Speaking of the car, where the hell had she parked? *Had* she parked? Or was it possible that she had forgotten to even stop the car before she had gotten out, and then the driverless car had crashed into the front entrance of the hospital, all without her real-izing it? No, that couldn't be. If that had happened, surely someone would have found her by now. It wasn't like she was the type of person who could become invisible if she needed to; her presence was always known, sometimes even before she arrived somewhere. Lilly King was a memorable person, whether she wanted to be remembered or not, and it wasn't always in the best light, as Owen used to remind her when she (frequently) embarrassed him in public. If only she could embarrass him now, just one more time.

But it didn't appear that anything was negotiable regard-ing her son's current situation—even something as min-imal as slipping a maître d' a twenty to get a better table at a restaurant like Barry used to do to impress her when they first started dating. Although by the time they actually started dating, a twenty probably wasn't enough anymore.

Occasionally, a maître d' would stare at the twenty as if they were conjuring a magic spell to make the denomination higher—a sure sign for Barry to dig deeper in his wallet. And Lilly had actually felt sorry for Barry due to the embarrassment he must have felt in those situations. After all, inflation wasn't *his* fault.

What *was* his fault, however, was how long it took him to ask her out on a date. Even with his bartender confidence—a paradox that she could never resolve, since he seemed to be so uninspired regarding every other aspect of his life. And despite his tips at the bar (and a usually busy bar at that), which she guessed would be more than sufficient for a boy his age, he seemed to always come up short when it came to paying his monthly bills—a likely sign that he had money management issues, but one which she chose, consciously or not, to ignore...until it was too late.

Just when Lilly was starting to lose hope that Barry would ever ask her out, he finally did—she wasn't blind as to the other girls at the bar he showed interest in, especially some of the waitresses—and they set a date to meet for coffee, yet another irony since Barry hated coffee. He didn't even drink tea, or at least have a daily need for it. Lilly, however, couldn't live without coffee—her overwhelming urgency for it every day, coupled with her unflinching routine (if it hadn't been compromised by sedatives and/or wine the night before), made her the kind of Starbucks customer whose specific drink was usually ready for her even before she exploded through the door every morning on the way to open her store.

In Barry's version of their shared history, however, it had been Lilly who finally asked *him* out, which she knew couldn't possibly be true. Doing something like that went against her better nature, not to mention it would certainly incite the almost violent disapproval of her mother, who didn't think it was a woman's place to ever be the aggressor with a man (and Lilly, back then at least, shared everything with her mother). According to Barry, though, she had asked him out for a drink, which she knew couldn't be possible either. To begin with, she hadn't kicked off her adult life as much of a drinker—it had been her friends back then who were mostly the drinkers—not to mention the fact that she never would have asked a guy, especially one she didn't really know, to go out for a drink (if she were to ask a guy out at all, which she had reminded her mother of on more than a few occasions throughout her early dating life). Plus, if that ridiculous story *were* true, how did they end up going for coffee instead? Although, admittedly, Barry did have a good answer for that; she just couldn't remember what it had been. As for the punchline in Barry's version of the story—which he never held back when they were at parties together—Lilly had apparently added, before he could respond to her daring invitation to meet for a drink: "You should know, I don't do no." And this last part had been said with "so much sauce" (according to Barry) that he couldn't help but agree to a date with her.

Less than a year later they would be married, and with Owen in her belly—"a total accident" if Barry happened to be asked, but completely intentional by Lilly. She would always refer to Owen as her "bonus baby" or "God's plan," depending on who she was talking to at the time, though the former tended to be confusing since Owen had no siblings.

Carrying this bonus baby to term, however, proved to be almost insurmountable for Lilly due to her having been born with a T-shaped uterus—a birth defect caused by her mother being prescribed a synthetic estrogen drug when she was pregnant—but after somehow making it through and delivering a healthy, happy Owen into the world, the still-newlywed couple once again deferred to the heavenly Father as the one and only reason for their miracle baby. This was yet another irony, since neither Barry nor Lilly were that outwardly religious, but unexplained phenomena can often make the most atheistic-minded people divine. At some point in a lifetime, everyone believes in magic.

Observing Barry in the intensive care ward now, as he sat nervously at Owen's bedside, over a decade and a half since their proverbial Red Sea had parted, Lilly noticed that life's recent challenges—the pending divorce, Owen being shot—had aged her once-promising husband-to-be. His once-thick mane was graying at his temples like the beginnings of a spider web, and his eyes had looming dark circles, as if sleep were as foreign to him as it lately had become for her. And when they were both getting coffee that morning (hot chocolate for him) in the hospital's cafeteria, after the doctors had kicked them out of Owen's room temporarily, she noticed that many of Barry's fingernails had recently torn cuticles, some of them still caked with blood, displaying to the world at least one of his secret torments.

"What did you do to yourself?" she asked, immediately regretting that she had said anything at all to him, especially about his damaged fingers.

"Huh?" he said, moving his introspective eyes over to her.

She caught herself from repeating the question, although her unintended downward glance gave her away. Still, it took Barry a few seconds to respond, his brain unwilling at first to register anything else but the tragedy of his son—especially something as mundane as his fingernails. She wondered whether his torn cuticles throbbed with pain, and whether he hoped that Lilly could somehow feel it too, like one twin vicariously undergoing the physical experiences of the other.

"Never mind," she said, diverting her eyes to the one long window in the room, a gesture intended to change the subject, even if that meant they would start talking about something as benign as the weather. Anything was better than talking about Barry's stupid fingernails or the fact that he couldn't stop tearing at them, even now in their son's hospital room, since she had apparently reminded his brain to begin doing it again.

There was a time, however, back when they were young and their hearts were like sponges, soaking up veiled dots of dopamine and serenity in exchange for the incorruptible love they felt for one another. Lilly did things for Barry then which most people wouldn't even think to do, much less actually do, especially in public where accidental observers would be given pause. Thinking about it now in the hospital room where their only offspring fought for his life, Lilly wasn't certain how she could have done such a thing, and, most of the time, do it successfully; it was an eccentric talent that even she couldn't explain (not that anyone would ever ask her). What she frequently did when she observed her husband chewing at one of his nails or cuticles for an extended period of time was put his finger-in-question into her own mouth, where, like the world's greatest athlete in the sport, she would tear off the bothersome piece of his micro-anatomy with her own teeth and spit it out. Always to Barry's wonderment—never could he believe that she'd done such a thing.

Lilly never bit off her husband's cuticles as a joke, sight-gag or parlor trick. She was sincerely helping him, convinced he wouldn't be able to succeed versus this minor dilemma that popped up like a whack-a-mole—or at least not in the reasonable amount of time she previously set without telling him he was on the clock. On the first occasion she did it, in line for a ride at Disney World where both of them were drenched in sweat, he thought she was just trying to be funny—and it *was* funny, *that* time, even to some of the other people nearby who had never seen such a thing. But his sudden embarrassment quickly dissipated when he realized that she had done it. She had bitten off the jagged piece of nail on his right thumb that his own teeth couldn't quite get a hold of (although he would be the first to admit that he was an amateur nail biter at best, even after years of practicing).

"Sorry," he said to her from beside their son's hospital bed, knowing that his own anxiety was most likely, as usual, driving her crazy. But then, out of nowhere, he exclaimed, "Fuck it, and fuck you," the growl of his voice sounding as if it came from an unseen fourth person in the room, allowing him enough time to jerk up from his chair and almost get completely through the open doorway before she could even think to respond.

"Back at ya!" she hollered at the now-empty space on the threshold of her son's room. Then, despite knowing she was only speaking to herself: "That's right. Fuck you...fuck you." She turned and stared at Owen's chest, which was heaving up and down, and not silently, as if trying to win back her attention.

She whispered the two words again, and to no one in particular. It was her new hymn, and she didn't seem to care who heard it—though she would later pray for an audience of some kind, even just an audience of one.

DOORS

Lilly carried too many keys, and she knew it. What she didn't know, however, was what most of the keys opened. She guessed that maybe she just hadn't discarded the keys she didn't need anymore at the time of not needing them. Maybe she had been distracted at the time, Lilly thought, and it was probably Barry who had done the distracting. Plus, he was always giving her shit that she carried too many keys, and she certainly didn't need him to tell her that. And he was also always telling her that the clothing she sold in her store was too "foo-foo," which she easily deflected as well, even though she knew she didn't need to defend herself or the clothing in her boutique, especially from him of all people, who had no fashion sense at all.

"Just because you say it isn't foo-foo doesn't mean it isn't," he'd said to her not too long ago, just before Owen was shot.

"You don't even know what foo-foo means," she fired back. "And I certainly don't give any credence to someone who only wears solid colors all the time, and most of them black…which isn't even a real color, by the way."

"A real color? What the fuck are you talking about, Lilly? Do you even know what comes out of your mouth half the time?" And then, before she could say anything to that, he said, "*Credence?* Wow. Am I supposed to be impressed that you use big words—"

"Big words? Credence isn't a big word…although maybe for you, it is." Instinctively, she took her key chain out and looked for a certain key that she wasn't sure she needed at the moment, but looked for anyway. It was a good distraction from continuing the absurd conversation she was having with the miscreant, even if the distraction wasn't real. Barry was probably too stupid to know the difference.

"You still carry all those keys?" he'd said, almost sounding genuine, like he cared how many keys she carried for her own good. "I bet you don't even know what half those keys open anymore," he continued, practically reading her mind—a trick he had carried through their marriage, and which, at first, was quite a turn-on for her, the final evidence that they were soulmates who were meant for each other.

Lilly found the key that her subconscious had apparently wanted and opened the door for the *other* backroom—the room that only she was allowed in and none of her employees, which numbered only two, and one of them only on Saturdays, her busiest day of the week.

She shut the door behind her, hoping that when she came out a few minutes later, Barry would be gone from the store. And then, as Lilly looked at the old Dell laptop on her desk, the laptop she really only used for internet dating, and which she kept secret from everyone (her employees thought the computer, which they could see on the server but required a separate passcode, was for the store's accounting, and that was why she didn't share it with anyone), she remembered a time back when she was in high school and had met this cute guy on a field trip to the Museum of Art. The guy wasn't a classmate of hers, and was quite a bit older—old enough, at least, not to be in high school anymore. He had been quietly studying the Manet painting, *The Execution of Emperor Maximilian*, while also trading stares with her. Finally, she stealthily left her group (a brave thing to do that was *very* un-Lilly-like of her—both her departure and her intended destination) and walked over to him. Then she said to him (another brave thing she was unaccustomed to): "I wonder what he did that made them so angry they wanted to kill him?"

He turned around dubiously yet deliberately, making the next few seconds come across in slow-motion.

"What who did?" he said, revealing a smile so wide and white that it almost seemed painted on.

She read the title of the painting. "The emperor guy," she replied. Then, realizing what she had said previously, added: "Well, I guess they're doing more than just wanting to kill him."

"More than just wanting to kill him?" he repeated, his smile a prisoner of his grizzled face.

"I mean, they *are* killing him. Not just *wanting* to."

He still looked perplexed.

"I said at first that they *wanted* to kill him...." Her uncharacteristic audacity was fleeting, causing her stomach to drop. She had to go to the bathroom, and sooner rather than later.

He laughed, and even though her colon was suddenly doing aerial tricks, she was still agog over him. Her crush would just have to wait a few minutes.

"I have to go to the bathroom," she said, not knowing why she had just admitted that. Couldn't she have come up with a fake reason to excuse herself momentarily? One that was a bit more romantic-sounding than going to the toilet?

He laughed again. "Okay," he said, though his tone sounded more like a question than an acknowledgment. "I'll wait for you."

"What?" she said, not expecting him to say that. But before she could wait for his answer, she needed to get to the bathroom, and as quickly as possible.

"I'll wait for you right here," he called after her, since she was already hurriedly walking away.

She managed to stop and turn around, but only for a

second; a second was all she had. "No, you don't have to wait
for me."

"That's okay." He smiled again. "I don't mind. Plus, I want
to study this painting some more."

"No, really, don't wait. Please don't wait."

He stared at her with a baffled expression on his face.

She started to turn back around toward the bathroom, or
where she hoped the bathroom was—she couldn't afford to
make a mistake that would cost any additional time—but
again he insisted that he would wait for her, wherever she
happened to be going.

"Seriously," she wanted to shout at him, but spoke at
normal volume, "please don't wait. I don't want you to wait."
And when she realized her pleading was doing no good, she
said, "Don't be here when I get back," a strangely intimate
thing to say to someone she had only met moments before,
as if she were breaking up with him.

When she did eventually return—hesitatingly at first, as
she was more than a little embarrassed for taking so long—he
was gone, and she felt bad for telling this guy to walk away
when he had every right to stand wherever he wanted.

Now, close to thirty years later, there she was hiding in her
secret backroom, praying that when she came out, Barry
would be gone, just like the boy in the museum. And he *was*
gone—Barry—which made her instantly worry that maybe
she would inadvertently shut the door on Owen someday,
and when she came out of that door, he would be gone as
well. Not only like the boy in the museum, or Barry, but like
everyone she had ever encountered (and presumably cared
about).

Her life had been made up of doors, she realized, both
opened and closed, though mostly closed. Standing alone in
the middle of her store that day, she wondered if she would
ever come across another door again, especially an open

one, knowing deep down that any open door in her future wouldn't stay that way for long.

Another door did open less than a month later—in fact, several doors—but they weren't the type of doors Lilly ever thought she would enter. They were jail doors at the county detention facility where the boy who had shot Owen awaited a preliminary hearing, and then, she hoped, trial (given that no deal resulted from the preliminary hearing). What she was doing at the jail, period, Lilly had no idea. She had been with Owen at the hospital for two days in a row, and one of his doctors had suggested that she go home, take a shower and get some sleep, then return to the hospital later, as Owen was probably going to be more or less the same for at least that long. If something did change, of course someone would immediately call her and let her know.

Lilly's intent had been to go home and do just what the doctor had ordered—though substituting a bath for a shower—but she somehow ended up at the county jail instead; as if, without explanation, someone else were guiding her against her wishes. Later she thought that maybe her controls had been taken over because she couldn't trust herself anymore to make the right decisions, so now the universe had decided that enough was enough and taken the reins from her—whether she wanted to relinquish them or not.

There was someone who was even more surprised at Lilly's diversion that afternoon, and that was Miles. At first, Miles thought the mother of the boy he had apparently shot had come to the jail to call him names, maybe tell him to go to Hell and spit in his face—or worse, whatever that might be. But surprisingly, she had not. Lilly was even astonished at herself for her constraint. After all, this was the boy who had not only shot Owen, but had most likely killed him (though she wasn't even close to accepting that yet). Thinking about this possibility, that she might lose her son forever, made her regret leaving the hospital at all, not to mention where she had diverted herself to instead.

Lilly was also taken aback by what the visit to the jail felt like. Somehow it didn't feel like she was the mother of the victim—mostly because it all seemed illusory, as if she hadn't really been there at all. How could she have been there?, she asked herself afterwards, in that concrete chamber of horrors that housed society's rapists and killers—the latter of which had taken her son's life, whether Owen died or not, because no matter what was going to happen around the corner, Owen's life would never be the same…which meant her life would never be the same either.

When the boy finally came into the area where the visitors waited—Lilly had been waiting for some time, as they all had to enter simultaneously to meet with whoever happened to come see them that day—she was alarmed at how young he looked. He looked even younger than Owen, she thought, and Owen still looked like a baby to her. This boy certainly didn't have the appearance of a killer—or rather, "the likely shooter," as the police referred to him.

When he sat down across from her, with the transparent partition between them, and picked up the phone so that he could hear her, Lilly was so taken with his long hair, flowing effortlessly from the top of his head, that her first thought, as strange as it seemed, was that he could easily be a transgender candidate. The night before, she couldn't sleep despite taking a healthy dose of melatonin along with the benign sleeping pill that one of Owen's doctors had prescribed her (not to mention her usual warm bath), so instead she watched TV late into the night, and eventually morning. One of the shows she had watched was some type of "reality" thing about transgendered people. Most of them—at least the men who wanted to become women, and despite all their surgeries and hormone therapies—still looked like men in drag to her, but this boy, this boy who had shot her son, looked as if he could make the choice of which sex he wanted to be without any need for a "transitional" phase.

"Hello?" he said again into the phone, since Lilly was still spaced out, thinking about the transgender TV show, and hadn't responded the first time he had addressed her.

Finally, Lilly came back to the moment, like a camera slowly focusing on its once-blurred subject, and said, "Hello," back to him, although she instantly regretted it, feeling that it was too friendly a greeting for the person who had shot Owen in cold blood. She wondered about the curious phrase "in cold blood," and then wondered if there were an unfriendly or less friendly version of the word "hello." Coming up short on both accounts, however, she left the greeting that had slipped out of her mouth as is, hoping that the boy wouldn't take her "hello" as any type of forgiveness for what he had done.

The boy was still staring at her, and another minute passed before Lilly realized that the onus of the rest of the conversation, now that "hello" was out of the way, was her burden. Still unsure of why she was even there, Lilly couldn't think of anything else to say. *What was there to say?* Of course, she could just curse at him, shout obscenities at him through the Plexiglas partition—but what good would that do? Also, she supposed that a guard or two would probably step in if she went down that road. But maybe that would feel good anyway, like a release of some sort, despite getting eventually shut down? Should she go ahead with that plan, she wondered, or would that just be a waste of time for everyone, including the boy? But what did she care if she wasted the boy's time? All he had now was time—and the ultimate justice was that a good chunk of it, if not the rest of it, was going to be flushed down the toilet, and he would have no other recourse but to stand there and helplessly watch it spiral away into oblivion.

But was this really the ultimate justice for the crime he had committed against her baby boy? Wasn't the ultimate justice death—"an eye for an eye"—like the Bible commanded? Like the "Old West" commanded? Or was that just in the movies?

Lilly was asking herself that question, the one about "Old West" movies, when the boy who had shot Owen tried one last time to greet her. He was probably wondering if she planned on saying anything to him; maybe she wasn't going to—not ever. Again, she thought, there wasn't really anything *to* say. And fuck him if he thought she *had* to say something. She didn't have to do anything, she decided. There was no script, no director telling her what she needed to do. In fact, if she wanted, she could just continue sitting there across from him, saying nothing at all—nothing at all—at least until visiting time was over. Or would he stand up before then, having figured out that she wasn't going to say anything to him, and walk out before visiting time ended? *Could he actually do that?* Wasn't he her temporary prisoner until she decided that he wasn't? Did he even know who she was? Lilly wondered abruptly, probably the most important question of them all.

Sometime later—or perhaps after no time at all—the boy did just what she thought he couldn't. Before visiting time was over he simply stood up and walked away, not even bothering to hang up the phone on his end. And Lilly was in such disbelief that he did that—both his walking away and the helpless phone he left hanging in the air—that she just sat there and watched the naked receiver swing from side to side, hitting parts of the antiseptic visiting booth as it did so.

Maybe even more surprising to Lilly was the fact that she herself didn't get up straightaway to leave once the boy had departed, as now there was most definitely nothing to say, and no one on the other end of the line to hear it if she did finally think of something. Although what frustrated Lilly even more was the simple observation that the guard standing closest to the still-swaying phone didn't bother to grab it and put it back in its place. She couldn't understand why he left it beating in the air like that, a throbbing metronome possessing time for as long as it wanted.

THUMB-SHUT

At first all he saw were eyes—hundreds of them, maybe thousands—and they were all looking at him. They weren't staring, he didn't think, although he wasn't completely sure. Owen didn't want to be stared at—that much he knew—even if it was only in a dream. The eyes were friendly, though, or at least seemed so. It was the other things he imagined, the other things he dreamed about, that might have had different intentions. But throughout all these dreams he had—if it indeed were several and not just one, which could have symbolized something scary—he never felt like he was in any type of danger. It was just the opposite; the images that swam inside his mind made him feel a powerful sense of tranquility that he had never felt before, as if someone were gently running a quiet stream over his body, a silent meditation that encompassed every religion, or none at all, which was okay either way. He felt a sense of calm beyond the restfulness of sleeping, as if it were somehow more important than anything naturally required by the human body—more important than food or sunlight, more important than water. There was always the water, which matched the sky, translucent blue. He envisioned rivers and streams, oceans and lakes, all bodies of water imaginable. And the water was ceaseless if he so chose, or converged with land should he prefer it. Everything was tangible enough that he could feel the water encompass his entire self, protecting him, but also absorbing his infinite will, God-like.

Relentless, these images continued as long as he wanted, or as long as he kept his eyelids firmly shut. And just when he thought he was seeing the last image, a new one would birth itself into his subconscious, as welcome as anything previous. But then there were the voices, the voices from people he recognized, and some he did not, all of whom were beckoning him to come back, in prayer or half-voice, as if the full volume of their utterances might inadvertently wake him up, despite the persistent irony that this was what they actually wanted him to do. There were things these familiar people or assorted strangers couldn't promise, however, even if they said they could, such as that he was going to be all right no matter what, that things were going to be okay for everyone on both sides of his consciousness. That was the thing of it all—the truth, opaque and immovable, was harder to rope than anyone could fathom; and truth's protagonist, time, was also ungraspable, the ghost of a magician who never erred.

Lilly also had a dream, but it was unlike Owen's. Residing in Lilly's subconscious was a young girl on a train, walking from car to car, laughing, maybe even mocking her. *But why was she laughing?*, Lilly wondered almost out loud. Why was this acerbic girl mocking her like this? Had Lilly done something to upset her? After all, everything was categorically Lilly's fault, she knew, including the fact that her son was so far away now yet still somehow lying in the bed before her. *But what was so goddamn funny? And why was this train girl going from car to car like that?*

But then, all at once, Lilly understood. It was *she* who was going from car to car on the train, and the girl was only trying to catch up to her. The girl was laughing because she knew the punchline—the punchline to the joke at hand—or rather, the end of the joke, the end of the riddle. The girl already knew the outcome and was trying to convince Lilly to stop running, as the train cars would eventually end and there would be nowhere else to hide—unless, of course, Lilly jumped from the fast-moving train. But where would she land, if she landed at all?

Now his hand was deformed and Owen didn't remember how this had happened to him. But maybe this hand belonged to someone else, and wasn't his at all? How could he tell, though, whose hand it actually was? Or perhaps it was simply another random image, a miscellaneous symbol to go along with the others....

But the others now didn't seem so random at all. In fact, now each seemed to perfectly align with the one preceding it, as well as set up the one that followed, like a perfect algebra equation—that is, without the correct constant or variable in the right place, the whole thing would fall apart. And Owen wanted more than anything for things *not* to fall apart, or at least *the* thing. Did anyone else know about *the* thing? he wondered. Were the people surrounding him, including the ones who knew him—*especially* the ones who knew him—aware of this *thing*? Or were they still trying desperately *not* to know the thing, even though it was staring them down like a mountain lion, waiting for just the right moment to pounce?

Maybe that's what had happened to his hand? The lion had attacked him and deformed it. *But why?* How did he even still have a hand to begin with? Wouldn't the lion have consumed it in totality, rather than leaving it deformed like this? Then Owen had a scary thought: maybe his hand wasn't the only thing that was now deformed? Maybe he had other body parts—parts he couldn't see or feel at the moment—that were also mutilated, surrendered to nature like an isolated tree hit by lightning?

Now Owen was in an enormous but empty house, drifting nervously down abandoned corridors looking for an open door—any open door, even just a crack—since every door he passed was not only tightly closed but also locked (and seemingly from the *outside*). Then sheer panic hit him like an oncoming wave, which he already knew was going to take him down when it ultimately broke ashore. But he innately understood the *apprehension* of this monster wave was much worse in the end than the wave would physically feel when it finally crashed down upon him....

At the end of one of the derelict hallways that he was anxiously bounding down, Owen found himself all at once in a small room like an enclosed office cubicle, staring up at a naked and dull saffron light bulb swinging precariously from side to side as if he were suddenly in the bilge of a ship caught in a torrential storm—a bilge, he realized, that he was now waist-deep into, engulfed on all sides by rising oily water which he feared would not stop until it devoured him.

And Owen was right, because he then heard someone, or possibly several people, on the other side of a door he would never be able to make it to, banging their fists over and over again against the callous steel hatch, begging for him to open it...

but then his light bulb burned out.

Barry was trying his best to sip the cold black tea he had just gotten from a vending machine without stretching his pinkie finger in the air. It was a peculiar thing, he realized, sitting in the hospital cafeteria, that most people, at least as far as he noticed, couldn't take a sip of a drink without doing this pinkie thing. He wondered whether this were a flaw in human design, a glitch left by whoever it was that created this strange circumstance of unintentional participation—or perhaps it only had to do with the size of the cup the drink happened to be in.

It was close to midnight—although it could have been later, he wasn't quite sure. As Barry looked around at the antiseptic tables surrounding him, he wondered whether the cafeteria ever closed. It was doubtful, he realized, since you obviously couldn't set specific hours around when people got sick or died—or could you? It made him remember an old college friend whom he'd eventually lost contact with, but who, in the swampy first years following graduation, had made frequent, likely habitual, stump trips to Vegas with Barry as his partner-in-crime. But it was their virgin voyage into that cesspool of lights that Barry remembered most—mainly just a simple question that his friend had asked the blackjack dealer who was finally allowing them to have some winning hands for a change. Although Barry, admittedly no Vegas expert himself (at least not yet), already knew the answer to his friend's dumb question and announced it before the dealer had time to reply.

"They never close," Barry had told his friend, which the dealer acknowledged with a more-than-noticeable nod, in such a way that his friend would have no choice but to believe it. Yet his friend *didn't* believe it—and this was a guy who usually believed just about anything. But this inarguable truth was somehow too much to comprehend for his gambling partner, who then followed up his initial inquiry with: "Really?"

"Yes, *really*," the long-suffering dealer answered as dryly as she could, beating Barry to it, as if his friend had just asked her whether the sky was actually blue.

"I still can't believe the drinks are free!" Barry's idiot

accomplice then remarked, throwing another log onto his already burning fire of shame. But this the dealer couldn't bring herself to acknowledge with even a simple nod of the head, probably too much energy to expend on such a fool.

Now, a full head of missing hair later, hiding in the barren hospital cafeteria, waiting to find out if his son would ever recover from a gunshot wound, Barry finally knew that nothing was free, not even the supposed drinks in Vegas. And as far as never closing, he knew also that the hospital cafeteria would never shut its frigid doors, with or without its staff—not as long as people kept dying and their family and friends needed nourishment along the way (even if only from a vending machine). Like desperate people hoping to win millions of dollars in a turbid casino, it wasn't something that would be changing anytime soon.

"The coffee's cold," a voice suddenly announced from Barry's blind spot, as if this person had just discovered the cure for cancer.

Barry turned his aching head far enough to the left to find a youngish-looking Hispanic man in scrubs, holding out his Styrofoam cup in the air as if pleading to the gods for a warm cup of coffee and nothing more.

"Are you actually surprised by that?" Barry replied, once again not even coming close to thinking first before any words dribbled from his mouth (which happened to be one of Lilly's chief complaints about him—amongst many).

The nurse seemed to contemplate Barry's answer for a moment while he stirred the chemical creamer into his tea. Just then, another voice came from outside Barry's peripheral vision, this time that of a female (and it definitely wasn't Lilly).

"Are you Owen's dad?" she asked flatly, causing Barry's heart to drop into his shoes, since he thought it might be a nurse who had found him to tell him the news he knew was inevitable. But when he turned his trembling head toward where the voice had come from, he was surprised to find a young blonde maybe around Owen's age, if not a few years older.

"Yes, I am," he said, feeling for the first time in a long time—possibly ever—like a truly proud parent (though he had no reason not to be proud of Owen prior to that moment).

The girl tried awkwardly to smile—a friendly smile, hoping perhaps to express she had come in peace. One hand strayed up to half-obscure her mouth before she forced it back to her side.

"Are you okay?" he asked, not only meaning her but Owen as well (although there was zero probability she could have caught on to the latter).

To this she started sobbing, which, again, she tried to stifle in an unnaturally grotesque way. He was inclined to stand up and physically console this wounded girl (an ironic act that, had he practiced it regularly with Lilly, might have saved their marriage). But he managed to stop such a gesture just short of embarrassing himself, and probably her as well, since that was obviously not her intention.

Barry was about to ask her again if she was okay—sticking to a verbal remedy as opposed to a physical—but he didn't need to, as she suddenly said something he never would have expected to hear from her.

"I killed your son," she said.

CELL

When Lilly learned of Owen's death, she decided to brush her teeth. And even though she knew this was something that would most likely haunt her the rest of her days— brushing her teeth instead of doing God knows what else— she went ahead and made sure her mouth felt as fresh as possible. On top of that, she wasn't even *with* Owen when he passed; instead, she was screwing around in her store, seven and a half miles from the hospital. She might have forgiven herself if she had at least been in the waiting room when it happened—sadly, though, she was not.

Thinking about it in the years to come—which turned out to be once a day, if not more—she would tell herself that the rest of her life back then had been one giant waiting room. "Life was a waiting room," she would eventually declare to someone she didn't really know, such as the person unlucky enough to be behind her in a grocery store line, or, more often than not, in one of her regular appointments with Dr. Stevens. "Life *is* a waiting room," she would then add, impressing herself immensely (if she said so herself). "Every minute, every day...."

But she hadn't been this deep or philosophical following Owen's death. Instead, all Lilly could do was tell Miles at his eventual sentencing that she hoped he would "just drop dead"—or, better yet, "get violently raped in jail" (as if any other type of rape existed in jail, so far as she knew) until he "slowly died" from the bloody complications of it. She had dragged out the two syllables of "slow-ly" for as long as she

161

could, perhaps hoping it would be more effective that way and Miles would actually do as she commanded.

It felt good to tell Miles that, as well as calling him some other choice words—until the judge politely asked her to stop, then threatened her with contempt when she didn't (she had wanted to get a few juicier phrases in first, naturally). And the cruelest thing of all—that she had to live the rest of her life without Owen—was simply not something she ever wanted to acknowledge, similar to the judge not acknowledging her that day.

Seeing that self-satisfied teenage thug in court getting sentenced—he looked like a younger, stranger version of Fabio, but with darker hair—only made things worse. She had literally wanted to kill him right then and there, even if it had to be in front of the judge in a courtroom full of other people; she didn't care about consequences in the least. As for the "other people" in the courtroom that day besides her and Barry, it was only a few select media and Miles' foster parents, the Kellys, who couldn't stop sobbing and whom Miles refused to acknowledge whatsoever, visually or otherwise. The Kellys themselves, following Lilly and Barry's example, refused to acknowledge the media who hounded them continuously outside the courtroom (especially the more aggressive ones, who bombarded them with questions concerning whether or not Miles was a racist and if the killing had been a "hate crime"—which the "Black Lives Matter" movement would presumably bring to national attention, though Lilly wasn't sure how she felt about that either).

If Lilly could take away any positive thing from the hearing, however, it was the fact that Miles was sentenced with the "delayed death exception"—meaning he would be tried for murder now, rather than just assault with a deadly weapon or attempted murder. She couldn't remember the exact initial charge against him; things had moved too fast at the preliminary hearing and hadn't really slowed down, particularly after Owen's death.

What Lilly *was* in touch with that day in court, though—or aware of to such a degree that she couldn't resist it—was the inextricable sense that this boy, now on trial for his life, wasn't smug whatsoever about what he did or didn't do (the latter of which he maintained to be true). He seemed somewhat timid as he faintly appealed for his innocence—not just to the judge but seemingly to the gods as well—with a sense that he knew his pleas of absolution would likely fall on deaf ears, mortal or otherwise. For the briefest moment, Lilly almost fell into a daydream that, in some parallel universe of a possible future, this boy might have actually been friends with Owen.

Any mercy she may have felt for Miles, however, was fleeting. In fact, she doubted that she had ever felt clemency toward him at all, for when he was eventually sentenced to fifteen years to life for second-degree murder, the only thing Lilly could think about was that he could potentially be out in fifteen years—or less, due to time served—while still a young man, and thus it was really no punishment at all. *What is he losing other than a decade, more or less? Which a kid like him would probably waste doing drugs anyways—or however else these kids spent their useless days.* This, nevertheless, brought her another horrifying thought: what if Owen had some kind of secret life—a life of drugs, or something else equally as bad—and she'd never had any clue, always thinking he was an angel of a son? But that was impossible; surely, she would have noticed something like that…right? Maybe, though, he had been *too* perfect, and since there was no such thing as too perfect, or even just perfect, she had been kept from the real truth due to the short-sightedness of her parenting skills. Perhaps Barry knew something about Owen that she didn't? If that were true, Barry had been keeping a secret from her as well.…

Lilly had been so lost in thought about those closest to her keeping secrets that she didn't even notice when the judge adjourned the court, the room emptying out so quickly she started to doubt it was ever populated at all. Even the kid was already gone, though not for good, as if he'd merely been one of several ghosts from her life she was only now beginning to realize still endured—always endured—just like the monsters who had hidden under her childhood bed. But if her adolescent fairy tales, including the scary ones—*only* the scary ones—had been true all along, and she was only now privy to this…. The idea terrified her more than anything, for it opened up a realm of possibilities better off safely contained in the starless shadows of her childhood bedroom, locked away in a pitch-black closet that should have stayed closed and locked forever….

"What?" replied Barry to the white, lanky blonde who couldn't stop sobbing. He was about to say it again, until she pointed to a corner of the cafeteria just beyond his right shoulder, her index finger seeming unnaturally long and crooked. Barry turned, almost expecting to see his son standing behind him, healthy as ever, as if he had never been shot in the first place, the whole thing just a very realistic dream or a hoax in bad taste that this blonde was somehow involved in.

But Owen wasn't standing behind him, not even as a specter, which Barry would have gladly accepted in retrospect. Instead, all he saw when he turned around was a large garbage pail standing alone, like a prize waiting to be won. More than a little confused, Barry turned back to the still-sobbing girl.

"Who are you?" he said, fairly certain that he had asked a

better question now, or at least one that had a better chance of getting answered by this girl.

"I'm Owen's girlfriend…*was* Owen's girlfriend."

Ignoring the *was* part, Barry said, "Owen has a girlfriend?"

"Well…okay…" she started, as if he had caught her in a lie. "It wasn't official or anything."

"Official?" he echoed, but not because he was confused by the word or its meaning.

"We didn't know each other that long yet," she explained further, like Barry was a cop interrogating her about her whereabouts during the hour a crime was committed.

All at once Barry realized that they were talking about the wrong thing—outrageously talking about the wrong thing—its unimportance almost grotesque compared to the very reason he was at the hospital. And this white girl had made him forget momentarily; this stupid white girl who had said—

Before he knew he was going to stand up, Barry was on his feet and filled with enough rage that he actually wanted to physically hurt this girl, especially if she were to blame somehow for what had happened to Owen. *She had even said as much, hadn't she?* But he didn't want to waste more time engaged in small talk about her possible relationship with his son. *What did that matter now? The first, and only, requirement of a relationship with another human being was that both people actually be alive. And if this girl were to blame somehow if Owen died, then she wouldn't be alive much longer either. Wait a second*—he paused, causing his blood to seemingly stop flowing. *She had said that she killed him, not that she might* have killed him…

was Owen already dead?

"Owen's dead, isn't he?" he asked her—but then didn't wait for the answer. By the time Elodie could reply Barry had darted out of the cafeteria, en-route to the bank of elevators that would take him back up to his son's room—where two orderlies had already been sent in order to remove his son's body; a room that his soon-to-be ex-wife was still inside of, sitting on the edge of the now-empty bed, head bowed in subjugation....

Elodie didn't follow Barry out of the cafeteria. She already knew what was waiting for Barry on the second floor, and she didn't need to see it again to believe it. *How could he not know?* she wondered. Only minutes before, Elodie had over-heard a doctor telling Owen's mother the news, although it hadn't seemed like the doctor really needed to say anything at all for her to understand. He was apparently so skilled at delivering such indecorous news that his face already told everything that needed telling. Lilly had collapsed into him (which he was ostensibly braced for), only regaining her own gravity when he informed her that she could go back in and say goodbye to her son if she were so inclined; she just had to wait a few minutes for the nurses to prepare the room (code, Elodie guessed, for preparing Owen's body, not just the room).

While the doctor delivered the news to Lilly, she had never once noticed Elodie, or so it seemed, who was standing just a few feet away—much too close for a stranger to be observ-ing such an intimate moment. But Elodie didn't consider herself a stranger, even though Lilly probably had no idea who she was at the time (if she *had* been noticed). As awk-ward as this scene was for Elodie, at least from her vantage point—she had no idea, of course, what it could possibly feel like for Lilly—she waited quietly until both Lilly and the doctor disappeared back into their present realities, Lilly running toward the ladies' bathroom at the opposite end of the hallway.

This mutual exit by Lilly and Owen's doctor yielded yet another player in this surreal stage play—a player who had done everything in his power to stay invisible, until it was no longer possible for him to camouflage himself in the presently empty corridor. And because Barry had seemingly witnessed the whole thing, Elodie was sure that he knew—but instead of waiting for the mother of his now-deceased son to come out of the bathroom so they could maybe console each other, or at least try to, he did something Elodie wasn't expecting: he retreated down the hall and took an elevator to the first floor, where he found the cafeteria. Just as she had silently witnessed Owen's doctor revealing the news to Lilly, Elodie secretly followed Barry to the cafeteria, initially due to her curiosity about where he might be headed, and not because she planned on confessing to him.

But Elodie *did* confess to Barry. He fled back to his son's room moments later, leaving her standing alone in the seemingly empty cafeteria. She walked over to one of the windows and gazed outside at the repressed rain-soaked traffic, the low hum of which vibrated her body upwards from her feet like a throbbing cavity getting drilled without Novocain. The more she watched the indiscriminate cars drip by, their headlights and brake lights coalescing into a cacophonous whirl of colors she couldn't escape, the more it felt like she was bleeding in the wrong direction from her raw mortal wound. But like a "good girl"—just as her father used to call her sarcastically when he was actually mad at her—Elodie remained at the window for as long as she could stand it, unflinching despite the rising torment inside her, as if she had to consummate the martyrdom or else succumb to an even direr fate.

Ultimately, however, she failed to withstand the frenzy of discomfort at the window, just as she told herself she had failed with everything in her life. *Add another one to the list*, she almost said out loud, which wouldn't have mattered anyway since she was still the only person in the cafeteria.

Doesn't anyone else have someone dying in the hospital right now? she wondered. Or rather dead, not dying, as was the case with her visit, and so she corrected the grammar of her thought—a weird thing to do, she realized, but she did it anyway. Maybe there was more than one cafeteria in the hospital, she decided, and she had picked the less popular one? There she was again, she wanted to admit to someone, making the wrong choice: the apparent core of her existence.

Moving away from the window, she noticed the lone garbage pail across the room, beckoning to her—the same one she had pointed out to Barry not long before. But Barry hadn't taken her cue, and she didn't blame him. After all, why would she be pointing out a trash can to him? Now that she thought about it, he probably thought she was nuts (her strange confession enhancing this impression), and she didn't blame him for that either. Maybe she *was* nuts. At the very least, she was responsible for Owen's death—that much was irrefutable.

Peering into the garbage pail to see if what she had thrown away earlier was still there—which it was—she had to stop herself from reaching in and taking it out. Now that she stared at it, sandwiched between a used Styrofoam cup and an empty bag of chips, it occurred to her that maybe she shouldn't have thrown it away. Maybe she had just been impulsive and should take it back out, especially since Barry was gone now and probably wouldn't have understood the ramifications of what he was looking at anyway, had he followed her pointed finger. Plus, in a few hours' time when people started arriving for breakfast, someone would undoubtedly take it if they happened to notice it—the odds-on favorite, naturally, was a janitor, since most people didn't look inside garbage pails in a hospital cafeteria...*or did they?*

But Elodie hadn't thrown it away for Barry to see, or for Lilly to see, or for anyone to see who would understand the meaning of it. The only one who might have understood the meaning of it was dead now, and, more importantly, was dead because of it. Regardless of what anyone told her—like a friend trying to console her, or even a shrink trained in such matters—she knew it was her fault no matter how the tale was spun, the object in the trash bin a (non-literal) smoking gun defining her guilt.

So Elodie decided to leave it there, just as she had that day in the coffee shop (though she had tried telling herself since then, unsuccessfully, that it had merely been an accident). What Elodie did get right, however, was the fact that in a few hours' time some lucky janitor started his day with the happy discovery of something he could definitely use, despite its bright pink-glittered case...

an almost brand-new iPhone.

GOBBLEDYGOOK

"There's no such thing as an accident," the public defender, Charles Holcomb, told Miles. "Especially for an appellate judge on a second-degree murder charge where an African-American kid bought the farm."

"Really?" Miles responded, perhaps too quickly, not completely believing that to be true, although he obviously didn't have enough experience in these matters to know for certain. "What about people who accidentally kill someone in, like, a traffic accident or something?" he asked, sounding suddenly defiant but not meaning for it to come out that way.

Holcomb paused, reflectively, for he apparently hadn't expected this particular client to challenge him. The boy wasn't a minor in the eyes of the court; to Holcomb, however, Miles was probably just another punk kid who had thoughtlessly taken someone's life, regardless of whether or not he had been sober enough at the time to be aware of what he had done (or hadn't done). Holcomb was just that, though—a defender—and the fact was, if he chose to only defend innocent people, he would be out of a job rather quickly.

This particular case, to be fair, wasn't that cut and dry. True, his client's fingerprints had been detected on the murder weapon, which was found at the scene not far from the victim; his client was later apprehended blacked out on the sidewalk a few streets over from the shooting, with no memory of what had transpired. But the gun also revealed the fingerprints of his client's friend—a friend who, according to his client, was with him at some point prior to the crime, if not during the actual crime itself, before his client's memory took a nosedive into an empty pool. And this friend—another punk, no doubt, named Sawyer—was at the very least an accessory to what had happened, if not an actual accomplice (particularly since, unlike his client, Sawyer had a record). But Sawyer was a ghost now, which had been another coil in the case. In Holcomb's experience, or even based on simple common sense, innocent people didn't run (especially ones with priors).

"This wasn't a traffic accident, son," Holcomb said, slightly shaking his head.

"Wait a second," Miles cried out, suddenly realizing what his lawyer had said just before that. "*Murder?*"

Holcomb stared back.

"I plead not guilty to *attempted* murder," Miles continued. "What do you mean—"

"That's old news," Holcomb said. "The victim died months ago."

"What?"

Again, Holcomb stared back. "Are you serious?"

"I didn't kill him…at least I don't think I did." Miles covered his face. "I don't know," he said into the palm of his hand, which was now sweating like a dam had broken.

"How can you not know?"

Miles shrugged.

Holcomb stared yet again; it was apparently his favorite thing to do, as if he trusted his eyes over his ears.

"I can't remember anything from that day…not really… not after we started drinking and stuff. It's all so hazy now." Miles looked down, like a sensitive child who had just disappointed his mother one too many times. "If I did it…and I'm not saying I did…I didn't mean it. It was an accident. I shouldn't have to spend the rest of my life in jail for it!"

"Like I said," Holcomb tried again, "there's no such thing as an accident. Not in this case. And you'll most likely get out in fifteen, minus time served." He stared at Miles for a long moment. "What do mean by drinking 'and stuff?' What exactly constitutes 'stuff?'"

"Haven't we already gone over this like a thousand times?" Miles looked away from Holcomb's piercing glare, like he was raising the white flag on a staring contest that hadn't lasted as long as he'd hoped, letting Holcomb claim victory yet again.

"Like I said a hundred times before," Miles said, forgetting the number from his previous exaggeration, "we did a bunch of drugs, too. I can't remember what exactly…" Miles turned and looked directly at Holcomb. "I thought you were on *my* side? Aren't you supposed to defend me, and not give me shit? You're not my father."

Holcomb laughed. "You're right. I'm not your father. I'm the public defender assigned to represent you, as you rightly pointed out, and now work on your appeal, but I'm only 'giving you shit,' as you say, because I can absolutely guarantee that the State is going to give you even more shit at the appeal, and if you're not used to this type of questioning—"

Miles was quiet.

"Listen, son," Holcomb said. He glanced around the room before continuing—and when he did his voice was much softer, as if self-conscious of someone overhearing him. "What isn't going to help your case, as I mentioned a few minutes ago, is the fact that the victim was African-American." He paused before saying to his client what he'd probably wanted to say ever since he had first met Miles more than a year before. "For your own good, I seriously hope you're not a fuckin' racist."

The public defender's use of a curse word, and the abrasive way it had come out of his mouth, somehow overshadowed the word following it, which was obviously the main intent of the question—if it *was* a question—and gave Miles such a start that he almost jumped out of his chair. Instead, he shifted uneasily and winced at the orange-colored light bulb above the table they were sitting at, as if its glare hurt him in some grievous way.

"We were both really fucked up," Miles said. "Like I told you before, I don't remember shit."

The use of "we" by his client seemed to remind Holcomb about the friend who was now in the wind. "Could your friend—" He looked down at his notes.

"Sawyer?" Miles offered.

"Yeah, Sawyer," Holcomb said, looking back up from the table. "Could Sawyer have been—"

"What? Been what?"

Holcomb looked down again and shuffled his papers. "In any case," he continued, not finishing his previous thought, "given the fact that the victim was black, and only a kid, and moreover that we can't find your friend, I'd say the chance of this appeal going anywhere is slim. We might be better off just taking the fifteen years."

Miles wasn't entirely following what Holcomb was saying, which was apparent by the expression on his face.

"Don't worry about the 'life' part…the fifteen years to life," Holcomb said, ostensibly trying to read Miles' mind. "You'll get out in fifteen, minus time served, as long as you don't cause a ruckus." He smiled, or at least attempted to do so. "Be a good prisoner, in other words."

"I shouldn't have to be a prisoner at all!" Miles cried, gasping for breath. The case against him, everything that had happened since he first met Sawyer in rehab, suddenly felt like an illusion, orange-tinged and endless, a nightmare so tightly wound that it had become him entirely, from skin to soul, and now he could only scream toward the firmament, to anyone who could hear him, to please rescue him from this suffocating expanse…

but no one would listen.

Lieutenant Colonel Ramirez had no idea where his son was: he hadn't seen him or heard from him in months, maybe a year. But right when he was going to file a missing person's report, he noticed that Sawyer's small blue suitcase was gone—as were, it seemed, a lot of clothes from his closet.

His boy wasn't missing; he had run away. Naturally, though, this wasn't what the Lieutenant Colonel had told the police when they visited him shortly after Sawyer's friend was arrested, for he knew something was very wrong, and he loved his son far too much. The retired military man even disavowed his allegiance to follow a code of honor he'd sworn his life to, no matter what the circumstance. But this was his blood—and blood, he felt, was stronger than anything else in this world.

Maybe, too, it was because of his military background that, when the police first showed up at his door, he thought his son had been killed—perhaps in a car accident or something similar, but nothing less than an act of God himself. In some respects, however, it was even worse, for they wanted to talk with Sawyer about a shooting that had been committed with the Lieutenant Colonel's handgun, which he had recklessly not secured (yet another thing to add to his growing list of regrets). Whether or not Sawyer was guilty of this crime, the fact that the lieutenant colonel had been so careless with his Walther P99 had, at the very least, caused his son to desert his life.

On the many sleepless nights that followed, Ramirez knew deep down that his only son must be guilty of something, for why else would Sawyer have fled? What was he running from? The fact that the Walther had been identified as the murder

RECKONER

weapon meant that Sawyer had been involved somehow, even if his son's friend had been the actual shooter (the truth according to the DA's office, which was just fine with the Lieutenant Colonel). But this still didn't explain why Sawyer had gone AWOL. If his friend had already been identified as the murderer—*and what kind of friend was that?*—then why had he disappeared? None of it made any sense.

Repeating what he had now said too many times, Sawyer's father told Sawyer's girlfriend the same thing when she showed up at his doorstep one afternoon—that he didn't know where his son was.

"You have absolutely no idea?" she asked again, after declining the coffee he offered her when she stepped inside the house, but only because he'd been in the middle of reheating a cup for himself when she rang the doorbell.

He stared at her for a few seconds, acutely sizing her up. "War has a way of making even the most devout soldier into an atheist," he finally remarked.

Elodie blinked, then looked around the sparsely furnished living room they stood in, as if digesting the edict he had just shared with her. But based on what she then said, it seemed as if she hadn't heard him at all (or was simply pushing on, regardless): "Did you file a missing pers—I mean... are you.... I assume you're looking for him?"

He would have laughed just then, but he was in no mood to laugh—not that he was a man who stepped lightly to begin with, even infrequently. "It's hard to find someone who doesn't want to be found," he said, taking a sip of the tepid coffee he'd made at the break of dawn that morning.

They took in each other for a long, awkward moment.

"What did you say your name was again?" he asked the rail-thin blonde with the accentuated mascara lines at both edges of her eyes—like Elizabeth Taylor's *Cleopatra*—expecting her to be the same girlfriend Sawyer had mentioned more than a few times, and likewise, hoping he would recognize the name once he heard it.

She stirred as if something had just bitten her beneath her clothes. "He didn't...he never said anything about me?" She sounded hurt, like a young girl who had just found out her playground crush didn't like her back.

The Lieutenant Colonel put his coffee down; he couldn't drink it this cold after all. "He said he had a girlfriend, but that was about it. I don't think he ever mentioned your name, although I guess it's possible he did and I just forgot." He looked at her sullen face and, had he been the apologizing type, would have said, "I'm sorry," just then, if only to make her feel a little better. But he wasn't in the people business, and let his silence say as much.

"We were sort of broken up anyway...." She seemed like she was going to add something, or perhaps subtract something, but then stopped.

"Broken up?" Ramirez echoed. He was still having trouble processing the idea of them as a couple, let alone a severed couple, a fact apparent from his facial expression. But what Elodie couldn't have realized just then, and wouldn't have accepted even if she had been told as much, was the fact that Sawyer's father had trouble processing anything as of late, especially if it seemed relevant to his son's whereabouts. For he did know that his son had a girlfriend—Sawyer had mentioned it every other sentence it seemed—and although he couldn't remember her name, and didn't know they had broken up, it was one of the only things he could reconcile these days—if and when it was necessary.

And it wasn't necessary. That said, the Lieutenant Colonel had no idea that even this was a lie. The truth had become the trembling ground beneath his feet—and although he couldn't comprehend the apex, or how much damage it might cause, he couldn't stop what he couldn't see. It was like a subterranean force that secretly terrorized him; the biggest irony of it all was that his son wasn't as far away as he might have imagined. Even though it was indeed hard to find someone who didn't want to be found, it was even harder, from the Lieutenant Colonel's experience, to find someone hiding in plain sight.

ORIGIN

He was sure he had just heard a woman scream—and it wasn't like the scream of a woman who discovered her favorite purse was on sale, or who had run into an old friend she hadn't seen in a long time. It was the real thing without question; he would have bet his life on it, whatever that was worth. For lately, the more he reflected on it, the more he realized he was simply a vessel of blood and tissue, muscle and bone—a meaningless cavity of meaningless things—although there was no way he'd ever admit this to anyone, consciously or otherwise. He had to keep up a front, the way he had for as long as he could remember, since showing any weakness, especially now, would surely elicit defeat. Like the one God he had worshiped for the past several months (after he accidentally came across the master's slim treatise at a used bookstore in downtown Raleigh), Sun Tzu, the uncontested master of war, proclaimed: "Appear weak when you are strong, and strong when you are weak." And Sawyer wasn't about to appear weak to anyone.

He knew the police were probably looking for him, although it was hard to tell from what the TV reported about the investigation. They had that dim piece of shit, Miles, in custody—from what he knew—and he didn't feel bad about that whatsoever. After all, Miles had been the one who pulled the trigger—and the police obviously knew that. What the cops didn't know, however, and never would (if he could help it), was that Sawyer had purposefully loaded up his unsuspecting "friend" with enough drugs and Jim Beam to get him to do just about anything. Even more fortuitously, Miles

wouldn't remember anything about it, including the fact that
Sawyer had stayed sober the entire time. It had been no less
than an Academy Award-winning performance by Sawyer,
who (if Miles ever happened to remember something at some
point) gave the impression that he was just as fucked up as his
completely clueless "partner in crime." And all of it—every
single molecule of it—to fortify the charade of who Sawyer
thought he was supposed to be in the sharp, tentacled world
just outside his densely curtained window.

In a lot of ways (Sawyer wouldn't admit this to anyone,
much less to himself), he wished that Miles had really been
his friend, for he had no one left now—no one to even claim
as a friend. And because it had to be this way, Sawyer had
misled Miles the entire time in order to set him up; although,
on some occasions with him, especially when they got fucked
up together (both of them, for real) prior to the shooting, he
daydreamed that he and Miles were actually friends. When
he was able to push, at the time, the oncoming crime out
of his head and just imagine the two of them as buddies,
Sawyer finally felt like he belonged in the world, that someone actually cared about his existence. It was evidence that he
was indeed roaming this Earth, proof that he couldn't deny,
no matter how hard he happened to try, during moments
of weakness. But then he would remind himself that Miles
wasn't truly his friend, that Miles was only in his life to serve
a singular purpose—that was it. Nothing more. Reminders
like these always kept him from feeling any guilt or remorse,
proving to himself, and eventually to others, that he had no
conscience.

What Sawyer didn't realize at the time, during their "courtship" so to speak, was that Miles was more than the friend
he never had, more than the fictional brother he'd always
dreamed about in his once-solitary, pre-pubescent mind. This
long-haired misfit, in his own seeming way and for his own

seeming reasons, would have done anything for Sawyer—if only to keep him as *his* friend (with or without an abundance of drugs and alcohol swimming around his body). For Miles was more like Sawyer than either could have imagined, despite their contradictory backgrounds leading up to their meeting at rehab, which now seemed like a lifetime ago.

"Do you want something, man?" the nose-ringed, wrist-tattooed barista asked Sawyer, who was next in line but had blanked out momentarily, lost in thought about the life he could have had had things been different.

The barista was staring at him. "You know, you sorta look like that guy who shot the black guy on the sidewalk right outside here," he said, gesturing through the front window at the now-famous landmark, where various strangers had laid messages and flowers for Owen. "I mean the African-American guy," the barista corrected, louder than necessary.

With the wig on, which Sawyer had purchased at a beauty store just down the street from the coffee shop, he did resemble Miles in a way, now that he thought about it, but it wasn't a deliberate choice—or at least, that's what he would have told anyone if asked. Even though the barista openly noticed the similarity, Sawyer still wouldn't confess to what he deemed a simple coincidence. He was trying to stay under the radar of this crime, so why the hell would he purposefully make himself look like the guy now in jail for it? Especially considering the fact—which, in retrospect, now seemed like an extremely bad decision—that he had determined not to run away to a different city. He'd figured that wearing the wig was enough, that he didn't need to disappear to somewhere else. And to make matters worse, he now stood in the very same coffee shop Owen had frequented, and had been shot just outside of. What had he been thinking, Sawyer asked himself, if he had been thinking at all? What kind of idiot was he? *Was there a word worse than idiot?* he almost questioned out loud.

"Oh really?" Sawyer answered the barista. Then, thinking

fast, he added, "I don't really know much about it, so I don't know what the guy looks like. I don't even have a TV." Before the barista could say anything else, Sawyer silently congratulated himself for coming up with three lies so quickly. It was maybe the only thing he was still good at—although, in the literal sense, he didn't really own a TV; technically, the Super 8 Motel owned it.

Sawyer looked up at the coffee menu hanging from the ceiling just behind the barista's head, as if actually perusing it to decide on a drink. "I'll just have a cappuccino," Sawyer said, trying to act like a normal customer on a normal day ordering a normal drink—a drink that, he now realized, he didn't even like. *But, oh well…such is the life of a criminal mastermind*, he thought, so proud of himself that his face had accidentally turned red, which the gay barista mistook for coyness, and then for outright flirting.

"I'm Jorge," the barista offered, furthering his misinterpretation of the scene with a smile.

"That's nice," Sawyer replied, voice sharp with crisp acrimony. As it happened, both Sawyer and Jorge were completely misreading the situation in their own idiosyncratic ways.

"Can I just get the cappuccino?" Sawyer said caustically, and with no apology to follow. He realized he was doing a terrible job of assimilating in public, which he knew was essential when the police might be looking for him. He had learned this from the true crime shows he'd been watching on an endless loop at the Super 8—especially since he couldn't sleep and had to find some way to pass the time. *The First 48* was his favorite by far.

Refusing to give up for some reason seemingly obscure to himself, and with his own provocative smile that he couldn't help but flash, Jorge said, gesturing at Sawyer's tattoo, "You a fan of Pee-Wee?" And then, without waiting for an answer, he added, "So am I. Big deal that he jacked off in a movie theater a million years ago, right? I mean, who cares?" But then, possibly realizing how he was coming across, he quickly said, "Okay, I'll have that cappuccino right out for you, sir."

"Sir?" Sawyer echoed without thinking, surprised that the barista had called him that, and in such a discordant way. It was what he called his father—what he *had* to call his father—but no one ever called *him* that.

Continuing this helter-skelter dance of awkwardness and confusion, and likely believing that Sawyer was now addressing *him* as "sir," Jorge blurted, "What?" back to Sawyer, not knowing what else he could possibly say at this point in the conversation—if their half-baked exchange could indeed be called such.

Sawyer sighed audibly, which apparently wasn't lost on Jorge.

"Okay, we'll have that drink out for you at the end of the counter," Jorge muttered, once again as though merely supplying information to himself.

Confused by the use of "we" since the barista seemed to be the only one working at the moment, Sawyer impatiently replied, "Is it free or something?"

"Is what free?" Jorge said, now so completely lost that there was little hope of bringing him back to any form of reality.

"I haven't paid y—" Interrupting himself, Sawyer turned toward the door. "Never mind," he stated matter-of-factly. Then he walked away.

"Wait!" Jorge called after him—clearly with no idea of what he would say if Sawyer actually stopped and turned around. *Had* Sawyer stopped and turned around, Jorge might have noticed that something was notably wrong about how Sawyer looked, for his copious long wig now hung askew on the top of his head.

What Sawyer wasn't counting on, however, was running into Elodie, by herself and on her way into the café to start reading the book she had just checked out of the library—a book she'd heard of from Oprah but never thought she would need, or even be curious, to read: Elisabeth Kübler-Ross' best-selling testament about the stages of grief, *On Death and Dying*. Consequently, when Elodie saw the wig, which was actually the first thing she noticed, she didn't even recognize Sawyer. He was the last person she expected to see at that moment—much less wearing a disguise. She wasn't in a "noticing" type of mood, anyhow; with her mind so many miles away, Elodie could probably walk past an alien who had just crash-landed their UFO nearby and not even know it. But walking past Sawyer—who, as far as Elodie knew, was of this Earth—she paused, his askew long hair looking too peculiar to ignore.

"Sawyer?" she said, maybe hoping it wasn't him; her overall tone, though, mostly revealing otherwise. "What the fuck?"

Despite Sawyer knowing there was no way out of this now (other than flat-out running off as fast as he could, which would only delay the inevitable), his ego wouldn't allow him to give up just yet. In his mind, he had barely started trying to be someone else, even if he looked like Miles' twin (which he would continue to tell himself wasn't intentional)—a feat he was sure he could accomplish, but nevertheless failed at in epic fashion moments later when Elodie ripped the sloppy wig clean off like a band-aid. To Sawyer, it had felt like she had taken his entire scalp off—physically *and* psychologically. Worse, her attack on his fake follicles attracted the attention of almost everyone in the coffee shop, as well as a few pedestrians who happened to walk by the window at just the right moment—or wrong moment, as it was for Sawyer.

"What the fuck?" he returned even harder than she had, on the verge of doing something violent due to the sheer shock of her sudden physicality toward him (although what exactly he might have done, he didn't know). It was now probably time to run, which in hindsight he knew he should have done a few seconds earlier, before she scalped him in front of everyone. But it was too late, he felt, even for that; the damage had already been done. The real question was whether or not anyone had just recognized him—though he had yet to see a picture of himself on the news, which he knew didn't necessarily mean he hadn't been on some other station, or that it hadn't been broadcast when he was asleep or away. The authorities could be looking out for him, regardless; there was no way Miles had kept mum about him, as there was definitely no love lost between them at this point, especially if Miles had somehow remembered anything from that day.

For now, though, Sawyer wasn't about to take any more chances, and decided it was best to vacate the premises as quickly as possible, with or without the wig, which presently lay on the floor next to Elodie's Chuck Taylor pink high-tops—a soon-to-be stepped on prisoner. Worse yet, when Sawyer arrived back at the motel there was a police car in the parking lot, and very near his room, which he assumed could only be waiting for him. How they had found him this quickly, he didn't know—unless they had recognized him from the coffee shop?

But he hadn't seen anyone following him, which didn't necessarily mean no one had. He was terrible at noticing that type of thing. Not to mention, if he had been followed, how had they arrived at the motel *before* him? Plus, on first glance (he wasn't about to look again), there was no one in the car—although this was almost worse, because where were they now then? In his room, waiting for him? Even if they hadn't followed him, and weren't waiting to arrest him as soon as he unlocked the door to his room, the whole thing didn't feel right. Nothing felt right anymore—at least not since he had run into Elodie at the coffee shop and she'd ripped off his wig.

No, this won't do, he thought, pulling out of the Super 8 parking lot and back onto the access road leading to the interstate. North Carolina was in his rear-view mirror now, as was everything that had preceded this moment.

But what Sawyer didn't realize, as he headed south toward Florida (since he had no idea where else to go and was already headed in that direction), was that something would eventually pull him back to the Tar Heel State—whether or not he wanted it to.

PATRON

Miles was dreaming about McDonald's when the high-pitched laughter of the dreadlocked, African-American cashier scared him back to awareness—or, at least, he thought it was a dream. Lately, he was never quite sure, although the chance he was actually at a McDonald's ordering a Big Mac was impossible since he was currently in prison and wasn't going anywhere anytime soon (that is, outside of the Polk Correctional Facility in Butner). The conviction had stated that he had "reckless indifference to human life," a phrase Miles took exception to, as he didn't feel this was an accurate description of his mindset the day of the shooting, despite his more than foggy mental state at the time, or any day for that matter, before or after the crime he had allegedly committed. He may not have valued his own life very much, which he would have admitted if he had been expertly cross-examined or forced to say so in some other manner, but that didn't mean Miles was "recklessly indifferent" to the lives of others—or at least he didn't feel he was that type of person.

The McDonald's dream, as feckless as it appeared, had been a reoccurring invention of his imagination, for the ordering of a Big Mac seemed to represent something more—something happy, something proud—between Miles and the man who played his father in this mealtime fantasy. It seemed to symbolize a rite of passage, as if no boy could handle such a sandwich; that only a true man could eat such a thing, much less request one. And though his "father" would appear differently each time behind his loosely closed lids, the man would always ask the same thing, verbatim, after

Miles ordered, which was: "Are you sure?" To which Miles would always respond, "Of course I am," as if the question itself was absurd to ask. But in the real world—as he couldn't attest to how real his world actually was, especially in its current manifestation, locked away in a cage—he didn't feel like a true man, or even a false one for that matter, despite how he was in the dream, and regardless of what type of food he might have ordered within it. The Big Mac, however, would never change—that and the high shriek of laughter that always followed from the African-American cashier (always African-American), as if Miles had just said the funniest thing they had ever heard.

If anything, what haunted him most from this reoccurring dream—which he now thought of as a nightmare instead, as he would usually wake from it with a start, sweating through the bed sheet—was the never-changing howl of laughter from the never-changing African-American cashier. After repeatedly hearing this high-pitched screech, it suddenly dawned on Miles that maybe they weren't actually laughing at his order of the Big Mac, which there was really nothing funny about, but, rather, screaming about something else—something far worse than two cheeseburgers sandwiched together with Thousand Island dressing.

The realization that the McDonald's employee wasn't really laughing at him revealed something far more disturbing once he examined it from a different angle, and that was the certainty that the African-American cashier was, instead, recoiling in fear from Miles, who, though ordering a Big Mac like a normal customer, actually held a gun in his right hand, and thus was anything but ordinary. And the fact that Miles ordered a Big Mac, rather than demanding the money in the register, rightfully horrified the employee even more. Not to mention, the "father" in the dream seemed to be disapproving of his son's true motive—a moral compass so to speak—which Miles countered unequivocally.

The most disturbing version of the dream, though, which he'd just had the night before for the very first time—and hopefully the last—was a social worker's wet dream, for when the angle widened out from the cashier's perspective, it was suddenly Sawyer holding the gun—and to boot, made up like Batman's notorious foe, The Joker, in his signature makeup, maniacal grin and all. And then, serving as the wicked punchline, when the camera flipped yet again Miles was now the cashier behind the counter, dressed to the hilt as a McDonald's employee. But unlike the previous cashiers in the dream, Miles didn't laugh when Sawyer amicably asked for a Big Mac (despite the fact that Sawyer continued to aim the gun at him) but, rather, took the order like he was helping a typical customer on a typical day. For Miles wasn't afraid—not even a little bit...

though he knew he should have been.

FLIMFLAM

One of the few things Miles remembered about that fateful afternoon when an innocent teenage boy was shot—supposedly by Miles himself, the one piece of the story he should have remembered above all else—was an idiot remark made by Sawyer following his piss stop on the side of the road, just after Miles had faked a call to his third and final step-parents, whom he had no intention of ever calling again (or even *pretending* to call again). This was an unfortunate circumstance, especially considering that the Kellys tried everything they could to make Miles happy, even attempting to visit him in prison several times and writing him letters that he refused to read—not that his previous two families didn't try as hard. But the Kellys were the ones that sent and paid for Miles to go to rehab—a proposition that Miles wasn't completely against. A surprisingly easy win for the Kellys, but more because he wanted to be around kids that might be similar to him, addict or not—which, in the theoretical sense at least, couldn't be anything other than perfect.

"You ever think about how much underwear there must be in the world?" Sawyer had said rhetorically after getting back in the car. "I mean, think about it, it must be a staggering amount...except Third World countries I guess, where they probably go commando most of the time." Absurdly, Sawyer was thinking of this while he was more-or-less sober, a feat which unintentionally made it more believable that he had exhausted the same amount of drugs and alcohol as Miles had—though the latter's intake hadn't fully kicked in yet.

Miles had been trying to put his cellphone back in his pocket, which seemed impossible to achieve—like he was playing with a kindergarten toy, attempting to force the wrong shape into the wrong corresponding hole by strength alone. "Can't you ever do anything like anyone else?" he had said, not really knowing if he was asking Sawyer or himself this question but expecting an answer nonetheless—hopefully one that would help him finally put his cellphone away.

This was the third piss stop they had taken since leaving Sawyer's house, although the first two were taken by Miles alone, and both on the side of the road as well—a curious point since Miles had just given Sawyer shit for doing the very same thing, as he'd already forgotten the first two stops. This was solely due to the drugs they had just taken—or rather, mostly Miles had just taken—which included a large dose of DMT and a generous splash of Old Crow. Whiskey was an unfortunate but necessary addition to the mix, to loosen Miles up—though mixing any alcohol with DMT, as far as Sawyer knew, could lessen the hallucinatory effects of the drug. Not to mention the combination could likely trigger a bad reaction, "bad" ranging from nausea all the way to death. Consequently, stopping to piss so frequently was the least concern of their afternoon festivities, or at least Sawyer's, as the two-to-one piss stop ratio was more than lost on Miles, who'd been led to believe his friend had taken an equal amount of brain-benders. Also lost on Miles was the fact that Sawyer seemed to have no trouble driving the car—an impossible accomplishment in his soon-to-be state.

After the third piss stop (the one Sawyer had to relent to), when their tan Mercedes finally made it to downtown—whatever "downtown" meant, as Miles couldn't think of downtown anything—they pulled over across from the bank because Miles had shakily pointed at the ATM, for no real reason other than that he had to throw up and couldn't think of the right words.

"How much cash did you get out?" Sawyer asked Miles when he returned to the car, if only to fuck with him, since it was obvious that Miles had gone nowhere near the ATM and had, instead, made a beeline for the side of the building—a curious fact since the side of the building was still quite visible from the street. Afterwards, as Miles was busy wiping at his already permanently stained T-shirt for any remnants of puke that may have landed there (only because Sawyer had told him to), and not coming close whatsoever, he began to think that someone was after him. Maybe even a whole consortium of people—"consortium" being his new favorite word solely based on the sound of it—and if he stopped at all, just to rid himself from feeling sick, it could potentially endanger his life. On top of which, he hadn't ruled out the likelihood that Sawyer was a part of this consortium and was telepathically informing the group on Miles' whereabouts. Illogically, while thinking along this vein, it didn't occur to Miles that, were Sawyer indeed a member of the consortium, he might be driving Miles right to their headquarters—if such a place existed, since they were such a secret organization—and thus, Miles would have been better off not only stopping to puke next to the bank, but then running off as fast as he could and hiding someplace where he would be difficult to find.

"Why?" Miles spat back defensively to Sawyer's question about money—and as a blanket question, since Sawyer had just unexpectedly turned into an anthropoid. As straightforward as the question seemed coming from a gorilla, Miles couldn't think of any number at all—the latter due to the fact that he was convinced numbers hadn't been invented yet—so he instead exclaimed: "Keep your stinking paws off my money, you dirty ape!"

At this, Sawyer could only stare back for a long moment, the urge to laugh somehow passing him by like a bus skipping a planned stop.

"What the fuck?" Sawyer finally said, repeating the three words that were quickly becoming his mantra.

"What?"

"Dirty ape? What the fuck are you talking about?"

Now Sawyer had returned to human form again, which allowed Miles to gain back a morsel of reality, but nowhere near enough to ground him completely.

"You never saw…" Miles couldn't think of the name of the movie now. "You know, the thing with the NR guy," he said, inadvertently leaving out the last letter of the acronym due to not remembering that either.

Sawyer mulled this over for a handful of seconds, as if actually attempting to figure out the movie Miles was referring to, despite the fact there was probably no way in hell he would be able to guess the correct one (although the quote, despite missing a word, did sound vaguely familiar).

"You know, the one with underpants guy…speaking of underpants," Miles said, as if reminding himself of a distant memory that he wasn't entirely convinced had really occurred. "Mark…Mark…Marky…" he searched.

"Marky Mark?" Sawyer finished as a question, not only to Miles but seemingly to himself, having likely forgotten what they were just talking about due to clear apathy.

"Who?"

"Marky Mark," Sawyer repeated. "Mark Wahlberg?"

"Wall?" Miles shifted in his seat and grabbed his eye, as if he'd been struck by a BB. "What wall?"

As abruptly as Miles' imagined BB shot—and once Sawyer had persuaded Miles to take another hit of the DMT, which didn't require much convincing at all—Sawyer pulled the Mercedes over to the side of the road again, throwing Miles in his seat as if someone had physically pushed him.

"The fuck?" Miles blurted, trying out Sawyer's new favorite phrase but forgetting to say the first word, dropping the baggie of whatever was left of the DMT on the floor.

"Get the gun out!" Sawyer suddenly commanded, not even waiting for the car to come to a complete stop.

"What?" Miles said, having heard him the first time but asking for a do-over only by reflex.

"Get the fuckin' gun!" Sawyer yelled again, in crescendo this time, as if both their lives depended on it.

By instinctive duty, like they were partners in some deep cover law enforcement agency, Miles flung the glove compartment open and was reaching inside to grab the gun when, for some reason near the surface of his otherwise elusive reality, it occurred to him what he was about to do, his hand freezing in mid-air. "Wait a sec…why do you need the…." Then, without waiting for an answer nor remembering the rest of the intended question, staring at the firearm as if it were somehow proof of extraterrestrial existence, he added, "Loaded?"—once again forgetting the other words necessary to form a complete sentence.

"Doesn't serve much purpose if it isn't," Sawyer said, reaching out for the gun—and not to shake Miles' hand (as it appeared to Miles at first), who started to extend his empty palm like he was about to be congratulated for something, even though he couldn't comprehend what he might have done to deserve it.

Had Miles' brief window of reality stayed open a minute longer he might have then asked something along the lines of, "What do you need it for?" But it was too late to impose any type of rationality on the unraveling scene at hand. Although Sawyer was still reaching out for the firearm, his hand searching the air as if the gun might materialize, he was also looking down the street at something—what exactly Miles couldn't tell, as his vision betrayed so many disparate things, so many competing apparitions, that it was hard to settle on just one (not the least of which was a tall, skinny blonde who manifested herself as a sprout of vanilla in the moist greenery Miles was concocting in his head).

"She doesn't have much of an ass," Sawyer observed, skating on the rink of Miles' perceived vision, sharing his reality of the vanilla girl.

"Whose ass?" Miles said, returning home to his transient psychosis, his squishy mind searching for pertinence despite compelling evidence to the contrary.

"I just want to scare him," Sawyer stated matter-of-factly.

"Him?" Miles echoed without any meat, as he really didn't comprehend anything coming out of Sawyer's mouth.

Then, like some kind of ninja, Sawyer suddenly had the gun in his possession, grabbing it so fast Miles missed the motion entirely.

Helpless, Miles was struck with a fear he couldn't come close to identifying—like Sisyphus, utterly unable to stop the gravity-powered boulder in its terrifying descent to whatever lay waiting at the bottom of the hill.

She had forgotten her phone yet again. He was planning on giving her shit about it, and for what seemed like the hundredth time, once he retrieved it from the coffee shop—her favorite place to leave it, apparently—but then wondered if he had worn this joke out already, especially since he couldn't tell if she understood that he was only messing with her. *So, what if she was a bit aloof, even with something as expensive as an iPhone?* It certainly wasn't the end of the world if she lost it for good one of these days—if he wasn't there to come to the rescue for some reason or another. Maybe it would even teach her a lesson, though he knew in the back of his mind that was doubtful. *Once aloof, always aloof. Wasn't that a saying?* he wondered.

It was no time to think about such things, however. Owen didn't know what it was exactly, but something felt off this particular afternoon. It brought to mind the old R.E.M. cover of "Strange" and its specific lyric: *There's something going on that's not quite right*—which Elodie had introduced him to only the week before. From the moment Elodie discharged an "Oh fuck!" upon the realization she had forgotten it (once again) to the moment he returned to the table they were just at, breathless, to retrieve it, he was constantly afraid it would be gone by the time he got back. Indeed, three kids who looked like students were about to claim it as their own—or at least the table the phone sat on.

These students were nice enough when Owen explained to them that his girlfriend had left her phone on the table—it didn't seem like it would ever get old, referring to Elodie as his "girlfriend"—and although everything was going according to the usual script (Elodie's iPhone retrieval script), he almost worried—and to such an extent that it bordered on a mental issue—that the students had somehow swapped out her iPhone for an older one before he was able to return to the table. He wouldn't know the difference, as a proud Samsung man himself.

"She forgets everything," Owen added as a side note to the three students, with a forced fake smile at the end to ease his own unwieldiness—though any further explanation was far from necessary. He was already spending far too long at their table, rather than just grabbing the phone and going on his way, perhaps due to his gut instinct of something not feeling quite right. So, he felt the need to stay there until his disquietude dimmed to something more tolerable. Conversely, the amount of unwarranted time he was spending at their old table allowed Elodie to walk further than she normally would have while waiting for him, thus getting too far away to clearly witness what would happen in a handful of minutes, and be over in even less time (a disproportionate equation that she would never be able to reconcile).

For Owen, however, things happened even faster and were

even more confusing. The sense of mortal danger can't be understood by those who have never undergone a similar experience, where life changes in an instant, like one has inadvertently walked onto a movie set where everything is supposed to be make-believe. *Supposed to be.* On a movie set the guns weren't real, and they didn't fire real bullets into real people: real people who could actually die. Consequently, Owen didn't believe anything he saw at first. He didn't believe that a guy was walking toward him with a gun visible at his side, not seeming to care at all that he was holding a lethal weapon more or less out in the open. Owen tried to ignore him due to thinking he was maybe smack-dab in the middle of an intoxicating interlude, a boyfriend (just like him) coming from the opposite direction, fetching a forgotten phone for *his* beloved. Although the closer Owen got—walking straight toward this doppelgänger boyfriend—he began to realize it might not be a smartphone in this guy's hand after all, because why would he be aiming an iPhone *at him?* This queer question didn't linger long enough for an answer, Owen's brain not registering the weapon with sufficient time to send a message to the rest of his body to flee.

But it didn't matter how long Owen's brain thought he had or didn't have, as there didn't seem to be enough time to react at all. The shock of what he had somehow walked into caused Owen to stop cold, like the proverbial "deer in the headlights"—paralyzed before his fight-or-flight response could be activated.

Ironically, the last thing Owen would ever see in life was a guy walking toward him like a murky dream; one in which the other person seemed to be dreaming, too, as if each of them were staring into the other's subconscious—a feat obliterating the lines of science.

Owen was a ghost and then seemingly prey—a boy who only wanted to return his girlfriend's iPhone to her...

and nothing more.

BRIDGE

"Bless you," Amos said to the young mother, who was sitting far enough away that she might not have heard him—but then looked around to find where the kind words possibly came from, not entirely convinced they weren't circling inside her head like most things did these days.

He smiled at her when she finally associated his gaze with his voice—and although Catherine wanted to smile back from somewhere inside her, it wasn't something she could do. Not even the infant she was holding looked happy, and this too shouldn't have been the case, as Amos knew all too well.

"I thought I was too far away to bless," Catherine said after a long moment, barely above a whisper, like she was going to make a joke but changed her mind at the last second, taking her voice with her.

He smiled at her again, in a way that seemed like it was a prelude to laughing—but it stopped there.

Is he some kind of pervert? she wondered.

"You're never too far away to bless," he said soothingly.

Maybe he's a priest or something, Catherine thought, wanting to ask him but then changing her mind. Besides, the baby was crying now, which made her realize that it'd actually been quiet for a spell when this stranger started speaking with her, almost as if the man had addressed her son as well, who stopped to listen even though he was too young to understand anything. Plus, the last thing she wanted to do at the moment was get into a conversation with this weird old man, who would probably turn out to be a sicko, like everyone else she met usually did.

Suddenly he was next to her. She spontaneously moved

away a few inches in her seat, still holding the baby close to her chest—an irony to be sure, as she hated the thing and wished she had aborted it when she'd had the chance, hating even more her instinct to protect it.

He was definitely a creep, Catherine decided; should he decide to attack her there weren't many other people in the diner at the moment, despite the fact it was prime breakfast time. There was a middle-aged couple in the far corner, who seemingly ignored each other as much as they were ignoring everything around them; a young Asian woman, perhaps a student, who was buried in a large paperback book; and the one apparent waitress taking a smoke break outside (discernible through a mesh screen door), along with the line cook, who didn't even smoke but was keeping her company in the obvious but very off-chance she might sleep with him after work. *It was a good time to rip off the place*, Catherine thought, *not to mention the few other customers* (but not with this fuck-ass old man bothering her).

"I'm sorry," he said, finally noticing that he was making her uncomfortable verbally, and perhaps physically (or vice-versa). "I come in peace, I promise."

"What do you want?" she said with intended acidity, losing the rest of her patience, which was in short supply to begin with and always had been.

Realizing that he was probably sitting too close to her—he seemed to make this mistake often, but it was never sexual—he moved to the opposite side of the booth across from her before she could say anything more, which was better for both of them (maybe all three of them, as the baby was still crying). But then Amos looked directly at the wailing boy and he stopped instantly, as if directed to do so by Amos' stare alone. Now the baby was smiling, or at least trying to—a sign that didn't go unnoticed by Catherine, for she had seen that face before countless times, and thus associated it with what was most likely happening: the baby was taking a shit and she would have to change his diaper. But she was out of diapers and, at this point, didn't really care if the baby's shit piled up in his generic Huggies. She couldn't afford the real thing—not that she cared one way or the other. After all, it was his shit, not hers, and maybe he would learn a lesson and dump less if she let him remain uncomfortable for a while.

"What's your baby's name?" he asked, ignoring her naked question, which he probably thought was rhetorical anyway.

"It says Miles on his birth certificate," she said strangely, and again with bite, as if she didn't like the name but it somehow found its way onto a legal document—if only to annoy her.

"Hi Miles," Amos said to the infant, turning to him and smiling.

This pervert won't stop smiling, she thought. *Is he planning on killing us both?* Because, at this point, she would almost welcome such a thing. Plus, if he killed them both, she wouldn't have to change a putrid diaper ever again. *Just make it quick*, she wanted to say out loud to the stranger, as she didn't want to have to endure any physical pain if this guy indeed intended to murder them. She'd had enough physical pain throughout her life. Not to mention, she only had one Percocet left, and no Klonopin at all—hence her persistent insomnia—which meant she couldn't even dull herself first.

Just then, a voice came out of nowhere, announcing to no one in particular that two planes had hit the World Trade Center. It was the waitress, back earlier than she wanted from her smoke break, with the line cook right behind her—the two of them like a perfunctory news team that couldn't contain this headline for a moment longer (though the line cook seemed to be trying to contain something else entirely).

Catherine wasn't sure what exactly this terrorist attack meant—CNN had apparently called it a terrorist attack—nor why it seemed to warrant such a flood of tears by the waitress, who now seemed inconsolable. And the line cook, whose lust for the waitress hadn't seemed to dissipate at all, regardless of the situation in New York, appeared inexplicably unsympathetic to anything that might be going on in the world. Unlike Catherine and the line cook, however, Amos did come across like he cared about the outside world at the moment, or any moment for that matter, though he didn't seem to be too surprised about two planes crashing into the World Trade Center—as if he expected such things, but was still resolute about the good in humanity.

But Amos didn't appear to want, and/or need, to show his true emotions or knowledge just yet, and tried to continue his conversation with Catherine as if the dramatic interruption by the waitress had never happened (to the latter's chagrin and, likewise, the line cook's).

"How old is Miles?" Amos continued, but then corrected himself. "I mean young, of course, since he shouldn't be lumped in with the word 'old' for a long time yet." Then he smiled again, without waiting for an answer to that question.

Is this guy just going to ask me a million questions? Catherine wondered, starting to worry that he would never leave her alone. "I don't know," she replied dismissively, then realized this answer made her sound stupid, like she didn't know how old her own baby was (which was actually true, despite giving birth not that long ago). And she hated sounding stupid.

"Two," she guessed incorrectly, as Miles was one (or in Mom speak, 14 months to be exact).

"He looks younger than that," Amos said, only lightly calling Catherine on her obvious wrong answer, which to a regular person would have been very puzzling—but not to Amos, who somehow understood innately why she made the number up.

"Did you two hear me?" the waitress interjected bitterly, like someone in the middle of an intimate fight with a romantic partner who made a habit of not acknowledging

her, especially when she was mad. Why she seemed to be sin-
gling them out, and not any of the other customers, Catherine
didn't know.

Amos raised his hand in the air to the waitress, as if to say:
Yes, we heard you, and thank you, but please leave us alone—
which seemed to work, at least for the moment.

"I don't know," Catherine said, not really meaning it as a
response to Amos' apparent challenge to Miles' real age, but
more as a hopeful end-stamp to their conversation, ignoring
the waitress' plea for attention and wishing she could also
ignore this man who wouldn't stop talking to her. "I don't
know" was the singular epitaph she might have had graven on
her soon-to-be tombstone.

"Maybe he's one?" Catherine then blurted weakly to Amos,
inexplicably returning to their previous conversation and
unknowingly guessing the correct answer. "I don't know," she
added quickly, just in case she was wrong again, repeating her
favorite phrase like someone testifying in court might plead
the Fifth Amendment. "You a doctor or something?" she asked
before he could test her again, thinking this was the only plau-
sible explanation for him knowing how old the baby was, as
if he had counted the rings of the infant like he would a tree.

He laughed, though she didn't know what was so fucking
funny. "No, I'm not a doctor," he replied, disregarding the
fact that he obviously knew he was getting on her nerves.
"Just a curious old man," he added, though neither adjective
was actually true—one a blatant lie, and the other a gross
understatement.

Outside, the wind stirred the trees like a shaded grave just
after a funeral, the prequel to a storm that would last for days
and keep the diner woefully under-populated. The waitress,
surrendering to the fact that she probably needed to find a
different audience, had now retreated to the back room to call
her mother with the shocking news of the planes (with the line

cook in tow, ironically matching his job title and responsibilities—at least reflexively).

The baby, evidently not wanting to be forgotten, reached out with one tiny hand and knocked the nearly-empty ketchup bottle from the table like it was his arch-enemy, causing it to spill most of its remaining contents on Catherine's left breast, with a small splash landing on Amos' outstretched, French-cuffed shirt sleeve. An even smaller amount landed on Miles, joining several other already-existing stains.

Catherine opened her mouth as if she wanted to say something, but then quickly closed it, unintentionally reminding herself of her mother—the ever-silent witness to her father's cruelty.

"No worries," Amos said, inadvertently stalling whatever she was about to say, even though there was no chance it was going to be an apology, as those two words didn't exist in Catherine's lexicon—nor in her parents' terminology, for that matter.

Ignoring his own soiled sleeve, Amos grabbed a nearby napkin and reached across the table to wipe away the tiny red blotch from the baby's T-shirt, doubtlessly hoping that his attention to it might also inspire Catherine to actually wash the infant's notably dirty attire sometime in the near future (an unlikelihood, which she communicated to Amos via a bleak expression that swam across her face).

"It'll be alright," he stated evenly, as if answering the desolate, unpremeditated gesture she had made. It was the most genuine thing she had said, without saying anything at all.

She wanted to ask him who or what was going to be alright—her or her son—as if she understood that he somehow knew this answer for certain. But she didn't ask—not then, and not later—for she could tell by his sorrowful eyes that only one of them would ever be alright...

and it wasn't who she thought.

Even though he knew what she was going to do—what she was *planning* to do—he didn't stop her. He could have, and quite easily. But he didn't. It wasn't his job to do that; nor should it have been. He could only serve as a mute witness, yielding to human intention—fear in its absolute.

And so, he watched her. He watched her as she left the diner with the baby almost unwillingly—with the baby, that is, as if she wanted to forget him too, along with the bill. He watched her as she stopped on the sidewalk for a long moment—a too-long moment—not sure where she wanted to go, or even a possible direction to head should the destination become belatedly apparent. And this pause gave sufficient time for the 9/11 waitress to storm outside and tell her that she "forgot" to pay the bill, as the first confrontation had to stay on the friendly side, just in case the patron had indeed forgot (which was *never* the case). But Amos knew she had purposefully run out on the check—a check that he had wanted to pay for her and the baby; but he just couldn't.

Catherine seemingly had no care in the world that the waitress had come out after her. Surely, a sane person wouldn't have stopped on the sidewalk outside the restaurant for so long, knowing they had just committed a criminal act. It was like a bank robber who wasn't concerned whatsoever after completing the hard part of the stick-up, nor in the least bit rushed to jump in the getaway car and escape before the authorities arrived.

Yet still, outside the diner, as Catherine went along with the "I forgot" excuse—more because it was the first one presented to her, and not because she was worried at all about the possible ramifications if she hadn't actually forgot—he wanted to intervene and save her from this undue trouble.

The kind of trouble that she could have prevented, were she so inclined...

but she wasn't so inclined.

And with a baby in tow, it wasn't so easy to run away—*literally* run away—if that was indeed her plan...

which, of course, it wasn't.

She had no plans to speak of, which made what she did next even more horrifying, like she was throwing an empty bottle into the closest trashcan, or some other pedestrian act...

but this was no pedestrian act.

It was an act that couldn't be taken back—a precipitous ending to something that hadn't yet begun, or even had the chance to begin, which made it all the more unforgivable; the kind of crime that couldn't be fathomed from any angle, unspeakable afterwards even as indigestible news; too inhuman to comprehend on any level of consciousness.

As it turned out, though, he had to intervene outside the diner. With Catherine nowhere near paying her bill—notwithstanding the fact that she couldn't pay for it even if she wanted to—he didn't want the scene to escalate any further than it already had, with the 9/11 waitress already threatening to call the police (and all over a bill that turned out to be less than ten dollars).

Not surprisingly, she didn't even thank him for stepping in; nor did she seem to notice that he had followed her to the bridge. Worse, the whole time he was following her, she had no idea where she was going or what was she about to do— not initially at least—but that didn't make what she eventually did any more conceivable.

Once they arrived at the bridge he stayed below, next to the running stream that wanted to be more like a river, as she perched above, extending the baby over the side like Rafiki declaring Simba king—none of which Amos could reconcile, even knowing human nature as he did. And surely Catherine wasn't replacing Miles with Simba in any symbolic way; if anything, it was just a last-second impulse as she happened to be walking across the bridge.

Miles was certainly no Simba, nor any other fictional character, but perhaps he stood for something else far beyond the surface of her present reality. When Catherine was a young girl, a few weeks before turning ten—"nine and three-quarters" as she had told anyone who asked—there was a platform nest of baby mourning doves next to the front door of the tenement house where she grew up; a natural refuge that the mother bird became less and less confident of due to the too-close-for-comfort traffic of humans that came and went all day long. Finally, her anxiety reached a zenith she could no longer tolerate and she felt compelled to kill the babies herself, leaving them on Catherine's family's front doorstep like some type of grotesque offering—a sacrifice the mother felt she had no choice but to make in order to some-how avert an even worse fate her babies might suffer if she remained passive.

But Miles couldn't be a sacrifice to the gods, as Catherine was in no way trying to protect the living creature that had come from her womb. Miles was more like a small piece of her clothing that she no longer needed, torn from her body in an unceremonious manner without a shred of grief; noth-ing more than a hopefully lucky coin, which she released as if making a wish upon it....

And just like that the baby was in the air, no longer secured in his mother's lofty bosom, unknowing of human evil or its own impending death, free-falling from the bridge into the rushing water below.

PART THREE
THE ABSOLVER

207

CADENCE

He'd been listening to Strauss' Death and Transfiguration, a CD he'd borrowed from the prison library after he dreamed about listening to some classical music—though which piece it was exactly he had no idea; probably a made-up one since he didn't really know any classical music—when a guard informed him that he had a visitor. He hoped it wasn't that mother again, the one whose son he had supposedly killed. She had been there a couple of times now, each time just sitting there staring at him, saying few words—and none that made any sense. He still didn't know what she wanted from him, besides maybe an apology. But what good was an apology—two stupid words, as meaningless as anything else that had supposed meaning attached to it—when it obviously wasn't going to bring her son back from the dead? Nothing would. Did she not understand that? Why did she keep coming?

He was trying to remember the mother's name—*Linda? Lisa?*—when he discovered that the visitor waiting for him was someone else, and not even a woman. He was afraid that other members of the kid's family would start visiting him, in addition to the mother—*was this guy waiting for him the father? He was much older-looking, so maybe the grandfather?*—if only to drive him insane with guilt over something he may or may not have done.

"Miles?" the visitor asked.

"Yes?" Miles answered, meaning something along the lines of "Yes, and you are?" but sounding more as if he wasn't completely sure of his own name.

The man, who was maybe in his seventies and dressed in a gray pinstripe suit that looked almost as old, picked up on the confusion that seemed to permeate the air between them and said again, "Miles? Miles Rockefeller?" .

"Yes?" Miles repeated, this time sounding more sure-footed, but still trying to figure out the possible relation this guy had to the shooting victim. *What was the kid's name again? Adam? Eric?* Miles couldn't remember, which was more than a little surprising since he had heard it announced so many times in the courtroom. But the caves in Miles' mind that contained his lost memories were becoming vast—so vast that Miles grew more anxious by the day that he had permanent brain damage due to his drug use.

"Any relation to John D.?" the man asked, with the type of grin which hinted that he knew the answer to this question already, an expert swimmer pretending to doggy paddle until a lifeguard came to save him.

Miles knew that he had a famous last name, but didn't know exactly who the *real* Rockefellers were; nor did he ever have the inclination to research it past what he already knew—mainly from a young social worker who wore too much blue eyeshadow and was more than eager to share her knowledge of the legendary industrialist. Apparently he was some old, rich guy that his first foster family had no relation to whatsoever, which was readily indicated by their lack (as opposed to overabundance) of money.

"I'm Amos," the man said, waiting to introduce himself until Miles had sat down across from him (and knowing that his John D. question was rhetorical at best).

"Yes?" Miles said a third time, now wanting to get whatever this was over with so he could get back to the Strauss, which was growing on him for some inexplicable reason, as was other classical music he'd borrowed from the library.

Miles was preparing himself to not pay any attention

above what was necessary to this likely grandfather of the victim—*necessary* constituting when the visit had run out of time—when the man said something Miles wasn't expecting at all.

"I knew your mother," the strange man said without ceremony, cutting to the proverbial chase.

"My mother?" Miles shot back, as if the word sounded foreign to him. The truth was that Miles hadn't ever *stopped* thinking about who his real mother was—or might have been. He had even recently wondered—*very* recently, in fact—if his birth mother also liked classical music, or had listened to it at all.

The man smiled again. "Well, you weren't Miles Rockefeller back then," he added, as if Miles might be curious what his original name had been (which of course he was). But the man didn't offer it straightway, even though it had seemed he would. Somehow, Miles felt he had to ask the man specific questions if he wanted specific answers to anything. First and foremost, naturally, Miles wanted to ask why his mother had given up on him. Had he not been worth caring for? Had he done something wrong, causing his mother to discard him? (He *had* been discarded, of course, but this was something Amos would never share.)

"She didn't know me," Amos said flatly. "Your mother," he clarified, as if Miles had somehow forgotten the subject of their—thus far—mysterious conversation (and once again referring to his mother in the past tense).

"What do you mean?" Miles asked, suddenly thinking that maybe someone was playing a practical joke on him—a very bad joke, and not a practical one at all.

The man straightened in his chair, as if that might somehow make what he was saying that much more understandable to Miles—although even he would admit that the last thing he'd said sounded more than a little confusing. He just wanted to make sure that Miles understood he was no friend of his mother's: maybe because being a friend by definition might condone what she did.

Miles was starting to feel like his eyelids were pulling apart, like Alex's in *A Clockwork Orange*; forced to watch images he didn't want to see, even if they happened to be from his real life—even if they *were* his real life. Miles had seen bits and pieces of *A Clockwork Orange* at Sawyer's dad's house, but never the whole movie at once. It was a film he had never even heard of before, though Sawyer claimed he had seen it more times than he could count, which Miles believed. In retrospect, Sawyer may have considered himself a real-life Alex DeLarge: a prisoner of the so-called world he was forced to live in. But Sawyer was no prisoner. Miles was the only one caught at the moment, as far as he could tell, serving time for something Sawyer was possibly more responsible for—though the truth remained veiled.

Both Miles and the old man sitting across from him realized, and at possibly the same moment, that a vital part of their conversation had somehow been skipped. As a result, the old man jumped in first. "You've been in the news, of course, and so I...." He trailed off, now sounding less confident than he probably wanted; not sure how to explain himself, or his possible motive, for visiting Miles.

"I've been in the news?" Miles said, having not considered the very real possibility that his crime might be significant in some way to society-at-large. If this was the case, though, then had Sawyer seen him on TV as well? If he had been in the news to the degree this old man was implying, then surely Sawyer knew what had happened to Miles.

That fuck! Miles almost screamed out loud, the sudden realization slapping him across the face, as if Sawyer stood right there.

I'm gonna kill that motherfucker when I get out of here!

I'm gonna find that cunt and make him pay!

And he's walking around outside scot-free, with no care in the world other than himself.

That asshole probably watched me on TV and laughed...celebrating that it wasn't him who got caught...celebrating with God knows what, hogging all the drugs for himself.

Miles had only recently finished getting detoxed—and getting detoxed in prison was no vacation. The doctors had withdrawn him like an animal, completely apathetic regarding whether they were draining him too fast—just as long as the end result was the same. The side effects Miles had endured getting there didn't seem that concerning to the medical staff either. Even a seizure here and there didn't matter. As long as he didn't die, that was good enough for them—though they would have preferred that he didn't have any seizures, if only because it complicated things a little, causing them to rethink some of what they were prescribing, or at least the dosages. The two things the doctors seemed to care about the most were possible seizures and any hallucinations—though the latter were okay so long as Miles didn't do anything to himself or any of the other inmates.

But Miles wasn't hallucinating anymore. A man who claimed to have known his birth mother was actually sitting across from him now; a man who maybe knew the answers to the questions Miles had always been too afraid to ask, for fear that the answers wouldn't be what he wanted them to be. But what did Miles expect them to be? After all, it couldn't be a surprise to find out that his mother had tossed him aside. How else would he have become a foster kid in the first place?

Maybe my mother recently died and left all her money to me, he suddenly thought. But this man couldn't be his mother's attorney, as he'd just said that Miles' mother didn't know him. *How could this be, though,* Miles wondered, *unless he was lying? How could it be possible? Isn't he here now visiting her son? How else would he know who Miles was?*

"What do you mean?" Miles asked the old man. "What do you mean, she didn't know you? My mother...."

"She didn't know me," he repeated, as though the second time might make more sense, if for no other reason than he'd said it twice. "Not really."

Miles looked around at the other visitors in the washed-out medicinal-smelling room. Everyone else seemed to be engaged in normal conversation; everyone else was seemingly making sense, the regular back-and-forth chatter like a dull, defensively played tennis match. So why was *his* conversation with *his* visitor so hard to comprehend? *Just speak regular!* Miles wanted to scream at the old man (whatever *regular* meant).

"You look confused," Amos said, finally saying something that made sense, and hopefully staying in the present long enough for Miles to understand what was going on—or, at the very least, find out who this man might be in relation to his mother.

Before Miles could answer, the man continued his allegory again—though, as a rule, whenever he spoke to strangers he always had a specific goal in mind, all his words chosen carefully, even the rhetorical ones.

Amos asked, "Do you believe in magic?"

Miles laughed. It sounded like the lyrics to a song. *Was it?* he wondered. It sounded somewhat familiar.

"You think magic is funny?" the man asked precisely, as if he had measured out the exact space between each word. His tone wasn't at all sarcastic or playful, but there was no hint of acrimony either. Almost as if he felt concern—like magic was as vital to Miles as oxygen, and he didn't want Miles to die due to any lack of it.

"What?" Miles said, as if he knew no other word anymore. He looked around the bleached room again. "Is anyone else hearing this?" he wanted to ask someone nearby—anyone. Was his visitor meant for another prisoner and not him?

Maybe that was why he didn't understand anything the old man said. But the man had addressed him by name, so....

"How do you know me?" Miles blurted. Then, trying to be more specific in hopes of getting a more specific answer: "How do you know my mother?" The word "mother" still sounded foreign to him, especially with "my" in front of it. Everything in Miles' life that had a "my" in front of it felt like a lie.

"You were very small..." Amos started, then stopped. This was uncharacteristic for him; he never stopped.

Before Miles could ask, "What?" again (the only question it seemed like he'd ever asked—and not just of his present visitor), a nearby guard announced that visiting time was almost over and to "Wrap it up." But how could he wrap it up? *There was nothing* to *wrap up, was there?* He suddenly felt very anxious, as if the most important moment of his life had just passed him by like a once-in-a-century comet passing the Earth, and he had neglected to do something as easy as look up.

"Too small," Amos added, not missing a beat despite the guard's coarse interruption.

"Too small for what?" Miles asked, clutching the words to his chest in such a way that it seemed he might never let them go.

Amos gazed around the room, which was now trickling with fragile goodbyes, uncertain farewells. He appeared to take everything in solemnly, but without judgment. After a moment he turned back to Miles. "It wasn't supposed to be like this," he said, adding a grace note of sadness, but then reversing his words like an idiot savant, as if starting the sentence from the opposite direction might make more sense (it didn't).

"Too small for what?" Miles asked again, ignoring the old man's hapless observation about what should have been, feeling like a stuck needle on a record player and not actually a live human being that could choose different words, forwards or backwards.

Amos looked away, his pupils dark and diluted, as if what he was about to say might not be for Miles but, rather, someone else who had been with them the entire time—someone whom he had neglected to acknowledge for fear they might look back at him, expecting something from him that wasn't possible…and never would be.

"Too small to die," the old man finally said.

PLACEBO

The white dog was back.

It had returned just like it had silently promised so long ago—or what seemed like so long ago, as time was as lost as the dog may have been; though something told her that this dog could never be lost. Like a ghost in its most translucent form, it knew its nature without fail; its haunting schedule as ironclad as the ticking second hand from a senile clock in a deserted hallway.

Once again flattened by her Xanax, wine, and customary evening bath (but with less effect due to her body growing stubborn against these once-potent ingredients), she was presently getting beaten by the latest Nicholas Sparks novel—a seemingly more effective sleep drug than any benzo her doctor threw at her. Worse yet were the movie adaptations; they could cure even her worst bouts of insomnia, with the exception of *The Notebook*, her all-time favorite movie. Though, lately, any movie could draw her burdened eyelids down—even the occasional good one that would normally hold her interest—most likely due to the combination of artificial darkness and psychological hot flashes that dominated her everyday life.

"Shoo!" she screamed, once again thinking that the dog could hear her through the thick windows; and even if it could, that it would actually listen to her. It was standing centered on her front lawn, like a clearheaded killer or devoted protector—she still couldn't decide which—somehow resistant to the stray golf balls that always seemed to find her outside, whether she was coming or going.

The one-year anniversary of Owen's death was approaching, like a coastal storm that couldn't decide where to land—but no less powerful from its hesitation. She still couldn't fathom the idea that he was gone and would never come back, as if he were simply a favorite sweater she had misplaced which would surface again in time somewhere; or, like a wave in the ocean that, by its very nature, *had* to return once it receded, like a rubber band pulled as far as it could go.

Never let go....

The white dog unsettled her—not that she was in any way settled before. She wasn't the type of person who was ever settled, at least in terms of the high-revving anxiety that was her default setting. Although, by a different definition, it could be argued that she had settled for Barry when the clicks of her biological clock had become too deafening. In its purest form, however, the word "settle" was not in her lexicon.

Naturally, like anyone drenched in the tidal wave that is grief, horrible visions of what her son might look like now haunted her. After so long a time in the coffin she had reluctantly picked out—been *forced* to pick out, as no coffin that day seemed right. Then buried half-a-dozen feet down in the earth, rotting away like discarded fruit, slowly digested by God-knows-what—such obsessive thoughts destroyed most of her "living" hours and made her dreamscapes hideous.

She had never had a fear of dogs—grizzly bears, maybe; cockroaches and snakes, definitely—and had grown up with large collies. Always two at a time, like highway patrolmen who rode their motorcycles side-by-side, lost in syndication. But this dog—the white dog—terrified her. It wasn't the typical fear of dogs that someone might experience, such as fearing getting bit by one, or it having rabies and then getting bit. She wasn't afraid of rabies or getting bit; she was afraid of getting *consumed* by it. She didn't even wonder if such a thing were possible: the dog eating her entirely, with nothing left of her at all.

That afternoon, after a bleak day at the store sales-wise, she had stopped at Starbucks to get her "usual" (though it wasn't "usual" to any of the employees for some annoying reason, even after ordering the same drink the same way every day at the same time without fail). *How can you not recognize me after all this time?* she wanted to scream at them when they gave her that daily dumb expression of "Hey stranger, what can I get you today?" accompanied by a shit-eating-fake-retail smile like she was just some commoner. She was NOT a commoner!

Then, at the counter that held the sugar packets, creamers and napkins—*was it called a counter because it was supposed to count how many things people took from it?* she wondered curiously for the first time maybe ever, wanting to ask someone else if they too ever wondered what "counter" actually meant. She stopped a nearby student, who proudly displayed a baby-blue Tar Heels hat over messy unwashed hair, also wearing a T-shirt that simply read: THIS WILL DESTROY YOU.

"What will destroy you?" she asked him, instead of the counter question, sounding more innocent than she felt or intended, and losing count of how many Splendas she had already used. She normally used nine—a compulsive spectacle that occasionally garnered sideways glances—even though her drink was too sweet as it was and didn't need anything extra added to it.

"Sorry?" the kid asked, maybe not sure if she was addressing him or not—and if she was, if she was serious.

She gestured at his shirt. "That!" she exclaimed, like a child who had only just learned how to pose a question.

"It's a band," he said, without a hint of sarcasm but with a biting tone, like her question was possibly the dumbest question ever asked in the history of mankind.

"Oh," she said dejectedly, not trying to hide her disappointment in his answer, if only because she thought his T-shirt was a heavenly message, acknowledging what she already knew to be true but needed validation for anyway. Lately, if not longer—though she would never admit this to anyone—it seemed as if she needed validation for just about anything outside of breathing; and there were days when even that was questionable.

She twisted her arm around so that she could see underneath her elbow, where she had a day-old scab from scraping it on the edge of the bathroom counter when she was bending down to look for toilet paper. The scab had barely formed yet, but this didn't stop her from ripping it off anyway as she stood there like a puppy watching its owner leave—the UNC student walking away from what he no doubt thought was a strange lady with an even stranger question, which he would probably recount to someone sometime as a funny Starbucks story.

But she couldn't let him get away. Not yet.

"Hey!" she hollered at him before he could get out the door, sounding like a completely different person than the one who had just asked him about his T-shirt.

Although he clearly knew this strange woman was screaming after him—based on the brief pause his body made at the door, as if only one small part of him heard her and hadn't convinced the rest of him yet—he naively thought he could get away.

"Hey!" she shouted again, as if she hadn't already won—now getting the attention of almost everyone else there, most of whom had previously been trying to ignore her. She couldn't be avoided; this much was evident to anyone nearby, and even those further away—some of whom even paused the music they were listening to in order to find out what the ruckus was about.

Sheepishly, the UNC student finally turned around.

"What?" he yelled back at her, reminding Lilly of her late mother, who also couldn't be reckoned with. Once, when she was a teenager and thus already embarrassed by everything her parents did, Lilly had helplessly sat in her mother's favorite restaurant as a waiter who had reached his limit shouted the same word, and in the same way, across the crowded dining room, frustrated that her mother flat-out refused to let him pay attention to any other table besides hers.

"Mom!" she had said to her mother as an aside, exasperated. "Order everything at the same time. You can't just add things every second and scream them out to him. You're not the only person in the world!"

But her mother *was* the only person in the world, and had remained to be, despite her passing over six years before. Although Owen, the virgin challenger in this other heavenly world, would probably take her mother's place at the throne, once Lilly could register her son as not coming back either.

"Do you know my son?" Lilly said to the student, who was still halfway out the door of the Starbucks as customers filed in past him, each one thanking him as if he solely held the door open for them.

"What?" he tried again, most likely hoping she would think he was too far away now to hear her, and already committed to leaving.

"Did you know my son?" she asked again, in such a meek way that she was barely audible. "His name was Owen."

Reluctantly, he committed to walking back through the door, like a guilty boy returning to his angry mother's side. "I'm only a freshman," he said, apparently hoping that would be enough to convince her there was no possible way he knew her son, especially if he was no longer a student there (based on her usage of the past tense—despite it implying that her son didn't attend *life* anymore, either).

She looked up at him blankly, as if confused by his addressing her; as if she had no idea whatsoever why this boy was standing next to her table.

"Your son already graduated, right?" he asked, his tone still impatient, caught in a conversation he wanted to end as soon as possible.

She still stared absentmindedly.

"Graduated?" she echoed, as if unsure of the meaning; forced to repeat it so she could try to make sense of it. But before he could answer her, she quickly added, as if anticipating his next question, "His name was King…Owen King," declaring his name, unwittingly, like James Bond would have (if he ever had the time to stop at Starbucks).

Now it was the student's turn to stare, his large pupils starting to dilate, vibrating back and forth like he was looking directly into a bright light. He appeared suddenly sympathetic to her plight, whatever it was; the fuck if he knew—though the compassion she thought he now felt was wiped out when he declared dismissively, "Don't know him."

She was expecting him to bookend a "sorry" after that, which he didn't, because he *had* to be sorry, didn't he? *Every-*one was sorry, or so they said to her more often than not. Then why wouldn't he have been, too, especially if Owen was once a classmate of his? But he was saying that Owen *wasn't* a classmate of his—that he didn't even know him.

He had to know Owen, though, didn't he?

"You don't?" she said aloud, wistfully.

"No, I don't," he repeated, enunciating each word as if he were talking to someone who couldn't understand otherwise. But then he appeared to feel bad, and added the only word she truly wanted to hear: "Sorry."

He unshackled himself from her then, triumphantly this time—an obvious win to those observing, their hurried footsteps escaping behind him in their own right.

SHIVER

The man in the public library had been staring at Catherine, who he probably thought was interested in him based on a few flimsy, sideways looks in his direction, though they were actually glances at the ladies' bathroom behind him, as she was waiting for its current occupant to vacate it—and preferably soon.

Christ, Catherine was thinking, *what were they doing in there?*

She had been so busy staring at the door to the ladies' room that Catherine didn't even notice the older-looking man sitting in front of it like a sentry—a man who was more or less the same age as her but seemed considerably older, likely due to alcohol and drug abuse—who couldn't move his eyes away from her (although the truth was that alcohol and drug abuse had imperfectly aged Catherine as well, so neither of them were going to win any beauty contests).

Catherine was frustrated, and getting more so by the minute, that this library only had one public bathroom. She didn't bother to ask anyone if there was another bathroom she could use for fear they might kick her back out onto the street, where, over the last few hours especially, it had become too cold for an average human being to survive, not to mention an improperly clothed one such as herself. She'd needed to go to the bathroom for the better part of the last thirty minutes, and refused to use the one down the street near the lake park that most of the other homeless people used, as she didn't want to pick up venereal disease again from an angry toilet seat, or possibly get raped again—the latter of which

223

had been compounded recently when she had to terminate another pregnancy herself, and in such a way that she had to be rushed to the hospital.

The single bathrooms, like the one in the library, naturally afforded much more privacy, which was why this particular one had also served as her surgical theater on several occasions; but now that she only needed to relieve her irritated bowels, the private aspect of this location didn't really benefit her—since she didn't care in the least about having diarrhea in public, as this wasn't illegal. Unsociable, perhaps, but not against the law. And she knew enough that her *MacGyver*-like self-abortions would probably not get looked kindly upon if she were ever caught.

When the unisex bathroom was finally surrendered— *renounced* was more apt—like General Lee's army at Appomattox, and with as much carnage left behind, a petite blonde woman revealed herself as the improbable antagonist. Even the nicotine-aged man (who went by the name Curtis, and who had been staring at Catherine), was briefly hijacked by the tiny blonde woman exiting the bathroom just behind him—a bathroom he seemingly didn't notice until someone came out of it, and not enough to realize that this was the main, and only, reason Catherine was looking in his direction. What was more, now that the bathroom had been relinquished, Catherine appeared to be walking straight toward him, his prayers apparently not falling on deaf ears.

But when Catherine then jumped into the bathroom— almost quite literally due to the urgency—and not into his arms as he might have imagined, Curtis was wrecked; and not just by the fifth of Stolichnaya that he had finished just before coming inside the library to find a bathroom himself, a quest which he had already forgotten about. Luckily for Curtis, however, though probably not as much for Catherine, she didn't take too long once inside the restroom. Perhaps she didn't take very long because she had no "operation" planned for that afternoon—not that they were usually planned for—and because it was easy for her to take care of business. She preferred it when things moved so quickly and easily. No fuss.

She hated fuss.

Outside the library, however, Catherine wasn't as quick. A bee's nest by the main doors caught her attention, but not because there were a considerable number of bees surrounding it. What caught her attention was the simple fact that there was a bee's nest at all, since she had destroyed one in the same location only days before with a long stick she had been using as a makeshift cane. The weather had been slightly warmer that day, and she thought she had batted it hard enough that it existed no more—but somehow it had reformed since she last visited the library. Surely it wasn't as big as before, but this was only because the bees hadn't finished building a new one just yet. It was a work-in-progress. Worse, they didn't seem the slightest bit upset, or surprised for that matter, that they had to start all over again rebuilding the nest. Almost as if they expected such a thing—and that was that. No big deal.

"But it *was* a big deal!" she wanted to scream at them. "You can't just start over again like that, and in the same place as before! Don't you see the danger in that? Rebuilding in the same exact area where you were annihilated before? Didn't you learn your lesson? How stupid are you!"

Nevertheless, the bees didn't want to listen to her; and now they weren't even trying to read her mind like they usually did. They simply didn't care. *But had they cared before?* she wondered. Maybe she had just thought they did.

These ricocheting thoughts concerning the bees allowed

for something else beyond Catherine's control. They gave Curtis enough time to relieve himself around the corner—near enough that he wasn't quite out-of-sight—and thus not lose a beat following her. He still hadn't realized that there had been a bathroom behind him inside the library—a warm place where his nuts wouldn't freeze off. But like the bees, even Curtis somehow survived—not to mention his balls—both due to shivering.

After the distraction of the bee's nest, which Catherine did destroy again, Curtis followed her for five blocks before he mustered up the nerve to say something to her. Catherine was so oblivious that she didn't notice Curtis behind her at any point, even considering his sheer ineptitude, which caused him to follow too closely. In Curtis' defense, there wasn't much he was good at, and this was only the third time he had ever followed someone—the previous two instances having not turned out well for either side.

She was thinking about the Pet Shop Boys for some reason—a rambling segue from the bees which, in her mind at least, flowed easily enough—specifically a song called "Love is a Bourgeois Construct," although she didn't know what "Bourgeois" or "Construct" meant. It had seemed to her that the song was simply about laziness, which was definitely something she could relate to; love, on the other hand, was *not* something she could relate to. Ever.

"Hello," Curtis said weakly to her after his body couldn't possibly follow her anymore, unintentionally interrupting her foggy reverie, which, unbeknownst to him, was her default setting.

"What?" she responded defensively; then, as a physical reflex, she turned her body away from him, as she was more used to getting attacked than flirted with.

"I'm just saying hello," he said calmly, as if not at all surprised by her reaction to him, this being his canned response to try and soothe her.

But instead of greeting him back with even just a nod of the head, Catherine responded to Curtis with, "Protractor says what?" An unusual response, even for her.

But like the true champion of inelegance that he was born to be, Curtis clarified his previous greeting accordingly and replied, "Protractor says hello," which he topped with a partial Myers-Briggs smile.

They looked at each other for a long, savage moment, but it wasn't a pause born out of awkwardness or shyness—though the former might have been expected due to their brief exchange about a measuring instrument mostly used in mathematics, and not, generally, an apparatus of courtship.

"The bees are back," Catherine said, her tone answering a question that had never been asked.

"I don't doubt that," Curtis replied. "They always come back."

In a way, Catherine was surprised by his response; in another way, however, she almost expected him to say this. And because he *had* said it, she was dangerously turned on—both by him and by what he had said. It was like she wanted him to keep saying what he had said over and over again, perhaps even while they fucked, which they would be doing in a matter of minutes.

"Why?" she asked him, although she didn't really want to know. It was one of those questions that she immediately wanted to take back out of fear it would actually be answered—and she wasn't in the mood for answers. She hardly ever was.

"Why what?" he asked, his tone also betraying his fear that she might, in fact, answer him. They were like hungry sharks swimming in a circle around something that wasn't really there, even though they could both smell it.

"Why do the bees come back?" she said, sounding like a child who had just learned what a bee was.

Curtis thought about this for a second while Catherine

anxiously waited, as she knew of no other way to wait, unfortunately.

"They just do," he said, sounding more sure than he actually was. Then he repeated these three words in the hope of at least convincing himself. "They just do."

She frowned and started to walk away, but then stopped, as if she had forgotten something. She gazed back at the library like it was the tombstone of someone she had once cared for but didn't want to visit anymore, its weathered bricks and withered wooden beams more distant now because they had walked further away than she thought. Brand new words started to form on her lips, although she had no idea what she was about to say. He didn't know what she was about to say either, but he seemed to like it that way. Somehow, though, she surprised them both.

"I'm a goner," she announced, as if strangely proud of it.

"So am I," he said, half-smiling but fully content.

BULWARK

They had beaten him up so badly this time that he almost died. He would have, had it not been for the intervention, yet again, of "Prison Drake" (a big fan of the Canadian hip hop artist, which also included emulating the rapper's famous beard), who usually seemed to be in the right place at the right time, at least as far as Miles' general health was concerned. Quite definitively, once Prison Drake stepped in whatever happened to be going on came to a dead stop. And those "concerned"—a dual meaning if ever there was one— would clear out as quickly as a human being could, all to avoid a thrashing by Prison Drake, which, more often than not, came to a stop only when the scent of death was palpable, the nearby guards merely looking on.

The inaugural savage bashing Miles received when he first arrived at the prison would have surely killed him—the so-called bashers a group of African-American inmates who didn't like the fact that Miles had committed a racially inspired hate crime (though Miles still maintained his innocence)—had Prison Drake not stepped in at the last minute. And the reason this most recent beating had gone on for too long—the prison guards, specifically the African-American ones, didn't seem at all inspired to break it up (the white guards, too, remained passive, barely watching for more than a few seconds at a time)—was because Prison Drake was busy breaking up another fight, defending a virgin inmate in the process of getting *his* welcome from an assortment of new friends. Prison Drake, not surprisingly, considered himself a type of superhero. He fought injustice whenever he saw fit, though sometimes he just stood by and observed, depending on who was on the receiving end of the violence.

The irony about saving Miles on more than one occasion was that Prison Drake, himself, was African-American; he just wasn't as quick as the others to rush to judgment. If there was any reasonable doubt at all, like there was in some of the other cases against fellow inmates, not to mention the one against him, he followed the book of law "to da teeth" as he called it. And no one was going to challenge Prison Drake's legal opinions.

The only fights that Prison Drake refused to break up, even if there was reasonable doubt involved—that he knew of—involved the pedophiles. "Deez sinners don't warrant no legal protections," he stated on more than one occasion. As long as one inmate accused another inmate of pedophilia— regardless of any evidence—that was good enough for Prison Drake. And if Prison Drake said it was so, then it was so.

This last time, as Miles was bleeding profusely from various orifices, and on Prison Drake to boot—the latter not seeming to mind—Prison Drake had to give a hard stare to one of the nearby guards in order to get his fallen brah tended to. Prison Drake referred to everyone as his "brah" no matter what their race happened to be, and "fallen" if they needed some type of help—especially from him.

"No wonder he mad," Prison Drake had been overheard as saying when the "Lord of the Underworld" came up in conversation, which was actually not as often as one might imagine—a free person's imagination, that is—considering the bleak backdrop the convicts all shared.

"He's probably more than a little mad," Miles had replied to Prison Drake when he was on the receiving end of this subject, even though he really didn't believe in that kind of stuff. Whenever you had a conversation with Prison Drake, you usually held your own beliefs aside—although he didn't like it if people just agreed with him out of the fear he might respond violently should he disagree. "And not *insane* mad, but *angry* mad," Miles clarified, then backpedaled a turn in order to better explain what he was trying to say. "Of course," Miles went on, "he's probably a little insane, too…." But then, thinking more clearly of what had just escaped from his mouth, added, "No offense."

"Offense?" Prison Drake repeated, as if not expecting that particular word to be tossed in his direction. "Why would I be offensed?" He smiled then, but not because he was trying to be funny—or clever or scary, as it seemed to Miles. "I'm not da Devils, obviously. You offensing him, not me." Then he said, in case Miles was still apprehensive, "'n you can offense him all day. No skin off my backs."

"Back," Miles corrected without thinking, then turned albino pale when he realized that might be the last word he ever spoke. But Prison Drake didn't kill him right then and there, as Miles was expecting. Instead, and to Miles' unmeasured relief, Prison Drake smiled again—and this facial expression couldn't be misinterpreted, even if the recipient was naturally averse to it.

"No skins off my *back*," Prison Drake tried again, somehow sounding pleased with himself. "Tank you."

"You're welcome?" Miles responded, though he wasn't really sure why he was getting thanked, especially since most of his mental energy was going toward preventing himself from automatically correcting the second-to-last word Prison Drake had just said. Miles seemed to have an urge to help Prison Drake—maybe to repay him for saving his life?—and couldn't have known that Prison Drake would have welcomed such an urge.

Miles had barely put a dent in his sentence when he was pounced on a third time, and saved yet again by Prison Drake—a man he would become unlikely friends with outside of jail, the seeds of their friendship sown amid adversity and mutual aid.

She was staring at him again and not saying anything. Miles was starting to get irritated—or, rather, *continuing* to be irritated. Lilly had visited him the week before as well, though "visiting" wasn't an entirely accurate term from either point of view, since to Lilly that meant "seeing a friend"— and a "friend" the killer of her son was certainly not. And to Miles, "visitors" were, at the very least, people who spoke— which didn't seem to be the case with Lilly. She apparently preferred to just stare at him, silently taking him in, trying to see what kind of person could kill another—or, more specifically, kill a man who was, to her, still a boy; to her, still a son.

"Why do you keep visiting me?" Miles said, destroying the silence with one violent slash and using the v-word as the jagged instrument. "I mean, don't get me wrong, I'm not complaining about getting a visitor, but if you're gonna come and just sit there, not saying anything…seems sort of pointless, doesn't it?"

"Pointless," she repeated, as if by accident; as if saying the word again, this time from her own lips, might somehow define it better—to her, to him, to the guard standing behind Miles with his back against the wall, seemingly holding it up for everyone.

She thought about the phrase "against the wall," which reminded her of when she first met Barry at the faux British pub he worked at. Because she wasn't much of a drinker back then and didn't yet know what kind of cocktail she might like, he had introduced sloe gin to her in a sweet drink called "Slow Comfortable Screw Up Against the Wall," with the "Against the Wall" part having to do with some big bottle of something which was usually kept flush against the back shelf of large bottles. But sloe gin didn't agree with her—not many sweet drinks did—and she ended up getting sick afterwards.

Thus, that "Slow Comfortable Screw Up Against the Wall" turned out to be her last, both literally and figuratively, as that sexual position was never quite comfortable for her— not even in her younger days, when she was more limber.

Lilly thought about the words "against the wall" in the environment she was currently seated in, and wondered whether the police had pushed Miles up against the wall when they arrested him for killing her son. If they had, had they hurt him? Looking across at him now, at his fragile youth and naïveté, both no doubt becoming swiftly hardened from living behind bars, she suddenly hoped that the police *hadn't* hurt him. *But why would she think such a thing?* she wanted to ask someone. Anyone. This boy had killed Owen. So why was she hoping no one hurt *him?* He *should* be hurt, and every goddamn day of his life, even after he got out of prison. *Actually*, she thought, *he should never get out of prison. He should spend the rest of his fuckin' loser life in this place!* Having just thought this, she surprised herself by what came out of her mouth next.

"What happened to your face?" she asked, noticing a slight discoloration under his right eye. *Had that been there last week when she was here?* she wondered. She couldn't remember.

He paused for a long moment before responding. This black eye, which wasn't so bad, was just from a minor pummeling in the showers a few days before, delivered by a new inmate who thought Miles had glanced at his ugly, uncircumcised penis. It was nothing out of the ordinary for Miles, of course, and nowhere near bad enough for Prison Drake to step in. Plus, someone else had interfered on Miles' behalf before it got too bad, since the guards didn't seem to care one way or the other.

"What do you mean?" Miles replied to Lilly, since, to him, his face was always in the middle of healing from some injury or another, whether from another inmate or self-inflicted—the latter of which was becoming all too frequent, often confusing Prison Drake. On a few occasions when Miles' own hand had been the source of a scratch on his face, or some other cosmetic wound, Prison Drake had been ready to pounce on whoever had done it, but after Miles explained that he had done it to himself Prison Drake eventually settled down, despite not understanding why Miles would do such a thing. The truth was Miles didn't know either, which he tried to tell Prison Drake when begged for an explanation.

"Nothing happened to my face," Miles added to Lilly, but then stopped himself, as he wanted to say more.

"Oh," Lilly returned quickly, though she didn't seem content about his answer. If Owen had ever come home with a face looking like that and answered her in the same way, she would have grilled him until she found out the truth; eventually, Owen would've caved in. She didn't know why, but she was fairly sure that Miles *wouldn't* cave in if she continued to question him—*especially* if she continued to question him—though this didn't stop her from trying.

"What happened to your friend?" she asked, as if on autopilot, the question hanging in the air like a trapped moth looking for light.

"Friend?" he echoed, like he was unfamiliar with the word. The truth was, as he sat there thinking about it, he didn't really have any friends—except for maybe Prison Drake. But Prison Drake was likely just a friend inside these walls; outside in the real world, he doubted the two of them—so very different—would ever be acquaintances, much less friends.

Lilly glanced at the guard behind Miles, who was still keeping the wall from falling. The guard looked down at his wristwatch, as if time itself could impede his job.

"What friend?" Miles repeated, possibly more curious about the *what* rather than the *who*.

Miles' voice brought Lilly back to the conversation and away from the possible collapse of the back wall.

"Oh…" she started. "The boy you were with…."

He waited, though now he knew who and what she was referring to—or at least he thought he knew. Nowadays he wasn't sure of anything.

She tried again. "The boy you were with when…." She got a word further, but only a word.

He waited again, but not with any malice. He wasn't trying to punish her by making her finish. He just wanted her to, and he thought that maybe she wanted to as well. But she couldn't—and not just because the guard behind Miles announced that it was time to wrap up. (*What would happen to the wall once the guard walked away?* Lilly thought anxiously. *Who will hold it up then?*)

"I don't know," Miles said, ignoring the fact that Lilly seemed more interested in something behind him. But then she turned her face toward him, so he said the three words again, definitively this time.

She looked confused suddenly, and he thought he knew why. Even though he had already answered her question—and twice now—they both seemed to understand that he was referring to something else entirely…

something else he didn't know.

INTERLOPER

No matter where he went, there were pregnant women. Always he would stare at them to such an extent that they would become uncomfortable, not that this was his intention. More often than not, they would think he was some type of creep who wanted to bed them. Accordingly, because these women didn't think any man in his right mind would be sexually interested in them due to their pregnant status—an assumption Amos could never comprehend—they would shift in their seats to make sure he could see their protruding bellies. This never worked for Amos, however, who was intent on them for other reasons—reasons which they could never know or understand.

He often used the name "Amos"—that is, if anyone happened to ask, as most would rarely get to the point of exchanging names, even if they stumbled into a conversation with him. Amos already knew *their* names, of course, so introductions were rather unnecessary as far as he was concerned. Like Catherine, who was one of the few who did talk to him, and for longer than most, the majority of women he decided to speak with, even briefly, would be too preoccupied to bother learning his name, which was just fine with Amos, since it meant one less lie.

Catherine was no different than the rest; Miles, on the other hand, *was* different, and not only because he happened to belong to an even more esoteric club: the offspring he would normally be finished with once they were born. But he wasn't finished with Miles, and although he knew why, he fought it just the same. True, young Miles had lashed out against figures of authority, which—not as an excuse of any kind—was "par-for-the-course" for a child growing up without a biological mother (or father, for that matter). But again, Amos knew this didn't give Miles a free pass to do as he saw fit. And now Miles was paying the price for it, serving out a prison sentence for something he may not have done in the first place; although, in ways that Miles couldn't understand, it didn't really matter if he had committed the crime or not.

Be that as it may, none of this mattered when Amos first visited Miles in jail—and Miles was more than a little puzzled. This was a normal reaction, Amos knew, especially considering the vagueness of it from the viewpoint of Miles. Here was a strange old man with no clear relation to anyone: the victim, the case in general, or even Miles' birth mother, who came up during the course of their conversation rather unexpectedly. Then again, was there *anything* Miles could expect? Was there anything *anyone* could expect? As it was, Amos had already interfered more than he was supposed to—especially since he wasn't supposed to interfere at all. This was the first rule, and he hadn't obeyed it.

This was bad. *Very* bad. And he knew it. So, when he visited Miles at the prison a second time, he really had no excuse.

But he didn't care. He wasn't supposed to care.

"You never answered me last time," Amos began after Miles finally sat down across from him in the Visitation Room—the latter only revealing the smallest hint of recognition, which the former wasn't even expecting. Most people didn't recognize him, although they often claimed they did.

"Answer what?" Miles returned quickly, already seeming irritated.

Amos stared back. It was obvious to both of them that there had been more than one unanswered question the last time Amos visited, which was more than two months before, but both remembered it as if it were only yesterday. For Amos, however, "yesterday" wasn't something he had to remember.

"The magic question?" Miles said, surprisingly, as that was exactly the question Amos had been referring to.

They looked at each other for a long moment, which seemed to be a favorite thing for Miles' visitors to do—his visitors being only Lilly and this old man—like he was a wild animal at a zoo they had come to see, and not a human being to actually talk to.

"Yes, the magic question," Amos said, revealing the first of several smiles that Miles would likely have to deal with.

Miles shifted in his seat, a simple folding chair the color of rust. "Why do you wanna know if I believe in magic? You a magician or something?"

Smile number two, and so quickly after number one. "Sort of," Amos said.

Miles shot a look of confusion over the bow. "Seriously?"

Smile number two was still lingering. "Well, not like the kind you might be imagining. I don't do kids' birthdays or anything." He chuckled, which to Miles was even more grating than his smile.

Miles then asked the question that had become his anthem of sorts. "What do you want?"

This time no smile. "We all believe in magic at some point in our lives."

"Well, guess what? I don't. And I never have."

"That's a shame."

"Not really."

"Oh?" Amos' facial expression froze. "Why's that?"

"Why's what?"

Amos was silent, meditative.

Miles looked down, as if the answer might be in his lap, like a crumb from a recent meal. "Because...who cares? Nothing's a shame, really."

"Oh?" Amos replied without the slightest pause. "It's not a shame that you're in jail right now?"

Miles thought about this for a few moments before answering. "Uh...I guess it is, but I probably deserve it anyway."

"Why do you deserve it?"

Miles closed his eyes heavily. He sighed, long and deep, as if gathering the energy to open his lids again. "Fuck, I don't know. All of us probably deserve it."

"Us being everyone behind bars?" Amos asked, even though he already knew the answer. He always seemed to know the answer, which was maybe why his questions all sounded rhetorical.

"You'll believe in magic at some point," Amos continued, as if Miles' protests were merely a gnat to swat away.

"I really don't think so, man."

"Amos."

"What?"

"My name is Amos. Call me Amos."

"Okay, *Amos*," Miles said, not even trying to hide his groundless animosity. Then he started to stand up, as if the guard behind him had called for time, even though nothing had been announced yet.

Amos smiled. "You don't want to stay for the rest of my visit?"

Miles laughed. "So, this is a *visit* to you? Doesn't seem like one to me."

"What does it seem like to you?"

"Fuck, man, now you sound like a shrink." Miles scoffed, then laughed again—although the laugh came out sounding like another scoff. "The magician shrink. He waves his wand over other people's problems and, *poof*, they all disappear." Miles was standing now, and made no effort to either sit down again or start walking back to his cell.

"Not exactly," Amos said, holding his tone without deviating one way or the other. "If only it worked that way—"

"What way?" Miles interrupted, his previous agitation no longer audible, but still standing in the same place, almost hovering.

"Good question," Amos replied, "although, sadly, I don't know how to answer it."

"What do you mean?" Miles tried again. "How can you not know how to answer it? Seems simple enough to me."

"Maybe you're asking the wrong question," Amos stated matter-of-factly, unveiling another smile, one which didn't seem to annoy Miles anymore.

The guard nearest Miles announced a time warning, but instead of wrapping it up as ordered, Miles relented to the conversation and sat back down. Noticing this, the guard repeated his announcement twice as loud, his eyes now focused on Miles.

"What's the right question?" Miles ventured, already seeming to know that Amos probably wasn't going to tell him but asking anyway.

"The question that should precede that one."

Miles shot up again from his chair, his aggravation with Amos returning just as quickly. "I can't deal with your vagueness anymore, Yoda. This is real life."

Amos laughed. "Yes, it certainly is."

The guard made his announcement a third time, as Miles and one other prisoner on the far side of the room had yet to commit to leaving the visitation area.

"I think I'm being quite clear, actually," Amos said, standing up on the other side of the partition in such a way as to prove how much he meant it.

Miles noticed the other visitor, who hadn't yet stood up from her lopsided seesaw now that the other prisoner had left. "That's who you'll be visiting next time," Miles said sharply, gesturing at her invisible relation.

"I hope not," Amos replied.

Miles nodded at the guard and started for the door, but then turned once more to face Amos. "Well, you probably like talking to ghosts."

"Not really," Amos said flatly, leaving Miles and the guard to stare at each other, dumbfounded.

Disney World was *not* "The Happiest Place on Earth," at least as far as Sawyer was concerned. It was actually not even close to "The Happiest Place on Earth," nor even on a *list* of happiest places (again, if Sawyer had any say in the matter). *But then*, he wondered, *who did? Who the fuck made this decision without actually asking anyone else what* their *opinion was? And these fuckin' athletes who just won the Super Bowl or whatever—why the hell were* they *in such a hurry to go to this God-forsaken place known as Disney World? If anything*, Sawyer thought, *it might just be the* least *Happiest Place on Earth, and thus a great place to kill yourself*—which was exactly why he chose it as the perfect location to put a bullet in his head.

He didn't have the Walther P99 anymore, as that was the so-called "murder weapon," which the police had found near Owen's body. There was nothing Sawyer currently had with him that he personally owned other than the clothes on his back, though even that was questionable; everything else was either his father's or stolen. As far as guns were concerned, Sawyer still had one of his father's 9mm Lugers, although it was a modern remake and not one of the more expensive WWII pistols that the Nazis had used. Lt. Col. Ramirez owned a few of those too, but they were kept in a safe that Sawyer could never figure out how to open, even if he had known the combination—which he didn't, despite some solid efforts to figure it out. It was *that* type of safe, the kind you needed to watch a YouTube video about in order to fully understand (Sawyer had tried that, too, but he was never very good at digesting "how-to" instructions).

Sawyer wasn't trying to be ironic when he chose the "It's a Small World" ride as the perfect place to kill himself. It was dark enough, and as long as he went on the ride during a non-busy time—if that even existed—it would work fine. Plus, what did he really care if a child accidentally saw him do it? It wasn't like *he* had been protected as a child. So why should he care about not ruining another kid's life? Although Sawyer felt suicide was the most honest endeavor someone could undertake, he was more than a little concerned that a Disney World employee would see him with the gun and call the police, which would surely prevent him from committing the deed. Of course, if an employee did happen to spot him before he was able to do it, they would have no idea Sawyer's only intention was to shoot himself and not harm anyone else—but once a person was seen with a gun in a public place, not to mention one ripe with children, it really didn't matter what the shooter had planned.

As macabre as it sounded—and in the end probably irrelevant, at least with regard to *how* dead Sawyer needed to be in relation to time passing—the one thing Sawyer had trouble deciding was *where* to shoot himself. He knew that through the roof of his mouth and into his brain was the quickest way, but it seemed so graphic with all that shit blasting out the back of his skull. Then again, what did he care? He would be dead, after all, and it would only suck for the person who had to clean it up. *What a shitty job that was*, Sawyer had thought as he slowly walked toward the "It's a Small World" ride, still unsure of how he would carry the whole thing out.

In the end, however, as far as that day was concerned, it was goddamn Steven Spielberg who ultimately stopped him from doing it; and not, as it should have been—at least location-wise—the popsicle of the man who once was Walt Disney (and arguably, since his body was currently frozen, *still* Walt Disney). It was all the shit-ass grinning children everywhere, each of whom seemed like they were living in a fuckin' magical Spielberg film where nothing bad could possibly happen. Or, if it somehow did happen—the bad thing—it would be eradicated almost as swiftly as it occurred, thus leaving the happy ending as intact as usual, with the standard sprinkling of John Williams' fairy dust to go along with it.

In hindsight, Sawyer wondered how all these happy-go-lucky children didn't affect him in another way, motivating him even further to be rid of this densely powdered, high-fructose world. There was too much friggin' hope in the air, clinging to everyone like angry pollen. And hope was one thing that Sawyer couldn't deal with, as it usually reared its ugly head at the most inopportune times, just when it didn't seem right to battle it. Sometimes, Sawyer knew, whether you wanted it to or not, you just had to let hope win out.

MURMUR

She had just put a pillow over her face to dull the sound of her moaning when the phone rang, interrupting her orgasm so abruptly that it was almost like she never came at all. The guy she was with, whose name she couldn't remember, didn't even stir when her phone started ringing, likewise making no effort to move his large-framed body off of Elodie so that maybe she could answer it, were she so inclined.

Which she was, removing the two immediate obstacles—the pillow and him—and grabbing the call right before it went to voicemail.

"Hello?"

She was silent for a moment—listening, concentrating—until her breath became known; her inhales competing with her exhales, and losing. Still, the guy who just moments ago had lain on top of her, was just a moment ago inside of her, made no movements at all. Even as she started to cry, wail, burst at the seams, he continued to not defer to her or commiserate with her whatsoever. Like the phone call was a temporary nuisance that would be over soon enough, and then they could continue fucking, maybe even get her to come again—this time hopefully without the pillow over her face.

She quickly turned to him, as if seeing him for the first time, like a cockroach she'd just spotted flitting away on top of the bed covers. "Get the fuck out!" Elodie screamed, not bothering to control her sonic flare of repugnance, or even pulling the phone away from her mouth—which she then had to account for. "Sorry," she said into the phone, "that wasn't for you."

She waited again, patiently listening to the voice on the other end of the line as if she were suddenly a completely different person—one who never lost their temper no matter what the circumstance. It was this, although not too swiftly, that turned out to be the tonic to get this strange man out of her bed and apartment; ignoring him, evidently, spoke louder than words. By then, however, she was almost off the phone, after learning that her father had died unexpectedly—*very* unexpectedly, and not just to her, but to 531 other people as well. The word "died" or even "passed away" didn't have enough synonyms for her. And a phone—especially a cell-phone—could never be intimate enough for such news, the end of a life indefinable with vulgar ones and zeros.

When Elodie hung up, it was like she was hanging up on her father, as if she had just snuffed the last of his life away by lightly touching the button to end the call. This was the first regret concerning her father's death—the one to kick it all off—but she couldn't *un*-hang up the phone. It was already done. Her life with him was already done. Her father was no more.

He had died of a heart attack on a plane—or so they said. Fortunately it hadn't taken off yet, but it was next-in-line on the tarmac. Her father had waited until the plane returned to the gate and the crew began the procedure for evacuating him before he took his last breath. Though this wasn't as rare as Elodie thought it might be, it still seemed too outrageous to believe; like the type of thing that only happened in movies. Fathers died—sure—but not on airplanes full of people.

"What did the other passengers do?" she asked her aunt later that day, when the family gathered at her mother's house.

"What does it matter what the other passengers did?" her father's only sister, Aunt Ray, replied. "It only matters what your father did."

"What?" Elodie said, almost yelling it. "What he did? He died, that's what he did!"

Aunt Ray laughed, which sounded more like an extended chuckle. *Why was she laughing?* Elodie wondered, wanting to scream at her aunt for doing so at such a time. *It wasn't funny!*

Elodie thought about what she would have done had the person sitting next to her on an airplane suddenly suffered a heart attack and died. It reminded her (rather shamefully, since it had been her father) of the movie *Weekend at Bernie's*. Was that the way it would have been, having a corpse sitting next to you that was alive only minutes before and therefore still resembled a person, but which had no control of its own gravity anymore, flopping over from side to side in the seat, requiring a live person to push it back upright?

"I hear the killer of that boy you…" Aunt Ray searched for the right word.

"Dated?" Elodie quickly said, filling the space her aunt had left gaping like a new sinkhole. "My ex-boyfriend, you mean?"

"*Please*," Aunt Ray squeaked out, as if she suddenly smelled a bad odor. "That colored boy wasn't your boyfriend…dear God!"

Elodie was already walking away, but couldn't help herself from turning back to face her aunt. "*Colored? Really?*" She walked a few more feet, then stopped and turned again. "This is the 21st century, Aunt Ray. People don't use that word anymore."

Seemingly ignoring the distance her niece had carved out between them, Aunt Ray said, "Oh right, what is that word you young people use now? I mean, this whole *politically correct* thing is just absurd! 'African-Americano' or some such nonsense? They aren't from Africa any more than we are!"

"It's African-Ameri*can*, and actually—"

Elodie's mother interrupted them both then—sounding, as she usually did in these situations, like a game show host. "What are we talking about over here? I think people can hear you two all the way to the west coast!" Her mother also liked to exaggerate.

"Blame *her*, Mom," Elodie said. "*She's* the racist."

"I think we're all racist, honey," her mother returned too fast, still sounding like Bob Eubanks talking down a suddenly embarrassed newlywed. But then, realizing that other people may have overheard her, she added, "At least a little bit."

Elodie could only stare at her mother, unable to even mumble a syllable.

"That's true," Aunt Ray commented, as if someone had asked her opinion. She frequently offered her conclusions this way, like they were vital to recorded history.

As Elodie successfully walked away this time, she thought about what her aunt had probably started to say a few minutes before: that Owen's killer might be getting released from prison. She had heard that, too, although she didn't know why it was happening, since he had hardly served out his whole sentence. Regardless, it wasn't fair. To only serve a few years for murder and even be *considered* for early release? What kind of a world was this? Maybe her mother and Aunt Ray were right. Maybe the world *was* racist. After all, Elodie was almost sure that had it been the other way around—a black boy killing a white boy—the killer would probably be given the death sentence. *The whole thing's a fuckin' joke*, Elodie thought.

It reminded her of a short story she had written when she was in ninth grade. She didn't remember much about it other than the ending, not even the title, and she usually remembered things like that. What Elodie hadn't forgotten were the last two or three sentences of the story, which was only a page and a half in its entirety, double-spaced:

He got in bed next to his sleeping wife and turned the light off. Then he laughed, finally getting the joke his co-worker had told him that day. And his wife didn't even wake up.

Standing alone now in the middle of the room, everyone dressed in black but her—she was more in an *off*-black—she thought of Owen's laugh and started to cry. But then she stopped. It didn't feel right to cry for Owen after so much time had passed, especially since today was specifically meant for her father. She was supposed to be crying for *him* and only him. But when she thought about her father's passing, all she could think of was, *Where was he going?* Like, *where was the plane flying to?* And why wasn't her mother with him? He had long been retired. And, *what airline was it? American? United?* Why hadn't anyone told her? This was important information! Maybe it was worth speaking with the passenger who sat next to him—but what if her father wasn't on the aisle, or next to the window? *Maybe it was only two seats?* But if it was three seats across and he was in the middle, then there were *two* people sitting next to him, which meant there were two people she needed to talk to. Why didn't she know, though, which seat her father preferred? *Window or aisle?* Although, she realized, it was possible he preferred the middle. Why, she would have no idea, but she supposed there were people that just preferred the middle for some reason. She would see them sitting there on half-empty airplanes and always wonder what was up with them. *Were they retarded?*

"Where was he going?" Elodie yelled to her mother, who was in the middle of a conversation a few feet away. She didn't recognize who her mother was talking to. *Wasn't this gathering only meant for friends and family?* Elodie wondered. This guy her mother was speaking with was neither—or, at least, she knew he wasn't family.

Her father had *friends?*

Elodie's mother flashed one of her real estate agent smiles, which was code for "Please don't embarrass me"—but this was nowhere near enough to keep Elodie from asking the question again, and *again*, until a sufficient answer was given. Both of them knew this.

"Why weren't you sitting next to him? Where were you?" Elodie shouted, as if her mother might have saved her father had she been on the plane with him. But she hadn't been, and now her father was dead—just like Owen. Heaven was too big for the two of them to run into each other; not to mention, her father didn't even know Owen. She had wanted to introduce him, and to her mother as well, but it was too soon—too soon to ask it of Owen—although she was sure he would have done it if she needed him to. He was that type of guy—the type of guy she would never meet again.

"Stop it!"

Her mother was suddenly standing next to her, cloaked in black—real black—the strange man she'd been talking to no longer in sight, as if he had only been an apparition.

My father's an apparition now....

"Stop what?"

"You know damn well."

So is Owen....

"I was only asking a question—"

"A ridiculous question."

Will I be a ghost, too, when I die?

"It's not ridiculous. *You're* ridiculous."

But her mother had disappeared now, off the wrestling mat but with no points given to either side, set adrift back into the sea of black.

Elodie was so tired of everything: fighting with her mother, going to sleep at night, waking up in the morning, taking a shower, blow-drying her hair.... She didn't want to do any of it anymore. Her father couldn't fly on an airplane without dying, and it hadn't even crashed. *It wasn't even in the air!*

How does that happen? And why had she never heard of anything like that before? Her friends' dads died of cancer and car accidents and things like that; things that were common and explainable. She had never even heard of anyone dying like this in the movies—and that was make-believe! Writers could imagine anything happening on the big screen, but they had never imagined anything like this—at least as far as she knew. She was actually embarrassed to tell her friends how her father had died. Hopefully, they wouldn't ask. It wasn't such an easy question to answer, or probably even ask. Even the way Owen had died—although fitting for Hollywood—was just as preposterous. *He wasn't a rapper for God's sake, involved in some type of drive-by! He didn't even have any enemies*—as far as she knew—*so how and why had he been shot and killed in broad daylight? And by a white boy, no less?*

Elodie had heard that the boy serving time in jail for the crime—the one who might be getting out soon—was white, but he wasn't the same white boy that the media first reported as the shooter: a kid with a Pee-Wee Herman tattoo, who also happened to be her "ex"—if you could even call him that—a fact she kept from the police even though she never stopped thinking that maybe Owen had somehow been shot because of her (and not just because he was retrieving her iPhone). They had barely dated—her and Sawyer—and had never slept together. Not totally. He didn't seem interested, which, at first, she took personally, but then realized that maybe she just wasn't his type—if his type was female at all. Initially, the DA had mentioned on TV that the guy with the Pee-Wee Herman tattoo was "in the wind"—a phrase she had never heard before—and had left the other guy "holding the bag." But as far as Elodie was concerned, since the killers were supposedly friends—"ex" or not—they *both* deserved to die, or at least rot in jail for the rest of their lives, no matter which one of them had actually pulled the trigger. But now they had found some new evidence to bring Sawyer in and keep him there, or so she'd heard, and a massive manhunt was underway. Someone came up behind Elodie then and hugged her. She wasn't even sure at first who it might be, as in the past this role was performed mostly by her father; he was the one usually sensitive to her feelings, wanting her to feel better above all else. When she was little and cried a lot for no particular reason, he was the one who always offered to take her for ice cream or some other sweet errand. Not that he was always on her side—"Elodie's great defender" as her mother put it—because if she messed up, he would also be among the first to let her know. He just wanted her to be the best human she could possibly be, to learn from her mistakes as well as her successes. She had often asked him what she could learn from her successes, since learning from her mistakes seemed an obvious one, and he had told her that, "Sometimes, learning from your successes can be even more fruitful than learning from your mistakes." This coming from a man who, at the time, was making plenty of mistakes himself—at least according to her mother—leading up to the divorce. And then, before the divorce was even final, he decided to have a fatal heart attack on a commercial airliner. The divorce papers actually arrived two afternoons later, indifferent as to whether both recipients were still alive or not.

As for the person hugging Elodie from behind, it turned out to be a semi-stranger, or at least the last person she expected it to be: an outsider with a taut body and large, muscular hands...

and a tattoo of Pee-Wee Herman.

But then she woke up from this horrible nightmare, her sweat-drenched body stuck to the bottom sheet like an insect trap, the only webbed fragment still lingering that of her father dying on American Airlines flight 2025 to New York...

the one part that wasn't a dream.

UMBRELLA

He had learned in prison that people with scars usually have a story to tell. And now he had scars. Maybe not visible ones, but he definitely had a story to tell. The only problem was that no one would listen, for when he walked out of jail with summer still officially lingering, no one would be waiting to greet him other than the premature fall weather (and perhaps the media, who his lawyer had mentioned after they won the appeal).

"The court has decided in your favor," Holcomb had said that day, "but that doesn't mean the public has as well...or will."

"But the evidence against me is circumstantial," Miles had pleaded, showing off one of the legal words he had learned. "Sawyer pulled the trigger, not me. They know that now, which is why I'm getting out. Isn't that what you told me?"

"Everything's circumstantial in this case, son. I'm not even sure they can convict your friend."

"He's not my friend."

"Sorry, I mean the other kid."

"They're still gonna arrest him, though, right?"

Holcomb laughed. "If they can find him."

And now Miles was getting out, and he should have known there wasn't even an off-chance that someone would be waiting to receive him in the real world—for one simple reason: he didn't know anyone anymore. Certainly, his foster family wouldn't be there; in the five years that had passed, the Kellys had probably adopted someone else and forgotten all about him. And the Rockefellers—*his* Rockefellers, the poor ones—were long gone; as were the Levensons and anyone else who might have cared about him. Not "dead" gone, just "Miles" gone.

Though he didn't consider himself as someone who had seen a lot of movies, Miles couldn't help but think of one as he walked out of the prison that day—a free man (*was he a man now?*)—but even in the movies, there was always someone waiting; it didn't matter how bad the guy was who'd served the time, or what he had supposedly done to be locked up in the first place. There was that word again: "Supposedly." But Miles knew, just in time for "day one" back in the real world—a term Prison Drake (who would be getting his own walking papers soon) liked to use—that adverbs couldn't be part of his life anymore. This, too, was something Prison Drake liked to dwell on, despite the fact that he didn't know what an adverb specifically was. He just knew it wasn't the right way to think if you wanted to move forward. As much as Prison Drake liked to learn new words and new things, he knew enough that looking backward served no purpose. It brought anger and resentment and "God know what else" (as Prison Drake often said, declaring furthermore that, "Some tings betta left wit' da Lord Almighty").

After his personal effects were returned to him (consisting of the wages he was due, an almost-empty pack of unfiltered Camels, and a porcelain monkey key chain with only one key on it, which he couldn't remember the purpose of—nor where the porcelain monkey came from), Miles walked out into the autumn-like world awaiting him, making his way to an idling cab they had ordered for him—although he still had no idea where he would tell the driver to go. Not having a real-world destination yet wasn't a surprise for Miles, as he'd been worrying about this problem ever since his first day of freedom became a possible reality, but the way it made him *feel* was unexpected. He hadn't anticipated that the words

"I don't know" would have such gravity, such definition—
although the taxi driver didn't seem very surprised by this
confession, nor by the barrage of media waiting for Miles to
exit the prison, which almost prevented him from making
it to the cab's passenger-side door. It was like the driver was
prepared for such vagueness; as if this were a common issue
for newly released prisoners. *Did this same guy drive everyone?*
Miles wondered.

So maybe Miles wasn't the first or only one to be unwanted
anywhere coming out of prison, but that didn't make it feel
any better when he finally relented to saying the three words
out loud. He'd had five years to think of *somewhere* to go—
anywhere!—so confessing that he ultimately came up emp-
ty-handed sounded wrong in every possible way. The three
words "I love you" could be inflected from different directions, he figured, but not the three words "I don't know."
When you admitted to such a thing as that, there was really
only one way to say it.

Before the cabbie could drive off to "We'll just figure it out
once we get moving, okay, champ?"—*Did he say this to all
the convicts who had no place to go? Did he call them all champ
to boot?*—Miles began a seemingly endless song of coughing
and clearing his throat, as if the mucous he wanted to be
rid of flat-out refused to leave. It grew so annoying that it
actually bothered Miles more than the driver—at least as far
as Miles could tell. *Was the cabbie used to this type of anxious
behavior?* The address Miles had made up wasn't entertained
by the driver whatsoever, as if he knew the destination was
bullshit before Miles even stepped into the cab. *Did other
prisoners make up bullshit addresses? It wasn't as if they were
model citizens of integrity,* Miles figured, *so maybe no one in
the real world would trust their answers regardless, even if they
turned out to be true.*

What did pause Miles in his coughing fit was a knock on
the cab's window right by his head, just as they started to

move, startling Miles enough to make him jump. When he turned to find the source of this invasion and saw that it was Lilly, he just stared in profound bemusement, having no idea what the hell she could be doing there. Before he could ask her, however, Miles noticed a guard standing behind her. He seemed to want to talk to Miles, which only became apparent once he took over the cab window knocking privileges, and enthusiastically so.

"You have a visitor," the guard said, not even waiting for the window to be completely rolled down. And how could he have a visitor, Miles wanted to ask, if he was no longer an inmate?

...or was he?

"No shit," Miles almost said, but instead replied, "Oh?" as if he didn't see Lilly standing there.

"Do you need a ride?" Lilly asked without a pinch of irony. This was proven by Miles' driver quickly turning the engine off, as if he expected Miles to get out of the cab and didn't want to waste any more gas if he could help it.

Just as Miles hadn't figured out yet where he wanted to go, he was also unable to come up with an immediate answer to Lilly's basic-sounding question. *But what was she doing there?* he wondered. More importantly, why was she offering him a ride?

Before Miles could think too deeply about it, however, the cab driver interrupted again, this time with his voice.

"Sorry to break up the family reunion, but who's gonna pay me for waiting?"

As he and Lilly drove out of the prison—Miles in the passenger seat, like a dog as excited to be going somewhere as it was nervous where that might be—he half-expected the

assembled media to follow them outside the main security gate, or that their car would be swarmed by protesters
once they were clear of the prison's periphery. But this was
only because he had heard something about it from the
other inmates, who put it in his head like a bullet of anxiety
(although "other inmates" was really just Prison Drake).

But this time Prison Drake had been wrong, as the media
stayed where they were—in a clump—and the protesters
outside the gate barely broke single digits. And not because
the "Black Lives Matter" movement wasn't upset about Miles
getting released after only five years; it was more because
there had been so many thousands of hate crimes in the
last half-decade that demand for protesters clearly exceeded
supply—not to mention that the media severely suffered
from ADD, especially when other high-profile events followed each other too closely. The more stories the better,
especially after five years; also, it was no longer referred to as a
hate crime (despite the race card played in an attempt to turn
the case in that direction). Now it was generally accepted as
a senseless act committed by a drugged-out kid—or *kids*, as
it may have been—and that, cliché as it sounded, the victim
had merely been in the "wrong place at the wrong time." But
there was no advocacy group for unlucky people who were
born that way, or for people who *became* unlucky in some
form or another over time.

Surprisingly, Lilly appeared to read his mind and followed
his gaze. "You were expecting more angry people with signs,
huh?" she asked.

The question seemed rhetorical, but he answered her
anyway, as it was important to him that he acknowledge her.

"I would probably feel the same way," Lilly offered after he
told her that he'd had nightmares about it. She looked across
the vacant road at the ripe farmland passing by. There wasn't
another person or vehicle in sight, as if they were the last two

people on the planet after an apocalypse both had somehow survived—whether or not they had meant or wanted to.

He felt weird telling her about his nightmares, or anything personal for that matter, but he had sprung a leak. It was like he couldn't control what came out of his mouth—although it was inherently okay that it did, even if nothing made sense. He still wasn't sure why she had picked him up from the prison, or even how she knew that he was leaving that day. Then again, if the media knew it made sense that she would have known, too. But again, it didn't make sense that she was driving him now—and where were they going? She hadn't even asked him for directions. Did that mean she knew he had no place to really go? *How much did she know, anyway?* he wondered, grinding his teeth together in agitation.

They had driven several miles away from the prison before he was finally able to ask the question that he'd been meaning to ask her for five years—the one that hovered over all the rest. "Why are you being so nice to me?" he asked.

"Why *are* you being so nice to him?" Dr. Stevens asked. "He killed your son—"

"He *might* have killed my son," Lilly interrupted.

"Why? Because they're after that other kid now?"

Lilly sniffed and looked at the ceiling. "Even if he did, it doesn't matter."

"Even if who did?"

"It doesn't make a difference," she said, sighing audibly. "It's not like it will bring Owen back either way, will it?"

Dr. Stevens stared at her. She wasn't trying to sound clever, only pointing out the obvious. Why she was trying to point out the obvious to her shrink, though, she didn't know. *Wasn't that* his *job?* she wanted to ask. But like a shrink, or at least a good one—and reminded her of the reason she had continued to see him these past several years—he read her mind.

"Can't argue with the glaring truth of it," he said, a smile spreading across his face like the sun steadily rising above the horizon. "Another answer, and the one I prefer actually, is that he's letting you."

"What?"

"He wonders why you're being so nice to him—Miles—which I do, too, of course, because it's my job to. And your answer could be because he's letting you be nice to him."

Lilly stared at him blankly—not for the first time, and not for the last.

"It's from *The Breakfast Club*," he said, outwardly proud of himself like he usually was with his abundance of movie references. And he knew enough now that she didn't need to say anything else for him to continue. "Allison asks Claire: 'Why are you being so nice to me?' Claire was the princess of the group, remember? Molly Ringwald's character? And Allison—"

He stopped. Lilly's face was a blank screen.

"In any case," he went on, "Claire answers: 'Because you're letting me.'" He grinned at Lilly, not with childish pride in his '80s pop culture knowledge but, rather, a paternal softness that consented.

A long moment passed until the proverbial light bulb went on.

"Why wouldn't Miles let me be nice?" she said, both of them realizing that this was the first time she had said his name out loud in session (and unbeknownst to Dr. Stevens, the first time she had said his name out loud period, even to the subject himself).

Dr. Stevens shifted in his chair. "Do you think Miles forgives himself?" he asked, taking advantage of the fact that this was finally out in the open.

"I don't...I think he's confused. Like I said, he doesn't even know if he did it."

"He knows whether he did it," Dr. Stevens interjected.

"But the drugs—"

Dr. Stevens shook his head. "Even with the drugs. Maybe not at first, but by now—"

"So, memory comes back after a time?" she asked.

"It can," he said, his backstep not going unnoticed by either of them. "But I think he knows...." That mischievous smile again. "Call it an educated guess," he added.

Silence.

"I think you know what my next question is going to be?"

She sat up straight. "Whether I forgive him?"

He waited.

"I don't know..." she started again after a long moment. "I want to, but only because—"

"He needs you to?"

She laughed, and he joined her.

"Did I read your mind?" he asked.

She continued to laugh, but then stopped abruptly, as if she had just remembered that she wasn't allowed to laugh. Her son was dead. He wasn't coming back. Ever. Laughing wasn't a luxury she could afford anymore.

"It's okay," he said, and repeated it as her laughs turned to sobs. But they both knew that he wasn't simply trying to console her. Like he often did, he meant something else as well.

SHOULDER

His biggest mistake was coming home.

Sawyer hadn't come back for Miles—at least not initially. He read that Miles was getting out of prison, but he knew this anyway because he had been keeping track. In fact, Sawyer had been keeping count on how much time Miles had left in prison more closely than Miles had been doing himself, although this was mainly due to the fact that Miles had discovered, like a lot of inmates, that time would move faster if he didn't think about it. Still, Sawyer's devotion to his former friend's circumstances never faltered during the five years of Miles' prison stay—and he did consider Miles as his friend (at least most days).

What Sawyer didn't know was that since Miles had been released, he had been seeing a hypnotist regularly to try to unlock his memory of the incident that had sent him to prison in the first place. Whether it was ironic or not, or just *how* ironic, Lilly had been the one who had referred Miles to the hypnotist, although she had claimed, mostly to Dr. Stevens, that it had nothing to do with her forgiveness of Miles' participation in the crime—regardless of whether or not he had been the one who actually pulled the trigger. Social media was still uncertain as well: the argument for each kid as the shooter went either way, and the public seemed equally divided.

Lilly hadn't even said the words "I forgive you" to Miles, despite the fact that he'd been living in her basement since he got out of jail; and though Miles didn't know why she had offered him this temporary goodwill, and maybe some compassion to go along with it, he had taken her up on her kind offer nevertheless, as he had no other place to stay. He knew it wasn't permanent, but as long as people were offering Band-Aids—or, in this case, just Lilly—he would accept them without questioning, too much, any possible motives.

After she picked Miles up on the day he'd gotten out of jail, Lilly had been ostensibly armed with canned answers should he ask questions like, "What the hell's going on?" or, "Where the hell are we going?" But he didn't ask either question, no matter how reasonable they may have been at the time; and though she was most likely overflowing with confusion about her own behavior, just as he was, Lilly did something she didn't think she could do, at least that day: she let it go.

Regardless of how much, or how little, was uncovered by Miles at the hypnotist, this was the one thing Sawyer couldn't do: let go. In some ways, the fact that Sawyer had come back was more surprising to Miles than Lilly picking him up from prison and offering him a place to stay—and without him even asking a single question, let alone the obvious one, which was easily the most fundamental.

Sawyer had come back to Durham for one reason—at least the only one he would openly admit—despite the manhunt that was underway: ketamine. In Orlando, he'd struck out finding "Special K" and was referred to a dealer in North Carolina—an irony he didn't share with the person who told him this, as it was nobody's business where he was from originally. Sawyer wasn't about to tell some low-level sweatpants-wearing O-town dealer whom he had found on Craigslist that Bull City was actually his home. It surprised Sawyer that it was so hard to find "K" in central Florida, as he remembered a trip there a few years before where it was readily available at most of the downtown clubs (at least the sublingual variety). But somehow it was hard to find now, especially with all the fake "K" floating around—some of which he'd heard was toxic. He didn't care, though, if he got a bad batch of ketamine; the chance of falling into a "K-hole" was worth it. And if that wasn't enough, it seemed to help his depression—at least at first. All told, it was quite possibly the best drug he'd ever taken. Injecting it right into his muscle made him feel like he had died—in a good way. It was as if he could feel his soul actually leaving his body. The disassociation between his mind and his body was simply beyond explanation, and the soul-leaving part made him feel almost religious, like there really was a God and everything that people believed was true.

Then again, maybe he deserved something toxic from a luck perspective. Sawyer didn't have time for guilt. It was all Russian roulette in any event, so maybe it was about time to load a bullet in the chamber.

As it turned out, Sweatpants' Durham associate also sold guns, and favored very casual wear like his Florida counterpart. "If I ever get pinched," he had joked when he noticed Sawyer staring at one of his Glocks, "I'll be going away for a long time anyway." He laughed then, revealing a David Letterman-type gap in the front of his teeth and a slight chip at the bottom of one of his canines. Sawyer had wondered whether the chip came from someone pistol-whipping him in the mouth—maybe even from one of his own guns. *Wouldn't that be ironic?* Sawyer had thought, but didn't end up asking him about it. He had gotten bored with the guy before their transaction was even over, and Sawyer ended up buying the Glock, too. *It didn't hurt to be protected*, Sawyer had reasoned with himself, especially since he had left all his guns down in Florida, planning to return as soon as possible. He didn't feel safe in Durham, as if one of his long-ago fuck-overs would be gunning for him—although which fuck-over it would be, he couldn't guess. There were too many that probably wanted to see him dead. But you weren't anything until you had enemies—or, at least, that was one of Sawyer's mottos, which he falsely attributed to himself (it was actually a hacked-up version of a Winston Churchill quote).

Back at his downtown motel after meeting the "Special K" dealer, as Sawyer was thinking about his Durham fuck-overs, Miles didn't even cross his mind at first—although, and arguably so, he had fucked over Miles more than anyone else. But then a news story came on the TV about a shooting outside a bookstore, which reminded him of Owen, and then Miles, and then that Miles had recently gotten out of jail. Maybe he should pay him a visit, Sawyer thought, only then realizing that he had no idea where Miles might be. And even if he did somehow find Miles, how would his old friend react to seeing him after all this time? *It probably wouldn't be good*, he realized.

As was Sawyer's customary flow of luck, on top of his need for caffeine—especially when he was regulating back from "K," which usually made him feel tired—he found Elodie at the same coffee shop that she used to frequent (and apparently still did). "Surprise, surprise," he had joked loudly as soon as he was close enough for her to hear his wan attempt at wittiness.

But when she turned around and recognized who it was, which took a few seconds (as Sawyer's hair was even longer now), she was anything but playful. "What hole did you climb out of?" she asked, hopefully rhetorically, then walked away before he had the chance to answer.

"Wait!" he called after her.

She turned around unwillingly, as if the slower she faced him the better the chance he might disappear back to where he came from. "What?"

"I'm just saying hi. That's all. Jesus. What the hell's wrong with you?"

"What the hell's wrong with *me?*" she repeated, as if she needed to say it again in order to fully understand it.

He changed tactics. "I just got back to town…was hoping I would run into you."

Elodie stared back, unsure of what she wanted to do or say next. "Well, congratulations," she muttered. "You found me. Hurrah."

"Seriously," he started again. "Do you live here? I mean, you're always here."

"I live down the street, so…what do you want?"

He stared back, finally registering that he might be running down her patience.

"You okay?" she said, softening a little. "You don't look so good."

"I'm a little dizzy," he admitted, not realizing just how dizzy he was until he said it out loud. "You don't happen to know where I can find Miles, do you?"

It was getting harder to talk, and the last question seemed to surprise her just as much as it surprised himself—the words escaping from his lips as if he had put too much food into his mouth.

"Who?" she replied too quickly, giving herself away. "Why are you asking *me?*"

He stopped. She was right. Why would she know where he was? *They weren't that serious, were they?*

"I think he's staying at *her* house," she said, accentuating the word "her" like he would secretly understand who she meant just by her nuance.

She was wrong.

"*Her* house?"

"You're really tan," she said, catching them both by surprise.

"Well, I live in Florida, and I work construction, so—"

"Your hair's still…" she started, but then stopped just as quickly.

He returned to reality as well, though not by choice—mostly because he was growing nauseous and needed to find a toilet as soon as possible. He still managed one last question, however, and arguably the most important one, before he felt the vomit sneak up his throat.

"Whose house?"

Sawyer's other mistake had been bringing his newly purchased Glock with him to Lilly's house. He was going to leave it at the motel, but then was worried that housekeeping might see it, despite the fact that he had hung the DO NOT DISTURB sign on his door—or at least he thought he had. And he didn't trust that someone wouldn't come into his room regardless, sign or no sign.

But he couldn't remember to a degree that satisfied him; consequently, his nervousness about whether or not he had posted the sign didn't let up. It wasn't until he squeezed the trigger on his Glock over an hour later that his worry over the sign finally dissipated, although he never would have defended the firing of the gun just for that purpose—to another person, that is. He didn't know it would temporarily quench his anxiety until he did it. And regret was something he had successfully removed from his life. There was never time for it anyway.

Lilly hadn't been home when Sawyer got there, and he found Miles almost immediately: his old friend was watering the bushes! Because of this strange sight, Sawyer didn't recognize Miles at first. *What the hell was he doing?* Sawyer wondered. But then he figured that maybe Miles was getting paid to do it; after all, gardening wasn't something Miles would volunteer to do, would he? Though watering some bushes could hardly be called gardening. Maybe Sawyer was just overthinking it. And anyhow, what did it matter?

"Hey," Sawyer called from a few feet behind Miles.

But Miles didn't turn around immediately. *Had he not heard him?* Sawyer wondered. Then he noticed that Miles was wearing headphones. When Sawyer looked at him from a different angle, he noticed that Miles was moving his lips, singing along to himself. But this wasn't Miles: watering bushes and singing! *Was the dude happy or something? What the fuck?* Sawyer wanted to ask him. Of course, Miles had recently been released from jail, so it made sense that he might be happy. And maybe this lady, Owen's mother, had put him to work, so Miles was getting paid to do what he was doing? *Seriously?*

Just then, Miles turned his head and almost jumped, presumably not expecting to see someone standing there, much less Sawyer of all people. He dropped the watering can and threw off his headphones—although he forgot to turn off the music, so Sawyer could still hear some faint drumbeats and an undertone of bass. *How loud was the volume, for shit's sake?*

"What the fuck?" Miles blurted. "What are you doing here? How did you find me?"

This last question was an unexpected one to Sawyer, as if it had been highly possible to Miles that Sawyer would try to track him down.

Sawyer awkwardly extended his fist for a quick bump, which never came. Instead, Miles just stared at Sawyer's outstretched knuckle as if it were a strange tentacle that didn't have human origin. Sawyer was so caught off guard by Miles not acknowledging his gesture that he held his fist out for an unnatural length of time, which only made it worse.

"What are you doing here?" Miles repeated, this time sounding even more agitated.

"Can't I visit an old friend?" Sawyer asked, with that fat grin of his that always irritated Miles—now probably even more so. "An old friend just out of jail," he added, in case Miles had forgotten.

The look on Miles' face betrayed Sawyer's next comment.

"You're all over the news. You're famous, man," Sawyer said.

Miles remained silent.

"Okay," Sawyer said. "Maybe not *all* over…not anymore. But you're still pretty famous. I mean, for just some white guy convicted of killing a black guy. I guess some people, mostly black ones I'm sure, think you should have served more time…maybe even gotten a jolt or two from the big chair."

A long pause, words exchanged that would never be said out loud.

"What?" Sawyer asked, preparing to answer the question that hadn't been posed but should have been—and long before. "You think I did it, but you served the time? Is that it? Is that what you think?"

But Miles didn't take the bait. He didn't have to say anything, as his silent look spoke again for him, this time spotting Sawyer's barely concealed gun.

Sawyer followed Miles' gaze. "What?" he repeated, this time accompanied by his shit-eating grin. "Did you think I would bring a gun to a knife fight?"

Miles let out a quick laugh, though it sounded more like a grunt. "You have it backwards, retard."

"No, *you* have it backwards," Sawyer quipped, his tone like a moody child.

"What?"

"You were pretty gone that day, that's for sure.…" He cleared his throat. "But not gone enough."

Miles made a sound in his throat, too, though it was unintelligible to Sawyer.

"I was just fucking with Owen…you know, pointing the gun at him. He was dating my ex, so I wanted to just scare him a little. But I wasn't gonna shoot him or anything. I was actually sober…mostly. You just thought I was as blitzed as you were."

"What are you—I don't understand. You knew Owen? I mean...*before?*"

Sawyer sighed audibly. "I was fucking with you, too, buddy. Wanted to see how you would react when I pulled the gun on him. But I didn't think you were gonna do what you did. That's why I made sure to fuck you up first...so you wouldn't do anything stupid." Sawyer shook his head. "But you went ahead and did something stupid anyhow."

Miles glanced at Sawyer's Pee-Wee Herman tattoo.

Sawyer seemed to read his mind. "Not a fan anymore, huh?"

"Of you?" Miles replied, hurriedly bending down to the bushes to throw up—the same bushes he had just been watering.

Sawyer laughed, then stammered as if English were his second language; when Miles didn't respond, he crouched down next to him. "Not such a tough guy anymore, huh? Too bad your prison friends can't see you now...if you had any friends in there, I mean."

Miles continued to puke all over the bushes.

"I think you're gonna need to water those again," Sawyer said, raising his voice as he stood up so his old friend could still hear him.

"Fuck you!" Miles muttered. But just then there was a loud pop...and all Miles could see was Pee-Wee Herman staring down at him.

MANNEQUIN

Lieutenant Colonel Ramirez wasn't sure whether his son was dead or just living in Orlando. That is, *still* living in Orlando. Naturally, he had filed a missing person's report several years earlier when he hadn't heard from Sawyer in over a month—they didn't have the type of relationship where they spoke to each other every day, or even once a week—and the police had actually traced him to Florida not long after, though they were unsure of his current whereabouts. But then the Lieutenant Colonel decided that if his son wanted to leave his old life, and his old man, so be it. He wasn't going to force his son to live in North Carolina if that wasn't what Sawyer wanted.

So, when he showed up at Ramirez's doorstep a few hours after shooting Miles, his father wasn't completely surprised to see him, though the former military man was more nervous than he would admit about the reported manhunt he had seen on TV. When the Lieutenant Colonel spouted some cliché about "what the cat dragged in"—since he hardly ever used clichés, explaining once that only weak people used them—it was obvious to Sawyer that something wasn't quite right.

"You gonna invite me in or what?" Sawyer exclaimed, already walking past his father and into the living room where the TV blared unceremoniously. Sawyer wasn't aware that his father had developed a habit of blasting Fox News almost twenty-four hours a day, as the Lieutenant Colonel had become more paranoid about the world since the last time they saw each other.

"Since when do you…" Sawyer started to say, but then stopped cold when he saw something on the TV that he didn't think would have made the news yet. Someone had found Miles, and since there was an eyewitness who had apparently seen everything, the cops now knew that Sawyer was back in town.

"Isn't that your friend?" the Lieutenant Colonel said, closing the front door and following his son's gaze.

"What?" Sawyer mumbled, his eyes still focused on the TV as if he only now realized the gravity of what had happened. "Is he dead?"

"You tell me," his father said, limping toward him.

"How should I know?" Sawyer shot back, his duplicity obvious, especially to the Lieutenant Colonel (who could smell a lie before it was even said).

He motioned for his son to sit down, and Sawyer knew it was useless to resist, despite seeming too weak now to actually make it to the couch.

"What happened?" his father asked in a strained voice. "And don't pussyfoot."

Sawyer started to shrug, but closed his eyes instead.

"You're fucked up right now, aren't you?"

Sawyer tried to open his eyes but couldn't—or maybe he just didn't want to—his father's voice unrelenting.

"Sawyer!"

"Okay, shit!" he exclaimed, his eyelids now dimly open but his legs wobbling like splintered toothpicks. He glanced at the couch, visibly unsure of what it had to do with him. "I don't know what…it just…." He couldn't stop swaying. "Bang."

"It just went off? Really? Why did you even—" A light flicked on in his father's eyes.

"Wasn't yours."

"I certainly hope not."

Still seesawing but anticipating the next question, Sawyer said, "Was a friend's—"

"You don't have any friends."

Sawyer winced, almost causing him to fall, but he received a pump of adrenaline instead. And the adrenaline seemed to remind him that he had the gun in question tucked into the back of his jeans.

"Really?" the Lieutenant Colonel said dryly when Sawyer withdrew the gun and pointed it at him. "Gonna kill your old man, huh?"

Sawyer sneered. "You're right about that. You *are* an old man…." He glanced at the TV, but the newscaster was no longer talking about Miles or the shooting.

The Lieutenant Colonel remained calm. "You got away with murder once already…maybe twice with your friend there…." He went to nod at the TV but realized, as Sawyer just had, that the news story in question was no longer on the screen. "And now, what, you're gonna go for the hat trick?"

"I didn't kill him. Owen."

"Who?"

"The black kid. I didn't kill him."

The Lieutenant Colonel closed his eyes.

"Okay," Sawyer relented, unintentionally letting the gun drop to his side. "But that was an accident, too."

"Once is an accident, twice is a trend, three times is enemy action," his father chanted, his words a twisted euphemism. Then, booming: "If you think I believe you, you're as crazy as you look."

Sawyer turned his head as if to see his reflection, but it was only his father's Bronze Star that stared back, hanging on the opposite wall.

"You're a sad…soldier," Sawyer said, still facing the wall.

Whether the Lieutenant Colonel had swung his walking stick in anger at his son, or had seen an opportunity to knock the gun loose, or had simply lost his balance—it wasn't clear, and Sawyer didn't stay to find out which one was the case.

After he slammed the front door behind him—the sad soldier now horizontal and powerless on the freshly stained carpet—the Bronze Star his father had so bravely earned could do no better than fall from its once-hallowed perch.

Sawyer didn't have a plan, but he still had the gun.

When he first left his father's house, he hoped to find out something more about Miles' status. Had he killed his long-ago friend? If he *had* killed him, he certainly hadn't meant to—or, at least, he didn't think he had meant to. He tried to remember what the report on his father's TV had said about it, but the news story had seemed to come and go so fast. *Or maybe there hadn't been an account about it on the TV at all?* But then, how the hell did his father know?

And why had his father been on the floor when he left? Had he pushed him onto the floor, or had his father just fallen there? He was pretty sure he hadn't shot him—but he couldn't remember. He couldn't remember much of anything, really, like how he'd gotten so fucked up in the first place; he couldn't remember how much he'd taken, or even *what* he'd taken. He didn't even remember why the hell he was back in North Carolina.

Sawyer noticed the gun on the seat next to him. Should he go back to see if his father was okay? That was probably risky, and he was in no shape for another confrontation with him—especially now that the adrenaline rush was gone. Without the aid of the adrenaline, he couldn't think straight. And it would be a while before whatever he had taken left his system. Although he didn't remember what he had taken specifically, Sawyer knew this much was true about almost anything he might have participated in, as he wasn't one who wasted time in the "lighter" column of street drugs.

Without warning, a wave of hopelessness washed over Sawyer so completely that he couldn't identify the feeling at first. Like he was suddenly the only person in the world and was going to die of loneliness. No one was ever going to love him again—if anyone had ever loved him in the first place. But that didn't matter, because now he was utterly alone, the chance of even seeing another human being again seeming implausible. He was going to starve or freeze to death, or perhaps die from intense heat. *Was it hot or cold outside?* Neither the A/C nor the heat was on inside the car, so he couldn't decide. Sawyer wasn't even sure whether he *was* hot or cold… or maybe he was nothing? *Was that even a possible choice?* But if he was indeed nothing, or, rather, feeling nothing, was there something inside the car he could flip on that would remedy that? Not A/C or heat but…something else?

He started to look for something on the front panel—a switch, anything—but then Sawyer caught sight of the gun again out of the corner of his eye, lying on the passenger seat as if someone had only just left it behind—someone who had been there with him mere seconds ago: a hitchhiker, a friend, maybe even someone who gave a shit about him and cared whether he lived or died.

Sawyer was still looking at the gun, trying to decide whether it was real or not, when he plowed into the car in front of him. It was a hard collision—hard enough that it would have deployed the air bag had he been in a newer car. But there was nothing to cushion the blow, the impact enough to gash Sawyer's forehead and break four ribs.

After struggling out of the car, blood from his forehead dripping onto his shirt, Sawyer didn't bother to see if the other driver was alright. He didn't even turn his head to look, as he was too busy clutching his chest; but since no one was getting out of the other car, at least straight away, he knew there was a good chance the other driver might be seriously hurt. And he simply didn't care.

There was a convenience store at the corner, which Sawyer limped toward, as there now seemed to be something wrong with his left leg. When he eventually made it there, however, he didn't go inside—at least not at first. Instead, he gimped his way to the back of the building and slumped to the ground. A light, dry wind brushed across Sawyer's face, which felt good on his cut forehead, like it was somehow healing it, even though he knew deep down this wasn't possible. He wondered whether he should put a little snow on it or something, but then realized there wasn't any snow on the ground anyway. He wasn't even sure whether there was *supposed* to be snow on the ground, as the current season evaded him. It didn't feel like winter; but it didn't feel like summer either. *Were there only two choices?* he wondered. Wasn't he forgetting some others? He wasn't sure, and there was no one nearby to ask. And even if there were, he didn't want to sound stupid. He just couldn't remember, and no one would understand that. They would just think he was some kind of idiot.

It was then Sawyer realized that in his other hand, the one not clutching his broken ribs, he was somehow holding the gun. He didn't even remember taking it from the car after the collision. But maybe that was a good thing: taking the gun with him. After all, the cops were surely going to arrive at the crash scene and he didn't need them finding a gun in his car. Finally, it seemed, his subconscious had done something good. But what was he going to do with it now?

For the moment, Sawyer set the gun down on the ground next to him. More importantly, he needed that hand to look in his pockets to see if he had any coke left. He needed a lift, needed to think clearly, figure out what to do—and if he still had some coke, that would sure as shit do the trick.

And as if God himself cut Sawyer a break at long last, there was indeed some coke in his pocket: not a lot, but enough for a quick pick-me-up. So, he emptied the contents onto the underside of his long pinky nail and snorted most of it into his left nostril, then finished the rest into his other. He flicked his nose and licked his finger, scrunching his face at the salty taste of his sweat. Then, on impulse, Sawyer picked up the gun and put it to his head, trying to think of that famous movie where they played Russian roulette, but he couldn't remember. Should he play a round? A queer grin crossed his face. *It might be fun just to try it*, he was thinking—and hell, if it was his time, then it was his time. He had nothing to lose if the gun was completely loaded. He had never thought to check. He could look now, but wouldn't that ruin the excitement of it? Not knowing if there were any empty chambers in the magazine lent the exercise an extra thrill.

He set the barrel to his temple, put his finger on the trigger and, with his free hand, flicked his nose again and sniffed.

"Fuck it," he said, and pulled the trigger.

It was a cosmic joke. Nothing happened.

Then he squeezed the trigger again. *Click.*

And again. *Click.*

Then again. *Click.*

Click.

Click.

Click.

Click.

He laughed. *What the fuck?*

He took out the magazine to confirm it. No rounds. Of course not.

He inserted the empty magazine and slid it back into place. So maybe he couldn't kill himself at the moment, he thought, craning his neck to see what convenience store he was behind. No one would know that the gun wasn't loaded. And he could use a pack of smokes; some cash wouldn't hurt either.

He stood back up and was immediately reminded of his broken ribs. "Fuck!"

He waited a moment for the pain to subside, at least a little, and tucked the gun into the back of his jeans—the required twist of his shoulder, in order to reach behind him, had hurt his chest even more—then limped around the side of the building to the entrance.

What the fuck was he doing? he thought, realizing that he hadn't robbed a store in some time, especially by himself. He had never done anything like this by himself. The last time Sawyer had done this, he'd been with Miles. He'd had a wingman.

But today he had no wingman. Today, he only had himself. The only question was whether he alone was good enough, capable of accomplishing something all by himself. But maybe that had always been the case, and he had fooled himself into thinking that he wasn't alone—that he was never alone—when, in actuality, there had never been anyone by his side other than someone pretending to be.

COP

Sawyer waited for the redneck couple to exit the store before he went inside. He knew from experience that he couldn't trust rednecks; they were wasted half the time and you could never trust someone who was wasted, especially when you were about to commit armed robbery. Not to mention, since they were in North Carolina there was a good chance they were packing as well, and he didn't need to risk that either. The fact that the cashier might be prepared behind the counter was scary enough; Sawyer didn't want to have to worry about more than one gun being pulled on him once he revealed his.

When the rednecks finally came out, though, there was something odd about them. They were laughing about something, but laughing in such a way as if no one other than them would get the joke, and that made it even funnier to them.

Sawyer thought again about the risk of someone, like the cashier, pulling a gun on him. But he had just played Russian roulette with all eight rounds of his gun and won. What did he care if someone pulled a gun on him at this point? *Fuck it*, he thought. If that was the way it might go down, it would be a cool way to go out—rather than a self-inflicted gunshot to the head in an empty lot behind a convenience store. The latter was just sad, pathetic even. But getting shot while robbing a place? That wasn't half-bad.

Once inside, after a jangling of bells announced his entrance, Sawyer didn't even bother to walk around the aisles first and scope it out, just in case someone else was in the store he hadn't accounted for. He went straight to the cashier, pulled his gun out, and said, "Okay, fucker, give me everything you got. And no games. Just do what I ask and you won't get hurt."

Sawyer glanced behind him, as if he were about to talk to his partner who had perhaps been too scared at the last minute to come in with him, but he was really making sure there weren't any other customers he had overlooked, like maybe in the bathroom. But it was all clear; he could see that the bathroom door was ajar, and dark inside.

Sawyer turned back to the cashier. "And a pack of Camels, unfiltered."

The cashier—a stick-framed, light-skinned guy whose race was hard to discern—could only stare, wide-eyed and unmoving, as if he had just been shot with a stun gun and was now encased, like Han Solo, with no way to get out.

"Is this a joke?" the cashier finally said.

"Excuse me?" Sawyer replied, not hiding his surprise at the balls the guy seemingly had.

"I'm being punk'd or something, right?" the cashier said, looking around the store as if he expected to find cameras he hadn't seen before—maybe even Ashton Kutcher.

"Hilarious!" he added, allowing himself a nervous smile.

Sawyer closed his eyes and vigorously rubbed his eyelids, then slowly opened them again as if anticipating a different reality than the one he'd inhabited seconds before. "Are you fuckin' kidding me right now?"

Now it was the cashier's turn to be confused. He scanned the store again, like he had possibly missed something the first time.

Sawyer followed his gaze. "What the fuck you looking at?"

The cashier didn't know what to say, which was apparent by his facial expression.

"Hello!" Sawyer tried again.

The cashier swallowed hard, his Adam's apple appearing as if it might break through the thin-looking skin of his neck. "Those other people just robbed me!" he shouted. "Now you're robbing me, too?" He shook his head and lowered his voice. "This can't be possible. I can't be *that* unlucky."

Sawyer could only stare. "What?"

"There's probably better odds of winning the lottery than being robbed twice in a row," the cashier continued, more to himself, like Sawyer wasn't there anymore.

Sawyer turned his head, letting the gun relax to his side. It was then they both heard the sirens.

"You better get outta here, man."

Sawyer raised the gun again and pointed it at the cashier.

"Look, man," the cashier said, throwing up his hands, the fear now obvious in his voice, "I called them about the other people, not you. So as far as I'm concerned, you were never here, okay? I never saw you—"

"I'm not afraid of the cops," Sawyer said, half-believing it. "Now give me the fuckin' money and the cigs before I lose my patience."

"Hey man, I gave those other people all the money. I swear."

Now Sawyer understood. Why it had taken so long to make sense to him, he didn't know. Perhaps he had thought that the rednecks failed in their mission before his, but then he remembered how happy they had seemed when they walked past him. *How am I this much of an idiot?* Sawyer almost said out loud. *If God only knew*—though he supposed God already did.

He remembered the day he was going to scare Owen with the gun, and freak Miles out at the same time. He had gotten Miles wasted—wasted enough that he would eventually black out and then wake up freaked out—which was all part of the plan. What Sawyer hadn't counted on was Miles reaching for the gun as he was pointing it at Owen (stupidly loaded, which Sawyer could never rationalize to himself); so, in effect, it could be argued that they had *both* shot Owen.

But all of that was over with now, especially considering that his friend might be gone for good, and by Sawyer's own hand nonetheless. And what greater distance was there than the one between the living and the dead?

The sirens were getting louder....

"Dude, you better go," the cashier implored again.

"Dude? Really?" Sawyer replied. "I'm not your friend... and why do you care so much whether I get caught?"

The cashier shrugged. "Fine, suit yourself."

Sawyer turned to look outside, but kept the gun unsteadily aimed at the cashier. The sirens were definitely getting closer. The cashier was right about that.

"Can you at least put the gun down, man?" the cashier tried again.

Sawyer returned his attention back to the cashier. Grinning, he pressed the trigger.

Click.

The cashier flew behind the counter. "Fuck! What the fuck!"

Sawyer laughed.

Click.

"Are you fuckin' crazy?" the cashier screamed, crouching below the counter.

"I wouldn't rule it out," Sawyer said. Then he laughed again.

The cashier popped up from behind the counter like a whack-a-mole, nervously pointing the store's revolver at Sawyer.

"Whoa!" Sawyer yelled, throwing both his arms up in the air, if only by reflex, but still holding the gun tightly in his hand. "Mine's not even loaded!"

Behind Sawyer, several screaming police cars screeched into the parking lot, sirens throbbing like disco lights.

"You're fucked, man," the cashier stated matter-of-factly. "Just give up."

Sawyer didn't need to turn around to know what was outside, but he did anyway. And he knew the cashier was right. There was no way out of this. Like it had seemed his whole life, there was no getting out of the way of his obvious fate. He was doomed, and always had been. Even when it seemed there was some type of light illuminating the way out, or a possible way out, it was only a twisted mirage, for the darkness was all-consuming. The devil just liked to fuck with him, Sawyer eventually realized, and if he was already target-locked in the devil's periscope, it was over before it even began.

Outside, Sawyer could see various cops with their guns drawn, and on the perimeter what looked like S.W.A.T. getting into formation; and though it paled in comparison, he knew the cashier was still aiming the revolver at him, too.

The hour of judgment was finally here.

"You gonna shoot me in the back?" Sawyer asked without turning around, as if he actually cared about the cashier's answer.

"I wasn't planning on it," the cashier replied. "I just don't wanna be taken as a hostage or something."

Sawyer laughed, but still didn't turn around. "Well, I wasn't thinking of that option, but thanks for giving it to me."

The cashier pulled the hammer back to cock the gun. "Me and my big mouth, I guess."

Still facing the door, Sawyer said, "C'mon man, I was just fucking with you. You're gonna be fine. No worries."

As Sawyer raised his gun and started to exit the store, he heard one last plea from behind him. "Don't go out like that. They're gonna kill you!"

Sawyer swung the door open, causing not only a chorus of bells to chime above the threshold, but a choreography of guns and assault rifles to gather themselves into one long click that wouldn't stop reverberating.

"Your gun isn't even loaded!" the cashier called out.

Sawyer stopped for a second, if only to laugh again. "I don't think it's gonna matter, bro. I don't stand a chance either way."

"Why don't you just surrender?" the cashier tried one last time.

Sawyer turned his head and grinned. "I'm not the surrendering kind," he said, letting the tolling door swing shut behind him.

HALF-LIGHT

For most of her adult life, Lilly was never quite sure about the difference between irony and coincidence. The fact that Miles was put in the same hospital room Owen had occupied, and both injured from gunshot wounds—not to mention Miles had been the one to shoot Owen in the first place—wasn't lost on Lilly by any means. And without Barry there, or anyone else who could possibly link the two—other than the media, who had already moved on from Miles—she kept this coincidental irony to herself, especially since Barry didn't know that Miles had been living with Lilly in the first place. If he found out, he would never understand (though Lilly wasn't quite sure she understood it herself).

More importantly, Lilly didn't know who had shot Miles. Even the police had no suspects yet, outside of a "person of interest" whom they were unwilling to share with her. And if Miles knew who had shot him, he was keeping it to himself for some reason, so law enforcement had to start with very little.

Lilly had found Miles bleeding profusely in front of her bushes. He thought he'd been shot in his chest, he told her in staggering breaths, but then she noticed that most of the blood was coming from his shoulder. Fortunately, she knew enough as a mother—and maybe from watching too many true-crime shows—that his wound needed pressure, so she quickly pushed down on it with the pashmina scarf she'd been wearing, causing Miles to let out a scream. Then, with her other hand, which wouldn't stop trembling, she dialed 9-1-1.

The emergency physician didn't say much after examining Miles and, as it stood, wasn't going to say much to Lilly regarding his medical condition at a later point, when all the tests came back, despite her telling the medical staff that she was his aunt—as in the kind who wasn't blood-related but, rather, a very close friend of the family. This didn't stop her from visiting him, however, and one night, in the dim light of the hospital's version of sundown, before leaving a peacefully resting Miles, Lilly stood in the doorway and just watched him sleep—similar to how she remembered watching Owen sleep when he was just a boy. And although the circumstances were obviously different, she still felt the maternal pang of nature, watching Miles breathe in and out, afraid that if she looked away, even for a second, he might forget to live.

But she didn't look away until she had to, and when her eyes were no longer adrift on his sea of nothingness, he breathed just fine without her.

In his dream, Miles was driving an overly crowded school bus and wearing thin, black leather gloves that he somehow remembered seeing once. What became readily apparent, though, was that this was no ordinary school bus, nor ordinary school day. In fact, Miles wasn't even driving the kids to school. He was driving them *away* from school, *away* from the shooter who was still inside, walking the still-populated hallways and shooting any kid he came upon—a shooter whose main point of identification was a tattoo of Pee-Wee Herman on his right forearm. The odd thing about this tattoo, however, was that Pee-Wee was bleeding from its black-inked eyes like a crimson-teared statue of the Virgin Mary, as no one had yet been able to stop this shooter or injure him in any capacity.

But the true horror of the dream was the fact that Miles couldn't get any more kids onto the already overflowing bus. And at each stop, more screaming, terrified kids wanted to get on—*had* to get on—but Miles couldn't fit one more person, even the smallest child. That is, until one of the kids happened to be Owen.

"That's okay," Owen said, seeing that there were no more open seats. "I understand."

"No, you don't understand!" Miles screamed. "You don't understand!"

"Really, it's alright—"

"But it's not alright!" Miles exclaimed, the fear evident in his voice.

Owen smiled. It was a knowing smile of someone much older and more mature. "You can't save everyone," he said, his teeth such a bright, silky white that Miles was almost taken out of the dream due to not remembering this detail from real life (as it wasn't a detail from real life).

"I know," Miles admitted tentatively, "but I can at least save you."

Owen leaned inside the door to view the rest of the bus, as if to make sure he hadn't missed something. "But you can't," he said. "There's no room."

"Take my place then," Miles pleaded, not able to think of any other options and already getting up from his seat.

"I can't take your seat, man. Who would drive the bus?"

Miles sat back down, nearly defeated. "Can't you drive the bus?"

Owen laughed. "No, man, I can't drive the bus. I'm not even here right now."

"What?" Miles started. "What do you mean?"

Owen laughed again. "I'm dead, don't you remember?"

Miles couldn't say anything.

"You were there," Owen said. "Don't you remember?"

Miles sank into the driver's seat. "I'm sorry. I really am. I didn't mean to kill you."

"You didn't kill me," Owen replied, pointing to someone who was suddenly in the back of the bus. "He did."

Miles didn't need to turn around to see who it was Owen pointed at. Even over the spray of bullets and the smell of new death, he knew exactly who it was.

"I'm gonna kill him," Miles said hurriedly.

"You can't kill him," Owen returned just as quickly.

"Yes, I can," Miles said. "And I will."

"You can't kill him," Owen tried again, the whites of his eyes like reflecting pools. "He's already dead."

When Miles woke up he didn't remember much from the dream, only that Sawyer had been a ghost—at least according to another ghost. And after conceding to the police that it had been Sawyer who shot him—why he'd held that information back in the first place he had no idea—they then informed him that Sawyer was, as a matter of fact, truly dead. He'd been fatally shot after an attempted armed robbery. The two officers who came to the hospital neglected to tell Miles that Sawyer had actually committed suicide-by-cop—a detail they could keep from the public quite easily.

Miles didn't know how to take the news at first. There was, of course, the realization that he had somehow dreamed this, which now didn't make any sense. How could he have known? Then there was the harsh truth that he had no feelings whatsoever from learning that Sawyer was dead. And it wasn't just because Sawyer had tried to kill him. *Had he really, though?* Miles was simply apathetic that his one-time friend was gone. *Had he actually been a friend?* Or had Sawyer just used him from day one?

Though he didn't care at all that Sawyer was gone, it did make Miles contemplate life in general. A person could be there one minute—living and breathing and doing whatever it is humans do—and then the next moment, that person could be gone. Just like that. They would never eat again, never sleep again, never even go to the bathroom again. It was like this person just suddenly disappeared off the face of the earth, making their time spent roaming around arguably meaningless. Whether they were put into the ground to rot or made into ashes, the suddenness of this transformation wasn't even comprehensible. Owen was gone, Sawyer was now gone, Miles had almost died himself. And if he *had* died, what would his life have added up to before he disappeared?

Nothing, Miles decided. It would have added up to a big, fat zero.

PART FOUR

AGONIST

289

ARMADILLO

Amos was sitting at the end of the counter, a homburg hat pulled down almost to his eyes, turned away from the entrance and involved in the front page of the newspaper, when Miles entered, causing the door to chime.

"Excuse me, is anyone sitting here?" Miles asked, hovering over the only empty seat he could find.

"Please," Amos said, gesturing with his outstretched hand. "It's yours for the taking."

Miles set his things down on the counter as best he could, given the sling around his shoulder, and not realizing that he had so many things to begin with; the main one, or most important, a zippered black bag not unlike a man-purse, but not strapped to his waist like a fanny pack, that held his prescription pill bottles: Percocet, Oxycontin, Baclofen, Clonazepam and Ativan. Only some of which—the Percocet and Baclofen specifically—were actually prescribed upon his discharge from the hospital, as he'd "neglected" to tell his doctors that he had a prior drug addiction.

The waitress stopped by and asked Miles if he wanted a coffee. He waved a "no thanks." He didn't want to go up, just down—at least for now.

Amos turned to Miles. "Good for you. Caffeine will kill you."

"Never liked the stuff," Miles lied. He was in no mood to make conversation with a stranger—although there was something familiar about this man—and figured his curt answer would do the trick in terminating their exchange.

"Don't tell me you're vice-free."

"Excuse me?" He paused. "Do I know you?"

"We all have vices," Amos went on, ignoring the latter question, his disclosure uninvited. "Even little old me."

Miles picked up the menu and started to read it. Maybe the old man would get the message and leave him alone. He glanced at the omelets listed on the back. He was hungrier than he thought. The last good meal he'd enjoyed was months ago, just before Lilly kicked him out of her house. He almost wished now that he *had* been the sole killer of her son—not out of malice or revenge, but so he could understand why she had turned on him in this way. It hadn't seemed justified at all. She wouldn't accept any money from Miles for letting him continue to stay at her house during his recovery, so what did it matter what he did every day? It wasn't like he was throwing wild parties while she was at work or something.

Miles looked up for the waitress, but she was at the other end of the counter, bent down and taking someone else's order.

"You'll be lucky if she comes to this end again," Amos said, neatly folding the newspaper and setting it down. He was apparently more interested in making conversation with Miles—or at least attempting it.

Miles didn't answer; instead, he gazed at the other patrons. It occurred to him that he didn't really look at people that much anymore, and sitting down in this diner by himself was out of the ordinary. It seemed like he had all the time in the world as of late, yet he hardly ever found a minute to eat.

He glanced at his watch but didn't register the time. Then he looked around for the waitress again, but she was nowhere in sight. She had disappeared into "waitress-land"—that secret place, hidden away from customers. He had found his own waitress-land the last few months since he got out of the hospital, a kind of Siberia where he could postpone the intricacies of life as an adult.

Miles started to feel anxious. It was that internal alarm,

always precise, when the downers left his system and his body ached for replenishment. He needed to go to the restroom and fast, as he didn't want to start opening bottles on the counter.

"Can you save my place?" Miles asked the man with the newspaper. "I'll be right back."

"Of course," Amos said. "I'm not going anywhere."

Miles started to walk away.

"Don't you need this?" Amos said, holding out the zippered bag Miles had left on the counter.

"How did—"

Amos smiled and handed him the bag.

Miles had the bathroom all to himself, as it was one of those single-person accommodations, which was much better than hiding in a stall like he was afraid might be necessary.

After locking the door, he stood in front of the sink and unzipped the bag. He was trying to decide what to take when he realized he didn't have any water to rinse it down with. Sure, he could have just used the water from the sink, but that wasn't something he would normally choose to do. It probably tasted like shit, he figured, and had fuckin' zinc or some other type of metallic element in it that wasn't good for you.

He laughed. *Good for you.* None of these pills were good for him, he knew, so why was he making such a big deal over the water? *Water was water, right?* He popped several "Klonies" into his mouth, but then decided to swallow them without any water. *Should do the trick for now,* he figured. And it *was* a trick, he knew deep down. He was deceiving his body like a seasoned magician misdirecting an audience, making them believe something in one hand, while the other hand performed the real magic.

But he had thrown too many pills in his mouth, and without the aid of water he wasn't able to swallow them. "Fuck!" he blurted out loud, after spitting the half-swallowed pills into the sink. He shook his head at himself for wasting the pills, and for such a stupid outburst. If someone had been standing outside the door, it might have sounded a little weird for the person in the bathroom to suddenly shout, "Fuck!" to no one in particular. What could possibly go wrong in the bathroom to warrant someone exclaiming that out loud to themselves, other than the gruesomely obvious? It was sort of funny when he thought about it.

"Fuck!" he shouted again, just to enjoy it this time. "Fuck, fuck, fuck!"

Suddenly a knock sounded on the door, just like he had feared. "Are you okay?" a voice asked.

"Yeah, fine. Be out in a minute," Miles replied. *That was actually nice*, he thought. Someone had heard him and was concerned. Maybe there were some good people still left in the world? He wondered whether *he* would have knocked on the door to make sure someone was alright after hearing them say, "Fuck, fuck, fuck!" Probably not. He would have just minded his own business.

Miles glanced at his reflection in the mirror. He looked older, as if prison had aged him. Not to mention he was using again, and that probably didn't help. He had dark bags under his eyes and his skin hung loosely off his face, as if the adhesive that held his flesh to bone had come unglued. He was even starting to get crow's feet, which he only recognized because Lilly had once described them concerning her own face. He was getting old, he thought, and he was still in his twenties. He hadn't shaved in several days, or was it weeks? The unkempt beard seemed to point to the latter. *Fuck it*, he thought. Who was he trying to impress?

A polite knock again on the door. "You sure you're alright?"

"Yeah," Miles said. "Just one sec."

He looked down at the sink where the spit-up Klonopin was; it didn't even resemble pills anymore, just blue bile. He figured it could be worse. If he was truly an addict, he would scoop up the blue slop anyway and eat it to avoid wasting it. But he wasn't an addict, he reassured himself, despite scooping up the slop unceremoniously a few seconds later and plopping it into the back of his mouth.

Surprisingly, and somewhat embarrassingly, since he was in the bathroom for so long, there were three people standing in line outside the door. They gawked at him as he walked past them back to his seat—or, at least, that was how it seemed.

What the fuck are you looking at? he wanted to scream at them. Then, unsure whether or not he had literally screamed at them, he tried to smile, convinced that nothing resembling his intention actually appeared on his face.

As he walked back toward the counter Miles stopped dead in his tracks, even though he had done nothing wrong. A cop was standing there, talking to the man who had been reading the newspaper, hopefully chastising him for not embracing the digital age. Miles told himself that there was no way the cop was there for him, but even the smallest chance that he might have to go back to prison, regardless of whether he'd done anything wrong or not, was too big of a chance to take. Although, on the other hand, he didn't want to leave yet. And besides, some of his stuff was still over there. So, he decided to act casual and just go back to his seat like everything was normal, a more challenging job than he anticipated.

Miles had to say, "Excuse me," to the cop, who was standing too close to his seat for him to sit down. But then the cop smiled at him and moved out of the way. *Thank God*, Miles thought. *Paranoid, anyone?*

"It's a dangerous job you've got," Miles overheard the man with the newspaper say to the cop.

"Yeah," the cop replied, sighing audibly and shaking his head. "I lost a buddy not too long ago. A good cop, too, been on the force a long time."

The man with the newspaper nodded. "I understand. You hate to see someone die young, or before their time. It's very unsafe out there. You've gotta be careful, of course, and never take life for granted."

"Oh, I don't. Trust me," the cop said, patting the man with the newspaper on the back. "Nice talking to you. Appreciate your kind words."

The man with the newspaper told the cop he would see him later, then smiled at Miles, who had already reclaimed his seat. "How you doing?" the man asked, picking up the sports section but feigning interest.

"Okay," Miles said, but then wondered if he ever would be.

"You sure?" the man asked, as if he had read Miles' mind. "You don't look okay."

Miles stiffened.

Saving him for the moment, the waitress appeared out of nowhere. "Coffee?" she asked again, forgetting that he had already declined the offer.

"No thanks," he said, not without a little contempt. She must have thought he was a new customer who had just sat down, not realizing he was the same guy from a few minutes before and had just gone to the bathroom.

The waitress walked away before Miles could ask for another menu, since she had inexplicably taken his away. There were usually menus, from what he could tell, wedged behind the napkin holder, but he no longer had one. Did she think he'd already ordered?

Begrudgingly, Miles turned to the man with the newspaper. "You don't happen to have an extra menu, do you?"

The man shook his head. "I come here all the time, so I don't even need a menu." He laughed. "Plus, I get the same thing every time."

"Which is?"

He smiled. "Coffee. Black."

He obviously had a dry sense of humor; the kind Miles could never quite get. "They have good coffee here, I take it?"

"The best," the man said.

"I thought Starbucks was the best place for coffee?"

The man waved off his statement. "No, no, Starbucks isn't real coffee." He held up his cup in the air, as if it were a trophy. "Diner coffee is real coffee. That other stuff is just commercial goo." He laughed again, more like a chuckle. "I never get tired of saying 'goo.' It's one of the more fun words in the English language."

Miles escaped the conversation momentarily; his mind was in a million places and none at all.

"Plus," the man went on, as if Miles had asked him to, "a lot of the people who go to Starbucks are not as healthy as they look. They think they're healthy, but they're really not. They exercise a lot, and whatever else it is they do—Pilates or whatnot—but then they partake in other stuff that's bad, and which completely erases the good stuff."

Miles had only caught the last part, but was paranoid enough to think that the man was talking about him. "Are you a doctor or something?" Miles asked.

The man laughed again; he seemed to be fond of laughing. "No, I'm not a doctor. Do I sound like one?"

"What's your job then?" Miles inquired, more than curious now.

The man paused. "I help people deal with life…and death, too, I guess, since that's also part of life."

"Oh, like a therapist?"

"Sort of," he replied. "And what do you do for a living? Or are you still a student somewhere?" Before Miles could answer, though, the man went on: "Sounds sort of funny, doing something for a living. People *live* for a living, don't they? Working is just what they do. But I guess I see where the phrase comes from. Just seems strange to me, you know, doing something for a living."

"I'm a—"

"Wait, don't tell me!" he interrupted. "Let me guess…."

He shifted in his seat and pulled at the loose skin on his face. "Wow, you're a tough one. I'm coming up blank."

Now it was Miles' turn to laugh. "That's because I do nothing for a living. I'm a product of the State."

"Disability?"

"No. Prison."

"Well, I would call that a disability. A self-imposed one, sure, but a disability nonetheless."

"I don't follow," Miles said. "How did I impose prison on myself? It's not like I *chose* to go there."

"Ah, that's where you're wrong."

Miles turned to look for the waitress, then started to stand up from his seat, as if he meant to either go find her or walk out the door. "This is bullshit." He turned back to the man, who was feigning interest in the newspaper again. "And spare me your bullshit, too. Thank you very much."

The man smiled and picked up the business section. "You're welcome."

Miles grunted and shook his head, but instead of heading toward the door, he surprised them both and sat back down.

"You sort of remind me of someone," Miles said, staring at the man closely.

"I don't mean to get on your nerves," the man stated matter-of-factly, opening the newspaper fully with a loud snapping sound and then concealing himself behind it. "I'm really quite harmless. People never understand that about me."

Miles looked for the waitress again, but she was nowhere in sight. It was almost as if he had imagined her, like one of those lucid, drug-induced dreams which hopped around inside his head like crackling popcorn.

"I don't think I can wait any longer," Miles said, standing up from his seat again.

"Come on, sit back down," the man commanded, but not in a terse way. He folded up the newspaper and gently set it back on the counter. "You have a whole life ahead of you. Have some patience."

Miles hesitated, but then sat back down.

"You seem very nervous," the man said. "It's not good for you, being nervous like that."

"Who says I'm nervous?"

The man made a smacking sound with his lips, as if he expected the question. "You're one of those people that's always anxious about something, huh? Whether or not you even realize it."

"I gotta go," Miles said, standing up yet again.

"You seem angry," the man said. "Did I hit a nerve?"

"I'm not angry," Miles replied irritably, like a teenage girl trying to master sarcasm.

The waitress materialized out of nowhere and handed Miles a menu. "Coffee?"

"No, I don't want a goddamn coffee! Jesus Christ, man!"

The waitress snapped her head back and scrunched her face, as if he had just thrown water on her. Then she disappeared again.

"Sorry," Miles said to the man with the newspaper, then quietly sat back down.

The man nodded toward the other end of the counter where the waitress had somehow reappeared, as if she had just come out of a wormhole. "Don't apologize to me...."

Miles tried to get the waitress' attention but, just as quickly, she fled again.

He turned back to the man next to him, who had already returned to the newspaper. Everything was happening so fast it was as if there were multiple time zones on each side of him, separated by only a few feet.

The man must have felt Miles' gaze, because he looked out from behind the newspaper. "Something on your mind, son?" he asked.

Miles shook his head.

The man neatly folded the newspaper and set it down on the counter. "I'm a good listener…or so I'm told." He smiled.

Miles realized that his heart was racing and took a deep breath. "You sure?"

"Always," the man said, without a hint of uncertainty. "What would you like to talk about?"

A different waitress suddenly materialized at Miles' side. "Coffee?"

AWAKE

Lilly had just come out of the ladies' bathroom when she heard the phone ringing. But it wasn't her cellphone, as she originally thought; it was a payphone set directly across from the restrooms, screaming at her to answer it. She had just taken something to calm her nerves—why she was anxious, she didn't know—and was considering going to the bar for a drink when the phone started ringing. Lilly had never answered a public payphone before—she didn't even know that they still existed—but, for some reason, felt like she had to pick this one up. In her mind, the phone was ringing solely for her. She was *supposed* to answer it. Besides, no one in close proximity seemed to notice that it was ringing.

Lilly picked up the receiver and held it a few inches from her face. She didn't want the dirty phone anywhere near her ear or mouth. God knew where it had been.

"Hello?" she said, her voice uncertain. She almost expected to hear a dial tone in response. It was obviously a wrong number, and the person on the other end of the line would surely hang up when they heard her voice.

Someone walked by and gave Lilly a look. Had they seen her answer it? Were they wondering why she had answered a public payphone?

Why *had* she answered a public payphone?

Lilly couldn't hear anything in the receiver, not even a dial tone. The person on the other end didn't say anything; nor did they hang up. It was just dead silence. She was about to hang up herself when they finally spoke.

"Do you usually answer payphones in airports?" the caller asked.

"Airport?" Lilly repeated. "I'm not in an air—" Lilly looked around, realizing that she was, indeed, in an airport—but what the hell was she doing in an airport?

"Who is this?" she asked, starting to get irritated—but more at herself for picking up the phone in the first place (not to mention being in an airport for no reason).

The caller paused. "You don't know?"

It was a man, but she couldn't place him. His voice was familiar and unfamiliar at the same time. "No. Who is this? Do I know you?"

"Depends how you define 'know,'" he said. "You might know me, you might not. I'm not really sure which one it is."

She was losing her patience. "Look, buddy, I don't have time for this. I don't like playing games."

The woman on the payphone next to her gave her a look. Lilly hadn't even realized that there was another payphone—or that someone was talking on it.

"Can I help you?" Lilly said to the woman, posing it as a rhetorical question that was far from friendly.

The woman continued to stare, then hung up and walked away.

The voice on the other end of the line came back. "Are you talking to me?"

"No, I was talking to this woman next to me."

"Don't do that. Focus on me."

"Who is this?" Lilly exclaimed, exasperated. "I don't have time for this."

"Then why did you pick up the phone?"

"I have to go," Lilly said.

"Why? Are you late for something?"

Lilly breathed through her nose, then exhaled loudly. "I want to get a drink before my flight leaves," she said without thinking, as she had no idea what time her supposed flight was departing, nor the gate number. Was she even at the right terminal?

"Do you usually drink in airport bars?" he asked. "I didn't know that about you."

She didn't know how to respond.

"Plus, should you really drink after taking pills? I don't think that's a good idea."

Her wind was knocked out. She put the phone to her chest, as if to steady herself, and looked around the terminal to see if anyone was watching her. *This is crazy*, she thought. *Is someone playing a joke on me?*

She put the phone back to her ear. "Are you some type of pervert?" she asked, regaining her breath. "How did you know I took some pills? I did that in the ladies' room."

"You ask a lot of questions...but you were always like that. A truth seeker from the get-go."

She swallowed. "You don't know me."

He laughed, and then coughed. "Does anyone really know anyone?" he said, sounding almost rhetorical. "I don't think so. We spend our lives getting to know shadows. Our expectations of people tend to distort the facts. We overlook things as a result. And when the cuts aren't deep enough, no one truly bleeds."

"You're very philosophical for a crank caller," she said.

"Who said I'm a crank caller? I was calling for you, and you answered."

She was feeling on the verge of tears again, having just cried in the ladies' room. "What do you want?"

"I want to talk to you," he replied. "Isn't that obvious?" He cleared his throat. "I want to help you."

"Who says I need help?"

He sniffed. "I can hear it in your voice. Call it instinct."

She rubbed her eyes. Her mascara was running. She was probably starting to look like a raccoon. No wonder everyone who walked by seemed to stare at her.

"Why do you feel like you need a drink?" he asked. "Do you usually drink before you fly?"

"What do you mean *fly*? I'm not going anywhere, am I?" She suddenly thought that he might be able to clear things up; maybe explain why she was in an airport to begin with.

No response. *Had he hung up?*

"I need to go," she said, finally aware that she wasn't in control of her own words.

"Why do you need to go?" the voice returned, as if it had never left. "Are things not moving fast enough?" He cleared his throat again. "Grief is a slow process. You can't rush it."

She grabbed a tissue out of her purse and dabbed her eyes. "It's been years. How is that not slow?"

More silence. *Where is he?*

"I have to go," she repeated.

"Alcohol is a depressant," he said, coming out of nowhere again. "It's not going to speed anything up."

"Well, it speeds things up for me. It makes time move faster…or, at least, that's how it seems. I don't think as much when I drink."

"Is that why you took the pills?" he asked. "So you wouldn't have to think?"

"Yes, I took the pills to slow my mind down," she blasted like a temperamental teenager, belatedly realizing the irony of what she'd just said (or rather, how she'd said it).

"So, you're trying to slow things down and speed things up at the same time? Sounds like you're confused."

"I am," she admitted. "I *am* confused."

Another passerby stared at her. She turned around and faced the wall. *Why is everyone staring at me? Hasn't anyone ever seen a woman crying before?*

"Why are you confused?" His voice had changed; it was softer.

A tear ran into her mouth, tasting salty. "I just am. I'm so alone. I have no one." She began sobbing uncontrollably. The wall in front of her became blurry. She was afraid to turn around. She knew people were looking at her.

"You're not alone," he told her. "You'll never be alone."

She tried to regain her composure. "I have no one in my life. I'll probably never get remarried. I have no one to talk to outside of my therapist." Her tears were explosive; they drenched her face. And the sound that came out of her was unlike anything she'd ever heard.

"I'm sorry," he said, sounding genuine. "The death of a loved one is a hard thing to get through—especially your own child, who is supposed to outlive you."

Lilly took another tissue out of her purse and wiped her face. The tissue came back black from her mascara. She blew her nose.

"So, what am I supposed to do?" she asked. "How do I go on with my life?"

Lilly could almost hear him smile at the other end of the line. "You take it one day at a time," he suggested. "Baby steps."

"I can't do it," she confessed. "I don't have the strength."

"Sure you can," he replied. "I have faith in you."

She moved the phone to her other ear. "Why do you have faith in me? You don't even know me." She started to cry again.

"I know you, Lilly. I've always known you."

She coughed out the next words: "You know my name?"

"Of course I do."

The public address system came on. A flight was announced. Boarding would begin momentarily.

"They just announced my flight," she said, as if she knew without a doubt it was her flight that had just been called. "I have to go."

"What about that drink you were going to have?"

Lilly let out a quick laugh, which surprised her. "I guess I don't have time for that now."

A moment passed. "Be good to yourself," he told her.

There was no one on the line anymore. Even without the dial tone, which hadn't sounded yet for some reason, Lilly knew he wasn't coming back this time. After a few more seconds, she hung up the phone. Then she wiped her eyes with the back of her hand, since her tissue had disappeared.

The public address system came on again. The flight Lilly sensed she was supposed to get on was pre-boarding.

She started to step forward, and that was when she noticed it: a yellow sign hung just above the phone. It made no sense that she hadn't seen it before. She read the sign twice, not believing the words printed on it.

It was an OUT OF ORDER sign, and no matter how many times Lilly read it or stared at the letters, the words didn't change...

but she did. She woke up.

OSMOSIS

Miles didn't understand why people who left their cars on the side of the road hung white rags or white shirts, or even just white plastic bags, from their driver's-side windows. Was it a silent tribute to the Civil War that only pertained to Southerners? Or was it just a queer form of surrender borrowed from the rules of engagement? It seemed an unnecessary proclamation, as these wounded (likely deceased) vehicles were not war machines sidelined from some ferocious battle. They were just no longer useful.

Anything resembling inspiration or even slight encouragement didn't last long after leaving the man at the diner, whose name Miles never obtained during their marathon conversation, nor a way of making contact should Miles ever want to speak with him again. When they exchanged goodbyes outside the diner, Miles had joked that maybe he could engage this mysterious man's services with the "bat signal" should the situation ever arise. Or perhaps this enigmatic man was closer to "The Wolf" from *Pulp Fiction* (Sawyer's favorite movie of all time, which he'd insisted Miles see—and agree about), who had an uncanny ability to set things right, even when they were way wrong. That was the thing about this man from the diner. Although they had only met this one time, Miles got the impression that this man was a "fixer": that he could somehow make the bad things good again, or simply prevent them from happening at all.

Whenever Miles thought about *Pulp Fiction*—which Sawyer forced him to watch multiple times, especially when they were stoned—he often wondered which one of them was Jules and which one of them was Vincent. Sawyer seemed more like the Bible-thumping, wisdom-spouting Jules to Miles—minus the religion and wisdom. But then after his death, intentional or not, it certainly seemed as if Sawyer was more like curiously thoughtful Vincent, if only because they were both suddenly gone, sent into the void as swiftly as the flip of a light switch.

Once, when they were planning to rob a convenience store, Sawyer had even wanted them to wear dark suits like Jules and Vincent did, but then Miles pointed out two things. One, Jules and Vincent never robbed a store. In fact, they were trying to *stop* a robbery—or at least Jules was. Two, Miles didn't own a suit. He never had, and he never really wanted to—if only because he worried that he might like it and would want to buy another one, maybe in a different color, which, of course, he wouldn't be able to afford, even hypothetically.

The only thing Miles ever learned from school, nowhere near on purpose—and that he couldn't forget no matter how hard he tried—was the definition of osmosis: the diffusion of water through a selectively permeable membrane. But it was just a random arrangement of words that had no meaning or bearing to Miles' life; he hated that it wouldn't leave his mind. He wished sometimes that he could exchange this merciless fact for an even worse thought, no matter how bad, just to rid himself of something he had no business remembering in the first place. To make it practical for something, however, Miles eventually started using "Osmosis" as a password—originally all lowercase, then with a capital "O," then with capital everything. But everything couldn't be capital; this much he knew.

Outside his childhood bedroom window—the one from foster home #2—there was a giant willow tree. And though everything seemed to be giant at the age he was back then, as he got older he realized that most willow trees were large—or at least the ones he'd seen. In fact, the one outside his bedroom window almost engulfed the house itself—not to mention his dreams. The only thing that seemed to hold it back was permission, as if it couldn't deny its Southern genial roots.

In prison, Miles often thought of that willow tree; and though he knew it was an image of a childhood he never had to begin with, it was also a symbol of freedom, as he would need to be outside in the real world to actually see it. But when he finally did get out of jail, it seemed as if all the willow trees were gone. There wasn't even one on Lilly's ample property—at least that he could find—although he wasn't there long enough to know for certain.

While Miles couldn't bring back the "idea" of the tree, what he did bring back from prison was the inevitability that nothing was for certain—not even whether he was guilty or innocent. And he still wasn't sure which direction Lilly leaned. Perhaps she had kicked him out of her house because she finally realized that he *was* the killer of her son—a truth he was waiting for her to grasp as undeniably as gravity. But, was he the killer? If *he* wasn't even sure, how could she be? But then, it still didn't explain why she had thrown him out so abruptly. *Useful? Really?* How was he supposed to be useful if he didn't even know where he was going to sleep that night? Or the night after that....

He had been living at a hostel near downtown since leaving Lilly's house, but he hated sharing a room with two other boys, not to mention the bathroom. Now that he was out of prison, Miles didn't want to share anything with anyone anymore, especially the toilet. He was tired of feeling rushed all the time, especially since that was all he had now: time. *Fuckin' time.* It just kept right on going no matter what, which in prison was obviously a good thing. But outside of prison, it was the opposite. He *needed* time now. He needed it to move at his own tempo, no matter what it happened to be on any given day. Time didn't seem to listen, though. And the worst part was that Lilly had told him time just got more stubborn as a person got older. If Miles thought that time didn't listen now, "Just wait," she'd said. "You'll lose complete control of it…if you ever had control before, which you didn't. Not ever."

This was a complete contradiction to what Prison Drake had told him, as Prison Drake claimed that anything could be controlled, even death. "Ya have-ta-have control ova ya mind. Dat's da ting of it all," he'd said, like some wise and ancient Kung Fu master. "Da power's in ya thoughts."

"You can't control death," Miles had argued, having the courage at that point in their friendship to disagree with him. "It's impossible."

"Not impossible," Prison Drake said. "Look at me, brah. I alive still."

Miles shook his head, mostly because he knew where the conversation was headed.

"You can seez me, right? So, I mus' been alive." Prison Drake smiled, no doubt thinking he had just won the argument using his limited knowledge of existentialism, having recently read eight pages of Sartre's *Nausea*—not even consecutive pages—which, in Prison Drake's mind, meant he was an expert.

"Yeah, I understand the whole 'mind over matter' thing. I really do. But—"

"It not just 'bout mind ova matta, man. It 'bout faith. Da Lord know when it ya time, 'n it ain't my time yet."

Miles laughed. "So, the Lord will tell you when it's your time?"

"Indubsitably," Prison Drake said, or tried to say, while tapping his head with his forefinger. Then he laughed, too.

◻

Miles had only recently made rye whiskey his chosen poison as far as anything not in pill form, which was exactly how the girl who worked at ABC Liquor had said it would be: that he would grow into it; that it was for men, not boys. "Boys drink beer, men drink whiskey," she'd stated plainly, as if it were up to her to officially separate the two. Not rum, not tequila—"except for shots," she felt obliged to point out— and not vodka. The latter was for people who were afraid— afraid of having alcohol on their breath, afraid of a certain type of hangover, afraid to be creative. Whiskey even cured the flu. "It's homeopathic," she'd claimed; she didn't really know what homeopathic meant, but was convinced she did.

"I'm not sure all the doctors would prescribe to that," Miles replied, throwing his own incorrect grammar into the conversation. "Although I do," he added, partly because he sort of agreed with her, and partly because he was afraid he might have offended her.

"Sure-they-do-honey," she said, running the words together, and with a much stronger Southern accent than she'd used moments before—maybe because she'd used the word "honey" and didn't seem old enough to Miles to call him that. Whiskey as a drink for real men Miles could commit to, but calling someone "honey" was reserved for grandmothers and diner waitresses. Besides, he wasn't *her* honey—although he wouldn't need much convincing to apply for that job on the off-chance it was currently vacant. But she was too attractive to be boyfriend-less. And she wasn't pretty in the conventional way—whatever that was; in fact, Miles realized, he was probably in the minority of guys who found her good-looking. Considering the vicious streaks of purple in her already half-bleached hair, her various tattoos—including the large Chinese letters that fit perfectly between her shoulder blades—and her overall mutt appearance, she was definitely an acquired taste. This was exactly what he liked about her, though: she was unique. And she didn't even realize that her name, Hannah, was a palindrome. Of course, Miles had only recently learned (from a dog-eared waiting room magazine that held no overwhelming interest to him) what a palindrome was.

Their frequent conversations—as he was one of those regular customers who shouldn't have been—covered not only the true definition of homeopathic, and eventually the wonder of palindromes, but also their shared views on the ever-reaching claws of death—from an existentialist point of view, naturally. For they both liked to imagine, whenever they watched old movies, who in the cast might be dead now—*had* to be dead now—especially any dogs in the film, for they, Hannah liked to point out, were *surely* dead now. There was no question with regard to that, Hannah would argue; whereas the human cast, in general, could just be very old now—although Miles would contend that the *already* old people in the cast at the time the movie was shot were no different than any dog captured in the frame, as whatever remained of their lives in terms of years had to be around the same vicinity as a dog's—or closer in some cases.

And once they started dating in real life—Hannah didn't consider the inside of the liquor store as part of real life—they developed a habit of watching old movies together so that they could argue about specific actors, and dogs even, especially if the latter were only puppies, for that made the math go a little deeper, if only by a few years. These "viewing parties," as they affectionately referred to them, had to be held at her apartment, however, since he had too many roommates at the hostel—more than she did, at least—not to mention the lack of a TV. And though Hannah's roommate, Erica, occasionally tried to get in on their existentialist math problems, it was clear this game only existed between Hannah and Miles, even though most of it could be settled by a quick Google search, as Erica liked to remind them. She didn't get that finding out wasn't the point, for Hannah and

Miles liked to argue about things, regardless, with the one clear exception of his ever-growing dependency, yet again, on mood-altering substances—whether on the "boy" side of things or the "man" side—as it was almost a sort of foreplay only the two of them could understand.

The Adderall was beginning to take effect on Miles when he opened the front door at Hannah's apartment—a place he spent most of his time due to the unappealing nature, and strict rules regarding female guests, of the hostel where his belongings still resided. Yet, as new as his relationship with Hannah was, Miles threw open the front door as if he lived there, and had for years. A sore point for Erica, no doubt, even though she had been staying at *her* boyfriend's apartment as often as she could.

"Where's this girlfriend of yours at?" a dark mass said from just behind him, standing in the now-open doorway.

"She's out of…. How'd you find…." Miles could only stare, his jaw bones slacking as if they were suddenly diffused. "When'd you get out?"

Prison Drake's laugh came from deep within his diaphragm, a sound like Santa Claus would make—and just as jolly.

IRIS

He had almost died and Lilly wasn't there. But it wasn't her job to be there anymore, she had tried to reason with herself on the way to the hospital. And when she finally got there—the traffic on the 40 was horrendous, even by her standards—Barry didn't look like himself. His face was bloated from all the infusions the doctors had likely done to clear his clogged veins, and due to the bypass not succeeding as much as necessary. The surgeon—a wavy-haired guy with a metal clipboard, who didn't look old enough to practice medicine—informed her that it was one of the worst cases of advanced heart disease he'd ever seen in a person who wasn't technically obese. Although Lilly wondered later just how long "ever seen" was for this Doogie Howser-looking kid trying to pass himself off as an adult.

"*Obese?* What the hell do you mean by that?" Lilly demanded.

The doctor sighed loudly, like a dog who was bored. "Well, even with the standards for obesity, which have dropped considerably the last few years, your husband was still twelve pounds—"

"*Ex*-husband," she corrected.

"Right. *Ex*-husband," the doctor said quickly, like the correction was a bug he wanted to shoo away. "Regardless, he was—"

"You keep saying 'was,'" Lilly interrupted. "Is he dead?"

The doctor sighed again, this time as if from self-directed aggravation, like he was mad at himself for going off-script. "Not yet."

"*Not yet?*"

"Sorry," the doctor said, his demeanor now calm, as if he were trying to soothe a child. "I meant to say he's alive, but in very critical condition."

"*Very* critical condition?" Lilly repeated, as if she were just beginning to learn new words and felt unsure about this one. "I didn't know there was a level *below* critical condition… other than death, of course." When the doctor didn't respond immediately, she added, "It's like the terror warnings with all the damn colors. What color is *very* critical condition, by the way?"

Lilly felt bad for him for a moment, but then realized he'd probably heard much worse, so she let the intended apology slip away. Besides, what did she care about his damn feelings? He was a doctor, and probably an overpaid one, so he could get over it. She was over it, that was for sure.

"Your hus——*ex*-husband is in bad shape. That's what I mean. We can't make any promises, obviously, but if his heart can get some strength back, and he follows up with regular exercise, and watches what he eats…oh, and takes his insulin."

"*Insulin?*" Lilly repeated, then said it again, as if she still couldn't grasp any words coming out of his mouth.

"For his diabetes…" the doctor began, but then seemed to realize what was wrong based on Lilly's face. "Your…Barry has diabetes, and needs to take care of it. Like I said, he needs to take care of himself, period. And see a doctor regularly."

He smiled unexpectedly, which instantly made Lilly feel better. Something she realized as she got older was that people, regardless of their natural attractiveness, always looked better when they smiled. It made her wonder what people like Hitler and Jeffrey Dahmer looked like when they smiled—*if* they smiled, which they probably didn't. Maybe that was why they became monsters: because they didn't smile, or know how to.

"Your husband doesn't seem like a big fan," the doctor added, interrupting Lilly's crazed thoughts, which were probably due to a recent bout with insomnia. Was her lack of sleep due to knowing ahead of time that something was wrong with Barry? She did seem to have an additional sense, ever since she was a child, but it mostly involved having premonitions of other people's deaths, like her father's sister and her second cousin, or celebrities like Michael Jackson and Prince—the latter two simply because she couldn't imagine them as old men. *But did this mean Barry was going to die?*, she now wondered.

"I mean *ex*-husband. Sorry," the doctor said, but then seemed to realize his apology was unnecessary. She wasn't even paying attention.

"What?" Lilly said, snapping out of it as if an alarm clock had gone off.

"I was saying that I don't think your husband is a big fan."

"A big fan of what?" she asked, back in the conversation but still not following everything he said (or the fact that he'd said "husband" again).

He smiled a second time, revealing crow's feet, which made her realize that he wasn't as young as he'd first appeared. In fact, now that she was taking a closer look, he wasn't that young at all. Not old, but not young either. It was how she perceived herself, and how she hoped others perceived her— at least the first part. She wasn't going to correct anybody, of course, if they thought she was younger than she looked. She might even participate in the lie, as she'd already done on several occasions. Although, now that she thought about it, that was mostly with men who probably just wanted to sleep with her. But that was okay, she decided, in order to put the creeping negativity away. "A compliment is a compliment," as her granny used to say, making sure Lilly was listening by loudly fake coughing after (Lilly's bad habit of not listening started as early as childhood).

"A big fan of doctors," Crow's Feet answered. Then, realizing that she wasn't paying attention again, he added, "Just make sure he's more vigilant about his health, and he should get through this."

"Can I see him?" she asked.

"Not yet," he said, throwing another smile at her as he walked away. "They'll let you know."

"I hope so," she called after him, though her words were lost amid the continuous buzz of the crowded hallway.

"Am I dead?" Barry asked after opening his eyes and recognizing Lilly, who was sitting at his bedside. The fluorescent light above his head gently flickered and hummed, sounding almost like a whisper.

"Well, if you're dead," Lilly said, relief painted in her smile, "then I must be, too."

Barry's face scrunched in confusion, like the expression a baby makes when it empties its bowels.

"Do you have to go to the bathroom?" Lilly asked instinctively, as if she were talking to baby Owen and not her ex-husband, who was six years older than her.

Barry's face wrinkled even more, this time taking his eyes into the fold, reminding Lilly of the heart surgeon whom she had spoken to a few hours before.

"You're not dead," Lilly said, partly easing her ex-husband's facial expression. "You've been in surgery for several hours, and the doctor said it might take a few more for all the anesthesia to leave your body...." Barry continued his blank stare. "That's why you're groggy," she clarified, much louder than before, as if she were talking to someone considerably older who was hard of hearing.

Lilly stood up and hovered over the bed, as if she were

looking for something. His eyeballs followed her like a living painting in an old horror movie. She bent down and gently kissed his forehead. It had been years since she'd kissed Barry anywhere on his face. It felt like kissing a stranger for the first time—their skin unbroken and new, soft and perfect.

"Go back to sleep for a little while," she said. "I'll be back later. I'm just gonna go to the cafeteria and grab a coffee, and maybe a bagel or something."

He reached out his hand, but didn't say anything.

"You can have tea when you wake up. You need to rest now."

His hand stayed in the air.

"What?" she asked, softer but still intent. "Do you need something?"

He grazed the top of her fingers with his own. And she knew the only thing he wanted was to hold her hand.

She was waiting for the elevator when she heard her name shouted from behind her. But when she turned around, it wasn't someone from the medical staff as she supposed it was; or, rather, like her heart supposed it was, since it had momentarily stopped beating out of fear that something had happened to Barry during the brief time it took her to walk down the hallway to the bank of elevators.

"You're Owen's mother, right?" said a young woman in a hospital gown. She was quickly making her way toward Lilly despite the obvious protest from her mobile IV, which seemed to be chasing after her. Lilly wasn't sure if the young woman was walking fast to escape from the IV or get to her quicker—or maybe both.

Regardless, Lilly turned her attention back to the elevators to see which would get to her first, a way out or the young woman.

"Please wait," the young woman pleaded. She had stopped so abruptly that she almost lost her balance. "I knew your son."

Lilly spun around to the young woman again, her motion timed exactly with the arrival of the elevator—though the latter didn't have the patience to wait for her, sliding shut after a few seconds. "How do you know my—" Lilly started. "Oh, of course, I forgot I was a celebrity," she said, not without a little malice, only then noticing that the young woman was white, since her mind was apparently still catching up with her. "Funny how the death of your son can make you a media star, especially when he's black...*was* black." Lilly turned back to the elevators and pressed the button again, hitting it several times out of frustration, as if doing so might make it come quicker. "That's another two bucks for idiot tax," Barry used to say when they were dating. Only then did she realize who the woman might be.

"You were his friend...at the end," Lilly said, turning back to her and naturally missing the next elevator that arrived.

"*Girl*friend," Elodie corrected. "We were—"

"You were there," Lilly stated evenly, her jaw twitching. "You saw—"

"No, I didn't."

"That's what you claimed back then, too," Lilly said, trying to fight back the same frustration that owned her when Miles was first arrested and she saw something in his eyes that betrayed his innocence. The girl was an eyewitness—the *only* eyewitness—who had not really witnessed anything at all, or so she professed.

"How can she be an eyewitness if she didn't see anything?" Lilly had berated the police repeatedly, getting pretty much the same answer every time.

"She's the only *possible* eyewitness," they clarified. "So far, at least."

"What?" Lilly had said, still not getting it. "She's gonna remember something later, just out of the blue?" Which triggered their favorite word again: "Possibly." Then, adding the craziest thing of all: "Or the suspect will remember. The one in custody."

But she'd never understood why they had said that about Miles. Even if he really couldn't remember anything at the time—which she ultimately believed—it wasn't like he was going to incriminate himself if his memory eventually revealed that it *was* him who had pulled the trigger. She'd told the police this very thing, to which they had responded: "He's already going to prison. Remembering would only be for his conscience now...and for you, of course."

But she still didn't get it. "So, there's a chance he's innocent?" she had said, which seemed to push their buttons every time she brought it up.

"We don't make it a habit of sending innocent people to jail, ma'am," the detective-in-charge had responded tersely, hitting "ma'am" with a bullet, as if such a possibility were so ridiculous that it wasn't even worth his breath.

"Because it's the truth," Elodie now said to Lilly, who had just missed a third elevator.

Lilly stared at Elodie, noticing that both her wrists were wrapped in bandages. "How do I look to you?" she said, her words so raw that a nearby couple looked over at them.

"What?" Lilly replied.

"How do I look to you?"

"Well, you...." Lilly's eyes focused on Elodie's bandages again.

"No," Elodie said, as if Lilly had physically reached out to touch one of them.

"How do I *really* look to you?" Elodie tried again.

Lilly considered it for a moment. "Sad?"

"You mean pathetic?"

"No, not pathetic. Just sad."

"Me or…."

"You," Lilly said, her tone shifting for the first time in the conversation. "What you did to yourself doesn't define you."

"Well, I think I cut in the wrong direction anyway," Elodie confessed.

"They told you that?" Lilly said in disbelief.

"No."

"Then how do you—"

"I just know…I think."

Lilly nodded. It made sense. "This isn't because—"

Elodie shook her head, her eyes two hazel pools.

"Then why?"

"Because," Elodie said, looking away. "Just because."

RESIDUE

Catherine was pregnant again. Not counting Miles, who was the first born—as well as the one she never wanted to count—this was number nine, although she only had three at home. There had been two stillbirths—one before Miles and one after—and she insisted on counting those in her mind since God had been the one to kill them; and she even counted the two she had terminated on her own—for health reasons, she had reassured herself—as well as the two she had given up for adoption (especially since she had been paid good money for them). In fact, had she known about this surrogate thing before having Miles, she probably would have cashed him in as well, since the option she ended up choosing for him—though it was more like an impulse—didn't turn out to be good for anyone, not least her. He was dead, despite her never hearing anything about the infant's body getting found by someone; and, as for her, the one sentenced to living, she had been plagued with nightmares for the several months that followed. In order to move on, however, Catherine came to realize that she simply had to notch up these dreadful nights as part of the many things she had been born to endure—yet another side-effect of having a shitty life was how she would put it, if it ever came up in conversation.

And it did come up in conversation—quite frequently, actually—though not the part about what happened to Miles (thankfully); only about her nightmares—about laying on her sweaty twin mattress all through the night, sticking to it like a flytrap, unable to even turn on her side. "For no good fuckin' reason," she would say about her insomnia. But there *was* a reason, and she knew it deep down; and Curtis, the guy she had met at the library—which was not the typical place she would meet men (thus why she remembered), and who she was somewhat confident was Miles' father—would have known, too, had he not OD'd a few weeks before Miles was born. Curtis would have known because he knew what Catherine was capable of—and from only the short amount of time he knew her. "She's a crazy bitch," he had told his drinking buddy on more than one occasion, but without saying what it was that made her crazy or a bitch. And his drinking buddy would nod in agreement because, to him, all women *were* crazy bitches, no explanation necessary.

There was only one other person who might have known about Miles, and that was the man she had met at the diner that same day (and only minutes before it happened), but then she had lost track of him after their brief conversation outside. It had felt like he followed her to the river, but she couldn't be sure, as every time she turned around, convinced he was behind her, there was no one there. Nevertheless, something still nagged her about him; it was like he somehow knew, even before her, what she was going to do.

He featured in many of the frequent nightmares that followed—always watching her from the riverbank—watching her but not stopping her. That was the part she didn't get no matter how many times she thought about it. Following her was probably easy. Men often followed her, especially after leaving bars; it was like she would invite them to do so without saying a word. But this couldn't have happened with the man from the diner, as he was old—too old even for her—unless money was involved, of course. She wasn't a hooker, though, or at least she didn't think of herself that way. She had to make money just like anyone else, and if the guy was unappealing or old—or worse, both—then she had to charge them, especially if they hadn't bought her any drinks or other desirables. If they bought her shit, however—particularly drugs, not just weed—then she felt obligated to spread her legs. It was only fair, and she would never argue about it. Nothing good ever came from arguing about it.

But that was the thing about this old man. He didn't seem interested in her in that way. He had seemed almost fatherly toward her, to be honest, though what that meant exactly she couldn't guess. It just seemed that way, like he was somehow looking out for her. But if he *had* been looking out for her (God knows why), and *had* followed her to the river, then why hadn't he stopped her? Maybe he just didn't have the time to stop her? Because, by the time he realized what she was doing, it was probably too late. But if that were the case, then why hadn't he reported it to the police? It didn't make any sense—unless he had never followed her to begin with; but somehow she knew he had. Somehow, she knew he'd also watched what she'd done. And though she couldn't be sure, she'd almost convinced herself that she saw him again after that—not right after, but just in general; here and there, every now and then. As if, in some way or another, he became a permanent extra in the movie of her life: mostly in the background, perhaps occasionally in the foreground, but never interfering, no matter what she did, even if that meant watching her throw her baby off a bridge and not doing a damn thing about it.

"Da South always have a story ta tell," Prison Drake said, sitting across from Miles in Hannah's living room. "Don't it?"

Miles wasn't sure what to say, as his shock from seeing Prison Drake out in the real world, and at his doorstep no less—or Hannah's, rather—had overcome him; as if his time in jail had only been one long dream. But seeing Prison

Drake now confirmed that all of it had really happened. And it wasn't that he didn't like P.D. or was unhappy to see him; he was simply thrown off by encountering him in an environment he wasn't expecting to see him in—at least not yet.

And Prison Drake read straight through it. "Ain't ya happy ta see ol' P.D.?" he said, also referring to himself as such, having told Miles that he liked the abbreviation better, as he didn't want to ever say the word "prison" again, no matter what the context. "It ain't good ta put dat kind of negative-ness out in da universe," P.D. had explained. "Da past is da past, 'n just like it sound, it pass, man. It ova. Done wit'... 'n I ain't going back no matta what."

"Of course, I'm happy to see you," Miles replied, forcing a smile. He was feeling bad that he'd possibly hurt his friend's feelings—and as it stood presently, outside of Hannah his only friend. "I just wasn't expecting you, is all."

Before P.D. could respond, Miles added, "How'd you find me, anyway?"

Prison Drake laughed again; it seemed like he hadn't stopped laughing since the moment Miles let him in. "Please, boy, you can fine anybody nowaday, so long you knows how da look."

Miles nodded, but couldn't hide his remaining apprehension. If P.D. could find him, anyone could. Paranoia was something he had unwittingly added to his arsenal since getting out of prison; chemically induced or not, he couldn't escape it.

"Ya really wanna know?" Prison Drake finally asked. "As I knows you ain't been datin' dis chick for a minute, which ya also tinkin' right 'bout now, huh?" He looked around. "Where she's at, anyway? She outta town or sometin'?"

Miles nodded again, afraid of saying anything else that might sound too unwelcome—although the question of how P.D. had found him was still hanging in the air.

Prison Drake read Miles' facial expression and grinned in response, as if he couldn't wait to say it.

"Facebook."

"People that cross our paths are like the tide. They wash in, and then recede to the sea."

"Recede?" Elodie echoed.

"Fade away," Lilly answered. "Disappear."

"Oh…like receding hair?"

Lilly laughed, catching herself off-guard. She wasn't allowed to laugh anymore. Her ex-husband was flirting with death three floors above them, and she was sitting across from a life-stricken girl who had tried to kill herself…

and her son would never grow old.

"Exactly like receding hair," Lilly replied, though no longer lighthearted.

"That's pretty deep," Elodie said, nodding, then poking her left earlobe with her pinky finger. "Seriously."

The two women sat silently for a long moment, each one seemingly wondering what the other was thinking, yet Lilly couldn't decide if she would want to trade places with Elodie and get another chance at life. Not that Lilly felt she was too old—just old enough where the decisions she had made were fairly final. Everything had been put into motion already. There was no going back. Whereas Elodie hadn't stamped all her decisions yet; things had surely *started* to happen to her— there was no denying that—but life hadn't really begun to unleash its *complete* fury. Elodie still had time to defend herself against it, or at least retreat down a different path, if such a route could be found. Elodie's father had died tragically, and under unfathomable circumstances; however, to Lilly, it was an act of God under the umbrella of *wrong place, wrong time*. It couldn't be helped. No one on that plane would have been able to save him, and Lilly told Elodie exactly that. It was as if her father had been struck by lightning, Lilly had also remarked. And Elodie had nodded like she understood. But what Elodie didn't truly understand, nor Lilly for that matter, was the crush of young love. Death made sense, love did not; when Lilly told Elodie this, the latter liked it so much she typed it into her iPhone.

"You're too young to have to worry about understanding love," Lilly had said, finally reaching for the Styrofoam cup of coffee in front of her, which had already turned cold. "Or death for that matter," Lilly added. "Things are going to happen to you whether you want them to or not. And sometimes you just…sometimes the only way to survive is to go along with it. Don't even question it, or the answer will put wrinkles on your face, keep you up at night."

"I'm already up at night," Elodie said with a laugh, as if it were some kind of punchline that she finally found funny.

"Sleep while you still can," Lilly continued, laughing along with her—this time letting herself do so without self-judgment. "Before the shit *really* hits the fan."

Elodie turned quiet.

"You okay?" Lilly asked after a moment.

Elodie hesitated, but then nodded her head.

"How's your mother?" Lilly said. "I can't even imagine what she's going through right now."

Elodie moved in her seat and opened her mouth slightly, but no words came out.

"Well, honey," Lilly went on, as if Elodie had said something after all, "you can't control what you can't control." She glanced at the time. "Oh my, I better get back up there. We've been talking for a while."

"Sorry," Elodie mumbled.

"It's not your fault, sweetheart. I've enjoyed talking to you." She paused. "Well, maybe *enjoyed* isn't the right word, but you know what I mean."

"Yeah," Elodie said, louder than before. "But I'm still sorry."

"Don't be. Time flies sometimes, and besides—"

"No," Elodie interrupted. "I mean about your husband."

"*Ex*-husband," Lilly said swiftly, reminding herself inadvertently of correcting Dr. Crow's Feet earlier. *Why bother, though?* she asked herself. *What did it matter if Barry was an "ex" or not?*

"Is he gonna be okay?" Elodie asked.

Lilly started to stand up from the table. "I don't know. Maybe."

"I hope so," Elodie said. "He seems like such a nice man."

Lilly stopped. Temporarily forgetting Elodie's morbid connection to her family, Barry's infidelity took center stage in her mind. "You know him?"

"Well, I wouldn't say 'know,' really. Just from seeing him on TV and stuff…like being interviewed? Right after—"

Lilly was free from the clutches of the table now. "Oh, I see," she said, not wanting Elodie to finish the sentence. She was ashamed of herself for going right to Barry's penis, not to mention forgetting how Elodie knew her to begin with—especially after the conversation they'd just had. *Am I getting senile already?* Lilly wondered, half-serious. As a child, she had memorized all the presidents in order of when they took office, as well as the capitols of all the states. Now she couldn't remember what body part she had or hadn't washed in the shower. Growing old was the twisted idea of a madman.

"Be kind to yourself, Elodie. Take care."

"But I don't know how," Elodie said, her voice cracking.

"Baby steps," Lilly shot back as if by reflex, though she realized before getting to the elevators that her reassurance was for herself as well.

ISH

"I don't think there's as many people in the world as they say there are," Miles announced, walking at a brisk rate into the living room.

"You sound like me," the shadowed figure in the living room said flatly. They sat on the couch with a lit cigarette in their hand; when Miles didn't immediately respond, they took a drag and exhaled a large plume into the semi-darkness.

Miles laughed, more out of some subconscious recognition, but then as he got closer, the person on the couch wasn't who he expected it to be—at all.

"Surprise!" the smoker said, suddenly animated like a comic book villain.

"What are *you* doing here?" Miles faltered, not believing what his eyes were telling him.

"I should ask you the same question," Sawyer said. "I'm fairly certain this isn't your place."

"Where's P.D.?" Miles asked, alarmed, since his prison friend was the one he thought he'd been talking to, and who should have been the one waiting for him to get out of the bathroom.

"P.D.?" Sawyer repeated, making fun of each initial like only he could. "You mean the police department?"

Miles hadn't ever made that connection. "No, Prison—I mean...Drake," Miles said, his heart dropping because he just then realized that he didn't know Prison Drake's real name.

"They shot me, you know," Sawyer went on matter-of-factly, sounding frustrated that Miles hadn't answered his question.

"Who?"

"The P.D."

"I know," Miles said, irritated, now convinced that Sawyer definitely shouldn't be there, sitting on his girlfriend's couch as if nothing had happened. "You're dead."

"Am I?" Sawyer shot back. "Are you sure? Because it seems like I'm sitting in your apartment right now. I mean, your girlfriend's apartment. Have you fucked her yet, by the way? I imagine you have if you're running around like you own the place. What does she look like, anyway?" He grabbed a framed picture off a side table, as though it had been placed there just for him. "Not bad, not bad at all." He set the picture back down with a thud. "Does she suck a mean cock?"

"I know you're dead," Miles said, swallowing so hard he was sure Sawyer could hear it.

And he had. "Gulp!" Sawyer shouted, then giggled like a comedian laughing at their own joke.

"You're not here right now," Miles said, more to himself. "This is a dream."

"You sure about that?" Sawyer asked, continuing in his mocking tone. "Because you don't seem so sure about anything these days. Take your girlfriend, for instance—"

"You're not here. You're not real."

"Whadya mean I ain't here?" Prison Drake's voice belted into the dream, waking Miles up. "I'm 'bout as real as dis shit ya took," he said, picking up a near-empty prescription bottle from the nightstand, then tossing it aside. "Yo need ta clean ya-self up, man."

Miles didn't know what was more of a relief: waking up from the nightmare or seeing Prison Drake there, still with him—although he didn't need P.D. to start stepping between him and his drugs. Taking care of him was one thing—like making him spaghetti earlier, just before he took a nap (a new habit due to Miles' professed 24-7 exhaustion). And P.D. even put brown sugar in the tomato sauce—something

Miles had learned from Lilly's recipe and had relayed to his initially resistant cook/friend, who had remarked, "Brown sugar ain't gots no place in anyting but oatmeals." Then he wouldn't admit he liked it, which was more than apparent from the big sloppy smile on his big sloppy face.

"Yo tired all the times cause ya gots a leaky gut," P.D. went on now. "Yo need some of dats probotic shit."

"It's pro*biotic*," Miles corrected his friend, only knowing the word because he'd heard it come out of Lilly's mouth almost daily. She had even brought him a bottle of it on one of her prison visits, just weeks before he got out when her motherly instincts were beginning to take hold, although the guards wouldn't allow Miles to keep it.

"I pretty sure iz probotic," P.D. said.

Miles laughed, which helped him wake up a little bit more, since he was still lying in bed, rubbing the dark bags under his eyes. "It's not a robot, dude," Miles said. "It's like the good version of bad shit for your body."

"Yeah, I know what's iz," Prison Drake boomed, his voice in crescendo as if he suspected the person with the louder voice might ultimately win the argument.

"You don't know shit," Miles said, finally feeling enough strength to start pushing himself out of bed.

"I knows you shouldn't been taken all *dis* shit," P.D. said, spotting another bottle—this one far from empty—and sweeping it off the bed as if it were a rodent, the top popping off and its navy blue contents spilling all over the floor and under the bed.

"Fuck, man! What the fuck!"

"Gets yo shit togetha!" Prison Drake growled, stomping out of the bedroom and slamming the door closed behind him, an as-yet-undiscovered pill bottle bouncing up from the bed in response, the mattress acting as a trampoline.

"Learn how to speak English!" Miles shouted at the closed

door, though he suspected his comeback was too little, too late.

And he was right; nothing but silence.

He grunted and gazed stony-eyed around the room, then flopped down on his sweat-stained pillow, his head like an anchor dropped from a ship—his mind racing, praying with all his might that he wouldn't fall asleep again.

He dreamed that he had woken up, even though he hadn't. He'd fallen into one of the deepest slumbers of his life—one so heavy that when he finally did wake up in a pool of spittle, which smelled like vomit and cough syrup, Prison Drake was gone, and without leaving any note that Miles could find— not even how to contact him.

Worse, Hannah was coming back from visiting her parents in a few hours and the apartment was a mess—mostly due to the fact that neither Miles nor P.D. had cleaned up the kitchen after their spaghetti dinner the night before. The only good news was that Hannah's roommate seemed to be gone, too—perhaps still at her boyfriend's place since it was only Saturday, or so Miles hoped, as she often stayed with him on the weekends, especially with Miles ostensibly a permanent resident of their apartment. On top of which, Erica wasn't a big fan of Miles, or his drugs, and had apparently told her roommate as much on several occasions. (According to Hannah during one of her futile attempts to get Miles to stop partaking: "If not for me, then for her.")

"Why would I stop for *her?*" Miles had argued with Hannah when she finally shared this with him. "If I was gonna stop for anyone—not that I'm doing anything bad anyway—I would stop for you, not your stupid roommate."

"You should stop for yourself, Miles," Hannah had said,

which (ironically) stopped the conversation cold, as Miles knew he had no comeback that would do him any good. This much he knew for certain.

And now here he was, removing something resembling bile from her pillow, with his thumping head threatening a migraine, wondering how the hell he was going to clean up the rest of the apartment before Hannah came home. He wished he could just sink back into his last dream, or at least the location of it, since the main part of it had felt more like a nightmare.

In the dream, he was on vacation with his parents; or rather, a bland couple straight out of Central Casting who didn't even come close to resembling any of his foster parents, but were giving him a hard enough time that he knew what their roles were supposed to be. They kept calling out to him from the hotel's lobby restaurant, which overlooked the ocean.

Miles, however, was stuck on the beach, though not necessarily in the ocean—it was hard to tell from his dream perspective—and try as he might, he couldn't get back inside to the mouth-watering food that awaited him.

"Come back inside!" they kept screaming at him, in between bites of food. "Get back to the hotel!"

Yet they kept eating without him, and he just couldn't make it back.

When Miles finally awoke from this dream, starving, not even the spit-up on the pillow lessened his hunger; nonetheless, he tried to clean up as much of the apartment as he could before deciding what to eat. While he was scrubbing tomato sauce from the kitchen counter Hannah's cat decided to make an appearance, which startled Miles, as he'd completely forgotten about Miss Pennyworth (whose name had sparked more than one heated conversation with Hannah, even though Miles had only made his opinion about the cat's name known to playfully poke fun at her, not expecting for it to turn into a full-blown argument). The second time this occurred, when Miles blamed Hannah's exaggerated response on her monthly cycle, things didn't go well for him at all. This caused their first breakup—despite the new-car smell still permeating their relationship—but then they got back together the next day, after apologizing to each other: her for overreacting, him for his plain stupidity.

Having cleaned the kitchen as best he could, at least for the moment, he decided to have a bowl of cereal, accompanied by 650 milligrams of Vicodin and a bar of Xanax. The milk in the cereal, however, was a bad idea, as were the meds, and he ended up in the bathroom throwing up small chunks of Cinnamon Toast Crunch alongside the pills he'd just taken. Which meant they had been wasted; and he hated that more than anything, even more than puking. It wasn't easy getting pills these days—in prison it had been much easier (the challenging part was keeping it a secret from P.D.), and ever since Lilly kicked him out it had become even more difficult, as he had to spend the money he usually would have spent on drugs on food and shelter instead. Food and shelter: the bane of his existence, not just literally but figuratively as well. Miles was more than used to the literal things—those were the things he couldn't control. But the figurative things—those were the ones that kept him up at night if he wasn't properly medicated.

As he had gotten older, or perhaps since getting out of prison, Miles had noticed that almost everything he encountered, or at least thought about for any length of time, meant something bigger, thus requiring more attention, more analysis. For all the things Miles knew he couldn't control, everything else required a right turn or a left turn. Most of the time, which he would barely admit to himself, he was happy to just sit in the dirt at the dead end and not go anywhere. This way, and only this way, he couldn't make a mistake; mistakes were something he couldn't tolerate anymore.

"Don't be doing dis, man," Prison Drake had begged him after dinner the night before, having walked in on Miles taking enough Klonopin to knock two men of P.D.'s size out cold.

"What the fuck?" Miles had screamed back, more out of surprise than anything else, as he was sure P.D. was well aware of his drug-taking. Keeping secrets from his big friend, in or out of prison, was futile. And he knew it. He just didn't want to live by it.

"Youz gotta stops takin' dat shit. It poison. Yo body is a tem-"

"It's 'Your Body is a Wonderland,'" Miles interrupted, more acerbically than intended. "Not a temple."

Prison Drake stopped mid-motion, his mouth still partially open as if someone had pressed the pause button on him.

"The song," Miles offered, his tone much lighter than before. Then, seeing a lack of acknowledgment on P.D.'s face, he added, "John Mayer?"

"What?"

Miles laughed.

"Is dat some kinds of white boy music?"

Miles shook his head and continued to laugh.

"Ain't funny, man," P.D. said. "But if yo wanna jokes yo-selves ta def, go on." And then he slammed the door, rattling the mirror above the sink to such a degree that Miles thought it might come crashing down.

"Joke yourself to death," Miles muttered to himself. "Joke yourself to—" He stopped, then threw some of the pills that were still waiting in his open palm into his mouth, swallowing them with only his spit. He sniffed and carefully put the remaining pills back into a nearby bottle, having forgotten where he put the original bottle that he'd taken them out of just a few minutes before.

"Joke yourself to death?" he repeated, this time as a question, as if he were memorizing the feel of the words on his lips, but still not gaining the meaning of them.

He put the pill bottle back onto the shelf behind the mirror and shut the door, but the latch wouldn't catch. The mirrored door popped back out, giving Miles an unwanted glimpse of himself—his dead eyes staring back like they belonged to someone else.

And now, his only friend in the world, who he had no way of contacting—especially considering that he didn't know P.D.'s real name—had abandoned him, just like everyone else in his life.

Fortunately, though, when Miles walked out of the bathroom something caught his eye that he didn't think was there before. It had a bright yellow cover, and once he was close enough to see what it was, he knew it couldn't be Hannah's. She didn't like to read fiction, which she reminded him of at any opportunity, such as whenever they passed a bookstore, but only in an effort to get *him* to read something, anything, so long as it wasn't a novel. And this bright yellow thing on the coffee table was definitely a novel—of that much Miles was certain. It was a worn paperback copy of *Huckleberry Finn*, a book he was supposed to have read in high school but never did. How it had suddenly appeared there, Miles had no idea—until he picked it up and opened the front cover, which he only did out of some type of curious instinct that people have when looking at a book for the first time. He realized immediately that it was a good thing he did, because there was a note scribbled on the first page that had his name in the first sentence:

Reed dis Miles. It a good books but dont get no ideah bout dat slave Jim. I aint yo nigga like he is but I am yo frends. —P.D.

And under the initials, a phone number, which Miles dialed as quickly as he could, afraid that the digits might disappear forever if he didn't dial them now. Just when it seemed like no one was going to answer, Prison Drake picked up; and though he didn't say "hello" like a normal person would— as if committing to the call wasn't something he necessarily wanted to do—Miles knew without a doubt that it couldn't be anyone else.

"So," Miles said, unable to stop the smile from spreading across his face, "what's your real fuckin' name, anyway?"

JIGSAW

"No more food from gas stations," Lilly said, laying down the familiar law she had repeated to her husband more times than she cared to remember. "You hear me, Bare?"

She had put him in her guest room, since she didn't want to drive to his condo every time he needed something—and she knew he would need something all the time, at least for a short while, until he was back on his feet again. Barry had wanted to stay with her in the master, of course, but that idea didn't even come close to consideration.

"It's not like I go to the gas station every day or something," Barry replied, smiling like a guilty boy who couldn't deny that he was caught—relieved, even.

"Yes, you do," Lilly said, smiling back but trying to remain serious. She wanted him to listen to her, finally, be it the last thing he ever did—which, based on his recent hospital stay, could very well be the case.

"When was the last time you went to an actual supermarket?" she asked, this time without the smile.

He laughed, which turned into a dry coughing fit.

"Easy, cowboy," she said. "It's too soon for you to be excited."

"It's never too soon," he tried to say between coughs, until finally regaining himself. "Does that mean no sex yet, too?"

He grinned like a horny teenager, though he was visibly anything but that. He was thinner than he'd ever been—and not just while she had known him, but based on the childhood pictures she had seen of him growing up. This was also counting the day they first met, before he gained what she called "marriage tummy."

Lilly shook her head as if to say, *What am I going to do with you?*—which she nearly said out loud, forgetting for the moment that most of the things she ever said to him, or almost said, he already knew.

"Aren't I eating here anyway?" he said, with that tone she knew all too well. "Why are you lecturing me about gas stations?"

"You're staying here, and eating here, only for the time being. And I'm not lecturing you. I'm just trying to make sure you take better care of yourself when I unleash you back on the world."

He attempted a smile that demanded no words.

"Look," she said, backing off a little and trying to be jokingly firm. "We'll go over all that stuff in your aftercare instructions." She paused to see if he was with her, and he was trying to be, but his eyes were getting droopy. "For now, just rest. We'll worry about your choice of grocery store later."

She started to walk away, but then stopped to say one last thing, just in case he was still unclear. "Not that a gas station is technically a grocery store."

"You win," he mumbled, his eyes already at half-mast.

"You always gotta get the last word," Lilly said, exhaling dramatically for effect. Then she turned and walked out of the room.

Accommodating her ex-husband in the same room where Miles had been living before she threw him out wasn't lost on Lilly (nor on Barry, who had protested about not sleeping with her in the master). But she didn't need the room to remind her about what had happened, nor the guilt that still swam around inside her, which was two-fold. On the one hand, she felt terrible for kicking to the curb a young man who was obviously troubled and needed help with his addiction; on the other hand, she felt even worse for inviting the convicted killer of her son into her house, under the same roof, eating the same food, and only steps away from where Owen had slept. That hadn't been lost on her either, but very few things were lost on her nowadays.

She had known Miles was taking drugs before catching him in the act, tipped off by finding empty pill bottles in the bedroom when he was out taking care of the yard, her reasonable suspicions backed up by his flat demeanor and the lack of light in his eyes. And then, when he was caught, he didn't even try to lie about it or make up some excuse. It was almost as if he wanted to be caught, like he wanted help—*needed it* to be precise—but just couldn't bring himself to ask for it.

She was haunted by Owen, and it trumped everything else. If anyone was lying or making excuses, it was Lilly. The fact that she had opened up her life, and then her house, to the "suspected" killer of her son had finally caught up with her. And since she had stopped sharing all of this with Dr. Stevens, who thought the whole story was "delightful"— surely the worst adjective in the world for him to choose in this context—Lilly was on her own with her conscience. But finding out that Miles was a drug addict seemed to fall in her lap as the perfect excuse to turn him out—not including the death of her son as something attributable to her house guest—even before he had a chance to course-correct.

And now, two months after kicking Miles out, with Barry as his replacement, Lilly's life was becoming—*had* become— grievously unmanageable. To borrow from one of her favorite TV shows—she was addicted to police procedurals, though she would be the first to admit that they all seemed to blur together after a while—her life had gone "sideways," which, in her estimation, was far worse than straight down. Down was down; like gravity, it couldn't be helped. Sideways, however, was a choice and then a commitment, the end result neither good nor bad, which was a worse type of hell in Lilly's estimation.

She had been surprised that Miles left without any resistance or plea for help, without defending himself or searching for forgiveness, and was even more surprised that she hadn't heard from him since. She wondered if he was okay; she hoped that he had checked himself into rehab or found some other way to turn himself around, however unlikely. Once in a while, and undeniably more frequently as she got older, Lilly questioned the Bible as no more than a book of fables, and Jesus as no more than the fictional protagonist of an overlong historical novel. For who was she really praying to other than herself, since no higher power ever answered her?

In church on an occasional Sunday, surrounded by the heat of mostly strangers, it seemed more like an after-school club, an extracurricular activity that was really just adults playing in the sandbox after recess bell had already rung, rehearsing in full dress for a play that would never be performed. And as a parent who had somehow outlived her own child—the most unnatural thing there could ever be—and due to such a random act no less, it was as easy to turn her cheek from religion as it was to slip into an old pair of sweatpants. For there was nothing more real than Owen's empty bed, still made up as if he might get into it any minute—especially not some weathered book crudely organized into cryptic sentences, ultimately something pretending to be meaningful that could explain the unexplainable.

She just wanted to be left alone now, and maybe Miles had picked up on that signal, though Lilly couldn't be sure when she had started feeling this way. He was, despite his age and everything else, very keyed into her emotional states while he was staying with her—or at least it had seemed that way. He knew when to approach her and when to retreat, a characteristic that her own husband hadn't acquired even after all their years together. And here was this boy, this young man, who seemed to know her after only months, perhaps even days. *But why am I comparing Miles to Barry?* she wondered. If she compared Miles to anyone, shouldn't she mark him in the checkbox next to Owen? Or was that too simple? Too profound? Too…what? *Freudian?* Or was it the doctrine of some other famous intellectual, like the one Dr. Stevens had quoted once, whose name she couldn't remember? Something about not letting yourself grieve, because anything you lose comes around in another way. But wasn't that just the same bullshit as, "When one door closes, another one opens"? That familiar phrase people always chant to one another after losing a job or a boyfriend or experiencing some other completely normal bump on the road of life. Although, was losing a child a normal bump on the road of life? It couldn't be… *could it?*

And the one person she could talk to about this, outside of Dr. Stevens, who had been on the front lines with her for most of Owen's life, refused to even mention his son's name. But perhaps that was why Barry was paying the price now. Karma is a bitch—of this, Lilly was certain. The question, however, was how far would karma go? Would it eventually take Barry's life? And then maybe her own, for falling short as a mother? Or what about Miles, if (beyond a reasonable doubt) he had been the one to take Owen's life? Wasn't that the ultimate litmus test for karma? But then, how many killers were still walking around free, having gotten away with their crimes? Probably more than a few. And Lilly had possibly befriended one, shown compassion to one, boarded and fed one….

"Lilly!" Barry was hollering from the guest room, interrupting her curious reverie. *Oh God*, she thought, *what does he want now?* It reminded her of her late mother, who, always a thorn for those in the service industry, had once yelled for a waiter so many times that the poor man finally shouted back across a crowded restaurant, "What the hell do you want now?"

And what Lilly wanted now was just some peace and quiet, away from people who needed something from her. *Fuck Barry*, she thought. *Fuck everyone.*

Ignoring Barry's repeated demand for her, Lilly walked outside into the crisp autumn afternoon and stood beside the house, like a disaffected teenager mad at their parents. She wasn't sure where she wanted to go, or why she had even left the house; nonetheless, Lilly wouldn't walk back inside. That much was certain.

She ended up at the bottom of the driveway, turning her head this way and that, but ultimately not moving her body in any direction. Making decisions, even the most insignificant—now more than ever—absolutely sickened her. If she were to be granted any wish for the rest of her life, outside of bringing Owen back, Lilly would wish for the ability to never have to make a choice again. The idea of having everything already decided—from what to eat for breakfast in the morning to what time to go to bed at night—was a luxury she couldn't even fathom.

Just then, as if it were scripted by a greater power, a golf ball landed at her feet and rolled to a stop against her Crocs. Without thinking, she picked up the ball and hurled it back toward the golf range (along with an expletive), knowing full well it would never make it all the way there—and it didn't. It landed less than eight feet away, not even clearing the rest of her driveway. Frustrated, she kicked the loose gravel at her feet (with another expletive). *One of these days*, she thought, *I'm going to get hit in the head by one of these damn balls and killed*—but maybe that wasn't so bad? In fact, why couldn't a ball just hit her in the head right now? Why did it always have to fall short?

Still on autopilot—her favorite mode of the day—she walked over to the side of the house and leaned against the bricks, desperately craving a cigarette, which she hadn't enjoyed (not even a puff) since Owen started high school. It had been a promise she made to him in exchange for something on his side, which she couldn't remember now, except for the fact that it was a lopsided exchange. She remembered that her side of the deal had been much more substantial than what he had to do. *Perhaps it was merely a certain homework assignment?* No, that couldn't be. That sounded too unequal. *What was it then?* She couldn't remember, which was something else she hated, especially since it was happening more frequently now that she was getting older. She would even rent movies to watch that she had already seen before but didn't remember seeing; and worse, she wouldn't realize it until halfway through, thus committing to the rest of the movie in the same way she would commit to a book if she made it past the first hundred pages. It was neurotic, she knew, but no worse than her sagging memory, or anything else that pointed downward toward old age. She was even capable now of seeing the same movie a *third* time, not remembering either of the first two viewings—and it was usually a movie not worthy of seeing *once*.

What she did remember, though, leaning against the house she had once shared with her husband (and was now, somehow, sharing with him again; was he still calling for her, she wondered?)—was the smooth intake of a cigarette and the languid exhale through her nostrils. She was enjoying the memory of it as if she were smoking one now for real—but just like it had been during her marriage, she had to cut it short and snuff it out because she had to get back to Barry. He either needed her, if he still did from moments ago, or would be calling for her again soon—and the last thing *she* needed was hearing his shit about her smoking.

But just as she was stomping out her imaginary cigarette, Lilly noticed something white in her peripheral vision. It was probably another stray golf ball, she figured (and she was right about that); but what she didn't expect to find, when she walked over to look, was not one but several golf balls—enough to fill up one of those wire buckets that Barry insisted she could use as a flower pot (after accidentally breaking one of hers).

"But all the dirt will spill out," she had said to him, wondering what the hell he was thinking.

"Well, yeah," he said, clearly hiding his embarrassment. "But I meant the outside. Like around another container."

"Then why would you even need it if you had another container?" Lilly responded, still dumbfounded as to where he was going with this.

"I don't know," he stammered. "That's your department. I just thought it might look nice…you know, different."

She stared at him.

"Isn't different good?" Barry asked. "Change things up a little?"

"Thank you," she'd said, not really meaning to be grateful. "But I like things just the way they are."

And now here Lilly was, standing at the top of her driveway looking down at a bunch of golf balls that would no doubt fit in the bucket he'd brought home that day, but which she had thrown out soon after. This was one of her bad habits, she knew, especially since Barry had given her shit about it on a regular basis. She would always throw things out before they were ready to be thrown out, like food that was still good enough to eat (according to Barry). But doing it this way—her way—Lilly wouldn't have to decide if something had gone bad or not.

EGRESS

"So," ***Miles started,*** aware that he was finally about to say this out loud, "I think...well, from getting back my...I think I may have caused the gun to go off."

"Of course ya did," P.D. said. "Yo coulda saved all dat money wit da...wit da—"

"Hypnotist?"

"Yeah," P.D. said. "Whateva dat shit is. Spook ya past like dat. Stoopid."

"You mean my memory?"

Prison Drake grunted. "Same shit."

"I just thought..." Miles tried again. "I just thought—"

"You was innocent?" P.D. cut in.

Miles smiled without meaning to, knowing full well what was coming next.

"We all innocent," P.D. said, maintaining his sarcasm under a thin layer. "No one eva guilty at Club Fed. I told ya dat. Don't rememba?" He shook his head. "Maybe yo should get dat...ya know...spend mo money ta rememba dat!"

Prison Drake laughed.

"Yeah, I remember that," Miles said, not sharing in his friend's humor. "Everyone knows that."

"You don't," P.D. said, not laughing anymore. "You think you're better than everyone else. That's your problem. You act like your shit doesn't stink...and trust me, it does."

"No, I don't," Miles shot back, not concealing his hurt. "I don't think—what? What the fuck?"

"What? You thought I was just a dumb nigger?"

"I didn't think you—wait a sec. Since when do—"

"I speak like an intelligent person?" P.D. said, finishing Miles' sentence.

Miles was sure his mouth was literally hanging open.

"I went to Duke," P.D. said.

Miles still couldn't speak.

"I studied divinity, although I didn't finish. Got into some bad shit...got in with some bad people. And then it was just downhill from there."

"But—"

"Why?" Prison Drake said, beating him to it. "Come on, man."

"So—so people wouldn't fuck with you?" Miles said, just then figuring it out. "Easier to fly under the radar?"

"See, I knew you were smart."

Another light bulb switched on. "But I taught you how to read?"

Prison Drake bobbed his head up and down, as if in agreement.

"Man, I should've done that. Pretended to be stup—" He stopped, realizing that he might have just insulted his only friend. "I mean...I don't mean...."

Prison Drake shook his head, but didn't address the inadvertent slap that had just been delivered. "You're white. You wouldn't understand." He smiled with his lips closed. "You didn't need to understand.

"And I actually am Canadian," P.D. continued, spacing his words out evenly. "From Toronto, born and raised, just like my moniker."

"What?"

"Drake."

"Oh."

"And my real name, by the way, is Winn, short for Winnifred. I didn't lie about that on the phone the other day when you asked me, or about anything else for that matter." He looked straight at Miles. "In case you were wondering. But don't call me Fred. I'm still bigger than you."

He smiled again, this time with his lips open.

Miles grinned, taking a sip of his Grande Latte. "So, going to Duke doesn't fly in jail, huh?"

Winn laughed and grabbed his Caramel Macchiato, which he had let Miles pay for. "Not usually."

"Winn left," Hannah said to Miles, who had finally come out of the bathroom. "He couldn't wait anymore. I would've left myself if I didn't live here. Oh, and he told me to tell you to cut the shit."

"Come on, Hannah, stop being passive-aggressive. You know I hate that."

"Wow, a new phrase for you, which of course you're using incorrectly. Did Winn teach you that?"

"What? You're jealous of him? Seriously? And also, I'm not using it incorrectly. You're telling me how *you* feel by funneling it through him instead."

Hannah shook her head. "I'm not jealous of him. I like Winn and I'm glad he's in your life. What I'm jealous of is the drugs. They seem higher on your list than anything or anybody else…including me."

Miles walked away toward the kitchen. "Give me a break, man. For once."

"For once?" she repeated, following him into the kitchen. "Really?"

He opened the refrigerator and took out a beer.

"Really?" she said again, but in a different timbre.

"What? This?" Miles said, holding out the Corona like a baby about to be baptized.

Hannah snatched the beer from him. "Yes, *that*, and everything else!"

"What do you mean *everything else*? What did I do now?" He paced around the kitchen. "Seriously, it's just a fuckin' beer."

She lobbed the bottle at him, which he barely caught before it hit the floor. "You're right. It's just a fuckin' beer, and I'm just your fuckin' girlfriend, and Winn's just your fuckin' friend, and…what's her name? The mother of that boy you killed? She *was* your friend, despite what you did, which is out-of-this-world crazy. But she's a better person than I could ever be, because I would never forgive someone for something like that. And maybe Winn and I should join her as people you once knew. You don't deserve any of us." She walked out of the kitchen toward her bedroom. "Kudos to that lady for figuring it out first."

"Nice," Miles called after her, taking a long sip from the Corona, which he didn't even remember opening. He glanced down, looking for the cap. "Really nice. Throw all that shit in my face again…and her name is Lilly, by the way." A pang of guilt and self-hatred shot through him after saying her name. He had to remember not to do that ever again. He could depersonalize it when it was just "that lady" or "the mother of that kid"—though even that was getting harder and harder to do.

"Didn't you say that to me once? That you don't need any-body?" Hannah was saying, bringing him back to the moment. "Well, maybe your prayers will finally be answered. Oh wait, I forgot, you don't believe in a higher power!" She slammed the bedroom door and locked it—the latter sound much louder than he expected.

"You're only my girlfriend," Miles shouted back, glancing at the floor again for the cap, as if it were life or death stakes that he find it. "I never asked you to save me."

He floated over to the bedroom door and tried the knob in the unlikely chance it would turn, but it was useless, especially since she had locked the door minutes before, not seconds. Time was as blurry as Hannah's bedroom door.

"Come on, don't be this way. I'm sorry, okay?" He waited. "I shouldn't have said *only*."

He tried the doorknob again, even though he knew it wasn't going to turn.

Or was it? Maybe she hadn't locked it after all....

But it didn't turn. The knob was like a statue, the door a painting behind it.

"Hannah?"

"It's too late for 'I'm sorry.' You're always sorry. And guess what? You're out of sorries. You've maxed out."

"Hannah...."

"You don't even know what to be sorry for."

He waited, not knowing what to say. And where the fuck was he? Wasn't he still in her apartment? *Why did everything look different all of a sudden?*

"Get out!" she shouted through the door. "Get out of my apartment. Go home, or wherever the fuck you go. I don't care anymore. Do what you want. But get the fuck out first."

So, he *was* in her apartment still. Thank God.

"Hannah...."

"She told you to get out," a voice firmly said from behind Miles. "So, get out."

Miles spun around, expecting to come face-to-face with Hannah's roommate, who could have easily walked in without him knowing. It was something Erica excelled at, especially when he was fighting with Hannah and was preoccupied. But it wasn't her. It wasn't even a female. It was a *him*, a *young* him, still with a high tenor in his voice.

Miles gasped and gulped, his heart nearly stopping as he recognized Owen. "What are *you* doing here?" he exclaimed.

"She asked you to leave her apartment," Owen said. "Are you hard of hearing, or just stupid?"

"You can't be here," Miles tried again, working to wrap his head around the fact that he was talking to a dead person—a person who was likely dead *because* of him.

Owen laughed, the sound shaking Miles' skull, causing him to cover his ears. But this only made the sound of the blood rushing around in Miles' head even louder. *How could there be that much blood inside?* he wondered. And that was just in his brain. *How much was flowing through the rest of his body?* he wanted to ask someone. *Any*one.

"How much blood do you have," Miles said too evenly, his tone not going up at the end to make it sound like a question.

"What?"

"…blood do you have?" he tried again, this time forgetting the first half of the question.

"Blood do I have?" Owen returned, mockingly. "What the fuck are you talking about?"

"Like in your body…your whole body?"

"What the fuck, dude? And anyway, I would say the answer is none, being that you killed me. The funeral home probably drained me in order to put—"

"But I didn't mean to kill you," Miles said quietly, or at least he thought it was quietly.

Owen grunted, or maybe he sighed. Miles wasn't sure.

"That's such an overused excuse," Owen said. "It's—"

"But I didn't," Miles pleaded. "I was just trying to stop my…I was just trying to get the gun out of his hands. He was the one holding it."

"But you were the one who made the gun go off. Not him." Blood started to leak out of Owen's head where the bullet had entered, as if he'd just been shot all over again.

"I was just trying to stop him," Miles whined. "I think—"

"Therefore, you are?" Owen finished, grinning at Miles.

"I'm not sure. I don't remember."

"You don't remember thinking?"

Miles sighed. "I don't remember. I was seriously fucked up that day."

"But you do remember now. You remember everything. And come on, dude, you're always fucked up. You're fucked up right now. You're actually *really* fucked up right now, like emergency room fucked up. I don't know what you took before, but whatever it was, it's gonna kill you if you don't go to the hospital. And I mean ASAP."

"No, I can't...." Miles glanced around the apartment nervously. It looked the same, although Hannah's door wasn't closed anymore and the Corona was on the floor, its contents spilt on the carpet. She was going to kill him, if the drugs didn't do it first.

He turned back to Owen. "Wait, am I dead? Is that why I can see you right now? Did I die? Did I die!"

Owen started to laugh.

"Stop laughing!" Miles shouted. But this only made Owen laugh louder. "What's so fuckin' funny!" he screamed.

And just like that, Owen stopped. "You're ridiculous, dude. You really are. Do you even hear what you're saying? You should see yourself right now. You'd be amazed."

"Am I dead!" Miles screamed again.

"I can't answer that, but maybe they can," Owen said, gesturing toward a crowd of shadow-people suddenly standing in the room and bending down, like they were staring at the spilled Corona, thinking of how best to clean it up.

But why would they care about the beer he had accidentally dropped? Miles wondered. It wasn't such a big deal.

Or maybe Owen's blood had gotten on the carpet, and they were wondering about that? Still, why were they there?

Miles was trying to see if Hannah's door was open or closed, but for some reason he couldn't turn his head. The carpet cleaners were holding it; they were holding his head!

But *why*? It sounded as if the walls were crying—but he knew it was actually Hannah who was sobbing. Her weeping was unmistakable; he just couldn't see her. And it didn't sound like the way she usually cried, when she was emotional from a movie or upset from a fight. This sounded different somehow. Very different.

"You did this," said a voice that sounded like Owen. "It's all your fault."

But Owen was gone; Miles could sense that without seeing. He started to say something—anything—but nothing would come out. He realized then that he was laid out on the floor, but he didn't understand why. He tried to turn his head to look for Owen, but the cleaners were still holding him tight. He couldn't even move his legs to get up and search for Owen. His whole body felt like jelly. And now Hannah's crying was fading. Everything was blurring. The ceiling fan that Miles had apparently been staring at for some time stopped its cruel spin.

Then there was nothing at all.

CONFLUENCE

"I'm too tired to save the world," Miles mumbled, his body swaying from side to side like a metronome.

The nurse laughed. "You don't need to save the world right now, honey. Just rest." She finished hanging the IV bag and pointed at a button on the bedside rail. "You see this, doll? Just push this if you need anything, okay? It's like the bat signal. You hit that and Batman will come running in…or Bat*woman*, that is." She laughed again and tucked the sheets around Miles. "Let me get you another blanket, poor thing."

"Why's he shivering like that?" Hannah's voice came from the other side of the room, where she had been sitting quietly for the past several minutes.

"You can come up and sit next to him, honey," the nurse said. "He won't bite." She winked at Hannah. "Unless you want him to."

"Oh, okay," Hannah said, standing up and edging toward the bed. "I just didn't want to get in the way while you were… uh, setting up or whatever."

"It's all good. Just give a holler if you need me." Then she turned to walk away.

"Uh…nurse?" Hannah said.

The nurse chuckled. "That was quick!"

Hannah gestured at Miles, who was still trembling despite the warm stuffiness of the room.

"Oh, right. The shaking. Totally normal for a patient like him…." The nurse studied Hannah's face. "When they're detoxing," she added, her smile dimming and her tone dropping to match.

"But...can't you give him anything for that?"

"He still has a lot of drugs in his system. It doesn't all leave that quickly. Sorta like a houseguest who overstays their welcome, you know? Just can't take a hint." She returned to her lighthearted state, apparently unable to be too serious for more than a minute at a time. "Don't you worry, honey. We'll take good care of him."

"Thanks," Hannah said, watching the nurse leave and then sitting down in the chair next to the bed, as if it were a car and she a passenger taking over driving duties.

She turned to Miles, whose eyes were closed, though she could see his pupils darting back and forth through his eyelids.

"Can you hear me, Miles?" she said softly. "Are you dreaming in there?"

She reached over the side rail and touched his hand.

Miles wasn't sleeping—it was impossible to sleep—and he could clearly hear Hannah. But he was in some type of intermediate state, incapable of responding or even opening his eyes.

"I'll let you sleep," she said, leaning down to kiss him lightly on the forehead. She turned to leave, but then remarked, "I don't forgive you, and I don't know if you can hear me or not, but...." She couldn't finish and walked out the door, aiming for the ladies' room down the hall.

Before she could get there, though, a man in a pinstripe suit (who was standing in the middle of the hallway) said to her, "Love is a verb, and broken-heartedness is not shame."

"What?" Hannah replied. "Are you speaking to me?"

The man smiled in a way that made everything else disappear.

"Do I know you?"

"That depends," the man said, still smiling, his words clean and unburdened. "Do I know *you*?"

He glanced down the hallway in the direction she had

come from. Then he leaned closer, like he was about to tell her another secret.

"Miles will know the illusion soon, and the trick won't work anymore," he said, barely above a whisper.

As Hannah was walking back to continue her visit with Miles, after spending a good amount of time in the bathroom trying to collect herself, a voice stopped her just as she turned to enter the room, this time a female one.

"Are you Hannah, by any chance?" the woman said.

Hannah spun around to see a well-dressed African-American woman that she seemingly didn't recognize. "Yes?" Hannah responded after a moment. "Do I know you?"

"I'm Lilly," the woman said. When Hannah continued to stare blankly, she added, "You called me?"

"Oh, right!" Hannah said, visually embarrassed that she didn't remember. "I'm sorry. I—"

"How is Miles? Is he okay? Can I see him?"

"Of course! He's right in there."

Lilly followed Hannah into the room where Miles lay asleep—or at least he looked that way, for he was still lost in the kaleidoscope theater of his imagination, consumed by the same images in altered rotation, which faded in and out each time in the most surreal manner. Part of him wanted to know what they all meant, because he knew they *had* to mean something, though he was so spellbound by the way his brain was working that it almost overshadowed any inherent symbolism. He remembered seeing these images before; these same slides were projected in his mind back in rehab years ago, but the doctors couldn't explain why he was experiencing them. It wasn't something typical, as far as they knew, in terms of withdrawal from the drugs he had been taking.

Back then, Miles had blamed it on insomnia more than anything else, since that same insomnia had caused him to see giant, dark shadows behind other people, almost like monsters in their own right. He hadn't slept in four nights, and even had to get up from one of the required sobriety lectures to stand in the corner with his hoodie over his head because what he was seeing was so intense. And since he had been through the same thing the year before—four nights in a row without sleep—and had hallucinated then as well, he knew that the shadow monsters and psychedelic slideshow were probably due to the same thing, like crisscrossed wires in his brain reacting to a lack of active consciousness.

But he wasn't hallucinating now—*was he?*—and he wasn't suffering from insomnia either; at least he didn't think that was the case. So why then was he still seeing these bizarre images inside his brain? Was he dreaming? No, he couldn't be, as he could hear Hannah and some woman talking nearby…

although it wasn't just some woman. He knew this woman. But what was she doing there…wherever *there* was?

He didn't want to open his eyes to find out.

"I guess you didn't think I would actually come," Lilly said, trying to take a sip from her sweltering coffee. She had noticed over the years that the coffee in hospitals was either too hot or lukewarm at best. There never seemed to be an in-between.

"What?"

Lilly looked across the table at Hannah: a beautiful girl with a unique aura, like she belonged in a fairy tale. "After you called me? I certainly didn't mean to startle you."

"Sorry about that," Hannah said. "I had just met some strange man, so—"

"Oh?"

"Yeah."

"What happened?"

"It was just weird."

"Here? At the hospital?"

"Yeah," Hannah said, taking a shaky sip from her bottled water. "A few minutes before I saw you."

Lilly tried her coffee again, then glanced at Hannah's trembling hand. "Are you okay?"

"Yeah, no biggie. It was just surreal, like I was talking to a ghost or something. I hope you didn't mind that I called you." Hannah laughed. "I was glad I got your voicemail, to be honest. Wasn't sure if I could sustain a back-and-forth conversation, especially since I've never talked to you before. And Miles, of course, didn't even know I called you...still doesn't." She shrugged. "I just had his phone, and—"

Lilly reached across the table and gently patted Hannah's hand. "Well, I'm glad you did."

Hannah tried to smile, but started crying instead.

Lilly took Hannah's hand and held it. "It's okay, honey. I know this is hard." She scoffed. "I've known Miles a long time now, and he's a strong...man. He'll get through it." She caught Hannah's gaze. "He's lucky he has you."

Hannah snickered and wiped tears from her cheeks.

"He's had a hard life," Lilly said. "Miles."

Hannah looked up and slightly nodded. "Why.... Why did—"

"I forgive him?"

Hannah nodded again.

"I haven't forgiven him," Lilly said. "And I probably never will. But I...." She searched for the right words. "I didn't replace Owen with Miles, if that's what you're thinking."

"No, no, I wasn't thinking that at all," Hannah pleaded, her tone escalating. "I just—"

"It's okay, honey. I understand what you're trying to say."

She shook her head and sighed. "Hell, I would wonder the same thing, sitting across from myself."

Hannah waited.

"Because he needed me. That's why. He needed someone. Simple as that."

"But—"

"I don't look at him as the killer of my son." She shook her head again. "Not anymore at least. I see him for what he is: a young man who needed someone...needed someone on his side. That's all." She tried her coffee again.

"But how could you take his side?"

"Maybe side is the wrong word...." She searched for the right one, but couldn't find it. "Life isn't one way or the other. It isn't black or white."

Hannah stared out with a vacant expression on her face—her emotion, or emotions, cloaked for the moment.

"You'll understand when you're older," Lilly said. "Or maybe not. I don't know. Maybe I'm not like most people, which isn't a good thing or a bad thing really...." She laughed, which surprised them both. "Look, if I have to call some type of customer service for something, I generally lose it in under a minute, so I wouldn't call myself a patient or forgiving person. Like I said, it isn't that I forgive him. I just—"

"It's okay," Hannah said. Then, in a different tone, "I guess they did release him early...you know, from prison...or at least that's what Miles told me." She scoffed, as if just realizing that Miles could have easily lied to her, especially since she wasn't the type that would go research his claim. She wasn't a Google person, and Miles knew that.

"But anyway," Hannah continued, "it's not for me to be judge and jury. If that's what...if that's what works for you, then so be it. I'm happy for you, happy for Miles that he's on the receiving end of...whatever this is. Oh my—happy? That's not what I meant to say." She quickly covered her mouth, as if trying to push the words back in.

Lilly smiled, knowing that many people (most, honestly) tried to convince themselves that happiness was a sin. She knew this because she was one of those people.

Hannah removed her hand from her mouth. "What I'm saying is, I don't necessarily get it. But that's okay."

"It *is* okay," Lilly said. "It's all okay. You don't have to understand. Heck, I've been hiding my relationship with Miles since he—no, relationship is the wrong word. The media can be...you know, they don't...they probably wouldn't get it. People don't have to understand everything, and that includes me."

Hannah took a sip from her bottled water, this time without shaking. "They don't need to get it," she said. "Fuck those people!"

Lilly laughed. "Yeah, fuck 'em!"

Miles was still watching the cryptic slideshow on the back of his eyelids when he heard them again: three voices, all female. One was Hannah and one was Lilly; he was sure of that much. The third one he didn't recognize, although he vaguely remembered hearing it before. As for Hannah and Lilly, he didn't know if he felt happy or not to know they were there—wherever they were exactly. Maybe he was jealous because they knew where they were and he didn't—at least not yet. Regardless, he wasn't sure what to say to Lilly, or Hannah for that matter; and he was too intrigued by the extraordinary images cascading like dominoes inside his brain, even the fanged teeth and deformed hands. For they were all beautiful. Every damn one.

11:11

"Thinking about swimming to freedom?" the PSA said to Miles, who had been looking out across the water, watching the geese glide toward the small island in the middle of the bay.

"What?" Miles said, even though he had clearly heard the PSA, whose name he couldn't remember.

"The water's only ankle-deep halfway out, and you could probably walk the rest of the way if you really wanted to," the PSA said, as if Miles were seriously considering the idea. "But I don't tell most people that. Plus, you would first have to get down this cliff here without breaking your leg. That's the hard part."

"You don't remember me, huh?" Miles said, but then quickly added, "Well, it's been a minute, and you've probably met tons of people since then."

The PSA grunted in agreement. "Well, yeah, there's never a lack of addicts, that's for sure. Never will be. Sad, actually. And even sadder the ones who return, like you. No offense. But at least we have a higher success rate than most with regards to relapsing."

"So, you *do* remember me?" Miles said.

"Not your name, no, but I know you're a relapse," he said, like relapse wasn't a noun but a nationality.

When Miles didn't say anything, he continued, "Don't sweat it, man. I've relapsed a few times myself." He made a clicking sound with his tongue. "But at least you came back. And you're in the best place, too. Trust me. But you already know that, I'm sure. Whether you're here voluntarily or not."

"I'm here voluntarily," Miles said quickly, his tone almost defensive. But then he softened. "I remember you telling me that last time, about the water not being as deep as it looked." Miles glanced back at the sky, which was currently empty of birds. "You also taught me about bald eagles."

"Sorry, guy. I've probably talked to hundreds of people about the birds." He chuckled. "I probably shouldn't be telling people about the water level, though. Gives 'em ideas, right?"

Miles wasn't sure whether the PSA was trying to be sarcastic.

"Like you said," the PSA went on, "a lot of folks come through here, and if it's been a minute, then yeah, I probably forgot." He studied Miles briefly. "Did you have long hair before? Like, really long hair? You do look familiar somehow."

"Yeah, but not *that* long."

Miles laughed, trying to remember what he looked like with long hair—or hair at all, since he was shaving it almost down to the skin now. He glanced at the PSA's name tag. Why Miles hadn't thought to do that before, he didn't know. Miles was wearing one himself, which the PSA seemed to just remember, too.

"Miles R.? Yeah, that sounds familiar...." He fell silent for a moment, still looking at the badge. "From Durham, huh?"

"From everywhere," Miles corrected, but then laughed after hearing himself say that.

"I bet," the PSA said. "You look it."

"University of life, right? The best institution money can buy."

"I'm with you, man," the PSA said. "I studied there, too."

Miles glanced at the PSA's badge again, having already forgotten his name even though he'd just looked at it. It was Cash, or "PSA Cash" (as he was more often referred to); although, as far as Miles knew, there wasn't anyone else named

Cash at the facility. They must refer to all the PSAs as "PSA so-and-so," Miles figured, just in case there was an addict there with the same first name, as they obviously wouldn't want to confuse the two.

"No offense, by the way," Cash said. "I meant it more like you seem more worldly now, like you've been there and back. Besides…." He gestured at Miles' bald head. "You lost the 'do. You don't look like a headbanger anymore, which is good."

They both laughed, although Miles hadn't laughed because of the rocker comment; Sawyer had worn that out all by his Pee-Wee-Herman-tattooed self. It was the "worldly" remark that amused Miles—wherever "there" was in "there and back"—although he knew it wasn't literal. Wherever it was, he had been there. That was for damn sure. Although whether he was "back" now was open for debate—unless returning to rehab a second time counted as such. This time he was going to finish if it killed him—even if he happened to meet another Sawyer, which he knew was highly unlikely.

Sawyer was a lot of things—a lot of bad things—but he was definitely one-of-a-kind. And now that Miles was in rehab again, at the same place where he had met Sawyer, it was difficult to escape the ghost of him. Even the spectacular surroundings seemed hesitant to negate the spirit that was Sawyer.

"I get it," Miles said to Cash without turning his head from the skyline, as if he meant the words only for himself. "No offense taken." Though he *had* taken offense, not to Cash's comment, but at the fact that the unassailable nature surrounding them was completely lost on the narcissists there—including himself—all of whom had pissed their lives away. And for what? A momentary high? A fleeting numbness to mask their shitty lives?

"I understand," Miles said, though he was talking to

himself completely now, resolving that he would never disregard the birds again, nor the pure blue they effortlessly floated through.

Cody, the music-loving nurse, didn't remember Miles, with or without hair. Miles understood this; considering the number of people Cody administered drugs to in a month, let alone several years, why would he be memorable? Still, Miles hoped that Cody would have a flash of recall, since Miles had once correctly guessed a Nada Surf song playing on the nurse's iPad. But it probably wasn't much of a feat in retrospect, Miles realized. And he never once kidded himself about guessing a Rufus Wainwright song correctly, for Wainwright's voice was far too distinctive.

In the hallway outside the nurse's station, in the meds line, a girl called after Miles when he walked by, but not by name. She asked if he was a relapse—again, as if it were the type of person he now was—and when he said yes, she asked if he was Kirk's old roommate, whose name she did somehow remember, despite his former roommate's distinct lack of personality. And they couldn't go fully down memory lane without her then asking about Sawyer.

Before Miles answered, he glanced at her name badge. "Yeah, that's right. Sasha. I remember you," Miles said, though he only half-remembered her. What he remembered more was how young she had been, and how hard of a drinker she was for her age—it all came down, naturally, to "daddy issues."

"Kirk didn't make it," she said flatly, moving on from the Sawyer question that Miles had ignored.

"Oh," Miles started, not getting it. "He's back here, too?"

"No, he didn't make it. He died. Killed himself. Well, OD'd but...you know," as if OD'ing and suicide were more or less the same, intentional or not.

"Wow," Miles said, surprised that Kirk had done something that definitive, but sad for him just the same. He remembered the words written over the thermostat in their room ("KILL ME") and wondered if Kirk had actually been the one to write that, and not a former occupant like he'd supposed.

As Miles continued down the hallway, mid-conversation, not knowing what to say to her tragic news, Sasha said, "Wait for me. I'll walk over with you."

Miles was about to ask, "Over to where?" but then remembered there was an 11 a.m. lecture every day at the main hall (every day but Sunday, that is, since Sunday mornings were reserved for Mass).

Ten minutes later, when they were both walking in the crisp fall sunshine toward the main lecture hall, Miles told Sasha about what happened to Sawyer—leaving out, of course, his own time in prison, which he guessed she probably knew about already; pointing out, instead, that Sawyer had an unhealthy relationship with authority figures, as she probably knew well, and that it had finally caught up to him.

"Death-by-cop," Sasha remarked, as if what Sawyer had done was somehow an achievement and she was justifiably impressed.

"What about you?" Miles asked, trying to change the subject since he didn't really want to talk about himself or Sawyer, especially if she was going to make a saint out of the latter. And he wasn't going to ask her how she knew about Kirk. It didn't change the fact that he was dead, too.

"Well, I'm still here," she said without irony. "No triumphant end for me...not yet at least."

"You think suicide is triumphant?"

"Eh, it's a good story for parties."

"But you wouldn't be alive *to be* at the parties."

"That's true," she admitted, not in the least bit embarrassed about her seeming lack of logic. She came to a halt and turned to look out over the water, as if she just then realized its proximity. "There's too many people in the world for it to mean anything," she said, after some silence had passed between them.

"What do you mean?" Miles asked.

She turned back to look at him, her face expressionless. "Way too many," she said.

Some weeks went by and Visiting Day finally arrived—a day that Miles had let pass unceremoniously the last time he was in rehab, since he had no one to put on the guest list before. But today he did, as P.D. came bounding in from the parking lot—or Winn, which he insisted he be called now—with Hannah and Lilly in tow, the latter two of whom had become good friends; although, the thought of what they talked about together when Miles wasn't around still spooked him a little bit. He knew there was no reason to be insecure, as there weren't any secrets anymore; just the same, he was working on not letting that get to him. It was a "work-in-progress"—a term he had learned from his first, and thus far only, session with Dr. Stevens, who, Miles had to admit, didn't seem that awful for a shrink. The session was meant to be an intervention of sorts, but it was plainly obvious to everyone, including Miles, that going back to rehab was his only option, especially since he'd already been detoxed in the hospital. Now it was just time and therapy he needed, so that he could learn how to stay sober. And he had promised Dr.

Stevens, as well as Lilly and Hannah, that when he got out of rehab he would come in regularly to maintain his sobriety and maybe work on other stuff as well, if Miles felt so inclined, which he already knew he would.

The four of them walked around the grounds together as Miles proudly shared his ornithological knowledge, pointing out several different species (including a pair of bald eagles, which most intrigued Winn).

"I'll tell you what," Winn said, after Miles singled them out. "You can keep calling me P.D. as long as I can call you B.E."

"I can't agree to that," Miles said, "although it's quite tempting." He grinned. "And I'm bald by choice, by the way."

Winn laughed. "No, it stands for 'Bad Example.' I don't know what you were thinking," he said, patting Miles on the shoulder.

"Ugh, men," Hannah said. "Can never be real with each other."

"Not these two," Lilly agreed, smiling. "And I don't know if I would want them to be. I don't think I could take it."

Miles wasn't paying attention to them anymore, and when the others saw what he was staring at, no one said anything. They laughed instead, almost simultaneously, when they realized why Miles seemed to be so mesmerized by a septic drainpipe coming out of the ground. It was camouflaged to be something else entirely, something far more pleasing to the eye and spirit.

"I'm going inside," Lilly said after a minute. "I'm freezing."

Winn agreed. "Me, too."

"Do you want me to stay out here with you, Miles?" Hannah asked, her arms tightly folded across her chest in an apparent effort to keep warm.

"You can go in with Winn and Lilly if you want. I'll be right there," Miles replied, still staring at the drainage pipe, wondering if anyone ever tried to use it mistakenly—though only the staff could carry personal items. Miles was forgetting about visitors, however, who definitely had good reason to attempt such a thing.

As the other three walked back toward the main building, Miles continued to focus his attention on what enclosed the drainage pipe, as he only wanted to see it for what it was truly meant to be:

a wishing well.

ACKNOWLEDGMENTS

I would like to thank the following people who literally saved my life in one way or another: John Sutherland (also an early reader), Eric Mares, Rob and Shelly Warren, Kevin McSpadden, a stranger at the Peppermill Casino in Reno, Nevada who gave me half of his sandwich after he overheard me tell someone I was homeless; also, a stranger on a public bus in Oakland, California who escorted me to a nearby pawnshop he knew so that I could sell my leather jacket to afford some food; and, in general, the kindness of strangers. It made me realize that people *don't* actually ruin everything....

I would also like to thank Al Watt, who helped me workshop the first draft. Additionally, I would like to thank North Carolina Public Defender Chris Caldwell, who helped me with some of the legal details.

I would also like to thank Doug Weaver, Heather Shaw, and Hart Cauchy from Mission Point Press; also, Mark Pate for the fantastic cover design and Scott Couturier for his detailed editing.

And finally, my family and friends—you know who you are.

ABOUT THE AUTHOR

Douglas Rappaport was originally a classically-trained violinist and composer, having studied as a young man at various conservatories in the U.S. and abroad. During his college years, Douglas studied under famed protégé of Jascha Heifetz, Erick Friedman, and after graduate work at Yale University, went on to U.S.C. where he received an Advanced Studies degree in Film and Television Scoring. He also studied at Goldsmiths College (part of the University of London), Guildhall, and London International Film School, amongst others.

Concerning Douglas Rappaport's 2003 debut novel, *One Day the Weatherman*, Absolutewrite.com wrote: "Rappaport's work is very detail-oriented and his writing is extremely descriptive; it makes for incredible realism..." His second book, Victim of Circumstance, climbed to #2 on Amazon's Free Kindle bestseller list (non-fiction) in 2014. Douglas's short fiction has also earned several distinctions, including an invitation to the exclusive Sirenland Writer's Conference in Positano, Italy.

Rappaport is currently working on his newest novel, *Dead People.*